The Goodbyes
A novel of secrets and mystery

by Helen Gillespie

Paperback ISBN: 9781940758893
Ebook ISBN: 9781940758923

Cover design: Ginnefine Art

Published by:
Audecyn Books
Upper Marlboro, MD

I dedicate this book to my wife, Cathy, who has always supported my creative efforts.

The Goodbyes

CHAPTER 1

Too Much of a Man

Leisurely awakening late in the morning, Dianne indulges in a relaxing shower. Squeezing out the last watered-down drop of her favorite cream rinse elicits a groan of frustration. Living in college culture, she wore her lengthy brown hair like a trophy, gathering many compliments. A lack of cream rinse was, indeed, an emergency.

After grooming meticulously and donning a coat, Dianne plucked her car keys from a bowl on the living room bookshelf. She wasted no time driving to the largest store in the Marshfield area.

Her heart pounded with each determined step as she hurried through MegaMart, fighting off a pounding headache from hunger and dabbing watery eyes from the cold. The garish fluorescent lights and blaring sale announcements only heightened her urgency. Despite her determination, she was captivated by outdoor items hinting at the distant spring season. The alluring smell and shine of fresh red paint on a riding lawnmower captured the harried shopper.

"Can I help you, ma'am?" asked an enthusiastic young clerk.

"I'm only looking. Thank you," Dianne replied, trying to appear purposeful. The items symbolized summer more than carrying a genuine interest.

"Mr. Glossen bought one. Want me to fetch him?" the clerk said quickly.

Before Dianne could respond, the young man disappeared into the lawn equipment area. She hoped he wouldn't find Mr. "whoever" since she wasn't planning to buy a mower. Distracted, she refocused on finding her cream rinse.

"Yes, ma'am!" An energetic baritone voice called out. Dianne jolted around to see a stocky, muscular, and slightly taller man, stepping toward her. His carefree smile trapped her instantly.

"Yup, I picked one up just last week," he explained. "I'm store manager, Michael D. Glossen," he said proudly, extending his hand.

Before she could say more, "Michael D." as she would soon refer to him, explained what seemed to be every bolt on the machine. She tried to listen politely, although her stomach moans broke through the imprisoning sales litany.

"Whoa, I, I...I guess my stomach says I'm hungry." Dianne didn't want to hear another word from this man but was captured by his stunning eyes and lyrical voice. "Um, I don't want to be rude," she said, "but as my stomach announced, I'm hungry. I'll check this out another time." Despite her hunger, she found it difficult to leave.

"I know you can see this is a fine mower. I'm sure it's what you need, and it's easy to run for ladies," he insisted with raised eyebrows. "Here's my card. Come back and see me or call me if you'd like. That is if you have any questions. Or ya wanna say hi."

As she decided her first lesson in lawn care would never happen in MegaMart, Michael's stare drew her glance into his captivating eyes. Dianne put aside her hunger for an instant and was fixated on those eyes, crystal blue with brown specs radiating from his pupils like spokes on a wheel.

"Try that restaurant by the road...Kuntry Kitchen," Michael said as he leaned over the lawn mower seat closer. "They got the best trout 'round, 'cept for the ones I catch," he bragged.

He smiled, continued staring at Dianne, and seemed to pull at part of her soul. She slid the business card into her coat pocket and gave Michael D. a quick, nervous smile before escaping.

After selecting her favorite cream rinse, she hurried to the checkout and exited the store, trying to shake her uneasy feeling. Michael's talk seemed like a typical sales pitch with some flirting. Yet, his mannerisms made her uncomfortable. He was almost too handsome and talked too much. She buttoned her coat and set aside her intrigue and uneasiness for an immediate need to eat.

Chilled evening air and parking lot lights flickering on seemed to hypnotize Dianne, like the Christmas ornaments she had recently tucked away in her mother's attic. More relaxed, she marveled at the contrast of lights dotting a darkening, luminescent pink and blue sky. The descending darkness gave her a mysterious feeling like when she met Michael, yet she was comfortable, not pressured...or intrigued.

After a long sigh, she nestled herself into the driver's seat of her car, flinging her hair over her seat back as she started the engine. *I really don't want trout or any fish tonight. No, I need to hear and see people. Home would be too lonely.* She thought, inserting her key into the ignition.

Her indecision did not stop darkness from descending over distant hills. After starting the car, she closed her eyes and imagined herself sitting on a flour-white beach in warm Florida, watching the sunset. She often drifted off to warm sands since fate placed brochures in front of her in a campus lounge at the beginning of her last college semester. Stress often launched Dianne into a world of gulf beaches, bright sun, and chattering dolphins made real to her only through books, pamphlets, and her imagination. She often envisioned herself as what her mother called "a hippy" cruising down the highway in her old Volkswagen Beetle. She remembered her mother's worry about the car, so she was grateful to have a new, albeit last year's model, 1991 Subaru.

Damn I'd like to be there, she muttered to herself, *And I wish mom could go there with me. I don't know what I will do after she's gone. All I know is, I WILL finish school.*

Dianne's hunger stopped her from sorting through her mind's confusion and brought her back to reality. She considered joining her mother at the church's potluck dinner and country dance but didn't want to seem like she was checking on her, a switch of mother-daughter care.

Since her father died in a car accident when she was 17 and in her senior year of high school, Dianne watched her mother keep busy with church and craft activities without showing interest in dating. When her mother shared she was going to the church dinner with Ken, Dianne took the opportunity to gently tease her about finally spending time with 'eligible material'.

"It's not a date," Katrina protested when she announced her plans. "We're only going to the church potluck, and we're not dancing," her mother insisted while blushing like a young girl. Both ladies knew that Katrina, as much as she would like to, did not have the strength to dance.

With the drama of the setting sun over, she returned from her ever-present daydreaming to her hungry reality and decided to drive the short distance to Kuntry Kitchen.

During college, Dianne often daydreamed into a lack of focus, delaying action on assignments and responses. To her, this was healthy and resulted in abundant creativity, yet some professors viewed it differently. "As long as I eventually act on my dreams, what's the harm? Some people plan. I daydream." she frequently told her mother. Melting snow dotting the parking lot nearly prevented Dianne from parking properly. She yanked on the parking brake almost in defiance when she came to a stop. Carefully, she navigated the melting sludge leading to the restaurant door. Upon entering, a perky server invited her to sit at a small table a few steps inside the eatery. Ironically, it was the same table where Dianne and her mother sat last October during lunch after Dianne interviewed with Marshfield Elementary School's principal.

That day, she burst out the latest news to her mother. "He hired me on the spot, Mom! I mentioned you had just moved here and where you live, and then he asked if I would mind living here. The next thing I knew, he said fine. I could do my student teaching here. And guess what, Mom! I might have a real job here next year! Mrs. Porter, one of the learning disability teachers, is pregnant and might not return! Can you believe it? A job right out of school!"

Dianne could barely look at the menu, thinking about how excited she was that day. After four years of learning how to teach children who were slow to learn even simple tasks, she would soon do that. However, the excitement faded to disbelief when her mother shared what had happened during her last doctor's visit.

"Hi, I'm Janet. Are you ready to order?" the server yanked Dianne back into reality.

"Um...do you have any chili? Perhaps some without meat?"

"No, ma'am. Ours got meat."

"Oh, OK," she said with disappointment. "May I have a bowl of chili and cornbread?"

"Cornbread, ma'am?"

"Yes, I would like some chili with cornbread. Oh, and iced

tea."

"OK, it'll be a minute. Sweet tea?"

"No ma'am, unsweet," Dianne responded.

Amazed at someone trying to order chili without meat, with cornbread, and unsweet tea, the server seemed to know Dianne was not local. The same thing happened when she and her mother lunched there. People outside of St. Louis had crackers, not cornbread, with their chili. And, following a Southern tradition, the tea was almost always pre-sweetened. This is how things were done outside of Missouri's big cities and south of Interstate 70, the state's Mason-Dixon line.

Cultural discoveries like this helped Dianne feel like she and her mother were friends and mother and daughter, especially the last few years while she attended college in Springfield, about 30 miles southwest of where they lived in Marshfield.

Dianne endured many cultural adjustments, and now she had to adjust to losing her friend and mother to an inoperable cancer.

Before sharing with her daughter, Katrina had shared with her doctor that she felt constantly fatigued, but had thought it was lingering depression from losing her husband. The doctor ordered a series of tests not usually performed. When the results were in, Katrina decided to face the inevitable alone until it was the right time to share it with Dianne.

At this same table where Dianne and her mother had sat, her life's focus changed. Dianne instantly wanted to be the caregiver. She wanted all her mother's hurts to go away and, like mothers do, she wanted to make fairy tales real.

"So, you took my advice. I knew you would. I could tell when I showed you that mower you'd like the trout at Kuntry Kitchen."

"Oh, hi. You're from MegaMart. I didn't see you come in. You're um...Michael? Your last name starts with a "D", but I don't remember it. Sorry."

Michael's intrusion prevented Dianne from thinking further about the last few weeks and the melancholy Christmas with her mother. If she thought too much about the last few months, she may have to fight back tears again.

"Actually, "D" is for my middle name. My last name is Glossen. I'm glad I saw you again. I wouldn't want you to spend the rest of your life looking for Michael D. at MegaMart. Can I sit with you?" Michael said as he pulled out the chair opposite Dianne and sat spread-legged, encroaching into available floor space.

"I see you're not a man who takes no for an answer."

"Of course not! That's how I'm only twenty-nine and a store manager. Ya gotta reach out and grab what you want," Michael explained with a clenched fist, pretending to pound on the table.

He continued in the style of a motivational speaker, or was he in a Baptist Preacher mode?

Dianne soon tired of his pontificating. Yet Michael, with his mysterious eyes, was a distraction from thinking about her mom and the emotional baggage that came along with the thought of losing another parent.

"So, what got you interested in retail?" she asked.

"It was my old man. He said he'd whop me upside the head every day of my life if I didn't do something with myself. Didn't want to go to college with the rich dudes. Ya know college people ain't that smart anyway."

She was shocked at Michael's comment and amazed that, having just met him, he had already gone on three tangents. That remark especially didn't impress her. She tried to ignore his talking and focus on his intriguing eyes and captivating, lyrical voice, spiced with Southernisms alongside unfounded opinions. She had grown tired of him.

"Um Michael, Janet wants to take your order," Dianne interrupted.

"No menu for me, thanks. I'm gonna have the bar. You know I gotta get the trout and big hunk of slaw," Michael said as Janet lowered a steaming bowl of chili in front of Dianne.

"And sweet tea...tea as sweet as you are, my dear," Michael continued overstepping boundaries of politeness while winking at the server.

"You're a smooth one, Michael D. I guess you know everyone here," Dianne said somewhat sarcastically.

"Yea, I know them...and their husbands know it," Michael laughed and jumped up to grab a huge mound of trout and a pile of salad trimmings from a fully stocked food bar.

"Trout, now that's some muscle food. You gettin' some?" Michael said returning to the table, barely sitting before he shoveled a huge piece of fish into his mouth.

"No, only this bowl of chili. I don't feel like eating much," she replied.

"Oh, that's OK. You new in town?" Without waiting for an answer, he jumped up, nabbed a bowl of slaw from the salad bar, and plopped back to his seat. "Forgot some good stuff. You saying sumptin?" Michael garbled his words as he motioned with his fork for Dianne to continue speaking.

"Yes, I'm here for student teaching, but I've lived here on and off since last summer. My mom was raised here but moved back recently. Last Christmas was her second here. She said this is home. I'm living with her, then we'll see how things go."

"Oh, I know. You just waiting for the right man to come along."

"No, not quite. I'm finishing my education and helping Mom. She's very ill. I don't know how long she'll be with me." Dianne's voice faded as she swirled her chili to avoid eye contact with him. Spooning through the piping hot mix and adding chunks of cornbread also helped to hold back her tears.

"Oh. I guess you might be thinking I'm a bit outa line. I don't mean much bad about teachers and that's sad about your mom. I get to talkin sometime and roll all over myself. Didn't know my mom too much, but the woman who adopted me is a judge in Springfield. My daddy is some big shot guy in Washington with the president. He's my real daddy."

Most of Dianne's remaining conversations with Michael centered around how each was raised and compared big city life with Marshfield's. Michael was different from the guys she knew in St. Louis or college. She couldn't decide if he was older yet more innocent, more country, different, or weird. His over-abundant smooth-talking, led by his hypnotic eyes, intrigued her. However, she was still relieved to say goodbye eventually and didn't offer her phone number or make any plans to see him again. Because of this unplanned dinner encounter, she decided to buy a lawnmower somewhere else or, perhaps, continue using the lawn service her mother started.

Dianne arrived home exhausted yet happy to see the familiar surroundings of the home she and her mother had shared for the last eight months. The house was a simple, three-bedroom brick ranch style with almost half-acre land supporting a huge oak tree and a few saplings. Large yards and various trees were not uncommon in Marshfield, but in St. Louis, where Dianne and her mom once lived, an acre could provide space for four to five homes.

Life was different here; quieter, slower, greener during the summer, and much friendlier than the city's hurried existence. After reaching home and having trouble opening the door, she entered the living room and slung her coat across the sofa. She fell into an old, overstuffed leather recliner that seemed to harbor her father's essence as her shopping bag slid to the floor beside her. Her exhaustion melted with her father's spirit into a relaxed dream world shaken awake when a slightly off-key voice brought her back into reality.

"*-but don't tell my heart, my achy breaky heart …*"

"Mom, are you singing Billy Ray's song?" Katrina poked her head in the front door like she used to do when she played "peek a boo" with Dianne.

"Yes, it's me. And yes, I had a great time. I really like Ken. He knows my condition, and he's helping me live for the day!"

Mother and daughter laughed and hugged one another, each attempting to take in the magic of the moment.

"Ok Mom, tell me all about it. But first, why didn't you invite him in and introduce him? Like, what is his last name?"

"Sorry, I couldn't coax him in for an introduction. His last name is Simpson. He said sometimes he has some anxiety about meeting new people."

"Hmmm, do you know why?"

"No, I just accepted it," Katrina shrugged. "Oh, he started calling me his Trina tonight."

The conversation was a great reversal of roles for the mother-daughter team. They shared times when Dianne used to tell her mother about activities with friends, and now it was mom's turn to share. Dianne pressed her mother for every detail.

After almost an hour of talking and barely breathing, Katrina sighed.

"Well, this is a change. I remember when you went on and on about what you did in high school. I'm glad you and your friend

Nancy always double-dated. It made me feel a lot better. But don't think I'm going to double date. I want Ken alone and all to myself. I don't care what you might say about his belly."

"Oh, Mom, you little devil. Ken doesn't know he's fallen into your spell, does he? So, Ken has a belly?"

"Yeah, a little bit. What do you expect from a mid-forties man? We're both under the spell. I haven't heard about your dates since you left for college. Surely you weren't so busy with your studies and political life that you didn't have time for dating?"

"I mainly went out in groups, Mom. There really wasn't much to it. I did eat dinner with a man tonight. Wanna hear about it?"

"Really? You had a date too?" Katrina inquired.

"Not exactly, but there was this guy, the manager of MegaMart, who met me over at Kuntry Kitchen. Not on purpose, he just showed up and sat down."

Dianne filled her mother in on the details and was surprised when she started to frown.

"It sounds like you enjoyed him somewhat, but it seems to me he talked about himself a lot."

Dianne knew her mother was right. Most of the conversation centered around Michael, what he did, how he liked things and his accomplishments, and how much money and prestige surrounded his father in Washington.

"Did he ask you out?"

"No, it was one of those things short and not so sweet. I don't know if I would go out with him, Mom. His talking exhausted me. I can't imagine having enough energy to go on a date with him. He didn't ask for my phone number, where I lived, or any other information about me. And I paid for my own dinner. No, before you ask, he didn't offer to pay either."

"Well, if you ever go out with him, be careful about getting serious. Your dad was somewhat like that, always talking about his stuff. It took me years to make him realize there were two of us in the family. I must admit, though, he did work at it, and things turned out fine. I can't say the same for his two brothers. They gave their wives hell. I always felt fortunate your dad was willing to work with me, and he didn't drink like his brothers."

"Gosh, Mom. I thought Dad was always Mr. Agreeable, and I didn't know that about my uncles. Why did you marry him? He wasn't THAT good-looking, was he?" Dianne smiled at her mother, stretching out on the large sofa, using both coats to cover herself.

"It was the thing to do, I guess. And...well...I guess...I don't have a good answer for you. In the late sixties, women needed to get married, and I guess that was it. Well, and...I was sort of pregnant."

"Mom? I thought...Oh, that's right you did tell me awhile back you had a miscarriage."

"Yes, the timing was bad, and I think God knew it. Although you were a surprise. No, you were not a surprise, you were an unexpected blessing, and believe me, dear, I was very happy to bring you into this world. I think it's nice when people think of us as sisters. We used to be the same size, which helped the fantasy, but I shrank about half an inch. I'm down to nearly five-four," she said.

It was easy for Dianne to believe her mother was happy to have given birth to her. She felt very loved by both her parents. As a family, they often spent time together playing games, going out, and sitting together only to talk.

"Mom, I don't think Michael and I will date or even see each other, other than in the store. I don't even think he wants to date. He just chased me down to sell me a mower. But you know, he is good-looking, very good-looking. And no, I'm not buying a mower from him."

"Sweetheart, I know how things go. I won't be around, so I'm telling you. Be careful. OK? So, what makes him so good-looking?"

"His eyes are mostly a brown-blue mix, and he has a charming smile. He's almost too charming—like those bodybuilder guys on TV who sell protein powder. And believe it or not, he's not very tall. He's a little taller than me, about five eight, but not a hair taller."

"Oh, sweetheart. Be careful. I want to look at you from heaven and see you happy. Understand?"

"I understand, Mom. It bothers me to talk about life without you. I never know what to say."

"You don't have to say anything, my dear. I know I'm going to miss you too."

"Wait! Ken's in his mid-forties?" Dianne attempted to stop thinking about life without her mother by redirecting their focus. "You're older than Mr. Ken Simpson? You're robbing the cradle!" Dianne said with a chuckle as she righted herself on the sofa.

"Well yes, I needed a young man to run me around to all the treatments and doctor's appointments," she said, smiling.

"So, he's the friend from church who's been helping you? I thought it was a do-gooder society lady from church."

"Society lady? Do you think we're still in Saint Louis?" The women forced a smile that broke into chuckles. When their humor wore down, Dianne stood and looked at her mother in silence and hugged her tightly. Both wanted to cry yet remain strong for the other.

"Don't be sad, dear. I'll always be with you, and I think your dad is with us, too. Do you know that?"

Dianne nodded and held on to her mother. Katrina leaned back, "Well, it's past ten, so what do you say we turn in?"

"Yes Mom, I know our family will always be a team. Good night. I love you."

CHAPTER 2

Unseasonably Forward

Although dressed and ready for her first day as a teaching intern, Dianne wasn't fully awake. She was conscious only enough to start feeling anxiety about her first day at Marshfield Elementary School. She didn't need any additional stressors as she made final preparations.

"Michael! You call at seven in the morning when I need to be at school in an hour, and then you tell me you want to demonstrate a lawn mower? I know you don't do this for all your customers. MegaMart would close, or people here would burn it down," Dianne said, responding red-faced at the unexpected call.

"You're right. I don't do this for all my customers. I thought you were interested when you looked at them last night. It took me all morning to find your number and where you live, girl. Operator doesn't have your phone number," Michael whined in response.

"It's only seven, the sun's barely up. So how did you find my number?" Dianne was spooked by Michael's actions.

"I figured you'd need gas, so I asked John at the Texaco if he knew of a new woman in town whose momma was sick. He knew right away that your name is Dianne. And he told me where you live. I figured the phone number would be the same as the other folks who lived there since you just moved in. I knew those folks from the store. It takes a while to change things around here. Why you spell your name with two n's?"

"Geeze! Now I know I'm in a small town!" Dianne said in exasperation. "What's that John guy doing giving out my address?"

"Look, city girl, if folks 'round here don't know your number right quick, they'll just come knockin' at your door. Someone will know where you live."

"No! I don't need a lawn mower over here. I'm not even sure I want one! I have plenty of time before summer! I don't have time for this!"

"C'mon, girl. I spent all this time looking for you. I'll be right over to help you out."

After hanging up the phone, Dianne attempted to finish preparations for her first day at school. However, before she could leave, Michael drove up toting the bright red lawn mower.

Michael whined as he scuffed his feet on the England's front door stoop. "I gotta show you this," he said insistently.

"Michael! It's January! The grass will wait!"

"I promise I won't be here more than a few minutes. I know you got some leaves in your yard. This mower will chop 'em finer than grandma's pie. What you doin' goin' to the school today anyway? Schools are closed. Time for fun."

"I agreed with the regular teacher that I would start my internship the day after Rev. King's day, so today I arranged to meet her on the holiday and help fix up the classroom. Wait! Get out of here! I don't owe you an explanation!" Dianne caught herself giving Michael more explanation than he deserved.

"OK, I won't take long," Michael responded insistently.

"Michael, I don't want you here!"

"Don't worry, little lady. You'll change your mind."

"There's no stopping you, but you'd better make it quick And it's none of your business as to why two n's are in my name! I will find that John guy and give him a piece of my mind!"

Dianne heard Michael laugh as she slammed the door. Smothered with frustration after talking to Michael, she could barely speak when her mother called out. "Hon? Is everything OK?" Dianne heard her mother's weak voice from her room. She responded after taking a deep breath.

"I'm OK, Mom. I'm not going to let him ruin my day, but it's going to be hard. Sorry for slamming the door. I didn't mean to wake you," Dianne said as her mother appeared in the living room.

"What's the matter? What happened? Who was at the door?" Dianne took another deep breath and tried to explain it to her mother calmly, but her words became jumbled. All she could do was pound a pillow in frustration.

"You know, dear," Katrina said, sitting beside her daughter on the sofa. "If that happened in St. Louis, I'd probably call the police. But things are different here. I guess he's trying to get to know you a little, and he's clumsy about it."

"I don't want to know him. I want to do my teaching and be left alone. And! He showed up uninvited! Unwanted! Mom, you're always looking for the good in people and giving them a break. I sense nothing but trouble from that guy."

Katrina began stroking her daughter's hair. All Dianne could do was tilt her head to her mother's shoulder, sigh, and begin to cry.

"Hon, yesterday I made some lunch for you to take. Get ready to go to the school, and I'll have breakfast for you. OK?"

"You are so sweet, Mom." Dianne said, holding back tears.

Dianne didn't expect to see her mother up after being so tired the night before. Dianne kissed her mom's cheek, then decorated her oatmeal with an overflowing spoonful of honey and frozen blueberries. Dianne's coffee was instant, with enough coffee taste to help her get moving.

"You feeling better after eating?"

"Yeah, thanks Mom. I took out my frustration on the couch pillows. It helped that I took a quick minute to calm myself by writing a couple of sentences in my journal. You know how I like to scribble in there. I hope I didn't ruin it, writing so hard." Dianne looked up at her mother's tired face.

"Mom, did you overdo it last night? How are you feeling? I'm sorry. I was so aggravated that I didn't ask about you or even notice how tired you looked."

"I hope I don't look that bad. No, don't worry, dear. A friend from church is coming over today around one for a late lunch. And I thought I'd rest this morning. No, before you ask, it's not Ken. The friend visiting me is a lady who's part of a church ministry."

"Well...please, Mom, do rest."

"I think I did get a bit too rowdy last night, but I really enjoyed myself. And Ken, well, I guess he's my Romeo. Oh, speaking of Romeo, I think yours has unloaded the lawn mower from a trailer. He seems to be an insistent one."

Dumbfounded, both women stared through their oversized picture window. The sight of Michael with an old primer-gray car towing a new trailer with a riding lawnmower in midwinter was more than the city girls could handle. Both nearly choked on their laughter.

"Please, Mom, stop! My coffee is about to go through my nose! Don't laugh at the poor boy."

Dianne's pleading was in vain. Both continued to laugh and could barely hold back tears when Michael started the mower.

Dianne suddenly jumped from the table. "Mom, I've got to put a stop to his nonsense! Michael!" she yelled as she charged through the front door. "This is crazy! I'm in shock! Leave! I'm not interested in your damn mower!"

"I'm sorry. I didn't mean to make you mad. I really think this is a good mower and wanted to see you. You're a nice lady and all."

"Thank you, but I think we should leave things as they are."

"Now I feel bad. Least I could do is make your yard a little prettier by chopping up those leaves for ya."

"OK. Do it and get away from my house! And don't block the driveway. I'm leaving in five minutes!"

"Oh, howdy ma'am. This must be your momma," Michael said, turning off the mower and slowing his speech while walking toward Katrina as she stepped onto the porch.

Michael extended his hand. "Ma'am, your daughter is real nice, and I don't mean any harm by coming over. Can I take you two for some ribs in Springfield to make it up to you?"

"Well, thank you, Michael," Katrina said, shaking his hand. "Dianne may have told you I'm not well, and last night I overdid myself. I must stay in tonight, but if you want to chop up the leaves, please do it quickly and ensure it doesn't make too much noise."

"Miss Dianne, Will you give me a chance to make it up to you? I'll buy you some good ribs and a big ol' baked potato. What ya think?"

"I think I should stay with my mother tonight. Thank you. I accept your apology. Now pack up the mower and go away!"

"Miss Dianne, I can be a gentleman. Why don't I call you 'bout four? You going to be home then? If you want to go with me, then I'll pick you up at about 5:30. I know you'll love these ribs. I pick them myself. I'll leave you both alone rather than making a lotta noise. You can rest, ma'am and Dianne can go on over to the school. I'll mow later, when the grass gets green. Expect my call, Miss Dianne?"

Dianne didn't know what to say. Michael seemed sincere with his puppy-dog stare and inviting grin, but as Katrina said, he was clumsy with his words.

"Well, that's real nice. I'm taking the schoolteacher to dinner. Oh," he hesitated, and looked at Dianne directly. "Maybe, that is. I'll call you, then you tell me. Thank you, ma'am," Michael said, then reached for Dianne's hand and kissed it. "It's gonna be nice to spend time with you. You sure you gonna be alright, Mrs.—umm. Sorry, I don't know your last name."

"Our last name is England, like the country."

"Thank you, Mrs. England. I'll take good care of your daughter," Michael said as he started back to reload the mower onto the trailer.

"Michael! I haven't agreed to anything!" Dianne shouted, as Michael seemed to almost skip back to his car.

"I need to hurry over to the school, Mom," she said, retreating into the house to grab her coat and classroom supplies. Dianne wanted to get upset with her mother for making it easy for her to forgive Michael and accept his invitation but couldn't bring herself to it. She saw how tired her mother looked and didn't want to make things worse.

"Did I take away your excuse, hon?"

"Yeah, but it's OK, Mom. I know you like spending time with Ken, and I guess it won't hurt to spend a few hours with the redneck from hell."

Dianne was surprised at her own words. She had not agreed to go out with Michael.

"That's a good name for him," Katrina responded. "I hope he's not that bad. He really does seem sincere, only a little clumsy."

"Mom! He's not socially clumsy. He's from a different planet not yet discovered in this galaxy! Sorry, Mom. I've got to go—and yes, I'll be careful."

Dianne leaned over and kissed her mom's cheek. "You have my number in case you need me? I'll stop by the office and tell them you might call. A couple of the office staff are in for a few hours today too. During lunch I'll call you and make sure things are OK."

"OK, hon. I'll be fine, but I do wish your prince charming would have stayed to tidy up the yard. I was so worried about those leaves."

"I'm sure you were, Mom." Dianne returned the sarcastic tease and headed off to her first day in a Marshfield classroom.

Dianne arrived at the school as two teachers were in the process of opening the classroom doors. Pamela Millbrook, the classroom's supervising teacher, started her classroom introduction by explaining that Myra Porter would work with them only a few hours each day due to her difficult pregnancy.

"Generally, there are three teachers in the class. With Myra part-time, we could say we have two and a half." Pam smiled. "Opening the shades over there is Darla Smith." Pam motioned toward a woman securing shade ropes onto their anchors. "She has adult children of her own about your age."

Darla shared with Dianne that her oldest child had learning disabilities, but programs were not developed as much when her son was in school. She said she is relieved he can live on his own and support himself working as a cabinet maker.

"The children all call us by our first names because it's easier for them. I'm Ms. Pam and you will be Ms. Dianne," the supervisor said. "And when they're not around, just use our first names. We're a team here, and it makes the flow better."

During the day, Pam described each student's abilities and personality with such love and detail, it was as though the students had a second mother at school, guiding them in learning about life and basic schoolwork. Dianne helped Pam and Darla go through students' papers and redecorate the classroom for the upcoming Valentine's and Presidents' Days. She learned a little about her coworkers between student profiles and decorating, which made the morning go quickly. Pam was a Marshfield native and left the area for a short time to go to school in Springfield and from there she went on to do church mission work in Haiti. There she met her husband, Robert "Bobby" Johnson, who was born in Saint Louis but was raised in Marshfield.

"It's kinda funny how we met," Pam explained. "The National Guard sent him over to Haiti for two weeks, for security duty when they were having a lot of looting after the hurricanes. After we met, he decided to sign up for some construction projects the

Guard Engineers were working on near the village where I was teaching. I was due to go home in a couple of weeks when he arrived, but I stayed so we could get to know one another better. Neither of us is Catholic, but a priest married us there, and we stayed only a couple of months after being married. It was a short engagement, but so far, after 14 years, it's working nice." Pam smiled and continued. "I kept my maiden name and dropped the hyphen when I started teaching. It was rather difficult for some kids to say all my name."

"What's he doing now?" Dianne said wide-eyed.

"He's one of Marshfield's finest! He went on to the Police Academy in Springfield, stayed with them for a while, then joined the Sheriff's Office. It's less money, but he likes the community. Folks here have known him as Deputy Johnson since '88 when he was promoted."

"Wow! That's impressive!"

Pam smiled at Dianne's reaction. "Thank you. What about you Dianne? Do you have any children, or is anyone in your family a slow learner? I'm curious how you became interested in students with learning disabilities, or like we are branded here, as Educable Mentally Retarded students. I'm working to change that label. Even saying this is an EMR class doesn't work for me. Labels are meaningful." Dianne nodded in agreement.

"I wish I could explain. I was a little afraid of not getting a job after finishing school. I read special education teachers were in demand, so I started taking the right classes. But that's only a small part of it. I like helping people who don't have the same good life and abilities I do. I know that sounds a little snobbish, but I don't mean it like that. Speaking of weird sounding, isn't learning disabilities a little rough of a title? It seems to pigeonhole a student rather than provide an opportunity for their full potential. "Abilities focused" is how I like to think of our profession." Dianne smiled, looking intently at her coworkers for their response.

After taking a few seconds to consider what Dianne said, Pam responded. "You'll do fine in this field, and we'll work well together. But I tell you, some days are going to be frustrating. Like Darla and I, you'll go home to your husband and not want to hear anything he says because you are trying to figure out how to get through to someone. The good news is that the program here is excellent. I can do what needs to be done in this classroom without too much flak from parents or Mr. Richards, our principal."

"No husband to go to, but I can understand getting frustrated. I did some volunteer work in Springfield during college. I worked with challenged adults in the Good Citizens Workshop. Most days were fun, and I loved showing them new skills, but when they had bad days, I sometimes let things get to me."

"I understand," Pam nodded in agreement.

"You're not married? You have a special sweetie?"

"No, and I guess this class...and helping my mom will keep me busy. I met a guy last night, but I don't think we'll date more than tonight. That is if I go out with him. He's weird. This is a small town. You two might know him, Michael D. Glossen, MegaMart General Manager?"

"I kinda know his dad through my husband. They did political things together and didn't part company on good terms. That senior Glossen is a slick one. People need to watch out for him. The son, Michael, seems to have a good job but is strange with helping customers. He's almost too helpful and too much of a salesperson. Unlike his father, I don't know him well, but he seems harmless. He hasn't been in trouble, or my husband would know it. I'm not sure, but he might be adopted. I seem to remember something about that."

Dianne told Pam about meeting Michael, and how he came about asking her out that night. "I guess my mom doesn't want me to stop doing things just because she's sick, so she made it easy for me to go out with him tonight. I'm not sure I want to do that, though."

"It sounds like he's a strange one—too much a salesperson. I guess your mom cares for you a lot and wants you to keep on living your life and not worry about her. It's up to you, but I don't think the young Mr. Glossen will be a problem. Who knows, you might even have some fun! It's a bit past our usual lunchtime. Since we've completed most of our work, why don't you go on, even though it's early. It'll give you a chance to pretty-up for your date."

"Oh, I'll take my time, and I'll wear jeans. I don't want to encourage him. Yeah, I guess I'll go out with him...maybe."

"Well, tomorrow before class, tell me about it."

"Thanks. I think I will go home. See you tomorrow. Is seven a good time? And Darla, the next time we meet I want to hear more about you."

"Certainly! It will be nice to get to know one another. We'll all see each other at seven!" Darla said as she closed the shades she had opened earlier.

CHAPTER 3

Busted

After leaving the England's home, Michael stopped at JR's Truck Stop to grab "the best cup of coffee on Missouri Highway 44." Michael often told Betty her coffee and pastries beat anything along the highway, which was a joke since both knew Michael had visited very few restaurants outside of JR's. Besides, Michael rarely ate pastry.

The few times Michael ventured away from Marshfield, he preferred to take his own food—healthy food—another quirk Dianne would soon discover.

"Hey boys!" Michael's voice cut through a room full of conversation.

"Well, hey yourself!" JR snapped back as he distributed plates piping hot with mounds of eggs, grits, sausage, and plump biscuits to a line of truck drivers sitting at the counter.

"That wasn't you toting the lawnmower 'bout an hour ago, was it?" JR queried Michael as he set plates and collected others. "Didn't think folks were coming to the MegaMart for summer buying. Yet, there you are, toting one 'round town."

"Yeah, still got it on the trailer. I thought I had it sold. Betty, give me some of your love juice, will ya?"

"Looking for some broken teeth this morning? I bet that's one thing you don't sell in that store of yours," JR's voice boomed.

"Umm, Betty, ma'am, may I have some coffee, please? If your husband could get his legs to carry his big belly around the counter, it might be my last."

"Michael, I know you don't mean much by it, but ya gotta stop talking to women like you do. Someday one's gonna have a real mean husband who's gonna use one of your mowers there and chop you up like dog meat," JR warned him. "Now be respectful."

"Ferget the husbands! I saw this truck driver this mornin' over at the pipe place loading up. She'll knock you out and strap you to her hood for the fun of it," volunteered a voice from a line of truck drivers working on his plate full of country breakfast.

"I know the one you're talking about. She was in here a couple weeks back. Wasn't she JR?" Another hearty eater interjected.

"Yeah, that's Millie. I don't think she's ever been married, so no husband will get ya, but I tell ya...she can handle herself and knows her work. She came through here haulin' pipe sometime back and some come loose. Millie and one other driver cranked down on the chains and went on 'bout their business. She's a hearty gal," JR told the group.

"Now that's a woman for our friend Michael. Someone to put 'em in his place and keep him there," another of the boys volunteered in a sea of mocking laughs.

"I hope you're listening to these boys, Mel. Michael needs some straightenin' up. You up to it?" JR smiled, as he looked over to his 19-year-old daughter and bookkeeper.

"Alright JR, you guys too. Leave Michael alone. He's not like all of you think. He does have a gentle, respectful side," Mel said as she approached Michael and placed her arm around his shoulder.

"Thank you, darlin'. Don't listen to these boys. They've been overeating sausage this morning, and it's going to their brains," Michael said, giving Mel a quick squeeze around the waist.

"Ms. Betty, may I have another cup of your most delicious coffee?"

"Betty, better give him some coffee before he gets too good for us. And I gotta pay up and get outta here. The rest of you boys got loads to haul?" Duane, the burliest of truck stop regulars, said as he moved toward the register.

"Yeah, I guess we do. Betty, I'm leaving the money here for ya. I'll catch the change on my way back through."

"Yeah, me too," each echoed from the truck drivers exiting the restaurant.

Regulars at JR's always left much more than their bill as a way of saying thank you to JR and Betty, not only for food but for their continued kind deeds. The couple was known on Missouri highways for helping truckers in trouble along the road and at their business. Occasionally, a driver would feel sick or need a cat nap.

The couple let them rest in a "real bed" in a room off the restaurant. A few months back, a driver who caught the flu stayed for three days, and the couple nursed him back to health before he continued down the road. Like all regular drivers at JR and Betty's, he repaid the couple generously at his next meal. They didn't want to accept his big tip because they knew he had missed some deadlines, which meant missing some money. The truck stop's silent rule was that they gave a polite thank you and continued to help where, and when they could.

"I'm glad those boys are gone. I've had a rough morning, and I didn't need their mouth," Michael said, still standing and gulping the orange juice he poured for himself.

"Something happened with that mower you're toting?" JR asked Michael.

"Yeah." Michael didn't tell the whole story about his experience with the new girls in town until Mel retreated to finish some book work in the business office.

"The new woman who bought the Garrett place has a pretty girl who came into MegaMart last night to talk to me about buying a mower. She even sat down and ate dinner with me. This morning it was like she didn't know me. I tried to take the mower she was looking at over so they could see how it took care of the leaves. They didn't even let me in the house for coffee. The little girl got all upset 'bout my comin' over there."

Michael suddenly stopped ranting when he saw John from Texaco walking toward him from one of the booths at the window.

"Well, what did you think, asshole? You didn't even know them! It's January! Six damn thirty in the morning you come talking to me! In January yet, you fool! And you lied to me, you dirty bastard! You told me they bought that mower. What you doing bothering those nice ladies?"

"Oh John! I didn't see you back there. Who's running the shop?"

"Danny's in early! Now boy, why did you want to bother those ladies?"

After being caught, Michael tried to wiggle loose like any rat in a trap. He tried to change the subject. But from the look on John's face, Michael saw his evasion wasn't working.

"Well ..." Michael shifted from foot to foot, sipped on his

coffee, finished his orange juice, and again told Betty how good the food was. "Mind if I grab a pastry? These sure do look good this morning, Ms. Betty."

While Michael tried to escape John's confrontation, everyone left in the restaurant fell silent. The last truck driver to leave looked around at the silent group of "locals" staring at Michael, still standing with one foot propped on a bar stool footrest.

"Yewie! This man's not staying 'round here while the squealing hog gets barbecued. See you next time, JR, Betty," the last of the truck drivers said as he headed out the door.

"Bye! Now don't you worry 'bout anything. We know ole Michael's gonna find his way outta this one. He always does," Betty said with a smile while cleaning away some plates.

"Now, Betty, ma'am, nothing to get me out of. I was trying to be friendly, and John don't understand me sometimes. You know John, they're gonna be buying something before long. They're new in town, and I don't see any harm in being friendly. I coulda cut up those leaves for the women while the girl was teaching today, but her momma was sick, and I didn't wanna make noise. When I saw they were upset, I asked if I could take them both for some ribs in Springfield or wherever they wanted. Only the girl wanted to go, and I'm taking her over to Benny's tonight. I promised her momma we'd be back early. I'm doing it to be honorable. You know I didn't mean any harm. I want them to feel good about Marshfield and feel real comfy here."

"Comfy my ass," John came up to Michael's face. "You just looking for pussy! Get me away from this asshole. I've got work to do. Here ma'am. The change's yours," John tilted his grease-spattered hat toward Betty, then left.

"He's done figured you out. I keep telling you. Women gonna get you back, boy." JR looked intently at Michael.

"JR, he don't know a thing. I told you he don't know what I do, or why I do things. I'd like to see him run a big store like I do. He's my daddy's age and just got a little gas station. Look what you got, JR! You know how to think big business. I'm sorry, Betty. I don't think I could eat this. I need to get outta here anyway," Michael pushed the pastry away, and Betty scooped it into the trash.

"Go on, Michael, I didn't think you'd eat it anyway with your muscle-building thing going on. I don't remember you ever eating anything sweet. You going to work?"

"No, ma'am. But I did eat one bite. This is one of my few days off, so I will stretch out with some weights and try to shake John's nasty words. Maybe I'll run around the land," Michael started to make excuses for his behavior.

"Michael, they weren't nasty." JR quickly responded, "You know John's telling the truth, and it's like I've been telling you, you gotta start respecting women. It's almost like you think you own them and don't think they have lives and feelings."

"All the good-looking ones like Betty have lives with me in it," Michael said with his signature smooth smile.

"Michael! You're not listening to me. Go home."

Michael left a few dollars on the counter in front of JR, then rushed out and headed for his home a few miles from the truck stop. Michael's money was short on generosity, yet adequate.

As he reached home, Brandy, his "almost German Shepherd" dog, strained her rusty chain to meet him with a wagging tail, wiggling, and short barks. "Now bitch, let me put my shit in the kitchen, then I'll come and get ya." Michael wasted no time throwing car keys on the counter and placing his prized possession, a 9mm Glock, into a kitchen drawer before returning to Brandy. "See, that didn't take long," Michael said to the dog as he unhooked her from the old chain. "You know, dog, we gotta keep the gun safe where nosy neighbor folks, like Steve Colson can't see it. We can't leave it in the car."

After Michael released Brandy from her chain, she shook the dirt from her fur and followed Michael to the carport. Michael referred to his carport as a customized weight room. He lifted weights in the room surrounded by plastic sheets tacked to a 2x4 framing system under an aluminum patio cover. Erecting the plastic was a cheap way for Michael to make a winter exercise room covering half his driveway. The construction showed careful detail, which is typical of his work. Heavy staples appeared every three inches along the frame, and the heavy-gauge plastic was stretched drum-tight, smoothing all creases and wrinkles.

When Steve Colson had first seen the fine construction, he asked why he didn't build a "real room" for all the work he put into the plastic. "I'm thinking on it" was Michael's only response. As was typical, he decided what needed to be done without much influence from others.

He liked having his dog as an audience in the plastic room and rarely let her into the house. During heavy rain, snowstorms, or freezing temperatures, she stayed in the house, right off his prized makeshift exercise room. However, when the weather was nice, she was at the end of the rusty chain, attached to a small doghouse, placed on gravel with a small patch of grass nearby.

When Mel came to visit, Brandy received a reprieve from her small circle of movement. When Michael was consumed with weights or bodybuilding, Mel often played with, petted, and groomed the dog like she was her own. Sometimes, when Mel knew Brandy was alone for a long time, she took her for rides in the country or over to the truck stop. What Mel didn't know was that Michael ran with Brandy almost daily. Brandy was a lucky dog when off the chain.

Michael's time away from MegaMart was often spent lifting weights, talking to his canine pal, or going "Dutch" to car races with Mel. When he was alone, he liked walking or running around what used to be his family property but now belonged to a drive-through animal park. He enjoyed seeing buffalo, emus, llamas, deer, and the more dangerous wild animals in distant compounds or running free on the grounds.

After his runs, or a weightlifting session, he followed a strict routine. He removed his shoes just inside the kitchen door and tiptoed through his spotless kitchen as though he would drop sweat on an impeccably clean floor. He usually plucked a beer from a nest of fresh vegetables in his refrigerator and then continued his ballet moves to the bathroom.

A predetermined routine continued after his shower. He wiped the steam-drenched walls, dusting most surfaces and catching any loose hairs he found as he finished his beer. After every shower, he neatly hung his once-used towel on hooks behind the bathroom door. When his housekeeper, Julia, performed a weekly cleanup, she removed the hung towels and washed them exactly as Michael had instructed her, or so he thought. When out of Michael's site, Julia performed her work expeditiously, without regard to Michael's proclivities.

Before getting dressed, Michael placed his empty beer bottle in a designated box in the kitchen, retrieved a second beer, and then resumed dressing in his bedroom. In the same structured manner, the home's walls displayed trophies of Michael's life, collections of area wild animal pictures, and mementos. Each was hung with precision, and he took great care to emphasize to Julia how to clean each one. Per his instructions, she displayed clean and lightly starched clothes, all hung in the same direction and buttoned. Everything in Michael's home had an exact place, and Michael was proud to brag about his organizational skills to anyone who would listen. He was always slow to admit Julia's part in the unnatural displays of order. He never acknowledged that, without her, he could not maintain his routine or extreme sense of household order.

Refreshed, Michael always positioned himself on a reclining chair, much like one his father owned, but Michael was proud to say his was a little bigger and had a massager. He usually capped his routine by sipping beer in the easy chair and clicking through TV channels brought in from around the world by his satellite dish. This deviation from Michael's fastidiousness was a minor contention Julia had with Michael. She protested about the crumbs and occasional drink stains on the recliner every week. Yet every week, she restored the chair to a stainless condition.

"You have table!" she often yelled in a thick Spanish accent.

His standard response was, "Don't I pay you well?"

Michael did pay her well. She and he knew this, and they both treated the exchange like a weekly ritual. However, his generosity came with unwanted behavior beyond his passion for routine. On the days when she was there, he completed his ritual of exercise and beer and showed his fascination with Julia's form. He loved her shapely breasts and ample rear. He loved staring at her as she worked. When she bent over, he often took liberties, sometimes before he dressed, with feeling her butt, waist, and breasts. He seemed to like her protesting. His only response was always, "Don't I pay you well?"

Julia put up with it because he did pay her well, better than average. He never indicated he would take his attraction further than caressing, so she put up with it for the money. Despite her husband's anger at Michael's behavior toward his wife, he put up with it, too, for the money. His anger often boiled inside, but he kept it between himself and Julia because he had to keep his rage private so Julia could remain in the USA.

Michael decided today would be different. Instead of preparing a butcher-crafted burger and resting it on a bed of crunchy lettuce, tomatoes, and trimmings on a whole-wheat bun, he left out the meat and used an extra slice of cheese. He always used the finest cheese. This small change in routine was significant for Michael, although it didn't last beyond this one meal. He munched the sandwich and thought about the earlier stern conversation with JR and John. He admired JR and began to think about what he said that morning. JR seemed to be everyone's ideal father image, so it was understandable that even someone like Michael would listen.

Michael turned off his TV, stared at condensation forming on his beer bottle, and tried to imagine himself as a gentleman in JR's eyes. It was unusual for Michael to think about other people's words and opinions. As a result of his deep thinking, he unintentionally left Brandy untethered. His mind remained on his conversation with John and JR about his respect for women. Adding to the multitude of thoughts swirling in his mind, Michael received a phone call from a MegaMart department manager asking him to decide on store displays. The day that started uncommonly strange was beginning to unravel without Michael's strict routines.

"Damn asshole bitchin' mutt. Whataya doin'?" After slamming down his phone, Michael blasted out his kitchen door into the cold air still holding his beer and wearing only a shirt, pants, and slippers. Brandy intently tore at the membrane surrounding his weight room. The dog continued to tear at a corner, and the plastic quickly popped away from the 2x4s like a candy wrapper. Michael swung at Brandy with his beer bottle, and it nipped her hind leg. Before he could get her again, she yelped and ran toward neighbor Colson's home.

"Fucking dog. Don't you run to that house! I don't want him to claim I owe him money cause you diggin' his yard...or for anything!" Michael cussed and yelled at Brandy while chasing her like a football player shooting out of a formation and heading for the goalpost. If any animals in the adjoining park could see him, they probably had their own form of laughter, seeing a mostly naked man running after a dog in the cold.

"Alright, dog, come over here," he said, calming down when he realized chasing Brandy wouldn't help. She reached the neighbor's porch before responding to Michael's calmer voice. "Dog, c'mon. I ain't gonna hurt chu."

Michael wanted Brandy to come before his neighbor, heard the commotion and began asking him for money again.

"Oh man, your leg done swelled. I'm sorry. Are you ok? You seem to be walking all right. You come on. I gotta get to work and straighten a mess, then get ready to take a pretty girl for dinner." Without Colson noticing, Michael recovered Brandy. The stealth action seemed to calm his anger and Brandy's fear faded as he led her back to their home.

"Here you go, girl. You're back home. Here's your house. Let me look at that leg." Michael bent Brandy's leg without her showing pain, but when he touched the swollen area, she yelped and snapped toward him.

"Whoa, dog, take it easy. It's frickin' cold out here, and I gotta get dressed. You'll be alright. I'll bring you in the house. Here, you can even sleep in the recliner." Michael resumed his dressing routine, slipped a small ice chest into his car's back seat, then headed over to MegaMart to settle a dispute between managers in two different departments.

"Well, hey girls. What's the problem? Why do I have to be called in here to keep you two from scratching each other's eyes out?"

"Mr. Glossen, I think you're talking 'bout the sweatshirt display," department manager Marty explained. "We worked it out. I don't know who called you, but it wasn't a big deal. Look!" She took him over to the disputed area.

"Now that looks nice. You got the red sweatshirts over by the Valentine candy and all, and she's got those perty red silky lacy things there too. I like that, Miss Wendy. Did you think of this?" Michael asked, giving her a wink.

"Why yes, I did. I didn't mean to alarm you when I called. I just thought you might like to know what's going on in your store," she said, then glared at Marty as she pretended to straighten the sweatshirts. Marty stared back, knowing it was her idea and knowing that it was she who arranged the display. Marty was not a person to fuss over the small stuff, so after her intent stare, she returned to her department.

"You ladies take care. I've got personal business tonight." He touched Wendy's shoulder gently before leaving. As Michael left, he heard the managers continue to talk with some volume about the situation and quickened his pace as their voices began to get louder.

"Ms. Kelly, would you go back to the two discussing their business rather loudly and remind them the store is open and customers are still around?" Michael said to the head cashier as he left the store. Having dealt with the two managers before, Ms. Kelly knew it was a matter of Wendy taking credit for another person's work. She would discuss this with Michael at their next managers' meeting.

Damn! I'm supposed to call Dianne. I guess I better not just show up again, he thought as he opened his car door. Upon re-entering the store, he locked eyes with the previously quarreling employees. Fearing a reprimand, both ladies made instant busy work.

"Ms. Kelly, did you make the two in the back see Jesus?" Michael asked.

"I tried. You back to check on them?"

"Nah...I just gotta make a phone call I almost forgot about. They looked at me like I was gonna go back there and walk them both out. We'll talk about them in our next meeting."

Although Michael promised John he would throw away Dianne's address and phone number, he pulled the slip from his wallet and dialed.

He smiled and spoke softly when Dianne answered.

Then he mumbled after hanging up.

"She's coming to Springfield with me!"

His mumble was almost loud enough for Ms. Kelly to hear.

CHAPTER 4

From Man Came Ribs

Although hesitant, Dianne prepared for her date with more apprehension than she had earlier when she prepared for her first day in the classroom. Weirdly, she hoped she would be stood up.

"Sorry I'm late. The ladies at work needed me to stop by and help them," Michael told Dianne when she answered the door.

"Hi, Michael. Please, come in. Do people ever call you Mike?"

"Naw, ever since the second grade, there was this other Michael, and everyone called him Mike and me Michael. It kinda stuck."

"That's understandable. I'm almost ready. I will finish putting these towels away and be ready to go."

"Your momma okay?"

"Yes, she's in her room sleeping. Thank you for asking."

Dianne was surprised to hear Michael ask about her mother and not instantly jump into something about himself.

"See, I'm not as bad as you thought this morning." Michael stared at Dianne as though he expected appreciation for his politeness.

"I hope not," Dianne said, smiling while placing the last of the towels in a nearby closet.

"Dianne, you leaving?" Katrina asked faintly from her room.

"Yes, Mom. I hope I didn't wake you."

"No, I was getting up and heard Michael come in. Ken should be over in about an hour. He's bringing me something to eat."

Dianne disappeared briefly from Michael's sight into her mother's room to kiss her goodbye.

"You going to be okay, Mom?"

"Yeah, my boyfriend's coming over and bringing dessert," Katrina said, smiling and forcing her eyes open.

"Oh, Mom. You're supposed to let me tease you and admit to

nothing."

As Dianne squeezed her mother's hand, she noticed how tired she looked, which almost led her to change her mind about going to Springfield.

"I'm okay, Dianne," Katrina said as though she was reading her daughter's mind. "Go on. Have fun. Ken will be along soon."

Reluctantly, Dianne started to leave her mother's side. "Hon, I appreciate you living here and caring so much for me, but please don't put your life on hold. Don't hold for me, or for anyone. Will you honor me by living fully?" Katrina smiled at her daughter as she pushed herself up from the bed.

"Yes, Mom. And know I love you, okay?" Dianne left the room, choking back tears.

"I'm ready to go, Michael," she said quickly to her date without looking directly at him.

As they approached Michael's car, Dianne's mood suddenly changed. She remembered laughing with her mother at the sight of Michael pulling up that morning. She couldn't believe she was about to ride in the car, which had earlier been a source of their amusement.

What the hell? I'll think of it as a cultural experience, she thought as Michael opened the door for her.

"It ain't the prettiest around, but I'm gonna paint it or get a new one. I like my painting to be just right. I've been keeping an eye on this truck I like in Springfield, but I'm not sure about it yet, so I keep working on my baby here."

"Well, at least this one's clean. You're going to trade this in for a truck?" Dianne asked, thinking, *Who would want this piece of junk, no matter how clean it is!*

"Yep, trying to decide if I should go ahead and paint it first. I was thinking white. That's a good color. It should make it sell or get a good trade-in at least." Michael looked at Dianne, anticipating that she would want to talk more about the car.

Dianne didn't care what color he painted it. Her mind flipped back to how tired her mother looked when she was saying goodbye. Michael's car wasn't a concern in the least.

"And you know what else? I bet you didn't even notice...I'm trying hard to be a real gentleman. I guess those college boys always opened doors for you, so you didn't notice my helping you there. I'm just a country boy, but I respect a lady," Michael proclaimed as he looked at Dianne while starting the car.

"Well, I can only remember college boys doing that a few times. But thank you, Michael. I appreciate it."

"I hope you think I'm a gentleman and get to liking us around here in Marshfield. You might like to stay awhile, and I hope you like ribs because you're about to have the best." Before driving, Michael turned and opened an ice chest sitting on his back seat. "Ain't them beauties?"

"I thought we were going to a restaurant in Springfield," Dianne quickly retorted. She wondered what Michael was trying to pull.

"Yeah, we're going. I always pick my ribs from the store. Benny makes 'em nice for me. He knows I don't like any other thing a supplier throws in a restaurant. And they're flavored just right for us. I'm sharing these with you."

"That quick? Don't these things have to sit and smoke for awhile? Is that legal?"

"Legal don't matter. I don't know how he does it. It's the best. Look over here. See, there's enough fat to make 'em juicy. The ones I dropped by yesterday were like these. Put these beauties with a baked potato and sour cream, and you got yourself a meal."

"Did you bring your own trout to the Kuntry Kitchen last night?"

"Now girl, you are pulling my leg. They do fine over there. They get their fish from a farm outside of Lebanon up in the woods. Ever been there?" Dianne admitted she hadn't, which opened a floodgate of information about the area, fishing, and backwoods anecdotes, which made the trip to Springfield longer than usual. After listening to Michael, she decided Michael was one of the strangest guys she had ever met. She also discovered he seemed almost obsessed with food, its origin, and its quality, whether accurate or not. His babble seemed like an endless gospel of good health.

"The only thing I allow myself is a little beer now and then, but no sweets," he bragged.

"I guess we all have to have our vices," was all Dianne could say, realizing Michael's primary communication method was to recite endless chronicles rather than have a conversation.

"Looky here. Let me show you something," Michael said, wheeling into a car sales lot on the outskirts of Springfield. "Now THAT is a truck." Michael pointed to a perfect red full-sized Ford F-250 with an extended cab. "Now look at those big tires. That baby wasn't on the road long. Mr. Scotty told me it's the best truck they have had here in a long time. It's last year's model."

"Why in a car lot already?" Dianne asked.

"Man got killed. The ole boy got shot right there in the truck when he was hunting deer."

"Oh my God. I think I read about it a few months back."

"Yep. Man down the street fixed up the holes in the door. Now it's like new."

"Well, Michael Glossen. You come back to get your truck?" Mr. Scotty greeted the onlookers.

"Not yet. I was showing this beauty to my lady here."

"Ma'am, this boy's got some sense. This is a great truck, hardly driven. Told Michael we'd fix him up with it, but he'd need some help."

"You need help, Michael?" Dianne asked.

"Well, you see, I've only been at my job for less than a year, and they won't give me the money. I'm thinking 'bout asking my buddy JR to back me on this."

"He must be a good buddy. This truck's over 20K!" Dianne said with amazement. "You think you can ask him for the money?"

"Yeah, JR known me since I was a kid. He knew my daddy too. He knows the whole family. Oh, 'scuse my manners. This is my good friend Scott Hickman."

"Hey, beautiful lady. I don't suppose you could help this fine man out. Could you, Miss?"

"Oh my goodness! We just met last night. I'm not even out of college. Even so, a teacher's salary couldn't pay for such a nice truck."

"Oh no, ma'am. You don't pay for it. Michael makes the payments. We use your name. The finance company likes to do business with teachers. I've sold cars to lots of teachers like this. I could sell you one too. It'll be easier doing business in one place. I'll put you and your friend here in something real nice."

"I'll think about it, but we were on our way to eat, so we can't do anything right now anyway," Dianne told the salesman.

"Yeah, I guess I better feed this little lady." Michael winked at the salesman as he turned away and escorted Dianne by the elbow. He said he hoped to see him again in a couple of days with some money, although he knew JR, who knows Michael's lack of skill with financial matters, would not lend him money or even co-sign a note for him.

Michael quickly exited the car lot, which had more to do with his fear of Scotty saying too much rather than his concern for Dianne's hunger. He didn't want Dianne to start thinking his finances were bad, although they were.

"Hey, ladies!" Michael addressed the servers as he burst into the rustic tavern-like eatery with Dianne at his side.

"Well, hey you handsome man. What you bring us to eat?" A buxom waitress threw her arm around Michael's shoulder and pretended to ignore Dianne.

"Now take it easy, sweetie. I've got a date tonight. This is Ms. Dianne England."

"Hello. I'm sorry I didn't know you two were together," the waitress snipped, flinging her curly bleach-blonde hair over her shoulder while half turning away from Dianne to swoon over Michael.

Dianne felt she had been thrown into another world as she stepped into the strange-smelling building, with made-up women who sported dyed and teased hair, making them look like cheap Barbie doll imitations. This woman's attitude was an open invitation to Dianne for some competition, but Dianne wasn't sure of the trophy.

"Oh girl, you're looking fine!" Michael said, looking Mitzi up and down as she fluffed her hair. "Now be good, sweetie, and bring these on back. Benny's done fixed the ones I want tonight. Oh, I'm gonna get my lady some Coke, and you can bring me a beer. Unless you want a beer too?" Michael said, turning to Dianne.

"Oh, don't worry. A Coke is fine, either Coke or Pepsi, whatever you have." Dianne knew she should verify what kind of cola she wanted. Just saying "Coke" could mean a wide variety of carbonated beverages in some area restaurants.

"Michael, what is it I smell?" Michael took a couple of deep breaths and stared at Dianne. He had to think a minute to realize what she was talking about. Nothing seemed strange to him.

"It smells like something cooking, but it's not hamburgers. It's much stronger. Is it some type of barbecue sauce they're using?" Dianne asked as she grabbed a tissue from her purse to catch a tear leaking from her watering eyes.

"I know what you're talkin' about! That's venison. Deer meat. I bet Benny killed it himself and is cooking up a stew. Ya want some? I bet he'll dish some out for you. You crying?"

"Oh, I don't think so," was all Dianne could say. She wasn't sure she liked the smell and started to realize it was more than the deer meat cooking. It combined years of cooking smells, old cigarette smoke, and stale, long-ago spilled beer, making a unique perfume.

"No, not crying. The new smell affected my eyes, I guess," Dianne explained.

Michael pulled out Dianne's chair unexpectedly, which seemed odd, but she attributed it to Michael trying to be a gentleman. After Mitzi served the duo their beer and cola, Michael jumped up to feed an old jukebox endless quarters before sitting beside Dianne.

"What ya think so far? This is where I'm at home. It's almost like my family here. I have fun, don't get too drunk, and usually dance with all the ladies. But not tonight. It's just you. I hope you like to dance. We can get our food down better that way."

Dianne was still experiencing culture shock. She didn't think Michael wanted an answer, so she became occupied sipping on her drink to avoid commenting.

"OK, we'll eat then dance," Michael proclaimed.

"Well here, handsome. Here's your salad," the Barbie-doll waitress placed an ample salad on their table in front of Michael. She placed a similar, yet smaller, salad almost out of Dianne's reach.

"You haven't been around here before," Barbie directed her comment at Dianne while she stood against Michael, one hand on his shoulder.

"No, I lived in Springfield during my college years. Before that, I lived in Saint Louis," Dianne told the server. She looked directly at her and purposely over-articulated her words as though she were talking to one of her students.

"Yeah, Dianne here is a schoolteacher. She teaches up at Marshfield. She come in last night wanting to buy the best mower we got," Michael interjected.

"Well, Michael could fix you up with a nice mower...I guess. My apartment house cuts the grass, so I don't have to worry about it. That's kinda a man's job anyway," the waitress responded, obviously trying to snub Dianne.

"My daddy's not rich, so I gotta get back to work. You two have fun and let me know if you need anything. Okay, Michael?" The waitress smoothly turned away from the couple's table while rubbing against Michael's arm.

"Oooo ain't she something?" Michael said, smiling.

"Yeah, she's something all right," Dianne responded as she squeezed salad dressing from a little packet the waitress had placed on the table.

"Now, I hope you don't let her bother you. She's been kinda sweet on me and don't like it when I come in here with someone. She's got her boyfriends. I got my girlfriends, but she wants it all, I guess," Michael explained between chews.

"I ask them to wash this salad before bringing it out here. I don't like to have anything nasty on my salad," Michael said, directed his comment to Dianne, and continued without taking a breath. I'm healthy and intend on staying this way. They had better wash yours, too. I don't want you getting sick."

"You still eat meat," Dianne said, glancing up from her salad. "Don't real healthy diets recommend not eating meat, especially red meat or pork?" Dianne said with a smile.

"I don't know about that, but I do know we need our protein. You like vegetables?" Michael said, pointing his fork toward Dianne after he poked at a stack of iceberg lettuce.

"Yeah, I like vegetables a lot, and someday, I might become a vegetarian."

"What? I know what that is! They never eat meat." Michael seemed as though he was proclaiming vegetarians were not of this world. Indeed, they weren't of his world. It was Dianne's turn to go on a tangent about healthy food and living.

It didn't take long before she realized she was losing Michael and trailed off talking about vegetarians. Continuing the conversation was not difficult for Michael. He jumped in, talking about his store's groceries in a conversation that seemed to take hours.

"You see, I know about this stuff. Oh, I see our ribs coming," Michael voiced, taking a breath in the middle of his ranting.

Mitzi quickly set dinner plates in front of the couple without any more sass or snide comments. Suspicious of her behavior, Dianne cautiously cut into her meat with a knife, suspecting it might be under cooked. Michael dug in with fingers and teeth.

"Yours as raw as this?" she asked, prying the meat away from the bone.

"Hell, no! They ain't! Gimme that plate!"

Dianne couldn't respond before Michael grabbed her plate and headed to the kitchen. She could hear his voice echoing loudly in the kitchen as he yelled at Benny about the ribs.

"These ain't even the ribs I brought in. There's too much fat in 'em. What you trying to do to my lady, Benny? You didn't fix 'em and barely cooked 'em!"

"OK, OK! Calm down! It was a little joke Mitzi and I was playin' on ya."

"Unless you want your skinny ass fried up on that grill of yours, you better get my lady some good ribs, and everything else better be perfect!" Michael told the cook, grabbing him by his apron. Michael left the nervous cook visibly shaking. Before returning to sit with Dianne, he side-tracked to the checkout counter to pick a rose from the bunch displayed as last-minute temptations for customers to purchase.

"Wow, you got serious there. Your veins are still bulging from your neck."

"Yes, I did, and here's something beautiful, like you." Michael tried to shake off his temper.

"Yep." Michael said, taking a bite of his ribs. Before he finished chewing, he started into another meaningless rant. "Mel, a woman I know, tells me I look like the Incredible Hulk when I get mad. Remember that program?"

"Yes, I remember it." Dianne answered quickly. "Why did you get so mad at Benny? Oh, before I go on, thank you for the rose."

"Glad ya like it. It ain't just Benny. Mitzi put him up to it. I guess she don't like you."

"I kinda guessed that."

"The GOOD ribs will be out in a minute. Meanwhile, I gotta get another beer. You need anything, my love?" Michael seemed to switch instantly from Hulk to a European romantic.

"I guess that'll help calm you," Dianne says as she motions toward the beer. "I'll finish my salad and wait for dinner."

"You bet, my lady. Mind if I jump into eating?" Michael continued his meal without waiting for an answer

It wasn't long before Dianne's meal arrived, cooked to perfection, with a small slice of orange on the side.

"I didn't expect a garnish," Dianne said, again poking at her rib dinner.

"Ya mean the little orange slicey thing? Yeah, I think that's Benny's way of saying he's sorry."

"My meal is good now. Thank you, Michael."

The incident with the ribs was almost a cleansing for Michael. Now he could finish his meal, chat with Dianne, and share things without going on tangents. After both completed their meal, Michael announced it was dancing time and fed more quarters into the jukebox.

"You ever done a two-step?"

"No, but I'm willing to learn."

"C'mon girl, we're gonna do it!"

Michael was great at teaching Dianne the steps she had only seen while surfing through Country Music TV. He was straightforward to dance with and patient when she made mistakes. When Dianne realized she had stayed an hour past her self-imposed curfew, she was tempted to ignore the time and beg Michael to teach her more.

"Oh, schoolteacher, I know you gotta be in class tomorrow. We learned enough for tonight. You wanna learn to stomp next time? Some folks call it clogging."

"Sure!" was the only response Michael needed and that Dianne could give.

"Wait now, before we go, we gotta get something for your momma. I'm going to ask Benny to pack up some of the good ribs, a few baked taters, and yeah, this big ole lollipop here at the counter. Think your momma will like that?"

Dianne was shocked, partly because Michael would think of

bringing something for her mother and partly at his gift choices.

Good heavens! Mom is sick, she thought. *What will she do with ribs, potatoes, and an oversized lollipop?*

"Looky here, this candy's bigger than my hand," Michael proclaimed proudly while Mitzi packed the food and took Michael's money. Before leaving the register, Dianne saw Michael lean over to Mitzi and barely heard him threatening that the ribs they were taking better be the right ones, and he didn't want any funny business from her again.

"What you gonna do 'bout it, sweetheart? Spank me?" Mitzi shot back.

"Check with Benny," was all Michael could say as he escorted Dianne away. On the way back to Marshfield, the couple, mostly Michael, talked endlessly about country dancing and music as though an incurable country-dancing bug had bitten them both.

"Now, I'm not even gonna try and steal a kiss from you, Miss. I'm just going to walk you to the door and say goodnight," Michael announced as they pulled up to Dianne's house.

"Now that's really sweet of you," Dianne said, somewhat confused by his words. She was back in the real world and did not want any kisses, hugs, or even a handshake.

"You almost sound local, girl."

"Thank you, Michael. Oh, I was wondering something …"

"Now don't you go proposing to me. I never marry on the first date."

"No, Michael, I wouldn't do that. Mitzi might shoot me. What I want to know is, could you call me Dianne rather than 'girl' or 'schoolteacher' or 'my lady' or the other names you thought of tonight?"

"Oh sure, girl. Oh, I mean Dianne. Dianne it is then. You go out with me this weekend Dianne?"

"Yeah, I'll go out with you. But you know, a storm is supposed to come in, and we're getting some snow."

"Aww, the roads 'ill be clear. Don't worry yourself."

"Goodnight, Michael," Dianne said, pulling herself from the car.

"But lady, you didn't let me walk you to the door. Ummm, I mean Dianne. I gotta be a gentleman. And this! Ya gotta bring this to your momma!" Michael reached into his back seat for the carryout package Benny packed for them, then rushed around his car to walk with Dianne to her door.

"Thank you, Michael, for being a gentleman, walking me to the door, getting Mom a present, and all."

"OK, I'll call you before the weekend so we can set up a time. Maybe we can get together before then, and I'll teach you a few steps." Dianne agreed it would be okay, and when he looked at her, he had the same enchanting smile with those beautiful eyes seeming to stare directly into her soul.

"Goodnight, Michael."

"Goodnight, lovely lady, ummm, I mean Dianne, Lady Dianne, that's who you are, "Lady Dianne."" Michael returned to his car, almost skipping, as he did earlier when he paid his unwelcomed visit.

Dianne entered a quiet house, placed the take-out box in the refrigerator and propped the giant lollipop on a set of canisters decorating the kitchen counter. As she was undressing, she felt dread.

My God! I didn't check on Mom! she thought, then walked gently to her mother's room and cracked the door a few inches to peek inside.

"I wondered if you were going to say goodnight. I heard you come in."

"Goodnight, Mom. I love you."

"I love you too, Dianne. I hope you had a good time. Tell me about it in the morning?"

"Yes, Mom. I will. Goodnight."

"Goodnight, darling."

CHAPTER 5

Reality Drifts In

The radio blared, yanking Dianne awake from a sleep she didn't realize had overtaken her. Thankfully, Mother Nature would soon accommodate her with much-needed rest as the weather reporter declared a snow day for area schools.

"Central Missouri has turned into a winter wonderland overnight with the snow belt stretching from Kansas City clear to Saint Louis. Stay tuned for the six o'clock news and a complete list of school closings after this message."

Well, that's just fine. My first week of school, and I'm lined up to have a three-day work week, Dianne thought as she listened carefully to the school closings on the radio while trying to peel herself awake. The announcer confirmed her guess that Marshfield schools are on the list of closings. Along with the school closings, news reports filled the airwaves with reports of jack-knifed trucks, accidents, and other weather-related incidents.

A sudden day off with little to do was unusual. College classes were rarely canceled as most students lived in dorms or apartments in Springfield. However, the few times they did close last year, she was relieved to have the extra study time. Now, it was different. She looked forward to working with the children, Ms. Pam, and the other teachers.

After listening carefully for sounds that her mother might be awake, and only hearing the occasional branch fall to the ground from the weight of heaping snow, she slid out of bed. With eyes half-opened, she donned her warmest pair of sweats and nestled her toes into furry moccasins before heading toward the kitchen.

While making coffee, Dianne felt suddenly uneasy. Dropping the coffee can, scoop, and carafe, she flew to her mother's room.

"What's going on, hon? Getting ready for school?" Katrina didn't raise her head to talk to Dianne. She mumbled into her pillow, eyes closed and not moving a muscle.

"Mom? Are you awake? Are you OK?" Dianne sat down beside her lethargic mother. "Mom? You OK?" she asked, trying to stay calm. Katrina was silent. "Mom! Mom!" she said louder while patting Katrina's arm.

"Oh, oh, I'm alright. I'm feeling real tired," Katrina mumbled.

"Can you sit up? Should I call the doctor?" Dianne's voice became urgent.

"It's getting harder, you know. Help me sit up."

"Oh Mom, you do look tired. Want some orange juice or water or something? Or should I call the doctor or ambulance? It's snowing outside, so we can't wait until the last minute. Maybe I should drive you. Want me to drive you?"

"Let me wake up. I'll let you know how I feel, OK?"

"Am I getting carried away?" Dianne questioned while fluffing her mother's pillows so she could remain upright.

"Please don't fuss. I'll be alright. You say it's snowing?"

"Yes, Marshfield schools are closed."

"I guess because of the country roads."

"Yes, the roads are bad, Mom. You getting better?"

"Yes, just worn out. I hope this snow is gone by Saturday so we can drive to the family farm."

"They're calling for about five inches today and more Wednesday afternoon, but maybe it will let up a little tomorrow and melt some by the weekend."

"Hon, I'd ask Ken to drive us, but I really want it to be just us girls."

"Just because he's a man doesn't mean he can drive any better," Dianne sounded surprised and slightly irritated at her mother.

"I wasn't thinking 'man,' I was thinking older, 'more experienced' person," Katrina said dragging herself awake and adjusting herself. Katrina seemed more like herself, but her face was etched with the effects of over a year's worth of myriad cancer treatments and emotional ups and downs. She had come to peace with the disease and the knowledge of starting a journey to her final home.

"Nothing like a good argument, or rather 'conversation,' to energize you, Mom," Dianne said, laughing while pressing her forehead against her mother's.

"You know if you say something sassy at my funeral, you can bet I'm going to sit up and give you a piece of my mind too!" Katrina snapped back with mock indignity.

Katrina's statement hung in the air and tickled both women to the point of laughter, which soon turned to tears and a warm embrace.

"Oh, Momma."

Katrina struggled to speak through a hoarse, weakened voice. "What day is it?"

"It's Tuesday. Remember? Yesterday was MLK day, and I only worked a little because the children were out."

"Hon, I'm scared, but you have nothing to worry about. Sometimes, I wish God would take me home. You know, even when I lived in St. Louis and felt there still was hope, I kept getting the feeling I was on my journey home. I'm so sorry I didn't tell you about this back then. I really...well, I wanted you to keep your mind on your college life and not be burdened with me. I was so ugly, with my hair falling out. I was tired, scared, sad...you name it, it was awful."

"Mom, I would have dealt with it if you had told me. I would have gone back if I needed to leave school for a while."

"I'm not so sure you would have gone back. You're far enough along now that if God lets me open the door to heaven, you will recover and continue. And I want to live. I'm not afraid of dying. I feel like I have things to do, like seeing you graduate. And I know how you get distracted with things in life."

As her mother's voice trailed off, Dianne became melancholy, letting a tear drop from her eye and delicately splash on her hand.

"OK, daughter, where did you go?"

"Mom, you catch me in a daydream every time," Dianne smiled. "You first. Tell me what's on your mind, OK?"

"OK. I thought about the picture at the church where Jesus is knocking on the door. I guess we're supposed to believe that Jesus has already knocked and opened the door, so all we must do is walk in and see God."

"Yeah, I guess you could say that, but I have my opinion."

"I know you do, hon. I don't always understand all you've got to say, but I'm so proud of you for developing your own thoughts about life on Earth and beyond. I hope I have always kept my heart open to you and anything you want to share. Please don't ever hesitate to talk to me. Please, Dianne?"

Her mother's words were comforting as always, which often led Dianne to share her thoughts.

"Mom, do you want me to make some breakfast? We can sit in the living room, drink coffee, and watch the snow fall. Does that sound good? You can relax and let me take charge," Dianne said, hoping to force herself from the melancholy mood brought on by her mother's sickness.

"Yes...that's good," Katrina said, smiling as she squeezed her daughter's hand.

Dianne scuffed into the kitchen to cook oatmeal, brew coffee, and set several breakfast items on the table in front of the couch. It all looked perfect.

"Mom! Mother?"

Dianne walked back to her mother's room. Katrina had fallen asleep sitting up with the mountain of pillows still propping her. Dianne couldn't imagine how her mother could feel comfortable in such a position.

"Here, Mom," she said, taking away some pillows, "I'll hold your breakfast, and you can rest."

Dianne continued to assist her mother by arranging pillows and covers. She helped her mother snuggle back into a reclining position without uttering a word. Dianne could see how tired her mother was and how sick she had become. Dianne padded from the room, gently closing the door. Entranced by falling snow and pained by her mother's illness, she sank into the couch, ignoring the breakfast she had made. All that mattered was the pain of losing another parent.

No, no, no, it can't happen! she said inwardly, ranting as she slammed her fist into the couch. *I've got too much to tell her! I've got too much to share!* Her rant soon became a frantic prayer. *Please don't let it happen! I've got so many things to share with her. Please, please, let her live! Please, please!* Dianne pleaded silently.

It seemed an eternity as she lay on the couch, soaking a pillow with tears, praying, and asking for help. She prayed with passion, addressing a god she was not sure existed. Her eyes swelled and turned warm from her emotion. Her throat was sore, and her entire body was stiff with sadness. Grief lulled her to sleep.

As she slept, she dreamed she was a girl again, playing with other children. In her dream, Dianne saw her father, who held out his hands to lift her in the air. She saw herself floating over her father as though she were flying. "I'm here to take you home, Nightingale," he said. "Daddy, I can't go home. I stay with Mommy," the little girl told him. "OK. I will see you later." Her father smiled. "Don't worry, Nightingale. All is as it should be." Her father's voice soothed her, although she didn't understand what it all meant.

A sudden sound of rushing water awakened Dianne.

"Mom? Is that you?" Dianne said, stumbling to her feet.

"Yes, hon. I'm...I'm hungry," Katrina said, shuffling from the bathroom to the living room. "What time is it?"

"Gosh, I don't know. Let me see. Damn, it's eleven!"

"What a way for a little Nightingale to talk! Do you remember when your father called you that?"

"Oh, Mom, you're not going to believe this! I fell asleep and saw Daddy in my dream. Daddy called me Nightingale."

"Wow! That's weird," Katrina said, shaking her head as she sat. "You think he's looking over us?"

"Yes, Mom, I do. I think Dad has always looked over us. I wish he'd been nicer about it when he was alive."

"I guess he didn't want to spoil you, being an only child and all. His father acted gruffly, so he acted gruffly. If we had a son, he may have acted the same way too, I bet," Katrina said reaching with a shaking hand for the orange juice. She sipped without commenting on how tepid it was.

"I hope not. Maybe I could have trained a brother or beat him up or something to stop that from happening." Dianne smiled at her mother and gently held her hand.

"I doubt it. You wouldn't have beat up on anyone. You might have given him all you had in words, though. In the cabinet under the TV are some photo albums. Want to grab a couple, and we'll talk and eat a cold breakfast while we page through them?"

"I guess you're right. I'm a softie. Here, let me heat that. The oatmeal is like concrete, and you don't want to know what the coffee might be like," Dianne said, plopping the photo albums on the couch and grabbing the coffee cup to reheat.

"Just some toast for me, OK? And a banana. I think I could eat a banana. On second thought, no coffee for me."

"OK. I'll have some leftovers from last night. Would my eating them bother you, Mom?"

"No, that's fine. Get what you want."

The women ate, talked, watched the snow fall outside the large picture window, and thumbed through the collection of albums. Dianne listened intently as her mother told stories of her youth, parents, and brothers and sisters. Each of the five children in Katrina's family had a special animal to care for on their farm, and each had chores to complete before and after school. All completed high school and went on to college, with the older ones helping the younger. Katrina guessed Dianne received her giving nature from her side of the family.

"That's what I'd like to think, anyway," she told her daughter. "I was like that, always ensuring others were cared for before myself. I think your father liked that in me but took advantage of it, too. It appears ..."

Katrina paused, wondering if she wanted to share a painful past. After a deep breath, she continued sharing.

"After we were married, your dad changed a little for the better."

"Instantly?"

"No, it was gradual. At first, I jumped every time he came into the room. This got worse when I was pregnant with the baby before you. After I lost the baby, I didn't handle things too well. I went into a shopping craziness. I didn't care if things were new or used. I figured I needed stuff. Our house looked like a combined antique shop, thrift shop, junk store, or whatever. One day, your dad and I looked around and realized things weren't right. He had become gruffer, really mean. I had junk everywhere. Slowly, we began to heal ourselves. That sounds easy, but I had to make some tough decisions. It came easier when we discovered you were on the way. Neither one of us wanted you to be born into a house full of junk and a father who was angry all the time."

"Did you have to go into counseling or anything?"

"We probably should have, but somehow, we did it alone. You know, that wasn't done too often back then. Even after we started straightening ourselves up, remnants of our former selves remained. Instead of buying lots of stuff, every time I bought something for you, I had to study to ensure it was the best I could afford. Indecision is not good, you know. I often couldn't decide to buy even what I needed. Most of the time, your father was a nice guy through it all, but if he was worried about something or tired, he was a bear. It was like he tried so hard to be nice, but when he was too tired to hold up the mask, he became himself, an angry bear."

"Did he ever hit you?"

"Dianne! I'm surprised you asked!"

Katrina remained silent for a few moments. She wanted to tell her daughter something but couldn't find the words.

"I...I was pregnant with you. I cried most of the day. During this time, your dad and I were fully committed to changing our ways of excess. And too, I experienced the emotional ups and downs that pregnancy showers on a woman. Dad seemed helpless to cheer me up. He didn't know, and I'm not sure he even tried to understand. He started yelling at me. He said I brought it all on myself, and if I could realize how much I had, I'd stop crying and quit feeling so sorry for myself. This was a total shock to me. He quickly picked me up by my arms and held me about a foot off the floor against the wall, yelling at me, scolding me like a child, only worse than a child."

"Oh, Mom, I had no idea Dad was ever like that. Like...that awful!"

"Really, I'm not sticking up for your father. He seemed to feel bad afterward. He let me down slowly, asked me if I was OK, and then stared at me for the longest time. Suddenly, he began to cry and apologize. He was so worried that he had harmed me, and we might lose you."

Exhausted, Katrina paused, sipped water with a shaky hand, and continued.

"I was scared, and I wanted to divorce him right then. I couldn't help but wonder what this man might be capable of, and I was terrified. I calmly told him to leave the house. I needed to think through some things. I didn't know what to do at that point. I wish I could have called my mother, but by that time, both she and my father had passed."

"Mom, you must have been so confused!"

"I was. I didn't have close friends at the time, either. I felt alone."

Dianne could see that talking so much and revisiting a tough time in her life had exhausted her mother.

"Mom? You want some more water?"

"Yes, thank you, hon. I'm really thirsty. Don't bring me cold water, just from the tap."

Katrina gulped a glass full of water and asked her daughter for more.

"Wow, Mom. I've never seen you drink like that."

"I'm really thirsty talking so much, I guess."

"You want to rest? Am I wearing you out?"

"No, no, I don't want to rest. I want to be with my daughter."

"Thank you, Mom. I'll bring a pitcher of water for you, OK? Just take it easy."

"You're a good nurse. Thank you."

"So where did Dad go? Umm, do you feel like talking?"

"Yeah, I'm fine. He told me that he drove around a little, then called Gerry. He and Gerry were not close friends, but he knew Gerry had an extra room. We didn't talk to each other for a few days, except for your dad calling and telling me where he was. It was weird. He even bought an extra set of clothes, a toothbrush, and all that kind of thing so he wouldn't have to come to the house."

"Well, how did you get back together?"

Katrina smiled, breathed deeply, and began to blush. The thought of her husband returning home made her look healthier.

"He was quite romantic. He knew I ate lunch at the Uptown Deli in St. Louis on Fridays. He brought a dozen roses, a ring with your birthstone, and proposed to me in front of the entire restaurant. We all were impressed, people I knew and just strangers sitting near us. I still had my reservations."

"So what did you tell him?"

"I said yes but told him it wasn't easy. I asked him to come by the next day, and we would talk. He did, and I decided to take a chance with him, so he moved back to the house. Well, at least he and Gerry became closer, and I got to know Gerry's wife. She was a great help when you were born." Katrina took a deep breath and sipped water. "Oh, and the deli customers kept asking the staff if we got married. They had to put up a sign, 'Yes, they are living happily ever after.' I wonder what the regulars thought when they noticed my belly getting bigger in the following weeks."

Katrina smiled. "I'm wearing out. My stomach feels queasy. Oh, I hate this." Katrina reached for Dianne's hand as though it would be a lifeline for hanging on to her meager breakfast.

"You're getting pale, Mom. You OK?"

"I'll be alright. Are you going out with Michael tonight?"

"No, that isn't until Friday or Saturday. Just as Dianne spit out her words, the phone rang.

"Hey, Lady Dianne. I have news that might make you mad at me." She heard Michael's voice on the other end of the call.

"You do? What?"

Dianne cupped her hand over the receiver. "It's Michael, Mom."

"Figured." Katrina redirected her attention to the picture albums Dianne placed on the couch.

"With all the snow and employees not coming in and all, I gotta work more than I thought on through the weekend. It's gonna to be tough," Michael said, almost in a whine.

"Oh, that's okay, Michael. Don't worry about it. My mother's not feeling well anyway, and I should stay close."

"Well, I could come over one night after the store shuts down. I wouldn't want you two ladies to spend so much time alone with this weather coming in. You got a snow shovel to get out of the house?"

"Thank you, Michael, but a few months back, Mom arranged for a neighbor to come over and clear our walk. He's been over already, but it looks like it's covering up again. Anyway, it might melt off a bit," Dianne predicted.

"Yep, these country snows. Ya can't guess how they gonna act. I think we're gonna get about six tonight before it starts melting a little. Don't go anywhere. It'll be too dangerous for you two ladies."

It wasn't a surprise to Dianne that one minute, Michael ignored how dangerous the roads were becoming but now acknowledged the conditions.

"We don't plan to go anywhere until city and country roads are clear. By Saturday, they should be fine. Dianne didn't remember if she had said anything to him about going to her mother's family farm, so she did not bring it up."

Michael seemed oblivious to Dianne's statement hinting she was ready to end the phone call. He continued to talk about the dangers of snow and all the accidents that had taken place in the area due to snow over the years. Dianne started rolling her eyes in response to her mother's forced smiles.

"I was in the middle of making dinner for Mom. I've got to hang up, Michael. We'll talk later," Dianne somewhat lied.

"I'll be at the store. If I can, I'll come by later. You be a good girl. See you later, Lady Dianne."

"No. don't. There's no need." Dianne became stern but wasn't sure if Michael heard her before hanging up.

"Mom, why could I have so much fun with this guy Monday, but a day later, I want to choke him? You know what he said to me? He said, 'You be a good girl.' Like I was his dog or kid or something."

"You said he had a dog. Maybe it just slipped out."

"You're probably right, Mom. He's a faux pas waiting to happen. Oh, there's food from last night for you. Are you able to eat that kind of food?"

"No, no way. I think Ken can eat it for lunch when he comes over tomorrow, or Thursday. If you are hungry, you can eat it. Did you know Ken is calling me his Trina? Isn't that sweet? I like it."

Dianne didn't know how she felt about that, a man other than her father, being close to her mother. She thought her mother had mentioned it, but for now, she would ignore it.

"I am getting hungry. I'm going to fix a sandwich with some of it. Want anything? Anything at all?"

"More toast. I really can't handle anything else. My stomach's still acting up."

As the evening settled, magic seemed to descend outside. The day's grayness turned to black ink over a luminescent white ground cover. Clouds lightly veiled the sky, revealing a peek-a-boo moon reflecting on snow.

"C'mon, Mom. I noticed something." Dianne beckoned her mother to stand, and she secured Katrina's furry robe, took her hand, and led her to the front porch.

Clouds sheered by a tree's bare branches danced past the yard, making the fresh snow sparkle.

"This is beautiful, Dianne. Thank you so much. I didn't notice what was going on outside. The air is so still. It seems mysterious."

The women stood speechless, taking in the cold, quiet beauty. Katrina shivered, then a delicate wind chime hanging on the porch tinkled, snapping the women back to winter reality.

"I think we had better close the door. I'm getting cold," Katrina said.

They returned to their comfortable perch on the couch to continue quiet conversation and sharing, but it wasn't long before Katrina began to tire.

"I need to rest, hon. I'm worn out."

"I don't think you really even got up today, did you?"

"True, but this long dream I had about spending the day sharing things with my daughter was great." Katrina smiled at Dianne as she kidded with her.

"Mom, you didn't eat much today. Please, at least sit for a minute and drink some Ensure."

"Oh, OK, I guess I had better do what nurse Dianne says. I don't want to make her mad. And, before I sleep, will you help me bathe?"

"Ummm, sure, Mom. It might help you sleep. I'll run some water for you while you finish your drink, or are you too tired for a bath?"

"I'm very tired and my stomach is a little upset. Yes, I'll take a bath anyway. Or, better yet, I'll take a warm shower. Perhaps it will make me feel better."

Forgetting about giving Katrina anything to eat, Dianne obediently ran water until it became warm for her mother, firmly secured her seat in the shower, and plucked fresh towels from the closet. She positioned a portable heater so she wouldn't be chilled before drying off.

After helping her mom, Dianne shared, "Mom? I've got a confession to make. This is a little weird, helping you with a shower."

Katrina smiled as Dianne dried her. For a moment, her healthy spirit seemed to return.

"Yes, you've never seen me naked as a jaybird. I feel weird about it, too, but like you said, dear, I think I'll sleep better after cleaning up."

"Oh, Mom, you're shivering. Here's another towel." Dianne quickly wrapped her mother.

"Oh, toilet," Katrina groaned. She leaned toward the toilet as Dianne flipped up the seat. The small amount Katrina had eaten swirled into waste, making her chalky and weak. All Dianne could do was help her into a gown, help her brush her teeth, and walk to bed. Still shivering, Katrina lay under a pile of blankets and began to cry.

"I can't help it. I'm scared. I want it all to go away."

"Yes, Mom," was all Dianne could respond. She lay beside her mother, cuddled her, and stroked her straw-like hair.

"I feel sad too, Mom."

It wasn't long before Katrina shivered herself to sleep while Dianne stayed awake, occasionally feeling her tears drip onto the pillow. She tried not to let herself sink into further sadness. She forced herself up. Dianne tried to close the door gently, but Katrina stirred. "I want to go to the farm," Katrina's weak voice mumbled.

Surprised to hear her mother's voice, Dianne peeked into the room, expecting to see her mother awake. She hadn't moved.

I guess she's talking in her sleep, Dianne thought as she gently closed her mother's door and returned to the living room. With the evening still young, Dianne ate a few bites of leftovers and tried to finish a poem she had started writing a few days before. However, the home's quietness and her sadness sapped her creativity. She thumbed through several magazines and newspapers—anything to keep her mind occupied and off the thought of losing her mother.

She slipped into her mother's room a few times to check on her. Her breathing seemed shallow, but the color had returned to her face, which relieved some of Dianne's worry. Before long, it was time for Dianne to sleep. Knowing a little more about her mother and father, she felt peaceful. Tired, she completed her night routine and tucked herself into bed.

His Trina? OK, yeah, I think this is good, Dianne thought before drifting off to sleep.

CHAPTER 6

Mystery from the Farm

Dianne felt as though she dreamed every minute during the night. Reality blended with her slumber, entangling her in the bed covers. Perhaps a suppressed worry robbed her of a good night's sleep.

"Wake up, Dianne. Remember? We're going to the farm today," her mother's sweet voice called, beckoning her out of a dream world.

Dianne's eyes slowly peeled open. Blinking away sleep, she noticed the bright sunlight filtering past the opaque yellow curtains.

"Mom? You feel better?" Dianne called out sleepily. "Mom?" She hoped for a glimpse of her mother walking around the house, busily preparing coffee and breakfast goodies, but the house was silent.

"You okay, Mom?" she called louder as she slipped feet into slippers. Rubbing sleep from her eyes, Dianne robotically shuffled from her room to the edge of her mother's bed. She listened to the same shallow breathing she'd heard the night before and checked for a fever but found only a clammy forehead.

"Huh? What's the matter, hon? Aren't you going to school?" Katrina mumbled as she started to awaken.

"No, Mom, snow again today. At least it will be above-freezing for a little while. Did you call to me a few minutes ago?"

Katrina started to wiggle to an upright position. "No, I just woke up. The room is too bright. I don't feel like it, but I've got to go. Don't know why I waited."

"Go where?"

"The farm! I have to go to the farm," Katrina said impatiently as though Dianne wasn't listening.

"Do you know how bad it is out there? You know it's not the

weekend, right? The roads might melt off some with the sun, but there will still be black ice. It's only Wednesday. Didn't we plan this for Saturday?"

Katrina had a troubled look that started to tear at Dianne

"It's okay, Mom. We'll go. Think you can eat some breakfast?"

"I think I can handle a small bowl of oatmeal, but don't put any fruit in it, okay? The room is so bright. My eyes hurt." Katrina's voice sounded hoarse and strained.

"That's the sun reflecting off the snow. Coffee? OJ? Umm, I hate to say this, but do you want some Pedialyte?"

"No, none of it. Fix yourself some. I need to get up and shower." Katrina tried to stand upright but could only get her legs to the side of the bed.

"Don't you remember? I helped you take one last night. You need another? And no, Mom, I don't think I need any of your 'power water.' I don't understand why you drink that stuff when you could take something like green sports drink."

"The doctor said to drink it. I've got a bad taste in my mouth. I'll brush my teeth. I threw up last night?"

"Yes, Mom, you threw up."

Katrina's health seemed to have improved from the night before, but her disorientation concerned and saddened Dianne. She felt cancer was racing to claim her mother's body and prayed for the disease to slow down. At least for today, she wanted the disease to loosen its grip so they could see the farm where Katrina was raised and enjoy simple moments together. She didn't want to venture out, but her mother was insistent.

After Dianne helped her mother get dressed and coaxed her to eat a few bites of toast, she helped her nestle comfortably into a warm car. The women quietly reveled in the bright sun radiating through the still air. They drove through their small community, watching small patches of yard turn to working farms. Gems of sunlight bounced off glittering snowdrifts, lulling away their tension. The countryside's winter blanket along wet country roads exalted the beauty of the area's rolling hills. All was calm, serene, and relaxed, effectively hiding trepidation about driving in potentially slippery conditions.

"Mom, with all you were going through, why did you buy this

car?"

"It's your graduation present." Katrina strained to speak. "I didn't know if I would be around to give it to you. I drove it once. Okay, not for long. I wanted you to have something safe. You talk about a place in Florida."

"You know, Mom, visiting Florida would be much more fun with you."

"I would like that. Oh...I think I should have brought water. I hate the taste. That water I'm drinking is for babies, for God's sake!" Katrina's voice sounded more strained. I'm thirsty and sick. I've got to say goodbye to Momma and tell her she has a granddaughter. You would like your grandmother. She was like you. Born later, I don't think she would have had five kids."

"Don't worry, Mom, I packed some power water for you. There's a driveway up ahead. I'll pull over to give you a rest from the curves, and you can have a couple of swigs of your favorite beverage."

"Oh, she jokes with a dying woman," Katrina croaked.

"And you joke back. And you tell me about Grandma and many wonderful things. Thank you, Mom. Is traveling to the farm your way of saying goodbye to her?"

Katrina slightly smiled at her daughter's words as a reaction to a queasy stomach and fear of the unknown that kept shouting for attention. She confessed the Pedialyte, combined with not moving, was comforting. Katrina traveled and enjoyed Webster County's roller-coaster hills for most of her life. However, now, each hill and curve was challenging.

"Let me breathe some fresh air. I'll be okay."

Dianne turned off the engine, leaving the key positioned so she could lower her mother's window for a breath of cool air. Joking or reliving memories could not ease Katrina's helpless feelings. Only her daughter's gently placed hand on her shoulder could even relax her. The small gesture communicated love, empathy, and sorrow for a cancer-victimized woman who had to follow a path alone.

"Mom, look! Someone's coming from the house. I guess he thinks we've broken down or something. Gracious, I didn't know it snowed that much. It's over his ankles."

"Yeah, we always had a lot of snow here. We kids loved it."

Katrina forced a smile.

"Hey girls! You got car trouble?" the burly country farmer said as he adjusted a too-small coat around a belly trying to escape from worn overalls.

"No, believe it or not, we're out for a ride. My mother was feeling kind of sick, so we pulled over for a second. I'm glad you had a clear driveway."

"Oh yeah. I take the tractor out every time it snows here lately. Never know when ya need to get out in a hurry. My daughter is 'bout to have us a grandson, so I gotta be ready. Oh ma'am, you don't look too good. You wanna come up to the house and rest? Y'all could pull right up in here. You know it's supposed to snow later. Maybe you had better turn on back?"

"Sir, this is something we must do today. Mom was raised out here and it's important."

"I see," the man said, seeming to understand the woman's urgency. "Whereabouts?" he addressed Katrina.

"The England Farm," Dianne interjected.

"Yeah, you're not too far from it. The farm creek starts up there. It's the Hanover Farm now," the man said as he pointed up a small hill a few hundred yards away.

"The Hanovers are the people who bought the farm from grandma." Dianne almost sounded excited to learn the current owners' name.

"Oh, they got a mess of children up there. No one wanted to move off the land when the kids grew up and had kids. They pretty much keep to themselves, but I see them in Springfield at the farmers' market every so often, and lately, they've been bringing my family some goodies. I guess they're farmers, what ya think?"

Dianne smiled at the man's slight humor, then continued. "It must be in the creek water. Mom's family had five kids. Now, the ones still alive are scattered all over the world."

"You'll see them soon enough," Katrina mumbled.

Dianne took hold of her mother's hand. "Sir, thank you for checking on us. I guess we better get back on the road. I'm not sure how long Mom's going to be up to all this."

"Yeah, I understand. Look, you ladies honk the horn when you come on by again so I'll know you're OK and heading home. You live in Marshfield?"

"Yes, it's better for Mom's health."

"Oh, yes, Doc Johnson?"

"Exactly," Dianne said quickly. "He's better than any I've known."

"Yep. You ladies get on, and don't forget to honk."

"Yes, sir." Dianne made a mock salute and started the car.

"Really? You okay? You want to go through with this?" Dianne asked her mother.

"Yes. Turn left onto the dirt road before you cross the wooden bridge."

After driving less than a mile, Dianne saw a low, concrete bridge following an asphalt driveway winding around a giant oak tree and up a gently sloping hill. It all looked new.

"Could this be it, Mom? How long since you've been out here?"

"Ken took me at the beginning of last summer. We wanted you to come too. Everything's new."

"Oh, I think I remember. I was supposed to drive you but didn't. I should have come. They wouldn't let me off where I was working at the time, or I would have. They treated me like yesterday's trash there. I guess that's why I quit."

"I remember," Katrina replied. "This is it. New, but the tree is there. Stop."

"Oh God, I hope we don't get stuck in the snow," Dianne said, slowing to a stop.

"Get the little shovel in the trunk," Katrina ordered.

"Little shovel?" Dianne asked. "Mom, we're not stuck...not yet anyway."

"You gotta dig."

"Dig? Mom, there's nearly a foot of snow, and what if the ground's frozen?"

"If you can't do this simple thing for me after I've tried so hard to put you through school! I never thought of you as ungrateful, but I'm starting to see you. It's only a few inches of snow." Katrina suddenly sounded angry, which made her voice more strained.

"Uh, okay. I didn't mean anything by asking. I just thought...ummm, where do you want me to dig?"

Dianne was apologetic as she gently took her mother's hand to help her from the car. Her mother's sudden fiery words had surprised her. Why was this so important, and why would her mother suddenly spout the things she did?

After pulling the Army entrenching tool from its cover, Dianne received curt, exact directions from her mother, who was leaning against the car. Still wondering, but not wanting to heighten her mother's emotion, Dianne dug with a quiet, purposeful energy. Scrape...thunk...scrape...scoop...thunk.

"Good! I know it's there. I was so hoping!"

"Mom, what is it?"

"Just dig it out." Katrina emphasized her seriousness as she continued to prop herself against the car.

"Mom, it's okay, I'm digging it out. Please get back in the car. Thank god this ground isn't frozen solid...I'd really have a hell of a time. Good gracious, Mom, the snow makes this place muddy. Please, get back in the car."

I'm glad the house is up the hill, so no one sees me by happenstance, Dianne thought. Katrina's brow began to show tension. The cold, damp weather emphasized the lines and dryness in Katrina's face. Not only was Dianne unprepared for the manual labor involved in raising a wooden box longer than her arm, but she was also shocked by her mother's sudden mood change.

"Okay, Mom, I'm getting it out. Look, it's coming loose without a problem. It's a little scratched up. What is it? And what's wrong with you suddenly?"

"Nothing's wrong with me other than the same old shit." Katrina paused lowering her head. "First, Dad lays down the law, then your father lays down the law, and now some man in the sky is laying down the law. Can't I get any freedom from this? You're my daughter, and I expected your help," Katrina said nearly in tears. Her frustration flowed like air out of a released balloon, making her unable to stand. Her exhaustion had overtaken her.

"It's okay, Mom. I'll clean up the box with some rags from the trunk. Please go ahead and sit in the car. After I cover up the hole, we can open the box together. Is it okay to open it? How old is this thing? The wood is coming apart." Dianne dropped the box quickly into the trunk and grabbed her mother's arm, as Katrina's legs seemed to weaken. It was tough for her mother to shuffle back to the car door. As Dianne lowered her to the seat, Katrina's eyes spilled tears as she gasped for breath between sobs. All Dianne could do was hold her mother awkwardly from outside the car and try to remain strong without letting her own tears surface. Dianne's trembling hand reached past her mother for a box of tissues from under the seat.

"Here, mom. It's okay to cry. Do you mind if I cry too?"

Dianne didn't wait for permission. She stooped beside her mother, attempting to dry her tears while she shared her grief. Clouds started to billow in, first in puffs, then in heavier gray clumps, which seemed on the edge of releasing frozen tears in shared sadness with the women.

"Mom?" Dianne raised her mother's head with a gentle hand. "We can drive back, and you can tell me about it later. Okay?"

Katrina nodded. After securing the digging tool and the mysterious box in the trunk, Dianne finished drying her tears and looked over at her mother, whose tears changed to a distant gaze.

"You okay, Mom? Ready to go back?"

Katrina nodded, letting the memories from the day many years ago pull her back like a magnet. Memories of that awful day when she buried the box seemed buried far deeper than the box.

"I'm sorry, Momma. I didn't mean to do wrong."

Katrina murmured through sobs. Dianne didn't hear all of what her mother said, ignoring it for the moment as she concentrated on aligning the car on the road. The car's tires screamed as it bumped onto the pavement, then slightly fishtailed before straightening. Dianne was frightened for the moment, but her mother remained in a haze. Dianne sighed then patted her mother's leg.

"You okay?"

Katrina turned toward Dianne and blinked, then returned to a glazed stare. "Don't forget to honk," Katrina whispered.

"Okay, Mom. I'm glad you're back with me."

Katrina sat quietly. As Dianne passed the farmer's driveway, she slowed almost to a stop and firmly pressed the center of the steering wheel, making the car sing out loudly. The porch light on the farmhouse blinked, and Dianne knew she had been heard.

Now that's neat. This country stuff is good, Dianne thought. Her words barely slipped from her mind when she hit black ice, propelling the car into a never-ending spin.

"Oh my God! The box! Don't hurt the box!" Katrina said repeatedly with her strained voice, "Oh my God! Oh my God!"

They spun down the road, somehow managing only to graze the shoulders, and eventually stopped when a brick mailbox mount seemed to grab the car's rear bumper. Only minimal damage was done, but Dianne was scared stiff, and the car's back wheels wedged into a small crevice off the pavement.

"Hon! Are you okay?" Katrina broke her gaze and returned to her role as Dianne's mother.

"Yes, I'm fine, Mom. Look! The farmer stuck his head out the door! He's yelling something. Can you hear him? Let me see if I can get the car out of here. He's probably wondering if we're okay."

Dianne restarted the stalled engine and rocked the car through skillful gas pedaling. She seemed to be making headway.

"Now, you girls, hang on! I got a chain here. Me and the boy'll pull ya right out," the farmer yelled as he approached the stranded car.

It seemed only seconds until the women suddenly had company in their predicament.

The sure-footed young man climbed off the tractor and wrapped a chain around the car's axle before the women could ask questions.

"Now you can do it, little lady. Gently push on the gas when I get to pulling."

The farmer's tractor and Dianne's driving skills worked like magic, pulling the car back to the road and away from the bricked row of mailboxes.

"Now, girls, it's starting to sleet a bit. It would be best if you got going. If you got some paper, I'll give you my number. You let me know when you get home safe, okay? This young man's a deputy. He'll help if ya get in another fix. You two saw the farm, okay? Meet the Hanovers?"

"No, sir, we parked and reminisced between us."

"I understand. Come back soometime, and we'll all go up there and have some biscuits and gravy. This is their mailbox right here," the farmer explained while patting an oversized box. "Us neighbors teamed up when the youngsters kept hitting our boxes for fun. With the boxes all bricked in, no more problems. I give 'em a pig every year, and we have some of the best sausages around with big ol' homemade biscuits."

"That sounds great," Dianne lied.

"Now you get on, and don't forget to call. Don't worry 'bout the mailbox. Ya didn't do a bit of damage."

"It sounds like they know the Hanovers a bit more than they let on earlier," Dianne told Katrina as she tucked the farmer's number in her coat pocket and carefully drove off.

After the women arrived home safely, Dianne called the farmer to tell him all was well. She apologized to the kind man for not wanting to talk further because she needed to assist her mother.

Several times, Dianne gently invited her mother to eat during the bedtime preparations, but she didn't want to be too pushy lest she become upset like she did when they stopped in front of her childhood home.

After Katrina lay comfortably in her bed, she drifted to sleep. Dianne discovered the leftovers from Monday were still good to eat, and she was grateful Michael was generous during their date.

During her somewhat ravenous hunger, Dianne noticed a note from Ken stuck to the refrigerator.

Call Cindy. She's a great caretaker for your mom.—Ken

Below his note was another note.

I recommend her too. And I left some ice cream in the freezer for you.—Dawn

What? Does all of Marshfield have a key to this house? And who is Dawn? Dianne thought as she searched for the ice cream.

Just as she was about to pull it from the freezer, she heard a light knock at the door and rushed to see who it was before her mother awakened.

Dianne opened the door slightly without removing the security latch, securing her foot behind the door in a true St. Louis-style security move.

"I knocked softly in case your mother was sleeping," a stranger whispered. "I'm Cindy. Dawn and Ken told me to stop by. They said you might need help with your mom. I helped a lady outside Springfield for the last few months. It worked fine."

"Really? How do you have time to work with my mom if it

worked fine?" Dianne responded in a reserved voice as she released the security latch and motioned Cindy into the home.

"She died."

"Ummm. How did that happen?"

"Oh no! I didn't kill her or hurt her. She was sick. I helped her with food, bathing, reading to her, all that kind of thing."

"Oh, okay. Yes. Please sit down. Would you like a Coke or tea? I have some sweet tea in the fridge. And tell me, who is Dawn?"

"Oh, sweet tea? I used to drink it all the time when I lived in Alabama for a bit. The man I married finished up school there. 'Roll Tide!"

Dianne looked bewildered as she poured two glasses of sweet tea. She had to ask, "Roll Tide?" Laughing, Cindy shared how everyone who likes the University of Alabama, or at least the football team, says that a lot. Cindy suddenly felt like she had stepped in gum...or something. And she felt like she might have failed her interview.

"Oh, okay. Now tell me, who is Dawn?"

She's the preacher lady at the church. Your momma and Ken know her real well.

Dianne couldn't think of anything else to say or ask. "I guess you know my mom is very sick, and I'm trying to finish my degree. Yes, I could use help."

Dianne heard her mom heading to the bathroom and jumped up to help.

"Excuse me for a minute," Dianne said.

"Here, let me help you," Cindy said, rushing close behind Dianne.

"Mom, are you getting sick?"

"No, pee."

"This is Cindy. Mom. She's here to help us," Dianne shouted through the bathroom door.

"Yes. She's good," Katrina barely croaked out.

"Ma'am, looks like you missed the toilet a little," Cindy said when Katrina opened the door. "No one likes wearing big diaper pants, but it will help keep your sheets clean and your butt from burning. You might have some. Where?"

"Top drawer," Katrina choked out.

"Miss Dianne, I'll get your momma cleaned up, fixed, and back to bed. First, check to see if the sheets are okay, then hand me a diaper."

"Yes. Everything's fine," Dianne dutifully reported barely a minute later as she handed Cindy an adult diaper.

"Good. You go sit down. I'll take care of your momma."

Dianne completed Cindy's order while thinking, *Good heavens. Those Alabama women are bossy!*

CHAPTER 7

Dianne and Dawn

Dianne was relieved the following day when she awoke to see her mother breathing regularly and sleeping peacefully. She was confident that if her mother had a health emergency, she could call Cindy, who would undoubtedly revive her.

Dianne laughed at her own twisted, thoughtless fantasy. Despite the weather and students having another snow day, teachers were called for a faculty meeting on Thursday. Before the meeting, she planned to relax, write in her journal, and possibly revisit her poetry.

Her leisure time was suddenly interrupted by a knock on the door.

"Who is it?" Dianne called through the door.

"I'm your mother's friend Ken. How is she doing?"

"Oh! Hi Ken! It's nice to meet you finally! What brings you here?" Dianne said as she opened the door.

"I heard from Cindy your mother had problems last night. Is there something I can do to help?"

"It was a bit rough last night. Cindy took charge. She stayed the night and left about an hour ago."

"Yeah, she does take charge. Ya know, ya couldn't get better care than her. Are you hiring her?"

"I'm thinking about it."

"It ain't my business, but I'm jumping in here. Your mother needs care. You can't leave her alone while you're teaching school. Pastor Dawn and I can't be here all the time you're gone. You need to decide soon."

"Well, I haven't done this before. I must think about it."

"I said my piece. The responsibility is yours."

"Umm, Ken, will you stay here while I'm at the faculty meeting?"

"I suggest that you make your decision tonight. What time is your meeting? I'm sorry for coming on so strong. I think you already know how much I care about your mother," Ken said after a few moments of silence.

"It's at two. Are you available?" Dianne responded.

"I'll see you at one-thirty. Are we good?" Dianne patted Ken's arm, then, holding back tears, she said goodbye as she ushered him to the door.

"Let's see if our newest team member might have a suggestion. Fellow educators, this is Dianne England. She is interning in Mrs. Millbrook's EMR class. If her work here so far is any indication, she will be a great asset to Missouri Schools," the principal, Mr. Ralph Richards, said in an on-the-spot introduction.

Oh, busted, Dianne thought as she struggled to understand what to address.

"Can you describe the problem in more detail? Since I'm new, I only have a slight idea of what's happening."

"New or not, isn't it obvious? We have too many cars mixing with too many buses and too many children," a teacher shot back, glaring at Dianne while seeming to pull up a wayward bra strap.

"Now, take it easy. Ms. England is new to this school and new to teaching. It's not fair to put her on the spot like this. She hasn't even been here during a regular school day." Pam saved the day with her comments.

Did she know Dianne was zoning out? Or were her rescuing instincts jumping in to save the young and innocent? Another kind-hearted teacher interjected with a shorter explanation of the after-school situation, dimming the spotlight on Dianne until she felt comfortable with a response.

"Well, at other schools I observed, students using different types of transportation were dismissed at different times, and those who had parents or carpools picking them up exited from the back," Dianne suggested.

"We can't do that here," the disgruntled third-grade teacher retorted.

"I'm sure there's something we can do. Let's table this discussion until next week. I want to hear some workable solutions to this problem. Each grade come up with an idea. Then we'll decide what works best." Mr. Richards dictated his instructions and dismissed the meeting. "That's it for today. Everyone travel home safely. I think tomorrow will end up another snow day from the looks of things. I'll see you Monday," he added over the rumble of moving chairs and bodies.

"I guess we were a bit much for you today?" Pam said to Dianne as they left the library.

"Thanks for sticking up for me." Dianne gave a nervous smile.

"You'll get used to all the personalities here. I think everyone is well-meaning, but sometimes negative and long-winded. You didn't fall asleep, did you?"

"No, I was daydreaming a little about Mom getting more care and some about Michael D., no less."

"It sounds like that's not daydreaming, it's nightmaring," Pam answered, and both women laughed.

"Yeah, I think my mom is worried about my relationship with Michael too, but he's OK—at least he was the other night. And I'm not planning to get involved with him anyway. Good gracious, we've only dated once. Anyway, I was thinking about seeing him again but I'm not sure if I want to. Mostly, I was thinking about taking care of Mom."

As Dianne shared her thoughts, Pam looked concerned, which stopped Dianne from sharing about the box she dug up the day before.

After a short silence, Pam responded with concern. "Well, regarding Michael, make sure it's YOUR decision to date him and not something he's manipulated you into doing,"

"OK. And I need to hire someone for Mom. Her friend, Ken, and the new pastor at the Methodist church recommended a lady to help. Her name is Cindy. She came over to introduce herself and ended up helping Mom right away. She seems to know what she's doing but is so bossy."

"Bossy is not bad, especially when caring for a sick adult. Perhaps you should remove Michael from your mind and put him under a rock somewhere until you decide about your mother's care. You're so young, and none of these things are easy at any age. I'm glad you have Ken and the pastor to help you decide."

"I'll tell you how it all went on Monday," Dianne replied.

Dianne thought Pam's comment about Michael manipulating

her was strange. Did she know more about Michael than she was sharing?

Katrina was up and welcomed her daughter home with all the love she remembered throughout her childhood.

"I sent Ken out. I'm perfectly OK. I've had a good rest, and I might eat something when Ken brings us homemade chicken soup from JR's on the highway. That's his hangout and they like spoiling him there." Katrina said with a surprising amount of energy.

Suddenly the phone rang, snapping Dianne's attention from her mother. Before she could say "Hello," a voice blurted out.

"You OK? What's wrong? Momma OK?"

"Uh, yes, Michael. Thank you for asking. I was engrossed in some other things."

"Oh well. You want to talk about doing something Saturday night? You know, it was a while ago we went dancing. Benny's starting to like you, and Mitzi's been good lately. Why don't we pick up some ribs and do some dancing?"

"You know, Michael, I think I might need that."

"Ooooo, yeah! My girl's coming to dance with me!"

"Michael! How can you call me your girl? I barely know you. I know you have other girlfriends. You told me so that night at Benny's."

"Now who told you that about me and girlfriends? I know I didn't! I've been working. I'm trying to get that truck. You know the one. Scotty's still got it!"

After Katrina stared at Dianne with a scowl, Dianne said goodbye to Michael.

"You need to let go of that man. I think he's trouble. I bet Ken knows some nasty things about him and he doesn't want to tell you," Katrina admonished in a change of assessment.

"Oh, Mom, it doesn't matter. Don't worry. We just had one date."

"Don't tell me about worry! I know about it. It's a short hop from that dance floor to his bed and little white-trash babies. Don't you even think about throwing away your education to start popping out monsters from his sperm!"

"Mother! Please stop. I'm not throwing away my life or

education. I know you're concerned about me, but PLEASE! Don't be mean. Have some faith in me. Do you remember Cindy from last night? Is it OK if she helps around here?"

"So, you can go out on dates with Michael?"

"Mom, I don't mean to be disrespectful, but I must go out for some air. No, I'm not going anywhere near Michael. Will you be OK? I'll only be gone for about an hour or so. Ken's coming back soon. Oh, never mind! I'll wait until he gets here."

"Well, you go right ahead. I don't have any control over you. I wanna go to bed anyway after Ken leaves. Don't worry about me and any damned bath. You go and find yourself ten boyfriends if you want. I don't care anymore."

"FINE! I'm going out! I need to catch my thoughts. Anyway, I think Ken drove up."

Dianne stormed from the house, not knowing where she was going, and was unprepared for the icy wind that whipped through her when she stepped out the door. She hurried to her car and started it up without acknowledging Ken.

"Damn! Where does a person drive to vent some anger and frustration in Marshfield?" she mumbled. She wasn't going to risk driving at night in the country, especially considering how cold it was, and she knew first-hand about black ice.

Ah hell, I'll just go and get some coffee, she thought. She pulled up to the Kuntry Kitchen. The frosted-over door seemed foreboding, and she couldn't bring herself to leave her car. Tears began to pour from her eyes. She was out of tissues and had to use some crumpled napkins that she'd stuffed into her glove compartment. All Dianne could do was keep the car running and let her tears pour. A sudden sharp rapping on the car window startled her.

"You OK?" shouted a muffled voice.

"Who are you?"

"Sorry, I didn't mean to scare you, but you don't look well. I'm Pastor Dawn."

"Mom and I had an argument—or discussion—or whatever you want to call it."

"Oh, I'm so sorry. I know you two are going through some really rough times. Would you like to come in for some coffee and we'll talk?"

"I don't want to bother you with all this stuff. It's the cancer, and I'm stressing about school, and Michael, and Jennifer...someone I knew at school… and my new job at school and …"

"And it's too much to handle by yourself." Dawn replied. "It's a lot, but it might help if you're ready to share. I don't want you to feel pressured into talking to me, but you're welcome to come over to my home if you like. I've got some decaf Irish Cream coffee that I can brew up quickly. It's better than the coffee in there that will keep you awake! I bet you would like some chocolate-iced biscotti too. It's cold out here. You'd do me a favor."

"Yeah, your house. It must be better than this place's coffee and fried apple pie. Thank you," Dianne choked out her acceptance.

"Good. Follow me. Do you want me to call Cindy to check on your mom? She can pretend she left a book at your house or something."

"Please! That will be one less worry for me."

"Good. I'll ask her to bring an overnight bag. She can sleep on the sofa to help you in the morning too."

"Thank you, Pastor."

Dianne wiped her tears and her windshield, preparing for a challenging drive following an unfamiliar car. She was surprised about how short and straightforward the route was.

"I had no idea you lived so close to us," Dianne said wiping her feet as she entered the pastor's tidy frame home.

"Everything is close in Marshfield. You don't have a coat?"

"Kinda left in a hurry."

"Yeah, Ken told me that when he called me. He and your mom were worried about you."

"Oh. So I guess they approve of Cindy coming over?"

"Yes. Ken suggested it," Pastor Dawn said with a smile. "And I called Cindy before I left to try and find you."

"Sorry, there are so many boxes still around," Dawn said as they entered her home. "I had to unpack some of my favorite things first. That is, other than some basic dishes."

"Oh, look at that stein! It's so large and so fancy!" Dianne had not seen the somewhat common military souvenir before.

"My father had that from Germany. His troops gave it to him

after one of the big training events, I think it was called Reforger 87. He said that he managed a lot of equipment in a lot of mud. Both of my parents were in the military and stationed in Germany for a while. Mom was in some kind of supply or logistics. I forget what. It was a good upbringing, but I hated to leave my friends every time we moved. I got to know some chaplain's kids in Germany, and I think, to this day, that's what encouraged me to go into ministry."

"How did you get to Marshfield? Most people have never heard of this little town," Dianne asked.

"My parents' last assignment was at Fort Leonard Wood, an hour or so from here."

"Oh yes. I've heard about that place. They do Army Basic Training there, I think."

"Yes, it's a tough place. And speaking of tough places. I think you're in a tough place. Want to share what's going on?" Dawn didn't let Dianne change the subject. Without acknowledging the pre-planning for Cindy taking care of her mom or any more about Dawn's background, Dianne launched into her story.

"What's going on? My mother has never been like this. Oh, when I was a child, she was a bit overprotective, but as I was growing up she always seemed to have confidence in me. Now it's going down the toilet with all the puking she's been doing lately. Oh, don't answer that. I know it's just that she's sick, But I get so tired of it."

Dawn motioned for Dianne to sit at her kitchen table.

"Yes, your mom is getting sicker, and you both know it. Lying beneath all the arguing is the fact that you're both scared. You're both scared for each other. Am I going down the right path here?" Dawn finished setting water to boil in a whistling tea pot and pulled some biscotti and cookies from her freezer as the pot heated.

"Yes. That's so true. But Mom had seemed better. She ate a bit and is walking around more. But she's been irritable."

"I would guess too, from the list you spat at me when I saw you tonight, that some other things are going on with you, aside from your mother's illness."

"Yeah, there's Michael. What a piece of work! I don't understand him. I guess that's normal, 'cause I barely know him."

"And Jennifer? Who's Jennifer?"

"She's someone I knew in college. We were friends, real good friends."

"Are you saying you were lovers?"

"Aren't you direct!" Dianne snapped back.

"It helps to be direct in my business. Sometimes, too, people can't say what's on their minds. I found that if I could guess what they're trying to say, at least they could say yes or no. Do you like frozen Girl Scout cookies, or do you prefer the biscotti?"

"The cookies are fine. Do you always ask such personal questions? I mean, about friends, not the cookies." Dianne smiled at the potential misunderstanding.

"Depends on the person. Let's get back on track. Tell me about Jennifer and your friendship."

Dawn looked directly at Dianne and pulled a chair out for herself. Dianne was very nervous talking to Dawn. She didn't want to be judged. Dianne cleverly steered her story from Jennifer, to moving back to Marshfield, to the strained relationship with her mother.

"You left out some important parts about your relationship with Jennifer, Dianne."

Dianne felt like a criminal who had been caught with stolen goods.

"You're not ready to talk about it?"

"I guess not." Dianne paused and tried to organize her thoughts, but words spun.

"Tonight's problem is more about Mom and me anyway," she blurted out without thinking.

"Dianne, no problem exists in a vacuum. OK, we'll talk about something else." The pastor placed various cookies on a small plate and spooned instant Irish Cream coffee mix into their cups.

"OK, talk about your mom. And so you don't have another worry added to your list. As promised, this coffee doesn't have caffeine," Pastor Dawn smiled.

Periods of silence between each sentence seemed like hours of quiet to Dianne. If only she could keep talking and fill the uncomfortable voids, then she could figure out her thoughts about Jennifer and everything else going on in her current life. She would then never have to raise the subject again with Dawn, but she couldn't think of how to begin. Dawn poured boiling water over the coffee mix. The drizzling liquid's sound seemed to soothe the thick silence.

"Damn, I'm stressed. I don't know what the hell I'm doing," Dianne blurted out.

"About what?"

"Everything. Sorry, I didn't mean to sound so trashy."

"Don't worry about language. I've heard it before, and anyway, whatever helps to get out your emotions. Do you know your mother is going to die soon?"

"Yes!" Dianne sounded angry. "That's what all this shit's about, isn't it?"

Dianne was shocked to hear herself sound so rough, in front of a pastor no less.

"Go on, Dianne. If you need to throw in some rough talk, it's OK. Just talk. You haven't had anyone to talk to, have you? Spill it, girl! Your mother's dying, you're dating a guy, and you've got some kind of a relationship with a woman you can't explain." Dawn paused, slurped coffee, and stared at Dianne who could only look down at the table.

"I'll take one of those cookies now." Dianne snatched a mint cookie and popped it in her mouth, using her chewing as an excuse not to respond. The crunching sound seemed to break the silence comfortably.

"Oh, I see," Dawn continued the conversation, "If that's not enough, you're trying to complete your degree. Now it's my turn to pop a cookie and your turn to talk."

Dawn exaggerated Dianne's eating. Dianne looked up to view what she considered a dignified clergywoman, stuffing her mouth with several cookies. The sight was comical, and Dianne's stress began to break.

"Well, I can play that game too!" Dianne choked out as soon as she could pronounce words after upping Dawn's ante of mint cookies in her mouth with a peanut butter Do-si-Do.

"Can't do that," Dianne clumsily tried to form the words, discovering that she not only had a mouth full of cookies, but with the peanut butter factored in, she could not chew or talk, which threw both women into laughter.

"These things need a warning label," Dawn said, trying to keep her coffee from shooting from her nose. Dianne could only try to finish chewing without choking.

Finally, both women composed themselves. Dawn looked squarely at Dianne.

"It's time to talk. You OK?"

"Yes, thanks." She was able to respond after a few sips of warm coffee.

"And thanks for the laugh. I guess you know I needed that."

Dianne began to relieve the heaviness on her mind by relaying the story of the visit to the family's farm but said nothing about the weird box they unearthed. She switched from the present to the past, and back again while interjecting vignettes from her past. She shared with Dawn some wonderful moments when her parents were both alive, and some good times they had. She felt she had just gotten started when they realized it was close to midnight.

"People don't turn into pumpkins in Marshfield, but I think you do have school tomorrow, don't you?"

"Yes, I do. Wait, no, it's another snow day I heard on the radio on the way over. Country roads, you know. I'm so sorry I kept you up this late! I really didn't realize I went on and on so much." Dianne stood ready to place her dishes on the kitchen counter.

"That's OK. Don't you worry about the cup," Dawn gently removed it from Dianne's hands.

"Go home and get some rest. Will you come back soon, and we can continue talking?"

"OK. I will. Soon."

"Just give me a call. Oh, and about Michael. I don't know him, but please be careful. I was getting ready to be direct with you again about him, but from what you have said, it sounds as though your mother has already done that."

"Yes, she has. I gotta get going. Good night."

"Would you like to borrow a coat?"

"It's not far. I'll make it OK."

Dianne wished she had accepted Dawn's coat offer but was relieved that her trip home was quick. She was happy to talk somewhat freely with Dawn. Perhaps she could speak more later or "soon". For now, she had to get some rest. Rest would be easier after sharing with Dawn.

Dianne tiptoed through the living room to her room past Cindy who was asleep on the sofa. Dianne saw a note on her pillow as she pulled down her covers. It simply said,

I love you.—Mom.

CHAPTER 8

Insistence

Perhaps the reason Katrina continued to spit acidic words was a product of her illness. Her meanness seemed to increase by the day. Simple things seemed to throw Katrina into a rant, such as when Michael called. Her irritability began when the box was unearthed. What secrets did the box hold that tugged at Katrina and pull her gentle nature into irritable bursts? Dianne wanted to ask her mother about the box but couldn't for fear her mother would again become sharp. The box remained in the car trunk, and Dianne's curiosity mainly stayed in the back of her mind.

With snowfall ceasing, Friday was a good day for in-town traffic. The main roads were clear, and businesses were opening as usual.

"Mom, is Ken coming over today?" Dianne shouted toward her mother's room.

"Doesn't he always," Katrina said from the bathroom with as much voice as she could muster. Dianne jumped up, surprised to see her mother out of bed.

"Are you OK?" Dianne asked with concern.

"I want to get dressed. Will you help me get bathed and into some clothes?"

"I'm happy to help, Mom. Getting ready for your boyfriend? You know, the one who says you're his Trina?"

"Yes, that's right. He'll be here around noon." Katrina smiled with happiness, knowing that Dianne accepted Ken as someone special.

"I'm happy but tired. Ken is a kind and caring man. I'm happy to be his Trina."

"Mom, do you mind if I hire Cindy to help?"

"Now?"

"No. Perhaps a little this weekend and while I'm at school

teaching."

"You don't need to ask. You're in charge." Katrina's gentle words were almost like a magic wand for Dianne. She helped her mother bathe, dress, and comb her hair. She was in charge and would hire Cindy.

"It's almost like your old card parties, Mom," Dianne said as a group gathered around the kitchen table.

Katrina nodded her head with a smile. Too tired to chat, she contributed little verbally but seemed to enjoy the word volley with the other ladies and Ken. When the conversation leaned toward esoteric thought, Ken tried to interject light volatility to encourage Katrina to engage.

"Ladies, ladies, you think too much. If you had husbands, it would keep your minds busy, and you wouldn't have to worry so much about Bible talk, spirituality, and religion and all!" Ken said, then looked at each of the women. When looking at Katrina, he gave her a quick wink.

Ken didn't take long to back off after the duo took his bait and fired off their opinions. Katrina shook her head and smiled at her beau. The group's easy chatting made Dianne feel welcomed as a fellow adult. The only hint of Katrina's illness was a nearly untouched plate of food, which Dianne hadn't seen since before their trip to the England Farm.

A call from Michael pierced the group's merry time. Dianne had trouble convincing him she could not leave her company to meet him. Losing her patience evaporated her enjoyment.

"That man! Would you believe he wanted me to get up and leave you all to meet him? Are you sure you've never heard of Michael D. Glossen, Ken? His family's been in this area for a while. I think he's OK, but he's strange. Fun enough, I guess, but strange. I almost had to hang up on him. He kept babbling on."

"I said I know him a little, but that's 'bout it. He might have some distant kin outside of town, maybe near where you two drove the other day. Look, step carefully. Do to him what women have done to me. Spend all his money, don't sleep with him, and move on. Everything will be fine!" Ken laughed at his self-humor.

"Ken, don't you tell my daughter that," Katrina admonished, finally conversing. "Hon, be careful. OK?" Katrina said with as much energy as possible while picking at her food.

"This food's fine, but I think I'll have some oatmeal." She started to head toward the kitchen cupboard.

"Oh Mom. Don't worry. I'll make a bowl of gruel for you, and I plan to be careful about Michael," Dianne said as she lifted herself from her chair.

Dawn switched to other topics in hopes of relieving Katrina's worry. They walked through the area's history as they knew it, entertaining themselves far past the time to say goodbye to one another. Dianne was happy to know a little more about Ken and Dawn.

Ken fought in Vietnam, where he picked up a souvenir limp from "water feet," as he called it, along with some shrapnel. Ken shared that he, JR at the truck stop, and the Texaco gas station owner had all served in combat. He said they often support one another when they think about stuff too much.

"You think I can dance? You should have seen me before the Army got me," Ken bragged. "I didn't just get up and wiggle either."

"And I was quite the dancer myself," Dawn added, "in my dreams, that is. I wasn't about to get up and dance like your mother did after the potluck."

"Hon, don't believe them. I confess, Ken held me up. I didn't dance, but I liked the music. I'm starting to love country music. I don't remember when I had such a great time." Katrina admitted, then gave Ken a schoolgirl smile.

"I remember, Mom. You came home like a giddy teenager."

A second call from Michael cut the electric atmosphere the group enjoyed.

"I had to come to the store for a bit. I'm done, and it's pretty out. You want to visit for a bit?" Michael asked. "We can walk around here in the field."

With half seriousness and half entertainment after overhearing Michael's loud voice through the phone receiver, Ken gave his opinion.

"Oh, go on, Dianne. We sure don't want him mowing what's left of the snow! If you're not back by dark, me and some of the boys will hunt you two down and have more than a stern word with Michael."

"OK, Michael. What's your address? OK, OK. I'll see you soon."

Before leaving, Dianne called Cindy to arrange for her services. "Mom. I think it will be better if you aren't left alone. I'll be at work next week. She will be needed. And Ken, I'm leaving a copy of Michael's address here next to the phone in case you need to gather a posse."

Ken, Pastor Dawn, and Katrina could only smile at one another as Dianne called Cindy to arrange for Katrina's care. Indeed, it looked as though she was in charge.

Michael D.'s home was off the main highway to Springfield, which made it easy to find. Dianne was a little surprised at the long driveway. It was a house she had probably seen more than a hundred times while traveling to and from Springfield, but she had never taken notice.

"Hey, Lady Dianne. It's been a bear's winter since I seen ya!" Michael slapped Dianne's fender to get her attention. "I think you'll like a walk around the property since the sun's out."

Dianne heard Michael's muffled voice as he walked alongside her car. She pulled to the end of his driveway before responding.

"Is your place so big that you can walk around?" Dianne snapped back at Michael as she opened her car door and stepped on the gravel. "The size of this house! It's huge for just one guy. Where did you pop out from? You startled me when you pounded on my car!"

Michael smiled at Dianne's shock as he approached her car but didn't offer an apology or explanation.

"What's mine is not so big, just a few acres. Daddy sold off a bunch of land to the animal park. If we walk the fence, we can see the buffalo roam. You ever heard of that song?"

"Cute, Michael. Who hasn't? Please! No more jumping from nowhere. My nerves can't handle that."

"Now, girl, always pull over here," Michael said, pointing to where Dianne parked still ignoring Dianne's discomfort.

"When you come, pull to the back side of the driveway. I know some people's cars drip, and I don't want it all over the place. And people going down the road don't need to see my company."

Dianne could barely hear Michael over the loud barking of a

dog chained to its house.

"What are you paranoid about, Michael?" Dianne raised her voice over Brandy's excited barking. "Your neighbor is what? A hundred yards away? I'm sure they can check on you if they want to. And look, my car is new. It won't be leaking."

"Oh, that doesn't matter, I just want to keep my business from folks passing by. Now you quit, Brandy! This is Lady Dianne. You gonna like her. Get used to her. She's going to be spending some time around here."

Dianne noticed that the yard and area surrounding the house were eerily neat. It was as though Michael had instructed Mother Nature to melt the snow and arrange any fallen branches.

"The house has four bedrooms and a big ole kitchen," Michael boasted as they walked toward Brandy. "You like it, Lady Dianne?"

"Lady Dianne!" Dianne mimicked him. "Michael D., please! As I think I said before, my name is Dianne! Without the Lady!" Dianne said, scolding him.

"Yep, the property ends about where the lone cedar is." Michael started off, seeming to ignore Dianne's request. "I think it gets windy around here 'cause of the open space. C'mon over here and talk to Brandy. She thinks she's a tough girl. She's bad when she barks like that and digs up the grass around her. And you shoulda seen what she done to my little room here awhile back!"

"Oh, she looks fine," Dianne said, extending her hand toward the dog. "Look, she's calming down. Does she stay chained here most of the time? Wait...was that Mitzi who passed by? A car slowed down in front of your house. I thought it was pulling in here, and then it sped off. The lady driving looked like Mitzi."

"I don't think Mitzi lives around here. Probably someone who looked like her. Now, Brandy's got all that fur and a nice house too, so she don't get cold." Michael quickly changed the subject. "Don't want that mud in my house anyway. C'mon, let's walk the fence."

"Well, what do you do when it gets real cold? She's not a Husky, you know." Dianne let go of the topic of passing cars.

"Naw. She's a dog. I'm not mean to her. I got her a few months back. I take her in at night and when the weather is rough, like this week. Look, I'm doing an old girlfriend a favor by keeping her. The bitch...no, sorry...the woman didn't want her, so I said I'd keep her. I'm considering putting some little rocks around the doghouse and maybe surrounding it with hay. What you think?"

"Well, yes. That would certainly help. Oh, look, she's starting to get used to me. Yes, girl, I see that tail wagging! You decided I'm not so bad after all, right? She's a sweet dog, Michael. Take good care of her, will ya?"

"I take good care of all the girls in my life," Michael said, coaxing Dianne by her elbow toward the lone cedar in the open field stretching from his backyard beyond the rolling horizon.

"Daddy once had 'bout 1000 acres," Michael continued to explain his home's history while the two high-stepped into the expanse of wintered grass with dollops of snow. "Now, there's only three acres where the house sits. The wild animals in the park use most of the land, but we can still walk along the fence. You cold?"

"A little. The snow melted a lot around here. I'm surprised because you're just across town from me."

"Yep, no real trees to keep it cool, so the snow melts. The park calls it the Back Lands way up yonder in and around those hills. My property barely touches it. If it weren't cold, I'd walk you back there. Now I'm not trying to get fresh. I'm just gonna put my arm around ya to help you get warm."

Dianne thought this was a sweet gesture, and although she was suspiciously reluctant, she welcomed Michael's arm as a windbreaker. In close quietness, they walked over to a tall chain link fence that separated Michael's property from open fields with several types of generally wild animals.

"Yep, Dianne, I like this. It's my favorite way to spend a day," Michael said, staring off into the distance. "This is a great place. Ever seen zebras do it?" he continued.

"Do it?" she asked.

"Yeah, not too long ago, I was walking along here, and one jumped the other. Cool, huh?"

"No, I've never seen anything like that. I'm not sure I want to," Dianne said, half-smiling.

"Awww. Didn't mean to embarrass you. It's life. Zebras fuck like every other fucking animal on earth. All animals fuck."

"Thank you for the science lesson, Michael. How about we continue to walk, OK?"

"Oh, Lady Dianne the city girl. Oh, I mean Dianne." Michael amended himself quickly when he caught Dianne's sharp glance. "What we gonna do to get you into country life?" After shaking his head, he was silent during the couple's return walk.

The silence allowed Dianne's thoughts to melt into the scenery as she let the fresh atmosphere and soft, crunching grass purge Michael's vulgarities from her thoughts. As the sun began to lower, along with the temperature, the couple decided to step faster and vigorously return to Michael's house.

"You wanna come in and spend some time?" Michael's words floated from his Clark Gable smile.

Why didn't he just tell me he wants sex? Dianne thought. *That was about as obvious as a guy can get. He's trying to look like a vintage movie star, and he's looking more like a pitiful puppy. Or maybe he thinks he's one of those zebras.*

The day had been near perfect until then. Indeed, she didn't want to ruin her evening by stepping one foot into Michael's house. Dianne thought that as far as Michael was concerned, spending time with him in his house translated directly into an invitation for sex, and Michael was not what she wanted.

But perhaps a romp in the hay with the country boy might be kinda fun and release some tension, she thought. *No, absolutely not!* Her "better self" took over. Dianne couldn't let such a thing enter her mind and stay.

"No, thank you. Remember? I have some sweet children to prepare for and a mother that needs care. I've got to get home," Dianne responded.

"Lady—um, no, Dianne, you're breaking my heart. Here I share all my animals with you and keep you warm. Now you're leaving me alone with a broken heart."

"Oh, be serious. I need to go. Goodbye. And goodbye to your beautiful puppy," Dianne said while lovingly petting Brandy.

As Dianne left Michael's driveway, she again saw the car with the Mitzi look-alike. Although it was a mystery why Mitzi would drive by, Dianne felt refreshed after her walk with Michael despite his invitation.

Well, he adopted a dog he didn't want, so I guess he's not all bad. And if that was Mitzi, perhaps she'll stop in and give Michael what he thinks he needs, Dianne thought as she drove away.

Dianne was relieved she had not entered his house. When she entered her home, she discovered her mother had donned nightclothes and was sleeping in the recliner. Gently lifting her hand, she awakened her mother and assisted her into bed.

"Good night, Mom," she said softly as she covered her. "Sleep peacefully," she whispered closing the bedroom door, leaving only a crack to let a gentle beam of the bathroom's night light shine through.

CHAPTER 9

Bad Truck Dream

Dianne's mind began to wander during the school's typically arduous Thursday afternoon faculty meeting. After the humiliating incident during her first meeting two weeks ago, she promised herself she would never lose focus again. Today, she forced herself to scribble nearly every word, even if it meant pages full of mundane details.

At home, Cindy's take-charge personality was a godsend for Dianne. Cindy efficiently cared for Katrina and completed light chores, allowing Dianne to focus on preparing for her teaching and spending quality time with her weakening mother. Cindy's help, along with Ken and Pastor Dawn pitching in, also allowed Dianne a few precious moments for poetry and songwriting.

As an unexpected blessing, Michael canceled several dates. Yet, she thought it might be fun to dance at Benny's again and hoped to do so soon.

"Hi, hon. Sit here," Katrina said, patting the couch next to her. Katrina barely gave Dianne enough time to get in the house and lower her "teaching bundle," as she called the satchel of learning aids she carried into the classroom each day.

"I felt pretty good today so I sent Cindy home this morning. I need to tell you a bunch." Katrina said sounding urgent. "The money your father left is now in CDs...in your name. They'll mature in a few months, but you shouldn't have any problem accessing them when I'm not around. Funny thing, I've only spent a little money to pay medical expenses, and you may need some money to pay Cindy. The rest I put into CDs. You might need them to pay off school expenses."

"You did all this today? How?"

"I called the bank. They know me and our situation. It only

took a minute. Stop by the bank if you can. They'll explain everything, and you can sign anything that needs signing. Ken banks there, too. Don't hesitate to ask him for help. He's savvy about these things."

"Mom, what's a CD? I know the music thing. I noticed you got a player in the car. Thank you for that. Does CD have something to do with money?"

"Yes." Katrina tried not to show a bit of frustration. Surely, her daughter must already know what CDs are. She explained patiently, "If you turn some of your money into a Certificate of Deposit and plan to keep it there for a year or two, your money can earn more interest than a regular savings account."

"I feel stupid. I remember learning that in school. I guess they're more valuable than my music CDs." Dianne smiled.

After feebly trying to throw a pillow at her daughter, Katrina finished explaining the steps she took that day to assist her daughter. Her actions, and sharing what she did, exhausted her.

"I'm wearing down, and Ken's coming over to cook dinner. Are you joining us?" Katrina rushed through her words and started coughing.

"Mom, are you OK? Do you want water? Here, let me get you some." Katrina took a deep breath and sipped the water.

"I'm fine," she breathed out.

"And here's a folder with everything you need to know when I leave you," Katrina said with trembling hands.

"Mom! I can't believe you're so sick, yet you're so aware. You know I'm not capable of handling all this."

"Oh yes, you are. You must tell yourself that, believe it, and do it! Will you please honor me with good decisions after I'm gone?"

"I'll try my best. I hesitate to ask, but I must get a few things. I need shampoo, cream rinse and gas in the car. Also, when Michael called Monday, he asked if I wanted to go dancing this weekend. Not a late night, just over to Benny's, dancing to the jukebox like we did the other week. If it's like before, he'll cancel. Would it be OK if I left for a few hours? I'll make sure someone is here for you."

"Hon, you don't need to give that asshole any Valentine's gift. It would help if you stayed here with me. Don't you even care?"

Her mother's sudden outburst shocked Dianne. She knew she'd said nothing about getting Michael a Valentine's gift. Like before, she only wanted to run from the house. Instead, she froze, staring at her mother, remembering the time before she left the house in such a hurry. Katrina was starting to tremble.

"Oh, Mom! I didn't mean to upset you. Please, you'll start coughing again." Dianne held her mother while both women tried to fight back tears.

"Look at us. The waterworks have opened. Mom, I'll stay here with you and eat, OK? I'm so sorry I upset you. I know I should be more considerate," Dianne said through her sobs.

After the women began to calm down, Katrina tried to apologize.

"I want you to live a normal life. I don't want you to feel sorry for me. Please go ahead and take your drive. I know you need it."

"Mom, I can't! What if...what if …?"

"No! Don't talk like that. I'll be here when you get back! I'll stay up for you, like when you were on a date in high school."

"Mom, I never really dated in high school. And I'm buying toiletries. I may get Michael a card, but that's it. No gift!"

"Hey, girls!" Ken's strong voice shot through the door.

"Come in, Ken!" Dianne responded while quickly drying her tears.

"I made the mistake of getting off the sidewalk and getting mud on my shoes. Would you mind if I took them off over here?"

"Oh, please do!" Dianne could barely speak before laughing at Ken's holey and threadbare socks.

"Oh, my! We should have gotten him socks for Christmas!" Dianne laughed, which started her mother laughing.

"You girls always pick on me when I come over! And I brought some good food, too! Are you in the mood for something other than oatmeal tonight, Katrina? I thought I'd put some spaghetti together. Look! I got some 'mater sauce with veggies in it, in case your tummy can't handle real food. Yep! I'm quite the chef!"

"I see that you are! Instant, instant. Bottled," Dianne verbalized her observation while pointing at each grocery item.

"Will you at least boil the noodles?"

"Katrina, send your daughter to her room. She's picking on me."

"Better. I'm sending her to Springfield. She's going to walk around the mall. Right Dianne?"

"OK, Mom. But I'm not planning to go to the mall; I'll go to whatever store has what I need. Driving familiar roads sometimes relaxes me."

"Okay, young lady, get on with it and get out of here. Give me and my Trina some rest!" Ken smiled.

"Okay, Ken. Consider me gone." Dianne winked at Ken and kissed her mother goodbye before grabbing keys from a bowl on the bookshelf and sliding herself into the driver's seat, Springfield bound. Dianne felt better about leaving her mother with Ken's cheerful spirit to keep her company. Yet, she still wrestled with guilt.

Geez, I know she's not going to be here long. Shouldn't I have stayed? She worried. With her cyclone of worry, Dianne didn't notice she was approaching Springfield. She pulled into her old mainstay, Fantastic Drugs.

What on earth am I doing here? I need shampoo. I don't want to get Michael anything, not even a card. I barely know him, and he's too weird! she thought as she parked. Dianne had not shopped there in almost a year, so it was like a walk into nostalgia for her. For a distraction she roamed the aisles, caressing jars, candles, and other accessories for the home that she discovered long ago no one needs, but so many people want. Sometimes she does as well.

I can't believe this! They have socks here, nice, fluffy cotton ones. I think I'll get Ken a pair...and Mom a pair...and me! By golly, I'll get myself a pair, too! Look at me, the college girl. I'm a practical one!

"Getting those for your boyfriend?"

"Huh? What?" Dianne stared at the man next to her. He looked familiar, but she couldn't place him. He certainly wasn't one of her college professors or student teachers. He didn't look the part.

"You don't remember me, do you?"

"No," Dianne confessed, "I don't."

"C'mon! Surely you remember. I couldn't twist that lovely arm of yours to buy Michael Glossen the truck he's been drooling over for weeks?"

"Oh yeah, you're the sales guy. You're Scott Hickman. I believe Michael called you Mr. Scotty. Have you ever sold the truck?"

"No, I guess it's waiting for the right person to adopt it. It has a spirit in it that's waiting to be adopted. That Mr. Scotty thing, it's Michael's sense of humor left over from his Star Trek obsession."

"Yeah, that's Michael's sense of humor," Dianne agreed. Dianne was surprised to hear this salesperson talk so friendly and down to earth. She thought salespeople were all high-pressure and bull. She was shocked enough to tell him about her impressions.

"Yes, we salespeople can be kind. You know, Michael's wanted the truck since we got it in. It's a shame he can't get it. The bank won't help him. I don't think he'd have any problem paying for it. I almost signed for him myself. You're a teacher, aren't you? How's it going?"

"It's going fine. I graduate in May. I'm not an official teacher yet, but they're talking about hiring me if one of the special education teachers doesn't return after giving birth."

"Well good for you! You're a smart girl for going all the way through college. I know you worked hard."

"Thank you."

"You know what a good idea might be to help your friend?" Mr. Scotty continued before Dianne could say more. He couldn't let her say goodbye so quickly.

"Why don't you come over and just look at the truck? Maybe you can buy it and let Mr. Glossen drive it around. He wouldn't be mad at you for buying his truck, would he?"

"I can't do that. My mom just gave me a Subaru." Dianne gestured to the store's front. I can't sell it to buy a truck I don't need."

"That's smart. Here, let me get these socks for you as my graduation present. In return, I hope you can do me a favor, come to the lot, and look at the truck. Let me know what you think. You don't even have to start it up. Sit in the cab, check it out, and go home with nice warm socks and your Subaru. How old is the Subaru? You owe much on it?"

"It's about two years old, and no, I don't owe anything on it. My mother gave it to me for graduation. Look, I've got to get cards too."

"OK, get you a card to put with these socks, and I'll see you at the checkout. You sitting in the truck will be good luck for Michael." It didn't take long for Dianne to sift through the Valentine's Day leftovers and find one acceptable for Michael that was neutral, plus seventy percent off. It showed no drippy love, only a cute dog on the front. On the inside, a simple "Happy Valentine's Day." She put a little more thought into the cards she picked for her mother, Ken, and Pastor Dawn.

"Well, that's sure nice of you to let me get this for you. A card for Michael?"

"Yes, and for my mother and close friends. Tomorrow, we plan on dancing at Benny's. That's sure nice of you to buy this stuff for me. You buy socks for everyone who is looking at cars?" Dianne smiled.

"No, it's only smart ones like you who wrap me around their finger. Good thing I'm not married, my wife would have whooped me by now."

"Oh," was all Dianne could reply. *Gads, I hope this guy's not flirting with me. Men can be vultures,* she thought.

"Meet me over at the lot. I'll finish up here. Don't run away. I got your socks!" Hickman smiled.

"OK, I'll meet you over there," Dianne chuckled nervously hoping Hickman was not pulling anything.

On the short drive across the street, Dianne felt uneasy about Mr. Scotty, but at least she had free socks, cards, and the other things she needed. All she had to do was sit in a truck for a few minutes.

Hmmmm. And I'll be home as Mom and Ken finish dinner. Possibly I could hold off and eat some leftovers. Wow! I'll save some more money, she thought.

"You sure are a quick young lady."

"I only drove across the street," Dianne shot back to the salesman in a half-laugh.

"Here, let me help you into this beautiful truck. Here's your package. See how nice you would look in there after shopping with the bag alongside ya and a few tucked behind the seat. And look, you could put a couple of antiques in the back. It's a pretty truck, ma'am. You check it out. I'll be right back. I gotta go to the office."

He's turned up the pressure. I need to leave. This is a nice truck, but I have no business buying it. Let's see what's on the radio. To her surprise, one of her college friends was talking about an upcoming volleyball tournament. Dianne listened intently until she was interrupted.

"Like volleyball?" Mr. Scotty seemed to appear from thin air.

"Ummm, yes. That was a friend of mine from college talking about this weekend's game. She's the team captain."

"Yes, volleyball is a big sport for the girls around here. I've got friends who go to the games and bet on just about everyone. I saw you listening intently as I walked up. Hope I didn't startle you."

"A little. Did your friends ever win anything?"

"If they bet on the home team. You know we're the best."

"Good answer. Listen, I appreciate the socks and card and all, but I've got to get home. My mother is sick, and I don't like to be gone long."

"Oh, I'm sorry to hear that. Maybe take a second to drink this sodee I brought you from the office. Now, giving Coke is something we do for our customers. Check out that cup holder. Good huh! I can see a smart, nice-looking, sports-minded woman like you going shopping with a friend in this beautiful pickup truck. It's got good tires, too! You got the key. Start it up. You know this thing's gonna hum real nice."

Dianne couldn't believe she was sitting in the truck's cab drinking a 'sodee' as this fellow called it, and now listening to the engine. And was she daydreaming about buying the thing?

"Oh, no, wait. I've got to go! I've spent too much time here. I've got to get home," she hurriedly told the salesman.

"Yes, Ma'am, I understand. You gotta get home, and your mom's sick and all, I'd better get you on the road. You know your soul is not ready to adopt this fine child. Can you picture Michael in here? Ya think he'd keep it nice? He seems like a good, tidy boy."

"Oh yes, he's tidy, clean, and takes good care of stuff. There's no doubt about that. His house is impeccable, well, his yard anyway. That's all I've seen," Dianne quickly clarified.

"Yes, I think this truck's soul will match well with Michael's. He could trade in his half-finished car, then keep up payments. Hey, I know it's a long shot, but what if you signed for the guy? You know Michael would take good care of it, and it won't cost you anything. The man will have himself a nice truck to drive you around in. You wouldn't be at risk, 'cause you know he'll keep up with everything. All you need is to put your signature here and you're on your way, and everyone's happy." Hickman took a roll of papers from under his arm. "You know I wouldn't put you in a bad way, ma'am. Not that I could. You're a smart young lady who will make her way in life, and no one can pull you into something you don't feel comfortable about. This deal won't cost you anything. Let me help you from the cab, and here's a pen."

"How does the signature thing work?" Dianne asked without thinking.

"You sign this paper that says you trust Michael to make the payments. By tomorrow night, he's driving away from here. It's a safe deal. I'll get you out of here in minutes. Tomorrow, I call the bank, and tomorrow night he drives it. You even got until then to change your mind."

"Oh, OK. What the heck? Let me sign the paper, and if I don't like it, we'll tear it up tomorrow. I can tear it up, right?"

"Yes ma'am. I have it right here. Sign there and put your other information there. You are now fixed up. And Michael will drive you around in something you deserve. Here's your copy."

On the way home, Dianne felt a warm glow of satisfaction. Making a deal on the truck for Michael felt like giving him a Valentine's gift, and it hadn't cost her a penny.

Heck, I didn't even pay for the card, she mused with a smile. But as she drove, she felt a nagging sense of unease. She hadn't read the entire contract, and the ease of the transaction seemed almost too good to be true.

Her fingers drummed on the steering wheel as she replayed the evening's events. Something about its smoothness all felt off.

"I'll talk to Ken and Mom about it," she verbalized and hoped her mother would feel up for a conversation. It wouldn't be unusual for Ken to sit in the living room, absorbed in a TV show, while her mother, exhausted, headed to bed early.

"What on earth? What are all those cars doing at my house?" she uttered loudly.

Dianne rushed into her home to find Ken, Pastor Dawn, and Dr. Johnson fussing over her mother.

"I think we had a bit of a close one. Your mother passed out after dinner," Ken told Dianne.

"Is she OK? Oh, I felt bad about leaving her. I knew I shouldn't have done that. Where is she? I wanna see her!"

"Stop, girl. She told you to go out. You couldn't have prevented it if you stayed. She's going to be OK, so don't you let go of yourself. There's nothing you could've done!" Dianne was shocked to hear Ken talk so sternly.

Placing her arm around Dianne, Dawn said the obvious, "He's a feisty one."

Dianne couldn't speak. She was overwhelmed.

"What happened? Is she going to be OK?" Dianne shot her questions toward the doctor. "Never mind, I've GOT to see her."

"Leave her. She's resting," the doctor ordered.

"Yes, for now, she's fine. You know your mother is very sick?" the aged Doctor Johnson asked.

"Yes, I know. I feel so badly about leaving her tonight."

"Doc, her mom and I told her to leave. Don't blame the girl because her mom fell out. Dianne, I'm sorry I spoke to you like that," Ken said, laying a gentle hand on Dianne's shoulder.

"I'm not blaming anyone," Doctor Johnson explained, "I want to make sure everyone here is aware of what's going on. Ken told me a little about your mother's health. How's she been for the last week or so?"

"She's been to the doctor in Springfield a couple of times in the past, not this week. Here...here's her info," Dianne said, handing the doctor a file she lifted from a living room side table. "She's seemed better these last few days. We went to her farm a few weeks ago," Dianne explained with a quivering voice.

"In the snow?" The doctor looked over his glasses.

"Yes, she wanted to go. It wasn't snowing, only some on the ground," Dianne replied quickly.

"Folks, there's nothing more I can do tonight. She's resting well. I'll call her regular doctor tomorrow and set something up in case I'm needed again in a hurry. Look, folks, I've been around this town for a while. I'm not the springy thing I used to be, but it doesn't hurt to let me know what's happening. You can't jump up and run to Springfield every time she sneezes."

Doctor Johnson would have talked more if it weren't for Pastor

Dawn's gentle manner, which cut the conversation short.

"Thank you, Doctor. You were certainly a huge help tonight. May we confer with you tomorrow after you coordinate with Dr. Clemmons in Springfield?"

"Yes ma'am, you may," the kindly doctor turned to Dianne, "For you young lady, go in there and kiss your mom good night. I'll talk to everyone tomorrow."

Still carrying her package of socks and supplies, Dianne slid into her mother's room.

"Mom, are you awake?" She said in a loud whisper.

"Yeah. Ummm."

"You don't have to talk, Mom. Ken, Pastor Dawn, and the doctor told me everything."

"I'm cold."

"I bought socks at the drugstore, Mom. Do you want me to put some on you?"

"I'm so cold."

"OK, Mom. I'll put socks on you."

"That noise? It hurts."

"It's the plastic bag. I've got the socks out, Mom. I won't make any more noise."

After gently sliding each sock onto her mother's feet, Dianne laid next to her mother with a gentle hand on her shoulder.

"Oh, sick."

"Sorry, Mom. I didn't mean to rock the bed."

"Oh, sick. I'm cold."

After placing an extra blanket over her mother, she sat on the floor beside the bed with her knees hugged to her chest, whispering prayers to a God she wasn't sure existed. Random thoughts rolled through her mind like dialing through radio stations.

"Dianne!" Dawn's whisper floated through the ajar bedroom door. "Dianne, I'm going home. Ken said he'll stay here if that's OK."

Dianne gingerly stood up, trying not to make noise with her plastic bag and slipped into the living room. She hugged Dawn in a way that both women felt was the start of a bond of lasting friendship.

"Thank you very much for coming over and calling the doctor

and everything. You're a very big help and support."

"It was Ken who called the doctor. I'm not sure if I was much help at all."

"Ken, I'd love for you to stay," Dianne said, still in a whisper. "Here, I bought some socks for you. I think you know your way around the house. Get towels, food, or whatever you need. I will grab one of the cushions and sit next to Mom for a while."

Ken gave an uneasy smile and a slight chuckle about the socks.

"You're welcome, Ken," Dianne smiled, knowing that was his way of thanking her. "The socks were an impulse buy. I'll tell you about it later. I need to spend time with Mom."

After returning to her mother's room, she soon realized that her mother's bedclothes were wet. She called Ken for clean sheets. Both caretakers cleaned Katrina and changed the bedding. After returning to the floor next to her mother's bed, Dianne tried to stop chaotic thoughts from floating through her mind. *Only a few days ago, I would have been very embarrassed to do this. And a few days before that, I would have been embarrassed to help Mom in the bath,* Dianne thought as her mind buzzed with a mix of past and present. *I guess it doesn't matter now. I'm sad. I don't want to lose Mom, not tonight, not ever.*

CHAPTER 10

Midnight Ride

Dianne fully awakened later that night after sleeping only in spurts, nodding off at the side of her mother's bed. She was relieved to hear her mother still breathing. However, her relief was short-lived when she stood to check on her mother.

"Ken...Ken …" she shouted, running into the living room.

Dianne nudged the sleeping man on the living room couch. "Mother's soaked the sheets again. I thought she started wearing the diaper things. I'm scared, Ken. I'm...I'm thinking we should take her into Springfield."

Ken opened his eyes and stumbled to his feet. "OK. Let's check to see if we need to call the doc."

"Ken, before the doc, or anyone, comes, can we change her again? Oh no! She does have a diaper and she soaked through it! And there's blood in it!" Dianne exclaimed as she was already attending to her mother.

"Oh! Bless you, Dianne! I think she would want to be cleaned up too. You are so much like her, you know," Ken said, forcing himself awake. He agreed with Dianne that they should call Doc Johnson and possibly take Katrina into Springfield. Something seemed terribly wrong.

Ken and Dianne worked as expert nurses, calling Doc Johnson and preparing Katrina for a possible ride to Springfield. They changed her bed sheets and gown, cleaned her as best they could, and ensured she would be warm for the trip. As they finished tucking a blanket around her, Doc Johnson arrived with an ambulance seconds behind him.

"We won't have any trouble with traffic at this time of night, so the ride should go quickly," the doctor said, entering the England home. "Ken, you want to ride with me and let Dianne stay with her momma in the ambulance?" The doctor wanted to talk honestly with Ken. He thought the trip to Springfield would be a good time for some straight talk.

"Ken, this might be Katrina's last ride into town. The lady's very ill," Doc Johnson said as they followed the ambulance to the highway and over to Springfield General Hospital.

"Yeah, Doc. She's tried so hard not to let her kid get so wrapped in it all. The momma acts like she's going to the beach with the girls for a weekend, and Dianne shouldn't worry, but damn, Doc, she's dying! I'm gonna miss her. The kid and her mom don't seem like they're connecting! I'm not sure it's right. I mean, the kid's gotta grow up. She can't go riding off on dates, trying to finish school, and acting like nothing's happening. I'm trying to protect Dianne, but I can only do so much."

"Yes, but it sounds like that's what the momma wants. After leaving the ladies earlier, I called Springfield and talked with her oncologist, Doctor Clemmons. He said pretty much what you're saying but didn't say if the elder Ms. England had a husband."

"He died a few years back," Ken said, with a shaky voice and fighting tears.

"With her momma sick, the young lady's got lots to think about in the next few weeks. She needs to do a lot of growing. You watch out for her?"

"Yeah, me and the new preacher in town should be able to help her out. I'm not sure if she'll be able to get through school. There's too much going on."

"Get through school? Her grades OK?"

"She's almost finished, but I don't know her grades. She's learning to teach the slow kids over at the elementary school. After she's done teaching, she gets her degree and a job...she hopes. It depends if the other lady comes back from having her baby."

"Yeah, I think I know about that. My son's wife works with her. When the sun comes up, I'll call her. Young Ms. England needs to rest today and doesn't need to worry about going to school on Monday. I think they'll help her at the school, too. They're a good group of folks."

"That's nice of you. I'll tell her not to worry about it, and she can get some rest."

"Do you want me to wait around and talk to Dr. Clemmons, or

just leave you off at the door?" Doc Johnson asked.

"Doc, you have been very helpful. Beyond being a great doc, you're a great support. I appreciate that. Just leave me at the door. I'll find my way around. Again, I appreciate you."

Doc Johnson pulled into the brightly lit area. "Take care, Ken. I know I don't have to even suggest you take care of the England ladies. You will. But watch yourself. There's only so much you can do," the doctor said, slipping his car into park.

"Yes, doctor. I'll do my best." With genuine gratitude and smiles, the gentlemen shook hands and parted.

After hours of waiting, Dr. Clemmons talked to Dianne and Ken.

"She's a bit dehydrated and may have suffered a stroke on top of all she's going through. She vomited?"

Dianne barely let the doctor finish his sentence. "She peed the bed a couple of times and said she was sick. There was blood in her diaper...but no, she didn't throw up."

Dianne answered Dr. Clemmons as wholly and quickly as possible. Still, Ken felt responsible and wanted to answer all the doctor's questions for Dianne, but he thought about his conversation with Doc Johnson. It was hard for him not to take care of his Trina and now Dianne. He struggled to keep silent with each question the doctor asked.

When Dr. Clemmons left the room, Ken's fidgeting was obvious. "I don't mean to be jumping in all the time, young lady, really, I don't," Ken said. "I'm trying my best to be quiet and let you talk with the people. OK?"

"Ken, there's so much I don't know. It's as though I'm suddenly my mother's mom. It's weird. Oh, and a couple of weeks ago when I talked to her about Cindy, she told me I was in charge." Dianne gave a slight smile.

"You'll get used to it. I'll be here to help when you need me. Otherwise, you're the boss. OK? And you're a grown woman now. OK?"

"I...I...Don't know what to say."

"I'm going to be your friend, if you want me to, but you're in charge," Ken said, looking directly at Dianne.

Dianne settled into an easy chair near her mother while Ken

nervously paced in and out of the curtained room. It seemed like an hour before they spoke again.

"Oh, I think Doc Johnson is your boss teacher's father-in-law," Ken said finally.

"I'm not surprised. Marshfield's people have a lot of connections. I guess that means his son is Deputy Johnson, the top cop," Dianne said in a near mumble without raising her head from her arm's perch.

"Yeah, I think that's the way it works. Anyway, he's going to tell them at the school what's happened tonight, so you don't have to worry 'bout coming in until you're ready. Looks like you might need some rest."

Dianne barely responded with an affirmative grunt, fearing she might gush tears rather than words. Fear, supported by Katrina's every labored breath, blocked Ken and Dianne from real conversation.

"I'm going to the machine to get some crackers," Ken said. "Want some?"

"Yes, I guess. Thanks."

Searching for something to say, Dianne asked Ken, "Did I tell you about my dream?" She didn't wait for an answer. "I dreamed I was falling."

"Probably when you were falling, your head jerked," Ken responded. "That happens when you sleep sitting up. The shrinks may have more to say about your dream."

"Yeah, you're probably right. I can't believe how blue the sky was in my dream. I felt like I was near a beach."

"Young lady, you need your rest, and probably something to eat. Still want those crackers?"

Dianne barely grunted "Yes" as she nodded her head.

Ken returned with the vending machine crackers and jumped in to talk about the papers he had snooped into earlier that evening. "Dianne, You probably didn't intend me to do so, but I looked at the papers you left on the coffee table when you came home. Ma'am, I'll only stick my nose in your business about those papers if you want me to."

"Papers?" Dianne was puzzled for a moment. "Oh yes, I know the ones. I left them there when I rushed in. They say in a bunch of legal words that I trust Michael is an honest guy, and I believe he would pay for the truck. I'm glad you snooped. I want to talk to you about them."

Dianne shared the entire story with Ken. She went into detail, as much to share with him as to distract her from the immediacy of her mother's illness.

"Do you really want my opinion?" Ken was hesitant to ask after what he'd just said about letting Dianne make her own decisions and choices.

"Yes. It was my intention to talk with you."

"I'm very happy to hear that. Are you ready for the full story?" Dianne nodded.

"Well …" Ken was trying to choose his words carefully. "First of all, Scott Hickman bought those things for you and grabbed the package to lure you to his property so he could run a scam on you! Dianne, those papers pretty much say that you're going to pay Michael's truck payment and that you're responsible for insurance on the truck. And, if Michael gets into an accident with the truck, lawyers can take every penny you have if the insurance company doesn't pay up. I'm sorry to be so blunt, but I think I can help if you want me to do so. I'm willing, especially because you need to place all your attention on your mom right now. Did Michael put you up to this?"

"Oh no!" Dianne was shocked at Ken's words. "That guy, the car lot guy, made it seem like there was no risk. I thought I was just saying how I thought Michael was honest!" Dianne was tired, shaken by this news on top of her mother's situation. She stared at Ken.

"Like I said, I think I can help. Do you want me to do so?" Ken's caring was evident. "Please remember from this point, your signature has value! It's an important part of who you are."

"Yes, Ken, I need your help. I feel so ashamed."

"I, too, have been hoodwinked," Ken said. "That's how we learn about things like this. I'm just so glad you are willing to let me help. It's nearly four. The sun will be coming up soon. If you can get rest in that chair, do so. I'm going home to clean up, maybe nap, then talk to the crook. I'll stop by the house to get the papers."

"How are you getting back? Didn't you ride with Doctor Johnson?"

"I called Pastor Dawn when I got the crackers. She was sleeping, but she said she would be here at five to get me."

"I can't believe what you both are doing for Mom and me!"

"I think it's called, paying it forward." Ken smiled. "I'll catch that hug later today. Try to get some rest."

On the way back to Marshfield Ken explained to Dawn about Dianne signing for Michael's truck. "Oh goodness, Ken! What can I do to help?" Dawn asked.

"I'm not sure. And I'm so tired, I'm not thinking straight."

Although he had no answers for Pastor Dawn, he was relieved to talk to her about Dianne's predicament.

"If you don't mind, can we swing by their home? I need to pick up those trouble papers. After I shower and rest, I'll read over them again."

"Sure thing! Don't let them get to you. I don't have enough money to bail you out of jail," Pastor Dawn smiled as she stopped in front of the England home. Ken ran in to get the paperwork and dashed back to the car.

"Got them. I appreciate the ride home, Pastor," Ken said, getting back into the car and buckling his seat belt.

"Ken, I'll continue to do what I can. I hope you can get some rest with all that's going on with you and with these ladies you care so much for."

As they drove away from the England's home, Ken seemed to be deep in thought about how to proceed to help Dianne. "I'm worried. It'll be hard, but it's possible. I'm exhausted." Ken said as they rounded the last turn to his home.

"That's understandable. Now go rest and call if you need me. If I'm not home, I'll be at the church. That's what we pastors do, you know," Dawn said as they pulled up to Ken's house.

"Oh yeah, I know. See you later, Pastor."

Ken showered and stretched out on the couch, attempting to read the papers Dianne signed. It troubled him that some parts did not print well and looked off from the usual car contract. Despite his worry, he fell sound asleep. As nature tends to do, he had to visit the bathroom no longer than three hours into his sleep. Then his worry wouldn't let go.

Forget this. I'm going down to JR's to get some breakfast, he thought. *I'll read this over coffee and some good grub.*

CHAPTER 11

Encounters

Ken tried springing to consciousness after his rough evening, but he couldn't fool his friend and confidant. JR knew him too well and for too many years.

"Good God! What happened to you? You look awful! You OK?" JR didn't mince words when he saw how tired Ken looked.

"I'm OK, I guess, just tired, hungry, and I gotta talk some nasty business today to Scott Hickman at the car lot this side of Springfield," Ken said, obviously not his usual self.

"What? You gonna do business with that guy?" JR asked.

"Oh, it's worse than that."

After ordering his usual huge truck-stop breakfast, Ken shared the story about Dianne's encounter with Hickman and Mrs. England's trip to the hospital. He didn't know how he was going to handle it.

"Oh, I bet the boys around here would have some ideas," JR responded then described the situation to the line of truck drivers sitting at the diner's counter. "That Hickman crook did Dianne dirty trying to sell her a truck when her momma is sick."

"Tell me what you're thinking," Ken inquired, as he scooped up his breakfast like it would be his last.

"Don't worry about it, Ken. Duane, any boys going through Springfield around 11?" JR shouted across the counter.

"Think so! I'll raise 'em on the horn to see what we got. Ya think we need to park some trucks around the car lot—maybe check the oil, tighten loads, or break down for a couple of hours? Be a shame if folks couldn't see that car lot for a few hours...or days. You know, it's so hard for cars to make their way around our big rigs." Duane responded as he looked around at the other truckers.

"Yep, I think you're right about that," JR responded. "Ken, my friend, finish breakfast and nap in the back. I put fresh sheets on the bed this morning. Or you can go sit in my recliner. I'll wake you when we're ready."

Ken didn't know exactly what JR was planning, but he was too tired to think about it. He finished up the breakfast and accepted JR's offer. He knew it meant a belly ache to sleep on a full stomach but figured kicking back in a recliner wouldn't be real sleep.

"I'm taking the recliner, JR."

"OK, I'll tell the ladies not to make any racket back there."

"I heard that." Betty and Mel responded in unison from just beyond the room.

"Don't worry, Ken. Mel and I need to go over some books. Page rattling shouldn't be bad for ya," Betty added.

Mel grabbed a towel and washcloth from a closet and handed them to Ken as he made his way to the recliner. As Ken slept, JR implemented a plan while taking orders and picking up dishes.

"Ken, shake yourself awake," JR said, using a handy walking stick to tap the bottom of Ken's feet raised high in the recliner. "Sorry to only give you a couple hours sleep. Meet me out front. We got a plan." JR threw the towel on Ken's lap.

"Uh-uh. OK, I'm tracking." Ken was still incredibly tired but committed to getting Dianne out of her contract.

"Ken, you're riding with me! You're in no shape to drive. Bring your papers in and talk to Hickman when we get to the lot. You got those papers?"

"Be right there! Let me wash my face."

"Tell that fool you want the originals," JR said putting away a dish towel. "Don't let him give you any crap about us talking and taking care of things that ain't legal. If he tries to do that, ask him how long he wants those trucks parked in front of his lot," JR smiled. "You catch what's happening here, buddy?"

"Yep! You and the boys are a great help," Ken responded with a sleepy smile.

"Scotty boy might need some more convincing. We're bringing some convincers with us. You boys piling up in my delivery van?" JR directed his question to four guys finishing up some coffee in one of the booths.

"We're with you JR!"

"Sorry, gentlemen. Excuse me, please. I've been listening. You trying to get a lady out of a contract?" an unfamiliar voice queried from the counter.

"You bet we are! A creep trying to take advantage of her. She's a nice lady, and her momma's sick. The asshole vulture saw his catch," Ken explained, still half asleep.

"OK. I'm a lawyer returning to St. Louis after doing business in Springfield. You don't have any time for fancy typed documents, so make the guy write a release in handwriting you can read. If there's a general manager there, get their signature too!"

"Good information. You got a card? Someone around here might need you," Betty said as she came from the back after listening to the plan with the lawyer's offer of help.

"Oh, and make sure you get that original paperwork. I'm Fred McCall. It's a pleasure to meet such a group of caring folks. Here's a handful of cards. If you come to see me, let me know where we met. If you think of it, call me after all this shakes out."

"Gotcha. Let's do it!" JR motioned the team to the van.

Heading toward Springfield, JR apologized to Ken that he could only muster a couple of trucks, but it would be enough to get the message across.

"Holy shit!" JR shouted as they neared the business. "Where's the lot? Can't see it. Too many trucks!"

"One, two, three. Okay, I'm tired, but I count seven trucks right cozy around the man's lot," Ken laughed.

"I think I want to see this pickup that all the fuss is about. Ken, get the papers. We'll go like we're interested in it," JR said.

"Got the papers! Yep. I'm interested in this truck, alright," Ken said, finally awake as much as he could be. The truck stop team found the truck and buzzed around it like bees to a sweet flower.

"Hey boys! That's a right fine truck there! I'll make you a deal...$25K! Barely got any miles on it. I'm Scott Hickman. I'm so glad you found this place. I don't know what's happening with all those trucks parked there. They never did that before."

"I know who you are," Ken snapped, staring straight at the guy.

"JR! This is the truck that man got killed in," one of the group shouted out.

"Yeah, that was so unfortunate. God rest his soul. I'm trying to help his widow by selling the truck for her."

"He don't got a widow you lying asshole!" Stepping from the group, Texaco John exposed Hickman's lie.

"Hey boys! Betty told me you would be up here. Thought I could help," John greeted the group.

Suddenly Scott Hickman looked like a frightened cat.

"So, gentlemen, what can I do for you?" Hickman choked out in a nervous quiver.

"This!" Ken showed the envelope with the contract. "I want the original. You took advantage of a young, innocent lady with a sick momma the other night. She had no idea she was buying a dead man's truck from you. Get in there right now, pull the original from your files, and hand it over to me. And you will write a note in your own hand releasing her from this contract!"

Now wide awake and getting a second solid wind, Ken explained and very forcibly added, "If you got a general manager or owner, you need to get them in the office to do the same."

"I'm sorry, gentlemen. I think the contract has already been sent to our accountant. I would help if I could, but I can't," Hickman stammered.

"Whatever it takes," JR explained. "My boys here will wait. And so will the nice gentlemen in the trucks out there."

"Um, OK. Let me see if it's still in the outgoing mail. As far as that release goes, we'll need a lawyer to type it up and get it notarized. We can't do that now."

"Yes, you can. I got a pen. You can scratch it on the back of the envelope if you need to. You know how to write, don't you?!" Ken had enough of Hickman's excuses, following him as he moved toward the office.

"Mrs. Roberts, have the contracts gone to the accountant's office, or do we still have them?" Hickman asked, hoping Mrs. Roberts couldn't find any contracts, especially not this one.

"Accountant's office? We never send them to the accountant. We only send the numbers after the deal is done. And now, I send them right away with the computer. The contracts are right here in my file cabinet. The contracts you made over the last three days are in my inbox for the three-day waiting period if the customer changes their mind. I have the release form if that's what you need. I'll get my notary stamp." Mrs. Melisa Roberts proved herself a very efficient office manager.

Ken quickly jumped in before there was any more of Hickman's stalling. "Mrs. Roberts, thank you very much for helping us with this. You're a smart one with those computers and all. Can you find the contract with the name Dianne England? This young lady is under a lot of stress and cannot make any good commitments. Her mother is terminally ill with cancer. She asked me to help her."

"Oh my! Bless her heart, poor dear. I'm so sorry," Mrs. Roberts emphasized. "Here's the original. Why don't you take it? I'll put the release form in her name, Mr. Hickman's name, and here...I'll notarize it for ya."

"I don't know what you're doing standing there, Hickman. You have a paper to sign!" Texaco John walked toward the salesman, getting ready to push him over to the manager's desk.

"Well, I don't think …" He didn't finish his sentence when he caught everyone's eyes glaring his way and John approaching him.

"Oh, OK. There, it's signed. Now get away from my lot before I call the police." Hickman tried his best to sound as though he had the upper hand.

"You ain't calling no cops. I know you too much." John inserted, then gave a hearty laugh. "I gotta get back to my station. Unlike you, Hickman, I need to make an honest living," Texaco John said, pointing toward Hickman's chest.

Ken, JR, Texaco John, and the remaining gang of truckers followed suit with thunderous laughter as they walked back to their rigs. Only one trucker stayed behind.

"Um, Ms. Millie. You part of that gang?"

Millie stood silent, pointing an angry finger at Hickman. It was apparent she meant business.

"Yeah. What the fuck?" Her voice was more booming than usual. "You tried to sell me that truck the other day for $26K, a thousand more than what you told the men. And you never told me it was the shot-up truck. I knew something was off about that thing. That's why I walked. Are you trying to sell it to a young girl with a sick momma for her boyfriend? I haven't a clue what's wrong with you other than shit for brains and no conscience! If I catch wind of you trying to rip someone off again, my friends and I will come a calling. Bank on it, asshole!" Millie, a woman of her word, said exactly what was on her mind.

Millie left the dealership office with pounding steps that seemed to propel her with a flying leap into her rig's cab. To accent her anger, she revved her engine with long, loud, bellowing sounds, causing fuel-wasting soot to pour from the truck's exhaust pipes, blowing some of the residue across the car lot. Always one to make her point, she pulled the blast chain to make the rig scream a heavy-metal chorus with ear-breaking howls. No mistake— Millie meant business.

"My god, that truck was loud! Did you mean to rip off that girl, Scott? Especially with her mom sick and all?"

"Look, Roberts! You're a meddling sorry excuse for a worker and a piss-poor excuse for a woman! You always have a better way to do things. Why don't you shut your know-nothing mouth and high and mighty opinions and sometimes do what you're told? I'm your boss and write your paycheck! When are you gonna learn that?" Scott Hickman was enraged. Not only had he not sold the truck that had taken up space in his lot all season, but he felt humiliated by truck drivers, by his employee, and most especially, by a woman truck driver.

Hickman continued his tirade against Mrs. Roberts shaking his fist at her and trying his best to lower her to dirt. "I ought to fire you right now!" he boomed, pumping a fist at her. Roberts slammed down a stapler on her desk.

"Then do it! You don't got the balls! And treat me with respect!"

"You're fired! Pack up your girly crap and get out of here. You have five minutes!"

Mrs. Roberts kept very few personal items on her desk, only enough to fill a shopping bag she toted in daily with her lunch and coffee tumbler. She wanted to make sure she packed everything within Hickman's timeline.

Lunch, cup hot, cup cold, personal journal, sweater, yep that's all, she thought to herself.

"You done? I'm going to walk you out, and don't you dare try to take that stapler or those clips or anything," Hickman yelled.

"That stapler, the clips, the desk pad, the pens, the pencils? I bought those! I got tired of begging for what I needed! I guess I should be grateful you bought the computers! But look!" Roberts leaned toward Hickman. "I had to figure out how to use the thing! Walk me out if you want. Walk me to the end of the parking lot or the end of the earth. I don't care! You make sure my paycheck, full and complete, is in the mail within three days! And good luck figuring out the computer!"

"Get out of my sight, you piece of trash," Hickman shot back.

Mrs. Roberts calmly explained, "I've been studying law, and that's what you got, three days! Make it registered mail with a required signature. Don't you dare make it late like my other checks."

Mrs. Melisa Roberts left with her bag of "girly stuff" and drove slowly, almost measuredly off the lot. She was thankful she would not see the inside of the lot's office again. She would not have to conjure excuses for Hickman. She would no longer have to listen to him lie to customers. The office became stone quiet after she left. The quiet was piercing to Hickman, especially given the noise earlier.

The loud phone ringing jolted Hickman. "Uh yeah, hello, umm, North Springfield Fine Autos," Hickman managed to spit out.

"May I speak to Mr. Hickman?" the man's voice uttered. After a quick hesitation, Hickman jumped into his sales persona, thinking it might be a customer.

"This is Mr. Hickman. May I help you with a car today?"

"Oh no, no. This is Jerry Myers. Call me Jerry. I'm your security system representative. Was everything installed to your satisfaction? Today, our staff started monitoring your office and parts of your car lot. You're one of our very first customers to try computer monitoring. Each camera hooks into your phone line and comes alive when it senses motion. At that point, we see what the camera sees. Hold up your fingers, and I'll tell you how many." Hickman was baffled. What did Mrs. Roberts do? He held up his entire hand high over his head.

"Got ya! All five, Mr. Hickman."

"When did Mrs. Roberts have this installed, and what papers did she sign?"

"You signed the papers!" Meyers laughed. "It was a month

ago! I brought them in. Remember? You tried to sell me an almost new truck for $23K. It was a nice one. I just wasn't in the market."

"Oh, yeah, sure. I remember now," he lied, "We finished?"

"Oh no! You got a good package! Mrs. Roberts probably has the contract filed. How she doing? Now go to where the truck was parked and hold up some fingers. We can test the cameras some more. Walk to each side of the lot by the building. Hold up some fingers and come back to the phone."

"Sure," he responded hesitantly.

Hickman hated that the security camera representative would see that the truck hadn't sold yet, but perhaps he could talk the guy into buying it.

I'll make a deal with him for sure, Hickman thought.

Hickman held up both hands in the lot, waved them around a bit, then walked over to the other camera and back to the phone.

"Both times with both hands. Looks like your cameras work, Mr. Hickman," Jerry said. "Wasn't Mrs. Roberts going to send a check for the next 90 days of monitoring today? The check she wrote was only for installation and the first 90 days."

"Mrs. Roberts, can you pay the security company today?" Hickman yelled to an imaginary Mrs. Roberts, then turned back to his conversation with Jerry. "Looks like she can do it!"

Hickman lied with energy.

"OK. I'll look forward to seeing it in my mailbox soon And, if you will, please remind Mrs. Roberts to pull the cassette each morning and evening. She should keep those tapes for at least a year. I told her how to label them."

"Yes, sure I will!" Scott again lied with convincing energy. "Shit, I paid enough for this system and I gotta remember to pull tapes!"

The phone rang minutes later. Hickman hoped the security guy was changing his mind about buying the truck. He was back to himself and knew he could sell that truck.

"Hickman! I'm glad I caught you." Jerry said. "Don't worry about that check! Mrs. Roberts gave us a post-dated check when you signed the deal."

"Oh, oh. OK. Are you sure you don't like that truck? You know it's nearly new! The guy wanted something bigger, so he brought it in here. If you can't afford it, we got others and some nice cars for successful salespeople. That truck is the best, and I'll give you the best deal!" Hickman tried to keep his sales persona on high without success.

He remained angry with Mrs. Roberts and unhappy with the security guy costing the company money. He had planned to spend a wad of cash he earned over the last month on some women in St. Louis. Selling that truck would have made it fine. Now he had an extra bill to pay and an unsold truck.

"Damn bitch!" he yelled in an empty showroom. "I'm glad I fired her! I swear now that truck is cursed!"

His words echoed in the cavernous space. Hickman had no intention of paying for the security system, but his former employee had tricked him into it, and he never knew it. What other things had she done that he didn't know about? He had to act fast to get some money and get that truck off his lot. He had joked about it before, but now he thought for sure the truck was cursed.

"Michael Glossen! This is Scott Hickman," he said into the phone.

"Hey, Mr. Scotty. You gonna beam me over there and give me that truck?"

"I might. How much money you got?"

"You gonna let it go for $12K?"

"Not enough. Bank still open? Go down, get what you can in a cashier's check, and come by this afternoon. We'll talk. Ya need to get there now! They close early on Saturday. I'm not dealing if you make me wait until Monday."

"You can't beam me there? Yep. You know I'm playing with ya! I'll get to the bank. I want that truck. Something tells me someone else wants it and is trying to low ball you."

"I'm not saying. Call me when you get back and let me know what you got. I know there's another paycheck this week. If you been drinking, brush your teeth first."

"Yes dad." Michael laughed, finished his beer, and headed to the bank.

After the bank business, he didn't waste any time calling the car salesman back.

"Hey, Mr. Scotty! You got that spaceship running?" Michael was extra loud with excitement when Hickman answered the phone, causing Brandy to bark. "I got three. You giving it to me for that?"

"Assuming you mean $13K, all in a cashier's check. Clean up that piece of junk car you got and come see me this afternoon. Bring that check for $13K, and we'll talk," Hickman responded.

"I'll be there in my beautiful, fine-running, fine-tuned car. I'm going to pick up my lady from the hospital first. Her momma went there last night. I want her to be my first passenger." Michael said gleefully then hung up.

"Thanks for picking me up at the hospital, Michael," Dianne said as she got into his car.

"No problem. It was easy. You're not too far from Benny's. I gotta stop in at Mr. Scotty's. We might could make a deal on that truck."

"Oh, really?" Dianne did not want to see Hickman after what he tried to pull. Dianne thought quickly for an excuse to avoid the awful car lot. "I've got to get things at Fantastics. Can you leave me there while you go talk to Mr. Scotty?"

"I don't mind. You'd probably get bored anyway."

"Yes, I probably would. And I must get some things for Mom." Michael dropped her off at the store and drove across the street to the car lot.

"OK, Michael D. Glossen, here's the deal. Your girlfriend stopped by. She wanted to sign for you to get the truck. For Valentine's—a gift for you."

"Lady Dianne did that? I guess she got tired of riding in my gray beauty."

"Yes, she did. That's a good woman you got there. But the bank won't accept her 'cause she don't have a paying job yet and you two ain't married. Anyway, what's a classy lady like Dianne doing riding in your car? I hope the inside is good so we can make a deal. That girl deserves better!"

"Oh yes, it's good! I redid everything." Michael was committed to getting the best dollar. He hated to sell it but wanted the truck more.

"Let's look at that car. Lift the hood and start her up." Hickman thoroughly looked over Michael's car; undercarriage, trunk, lights, engine, every light on the dashboard.

"Looks good 'cept for that paint job. You even got the manual. This will work for me. Let's deal. Considering I gotta paint it, I'll give a thousand for it if you buy the truck."

"A thousand? I looked in the blue book. I can get THREE THOUSAND, FIVE HUNDRED DOLLARS for it!" Michael loudly accentuated his words, looking Hickman directly in his eyes. "The body is perfect. It runs perfectly!" His neck veins began to swell as they did at Benny's during his date with Dianne.

The men volleyed words with raised voices, showing strong emotion that could be heard across the car lot. After thirty minutes of heated discussion, they decided on a deal.

"OK, your car, 13K, and I'll take a note for 5K. And you'd be smart to marry that teacher girl," Hickman added. "Get her before she starts meeting some other guys in town. With her momma sick, she's going to need a shoulder to cry on and some good lovin. Maybe you need to make her pump out some babies so she's not running off. I got a contract here. Now sign!"

"Mrs. Roberts fixed you up I see," Michael had a bit of a smirk on his face.

"Yep. Then I fired her. She was a mess. You don't need to know the details. Sign here and get your crap from the car. I'll get you a temp tag and you get outta here before I change my mind. Deal?"

"Deal."

The men shook hands and signed the paperwork.

"Hey Glossen! Here's a bonus. I found this in the lot last week. It ain't worth much, but you can use it for the teacher lady. I checked it right quick. It looks like one of those rings girls wear at the bar when they don't want guys to talk to them." Hickman laughed as he reached into the desk Roberts once occupied and pulled out what could be considered an engagement ring. "Now get that truck out of here, boy. I swear that thing has the devil in it! Not gonna wait to find out. I don't want it on my lot."

"This will work! I'll go pick up my lady now in my pretty new truck. She'll be impressed. Who knows? She might marry me," Michael said with a new heart full of confidence, excitement, and what he thought was love. He joyfully drove across the street to pick up his lady in his big red truck, just in time for Valentine's Day.

CHAPTER 12

Back at Benny's

Pacing the sidewalk in front of Fantastics didn't help Dianne. She wanted the wait and the evening over.

Although dancing with Michael was fun on their first date, she was rapidly coming to the realization that a few hours dancing was not worth the stress she felt. Dating Michael seemed wrong on so many levels.

"Michael! I was getting a little worried," Dianne said. "I saw you over there yelling at Hickman. I couldn't hear you, but I saw you swinging your arms, and you were in his face. I'm glad I didn't have to walk over there or call the cops!"

"It's all good. As you see, I got the truck! Thank you, ma'am! You sure know how to care for a guy! Mr. Scotty and I just had to do a little more dealing."

Dianne didn't say a word. She was very worried and could only hear Ken's words of advice echoing in her thoughts about Hickman taking advantage of her. Was she committed to paying Michael's truck payments?

"You got the title?"

"Yes. Mr. Scotty didn't have to beam it over to me. He signed it right there. You know my joke, right?"

"Yes, I've heard it a few times. You mind if I look at the papers? I've never bought a car before, and I wonder what papers are involved." Dianne really wanted to see if her name was mentioned anywhere. Without an answer or permission Dianne grabbed the papers and almost immediately, began asking questions. She felt as though Michael was evasive, which worried her.

"Oh, I see we're a bit late in here tonight...the lot's almost full up." Michael redirected the conversation. "I hope Benny doesn't give me any mouth about cooking up these ribs. I might have to talk to him like I did the other week." Michael still seemed to be thinking about ribs and his new truck while trying to make conversation with Dianne.

"I don't think he'll give you a hard time with the ribs, Michael. He may even put another orange slice on our plates," Dianne replied with a slight smile. "So, this is totally your truck? You pay for it?"

"Don't worry girl! I worked hard for this truck. If he does give me a hard time, like last time, I'll make it right for you. You know, we are a couple." Michael paused and looked straight at Dianne, eye to eye. He was breathless. He rarely looked at a woman straight on, directly into her eyes. He knew what he had to do, and it wouldn't wait.

"You do know that don't you? I'm not going to let anyone mess with you," Michael half whispered to Dianne as they entered Benny's place. "Like I said, we're a couple. Hang on dear...I gotta go talk to Benny." Michael dashed off to talk with Mitzi and then to Benny in the kitchen.

"Here you go. You know how I like 'em," Michael said, as he handed the cooler of ribs to Mitzi. Dianne sensed something was up but couldn't guess what would soon happen. She saw Michael inside the kitchen door, first talking to Benny and his helper, then talking to Mitzi again, which seemed to upset the server.

"You're dreaming. It ain't happening!" Mitzi talked a bit too loud in response to Michael's chatter. Benny's had your ribs ready for an hour. Let him warm them a bit with fresh sauce, and I'll bring them out." Her follow-up laughter was heard across the restaurant as she walked toward Dianne.

"Here, hon. I'll show you where to sit. I'll take good care of you tonight. It's going to be special. I guarantee it!" Mitzi turned to Dianne and gave an uncharacteristic smile, then showed her to a booth.

"There you go. This is a nice, private little place. You sitting here or over by Michael so you two can cozy up?"

"Across from Michael is fine." Dianne couldn't understand Mitzi's weird kindness and became more concerned about Michael's purchase than happy for him.

"So, he accepted 13 K for the truck?" Dianne discovered the

purchase price immediately after reading the truck's papers.

"Oh, sweetie, don't chu worry about me. I got it all covered. It's not like it's costing you anything. I know you'd buy it for me if you could," Michael smiled.

Dianne was worried. She didn't know if Ken was successful talking to Hickman, if Hickman was fooling Michael, or if both Hickman and Michael were fooling her and possibly Ken.

"Do you have a song you want to hear my little sweetheart?" Michael said, trying to sound romantic. "How about something sweet and romantic?"

"Oh Mitzi! You bring us some beer and a soda?" He turned his attention to the server briefly.

"No problem, Romeo. You and your girl make yourselves comfy."

Mitzi seemed to be laughing at Michael's order. Dianne couldn't imagine what could be so funny to Mitzi, except perhaps Mitzi's own behavior.

"Mitzi, may I have a lemonade instead of soda?" Dianne asked.

"Why yes, hon. I'm happy to bring you some lemonade."

"Sorry Michael, I only know one country song. Do you know that song by Patsy Cline, 'Crazy Over You,' or something like that?"

"You reaching back girl. I don't know if that's on here. You dance with me if it is? Woman, that's before either one of us was born. I didn't know you were crazy over me." Dianne instantly regretted her limited memory.

"Michael, you seem weird tonight. You're kind of sweet, but strange. Sure, I'll dance with you if you find the song," Dianne said, hoping he couldn't find it.

Mitzi didn't have time for a lot of attitude toward Dianne, with many customers she had to serve. Yet, before Mitzi returned to their table, she approached each table with a reserved voice, unlike her usual style. With each customer encounter, she laughed a little, and the people smiled in return.

"OK, girl, you got it. It's right here!" Michael directed his full attention to Dianne. "Now, I always try to be nice to you. It has nothing to do with the truck. Patsy Cline is being good to you tonight, too. She's here. She just was hiding and waiting for us to get close."

"Michael, you know I didn't buy you that truck! Stop being so weird. It's not anything I did!" She blurted out, trying to hide her worry.

Michael didn't respond and spoke little when they danced. Dianne continued to worry about what she might have done and if Ken fixed it.

Michael, unaware of Dianne's worry, mulled over exactly how he would ask Dianne to marry him, which increased his weirdness.

Before talking to Scotty, he never considered getting married. However, he was smitten with Dianne and wanted to keep her.

Adding to Dianne's strange feeling, Michael seemed to know almost everyone in the place, yet no one spoke to him. They just smiled their way. Strange things always seem to happen around Michael.

Shortly after the jukebox finished and the couple returned to their seats, Mitzi delivered the couple's drinks and salads quickly, without a word, only a smile. She resembled a little kid who knew a secret they'd promised not to tell but wanted to do so. She carefully placed both of their drinks on napkins and left a few neatly folded on the table, different from last time when Michael had to beg for napkins.

"Let me know if y'all need anything else," she finally said with a bit of a snorting laugh. Dianne was concerned. Was Mitzi high, or perhaps planning a dirty trick on her and Michael?

Michael gave Mitzi a wink and a quick smile. Dianne thought he was ready to enter his usual flirtatious mode, but he veered away from his instincts and directed his attention to Dianne, increasing her uneasiness.

"You so sweet on me." Michael said to Dianne seeming to pull senseless thoughts from the air. "C'mon, here's another song. Remember, you're dancing this one with me." Giving her only enough time to barely sip her lemonade, Michael took Dianne's hand and led her to the dance floor.

"Crazy, I'm crazy for feeling ..."

"Again?" Dianne quizzed Michael on the way to the dancing space. Michael held Dianne close, too close and too tight for Dianne's comfort. Dancing with Michael before was enjoyable, but not tonight. Before, they danced side by side with prescribed steps. Now it seemed that Michael wanted to contain her, not dance with her. His stranger-than-usual behavior was scary.

Could Michael have gotten high with Mitzi earlier? She wondered.

After this second dance ended, Mitzi served the reheated ribs, complete with an orange garnish supporting a sprig of parsley. The dinner looked "picture perfect" and smelled inviting despite Dianne's nerves unsettling her stomach.

"Here, Benny sends these too." Mitzi placed a piping hot bowl of fried apples on the table. "Benny said he and Jenny canned them last fall, and it was time to finish emptying the cellar," Mitzi explained.

"WOW! Thank you, Mitzi." Dianne tried to be as kind and sincere as possible to Mitzi.

"You're welcome," Mitzi quickly responded with a forced smile and hurried off to another table.

"Not so quick—I need another one here," Michael shouted to the busy server.

"Michael, let Mitzi do her work. I know you can hold your booze, but remember your big red baby in the parking lot. You need to get her home safely, OK? You don't usually finish your beer that quickly and start clambering for another. What's up?"

Dianne wanted to clear the air and discover how Michael D. now owned the truck. She wanted the entire story.

"Oh, I guess I'm excited about my big red baby in the parking lot," Michael said, smiling, while kissing Dianne's hand. He switched to drinking water and started to pull apart the ribs on his plate. He smiled at Dianne and tried to comment about the crowd and the evening in general. He was trying to get at something but couldn't say it.

"I didn't ask you...how's your momma? She comin' home soon?" Michael attempted a conversation between chews.

After barely swallowing a bite of her salad, she replied, "She's not well at all. I'm praying she does come home. I have some good news, though. Well...perhaps it's good news. You remember meeting Ken at the house?"

"Yep," Michael replied while continuing to chew with lips decorated in a deep brown sauce. "That Ken, I see him at JR's for breakfast sometimes."

"I can't believe how full I've become," Dianne said after eating only a few bites of salad. "Before I update you about my mother and Ken, I want to know about the deal you made with Scotty."

"We can't keep eating, darling. Patsy's comin' back! You dance with me again?" Michael seemed uninterested in Dianne's inquiry or Katrina's condition.

"Oh! my stomach can't handle this," Dianne protested, but Michael didn't answer. He grabbed her hand and led her to the dance floor.

"Michael let's sit down! I'm going to say my piece!" she continued to protest. Seconds into the song, Michael stopped to caress Dianne's face, then kissed her—a long, full-mouth kiss. In total shock, Dianne did not enjoy Michael's passion. She tried to break away to return to her seat, but he moved closer and held her tighter with one foot directly behind hers, nearly straddling her leg. His tight hold assaulted her with his penis swelling. With surprise turning to anger, she broke away.

"Michael, Slow down!...and sit down!" she said, trying to be calm. "This is embarrassing, very embarrassing!"

She broke Michael's grip and returned to the table to think through her next action. She was depending on a ride back to the hospital in that dammed truck and felt she couldn't leave, yet Michael appeared out of control, and she was afraid.

"But hon, I want to marry you!" Michael shouted across the room as Dianne sat down. Michael followed and stood inches away, blocking a quick exit as fear and embarrassment ran through Dianne's every nerve ending.

"Please? Please!" he begged, pulling the car-lot ring from his pocket and attempting to present it while hovering over her.

"Michael! I'm embarrassed! I can't do this! I've got to go back to the hospital to be with Mom," she shouted. I'll wait for you by the truck. I assume you have money to pay for this!" Dianne said through gritted teeth and a fiery stare, pushing him away.

Dianne's stern declaration shocked Michael. Everyone in the restaurant watched Dianne exit to their extended chorus of "Awwwwww, poor fella."

"Ain't down yet," Michael shouted after leaving more than enough money on the table in crumpled bills. Mitzi rushed over to the table to count the money. Now she was in full laughter as she shook her head and straightened each bill.

"I get the best tips when this happens," she shouted, laughing at the customers' dismay. "I hate to see this good food go to waste."

"Hey! Any of you want some ribs? These things are barely touched. You can eat 'em or bring 'em to the dog!" A couple of hefty guys rushed to the table to collect the leftovers.

"Oh! Apples too!" the shorter of the two shouted in excitement. Customers laughed at the two making fools of themselves.

"I made you mad!" Michael caught up to Dianne in the parking lot.

"But woman! It's so early. I hate to leave here. And I gotta show Benny my truck. If you want to leave, OK. You keep going to the truck. I'll talk to Benny and be right back."

Without a word, Dianne continued to the truck.

Barely stepping back inside the restaurant, Michael encountered Mitzi.

"Michael! Go back to your girl!" Mitzi scolded. "You owe her a big apology for springing marriage on her like that!" Mitzi said, showing real empathy for Dianne.

"Benny's back there busy. You go on and take the girl back to her sick momma. She can't deal with all this right now! Tomorrow, you buy her flowers and apologize. I'm talking real flowers, not one of these fake things here! Go on! Go on before she finds someone to shoot you for acting such a fool."

Crap, I bet it's locked. Dianne's quick pace was not enough to keep her warm on a night like tonight. She wanted to get warm in the dammed truck and escape Benny's immediately.

Instinctively, she tugged on the door's handle. *Damn! He left it open! Someone could have stolen this thing, especially with the papers on the dash and spare keys on the seat! I hope he hurries up so I can get back to Mom,* she thought.

Dianne was surprised at Michael's carelessness. She contemplated crossing the street and calling her mother's room from the open gas station. Perhaps Ken would still be there, and he could come get her. Before deciding, she saw Michael's silhouette approaching the truck.

"Benny's too busy. I'm taking you to the hospital. Or I could take you home? How'd you get in the truck? I hurried back 'cause I didn't want my sweetheart to freeze."

"Michael, your truck was left open," Dianne snapped.

"Open? What?" Michael started to feel under the seat. "Yeah, there it is. My sweet thing is there." Michael pulled a 9mm Glock from under his seat to show Dianne, hoping to impress her.

"What is that?" Dianne became more than upset; she was scared.

"You go shooting with me sometime? It's nothing to be scared of. I keep it so no one messes with me. You wanna hold it?"

Now very nervous, Dianne panicked.

"No! Take me back to the hospital!" she ordered.

"OK, OK. Don't worry, darling. You're not the first woman to be 'fraid."

Dianne sat quietly, seething during the ride. Once safely back at the hospital, she only wanted to get out of that truck and away from Michael without any more drama.

"Well, here we are. Can we go dancing tomorrow? Benny's is closed, but we could find someplace."

"Michael, unlock the door." She ordered, fumbling for a door release. Dianne had a new voice and had shed any fear of using it.

"Oh, no! I'm coming around to let you out like a gentleman. You told me those college boys did that."

"No, I didn't. I'm outta here!" She found the door's release, and without hesitation, she slid from the truck to the curb.

"Don't bother coming around, Michael. And don't come around my house!" she said, holding the door open. "If you see me somewhere, go the other way. I don't want to see you!" Dianne punctuated her anger by slamming the truck door with the force of a thunderstorm.

"But I gotta kiss you goodbye!" She heard Michael plea as he stepped from the driver's seat.

"I don't know what the fuck you are talking about!" she said, slamming her gloved hand on the fender. "This is it! The end! I don't want to see you again! That means no ribs, no dancing, no fucking animals, no lawnmowers, and definitely, no no no NO marriage! We are not dating, we are not engaged, I am not your girl! Two months is way too long to have put up with you and all your weirdness!"

"Don't know what you mean, Sweetie, but OK, if that's how it is. I'll call you tomorrow to make sure. You gonna need a ride later?"

Dianne turned her back on his pleading and headed toward the entrance. The usually garish bright lights from the hospital entrance strangely comforted her. She felt a sense of relief and contentment, knowing she had one less thing on her mind. *I need to ensure that Ken has recovered the contract,* she thought as she started the journey to her mother's room.

"Miss! Miss! Visiting hours are about over." The security guard approached her with a tin-soldier stride.

"My mom is on the third floor, Room 312. Dr Clemmons said it would be OK to extend the visiting hours."

"Can I please get her name and see your ID? I'll check the list."

"Oh, OK. Room 312, as you said. We try to keep our patients and staff safe. The hospital contracts us. Are you looking for a job? The company pays well and has openings. I must confess, if you stay more than 90 days, I get $200. They're looking for women." Dianne smiled at the handsome young man's energetic and unexpected recruitment effort.

"Thank you. I have a job next year at the elementary school in Marshfield," Dianne said, relieved that the conversation had taken her thoughts away from Michael's craziness.

"All the best to you, Ma'am. Go on up and see your momma."

"Thank you."

The gentle exchange relaxed Dianne. Indeed, the young man's kindness was the angel to rid her mind of a truly awful evening.

"You made it. You're back early. Your mom was awake for a while, but she's sleeping now," Ken said, obviously happy to see Dianne return early.

"Oh, Ken, you wouldn't believe what a horrible night I had! I called it off with Michael. His weird self became too weird. I've got other things to distract me. I sure as hell don't need him. Honestly, I wish I had not agreed to the first date with him and definitely not this one."

"Hi, dear. Talk to me. How are you doing?" Katrina said, barely awake.

"I'm doing fine, Mom! I'm better than ever! I'm tired but feeling great. I'm no longer seeing Michael. I broke it off with him."

"Good. I think he's trash." Katrina spoke softly and then seemed to drift off again.

"My dear Trina, I'm saying goodbye now. I'm taking Dianne home." Ken kissed Katrina's cheek and turned to Dianne.

"Dianne, would it be OK to say our goodbyes and return to Marshfield? Wait! Before I forget...it's confirmed. We will take your mom home tomorrow. She should be out of here by noon."

"I will be happy to leave. It looks like mom could use the rest."

"OK, I'll get the car, and you can meet me in the front."

"OK. See you in a minute at the curb."

Dianne stepped over to her mother's bed and gently stroked her hair.

"You looking forward to going home, Mom?"

"Yes." Katrina shut her eyes and drifted off. Dianne held her mother's hand and said a little prayer:

> *Angel of God my guardian dear*
> *To whom God's love commits me here*
> *If I die before I wake*
> *I pray to heaven my soul to take.*

"It's such a morbid prayer, Mom, but it's one you said to me every night when I was a little girl."

Dianne thought her mother was sleeping peacefully.

"It's *I pray the Lord my soul to take.*" Katrina had awakened enough for a whispered correction and a smile.

"Good night, Mom. I'll see you in the morning." Dianne kissed her mother's cheek and left the room to meet Ken for her ride home.

CHAPTER 13

A Long Day

Ken was tired and anxious to get home. The poorly lit parking lot and surrounding area seemed to match his mood. As hoped, Dianne was at the curb when he pulled up.

"Have a good evening, Miss," the security guard said as he escorted Dianne from the hospital and opened the car door for her. "You come to see me if you change your mind about that job," he added.

"Thank you, sir, I will," she responded, smiling as she buckled herself into the car seat.

Ken turned to Dianne as he waited for the traffic to clear. "I hope you had more rest than I did this afternoon. Was your mother conscious when you left?"

"No, sleeping," she said softly, staring out the window.

"It's been a long day. I hope you'll talk to me so I can stay awake while we drive back to Marshfield."

Ken barely pulled into traffic when Dianne couldn't wait another second. "Yes, I'm going to talk to you. I'm worried. Did you help me with the truck thing? Mr. Michael D. got the truck and acted like I bought it for him. I'm worried!"

"I see now that I won't fall asleep at the wheel! Hopefully, you won't either when I tell you what happened. Today has been quite an adventure."

He adjusted his driving position and twisted his head to work his stiff neck. "Let me tell you about my day and why I didn't get much sleep," he said, stretching his neck. Step by step, Ken described the truckers' rally at the car lot and how he reclaimed the papers she signed. Whether he was tired or thought the situation was ludicrous, he had to laugh most of the way through the story, extending his telling.

Admittedly, he said the telling of the story was more

entertaining than being part of the melee. He shared that he was very upset about what Hickman had done and that stalling did not calm him or the truckers.

His storytelling spurred Dianne to laugh at their adventures after she shared what led to her breakup with Michael. Their laughing and adding quips to their stories kept them awake on the trip home.

Earlier, she was embarrassed and angry at Michael for what he did at Benny's. After Ken described his day at the car lot, she responded with full, snorting laughs that soothed her and Ken's emotional day.

"Ken, I was scared half to death when he pulled that gun from under the seat. I had no idea if it was loaded," she said after recovering from her laughter.

Ken shook his head. "Understandable. I don't know why so many young guys around here fear someone will ambush them. Did you see what kind of gun it was?"

"I don't know what kind of gun it was. And I didn't ask! I wouldn't know one type from another. It was a pistol sort of thing, but different from what I've seen in Wild West movies. It almost looked like a toy, but he said it was real. Could it be something like a clock? I think he said that. After seeing that thing, I only wanted to get out and run. I was pissed, then scared. I don't know what that guy is apt to do."

Ken smiled at her description as he approached the England home. He reassured her that she would be fine and that Michael would not harm her. He reassured her as though he was certain.

Dianne was far from certain.

"Your papers—your copy, the originals, and a notarized note getting you out of the contract—are in the envelope in the back seat," Ken said. "Now get inside and rest! There's another big day tomorrow. I'm marrying my Trina, the most beautiful woman in the world! And I want to see her daughter well-rested to witness it all. Oh, wait! Don't forget you promised Pastor Dawn you'll attend church tomorrow."

Dianne glared at Ken and tried to put words together as she exited the car. "Ken, she didn't really expect me to go, did she?" Dianne said as she opened the back door to secure the papers. "I'll be tired, and you know I don't like religious stuff."

"All I know is that you promised, and you are not a person to break a promise. I'll even sweeten the day a little for you. I'll buy you breakfast at JR's truck stop."

"Breakfast at a truck stop is sweetening the pot?" she continued the gentle protest as she closed the car door.

"Yes, it is," Ken countered. "Wait until you taste it! It's the place for truck drivers and locals to stop. It's out on the highway on the way to Springfield. Guarantee you'll love it! Sorry, they don't have tofu bacon for ya."

Dianne let out a hoot. "I've had a lot of laughs from you tonight, Ken. That was a big one. OK, I'll go, even though there's no tofu bacon."

"Alright! I'll pick you up at eight-thirty. We'll get to the church in plenty of time to meet people. I'm sure some people heard you were teaching at the school and would like to meet you," Ken encouraged. "At breakfast, you will meet more fine folks. Some are the ones who helped with that truckers' party at Hickman's. Surely, if anyone there went or knows about it, they'll have their own stories. That's the way it is over there."

"Oh yeah, another opening, another show all about God and surely not about the good Christians who gather to gossip about whatever and whoever," Dianne said, letting her sarcasm escape her thoughts. "Breakfast afterward sounds like it would make church palatable. Good night, Ken. I'll see you in the morning at eight-thirty."

"Good night, Dianne. I assure you that all will be well. I'll wait here until you blink the porch light. By the way, I believe the gun Michael has is a Glock, not a clock."

"Oh, thanks. That will make me sleep better," Dianne said with playful sarcasm. "Good night, Ken. Thank you for the lift home."

As Dianne stepped inside, the house seemed eerie. It was too quiet, too dark, too lonely. The day was too emotional, long, and life-altering for Dianne to comprehend the changes she was experiencing. She blinked the porch light as Ken instructed, and after a quick nighttime routine, she slumbered from pure exhaustion.

Sunday morning came quickly. Dianne awakened late and hurried to get ready for her church debut. Once there and still exhausted, she met gaggles of people receiving a constant stream of offering thoughts and prayers. Church was a whirlwind of regurgitated small talk without any real thought or prayer attached to many sentiments. She was dazed after the church service and hoped the breakfast Ken promised would be as good as he said.

Negotiating the truck stop gravel parking lot in her heels caused her to take slow and careful steps, which was difficult, as hungry as she was.

"I see you're having trouble there. Want me to get your sneakers from the car?"

"Ken, they haven't been called sneakers since before I was born." Dianne continued to step like she was walking on coals.

"OK. Athletic shoes. You want 'em?"

"Thank you, Ken. We're almost to the door. If you don't mind, will you get them after we eat?"

"After you, delicate princess," Ken teased as he opened the door for Dianne.

"Hey JR, I've got someone I want you to meet!" JR barely looked at Dianne before he took Ken aside.

"Mel's right in the back! You going to introduce the two girlfriends?" Before Ken could answer, Mel came from the back at a healthy pace.

"Hi! You must be Dianne! I'm one of Michael's buddies, and I work and live here! JR and Betty are my parents."

Without waiting for Dianne to respond, she continued. "Michael called me last night, and I blessed him out for what he did. I'm so sorry he put you through all that! The way Michael tells it, it looks like Scott Hickman put him up to it, or at least put the thought in his head." Mel extended her hand to exchange greetings officially, and the two ladies fell into conversation as though they had known one another all their lives.

"If y'all don't mind me taking a break, I'd love to sit and talk to Dianne," Mel said to JR and Ken. "What do you want for breakfast, or I guess, brunch," she asked Dianne.

JR, Ken, Betty, and Dianne were all shocked by Mel's greeting. Finally, JR found his voice. "Um, you ladies go over to the booth and sit for a chat. I'll bring some coffee. Dianne, it's a pleasure meeting you. What would you like to eat?" JR said after recovering from Mel's cheerful greeting.

"Remember, they don't have tofu bacon," Ken said and smiled at Dianne.

"Could I have two eggs over easy and some grits?" Dianne couldn't think of anything else.

"Got it. Two eggs and grits with a cheese slice. To finish it off, we'll add biscuits and some melon." JR winked at Dianne.

Mel waved her father away. "Dianne, don't fuss with him. He wants to make sure first-timers are well-fed. Come on, let's sit and talk."

The ladies didn't take long to jump into tales about Michael and some of his antics. Betty appeared with some appetizing plates sooner than seemed possible.

"Here you go, ladies. I whipped up things quick for you."

"Thank you, Momma! Dianne, this is my mother, Betty. She does about everything around here, and she's teaching me the ropes, the problems, and generally how to run the place."

"It's a pleasure to meet you," Dianne said. "You have a big job. The way I've seen Marshfield work, I guess you already know who I am, what I do, and probably when I lost my first baby tooth."

Nodding their heads, the women laughed at Dianne's impression of Marshfield. "I've been around a few years, so I can see where you'd say that." Betty smiled. "But honestly, we know so many people, but we don't know their whole story, just what people are babbling about at any time. I'll let you two talk. Exchange phone numbers so you can keep in touch! Mel knows a few of the gals over at the animal park. She will help you get to know some folks around here, Dianne."

"I guess you know I'm swamped tending to my mother right now, but I want to keep in touch. Especially with summer coming up. It will be great to have a friend."

"Sure thing!" Mel agreed.

Ken interrupted. "Dianne, did you know we've been here over an hour? We need to get to the hospital."

"Wow! That long? Mel, I didn't tell you something big. Ken and my mother have been spending time together for almost a year. He asked my mother to marry him! It's not a legal marriage; only one to show their love. Maybe it can be called a 'love union.' I don't know what else to call it. It will be in the hospital chapel and not a big thing. Mom is too sick."

"JR and Betty told me about your mom. I'm so sorry." Mel put her hand over Dianne's.

"Yes, Mel. It will be good to have some friends during this tough time." Although the two had just met, they hugged tightly. It was obvious to everyone around that, before long, they would be good friends.

"We'll stop by the nurses' station to see how close your mother is to leaving," Ken began. "No, you will check on your mother at the nurses' station. I'm only along for support. You're in charge, Dianne."

"Thank you, Ken. Oh, Dr. Clemmons!" Dianne spied the doctor leaving the area. "Looks like we caught you on your rounds. Is my mother ready to leave?"

"Yes," Dr. Clemmons said solemnly. "The nurses are getting her ready now. Do you have someone at home to help you?"

"Yes, her caregiver, Cindy, is coming over at two," Dianne said.

"Your mother is frail. I know you planned something in the chapel. I wanted to be there. But my suggestion is to take her home and make her comfortable. She may have already said all she needs to say for this lifetime. She only needs her daughter's love...alongside a very best friend."

"I understand, Doctor. Thank you."

Ken leaned toward Dianne in a near whisper. "Dianne, I'm going to say hello to my Trina, then I'll get the car. I'll see you at the discharge circle. OK?"

"OK."

Katrina looked small and helpless in the wheelchair, but she smiled at her daughter. "Mom, can you hold my hand? I'll walk alongside you. The nurse said she would help take you down to the car."

The nurse who assisted Katrina and Dianne to the car was a true professional, yet Dianne couldn't help noticing a tear forming as she closed the car door.

"Goodbye, Ms. England. It was a pleasure meeting you and working with your mom."

"Thank you, nurse. I don't know what I would have done without you helping mom during this time."

"My name is Jasmine Belk. You are going to have some tough days ahead. If you need a friendly ear, please call the hospital and ask for me."

"I will," Dianne said.

CHAPTER 14

The First Goodbye

After a quiet ride from Springfield that morning, the group arrived to see Cindy waiting. The three of them guided Katrina up the stairs. Her legs, close to atrophy, made the task precarious, and Katrina, barely awake, leaned heavily on them.

"Perhaps we should have taken the option to have an ambulance bring her home," Dianne mused while supporting her mother. Stepping carefully, she breathed heavily with her mother's arm around her shoulders as she lifted as much as Ken.

"I think you're right, Dianne," Ken said, panting. "I'm guessing this is her last trip from Springfield. If she had opened her eyes, she would have seen the shadows of hills and country homes, not medical equipment, and the faces of strangers. If it were me, that's what I'd want. Maybe we should have just let her be comfortable here."

"Ken...possibly." Dianne was overcome with emotion and could barely speak. After much effort, the three caretakers settled Katrina into bed with clean, crisp sheets, side lamps glowing gently, and some of her favorite music playing softly from a CD player.

"Cindy, how did you know Mom likes light jazz?" Dianne whispered.

"I saw some CDs out, so I figured. She has a few classical ones there, too. Oh, and I brought a Billy Ray Cyrus CD from home. Didn't you say he became a favorite of hers lately?"

"Yeah. She and Ken found it special." Dianne looked over to Ken, who possibly heard her, but his far-off glance clearly indicated he wasn't in the mood to respond. After settling Katrina in bed, the team sat sullen in the living room, each trying to think of something to say but not wanting to say anything. The house was eerily quiet without the usual heavy breathing from Katrina or chatter from anyone.

"No oxygen from the hospital?" Cindy broke the silence.

"No. Dr. Clemmons said it's best to let her be," Dianne spoke in a nervous whisper.

"I don't mean any disrespect," Cindy offered. "But I'm not sure Momma Katrina would want to see you two this way. Ken, grab a beer. Dianne, we're popping open some wine. We gotta talk...say something! Holding stuff in is no good." Cindy hoped her forwardness would be well received. She needed to break the silence for herself, Dianne, and Ken.

"Yes. A beer would be good," Ken acknowledged.

"Dianne? I found wine glasses. You up for it?" Cindy pressed on.

"OK. Thank you."

"Good beer, Cindy! I'm not going to finish this, though. I must marry my Trina." Ken burst through the silence, urgently declaring his wish as he headed toward Katrina's room as Dianne attempted to follow.

"Wait." Cindy extended her arm blocking Dianne, "Let Ken have his visit. OK?"

I guess I should have been in there before, Dianne worried but said nothing.

"Bring it with you, Ken. Your Trina won't mind." Cindy directed. "She'll be happy you're there! Bring a glass of wine or water for her if you like." Before Cindy finished her encouragement, Ken, with a beer in one hand and a small glass of water in the other, adjourned to "his Trina's" room.

Although Ken's Trina didn't stir, and he wasn't sure she could hear him, Ken whispered gently into her ear. "Trina, dear, dear Trina, I'm so sorry I couldn't spare you this journey. But please know that I promise to watch over Dianne and help her make good decisions. She's given me life as you gave her life. I nearly lost myself in a dark place, a very, very dark place. I never told you this, but I lost a great and close friend in 'Nam. I take the blame for it. I messed up. I don't care what the shrink says, I messed up. I decided this past Christmas if I couldn't save your life, I would join you on your journey. Now, I feel differently. I promise you. I'm not going anywhere. I will care for Dianne like she's my own. Don't worry now. Be at peace. I will protect her with all my strength."

Ken became silent, but he couldn't silence his mind. Memories screamed at him. Rarely had he ever cried. Now, he cried strong tears that had welled up in him for years. Katrina moved her hand to his shoulder then it fell back to the bed.

"Please help me! Somebody help me!" Katrina cried out. Ken placed Katrina's hand into his, which seemed to calm her. With further words unnecessary, Ken sat quietly, holding Trina's hand.

"I need to see her!" Dianne cried. "Isn't that what daughters do?" She asked with tears forming.

Cindy gave Dianne a sympathetic smile. "There's no right way to do things—birth, death, and everything in between. We need to play life one minute at a time. If you think about it, most folks do what they can at the time they are doing. You get my meaning?"

Dianne could only nod as she fought back tears, trembling with a cramp forming in her throat. Attempting to distract her, Cindy continued to speak.

"I meant to say earlier," Cindy went on, "Pastor Dawn will come after a bit. She needed to attend to things at the church, and she thought you and Ken would need some time."

"Yes, I'll wait for Ken to come out."

"Someone's coming up the walk. Want me to get the door, Dianne?"

"Please."

Cindy opened the front door to find JR and his family waiting on the front stoop.

"I hope we're not interrupting family time, but I knew y'all would need some easy food. Didn't think you'd feel like making dinner. And it's getting late for that anyway," JR explained as Cindy welcomed them in.

"Betty made potato salad, and Mel made sure we didn't put any bacon in it, tofu, or real stuff!" JR smiled at his attempt to lighten his own mood. "She cut up some veggies and made a special dip for you, Dianne. I hope adding us three to this group isn't a bother for anyone!"

"Oh, you're JR and Betty from the truck stop," Cindy said. "And I believe you're Mel, the finance and bookkeeping lady! You all know Dianne?" she asked, stepping in as host and accepting the group's generous offerings.

"We only met this morning. We didn't know what to do to help, so we did what we do. We brought food," said Betty.

"And you make very good food," said Dianne. "I'm not sure if I said so this morning, but I very much enjoyed my breakfast. And Mel, I thoroughly enjoyed our chat." Dianne seemed to escape from her grief for a moment.

"I've got a whole lot of chat left," Mel said.

"Dear, how's your mom?" Betty interjected, reaching a hand toward Dianne, then holding her young hand gently in her own. "I know it's tough. We want to be here for you, whatever you need. OK?" Betty said, looking directly into Dianne's eyes.

"My mother's not well," Dianne said after a pause. "I guess it's only a matter of time. Ken is in her room. He's torn up. I'm so grateful for him. He said he had to go in and marry his Trina." Dianne fidgeted and paced the floor, trying to soothe herself.

"That's how he always referred to her at our shop," said JR. "We came to offer our friendship, help, and our little bit of food, not to stay long," JR said as he started his family's exit. Cindy slowed them.

"Mel, do you want to stay for a bit? I'll run you home later if it's OK with Dianne." Cindy knew Dianne needed someone to level her emotions. She figured a new friend might help.

"Oh yes, you're welcome to stay, Mel," Dianne affirmed. Cindy was back to action after everyone said goodbye to JR and Betty.

"I thought Ken might be taking my place on the couch tonight. Is it OK if I move around some of those boxes in your third bedroom and set up a cot there? I doubt either of us will want to return home in this foggy weather. And it's getting dark," Cindy said.

Sleeping arrangements were far from her mind, but Dianne welcomed Cindy's idea, at least for a distraction.

"Some of that is my stuff from college," she said. "We can shift things around, and maybe I'll throw away some things."

"I'd love to help. I can see what kind of stuff college girls have," Mel joked. "We can start by turning on another light," she said, pulling a small lamp from the rubble.

The three women started working in the room, managing a few

laughs when they unearthed some of Dianne's keepsakes in a room of stored memories and a hint of faint mustiness.

"How many pompoms do you need? I think there's a dozen in here," Mel asked, bringing the trio to chuckle.

Dianne explained, "Some of my friends were leaving the area and thought since I was local, I would give them to volleyball fans at the games."

As the women were engrossed in their tasks, they didn't realize Ken had left Katrina's room and gone to answer a gentle knock at the door. Ken's voice boomed when he opened the door.

"John, you always show up at the absolute right time. We're feeling a bit gloomy here."

Welcoming John into the house, Ken called out, "Hey ladies, I hate to break up the fun, but John from Texaco is here! Dianne, you want him to take your car over, fill it up, and fix that bumper?"

John's visit helped to break Ken out of his melancholy and inject some simple comfort into the home.

"Katrina?" John asked hesitantly, his concern palpable.

Ken sighed, looking over at Dianne before responding.

"Honestly, we are all waiting," he said, his voice heavy with emotion.

"Yes," Dianne confirmed. She turned to John. "And you? You came all the way over here in this crazy fog to get my car?"

"Well, ma'am, I know you don't want my cookin' if I did any. And I'm not much for conversation. I can only see what folks need and treat them right."

"John, that is obvious," Dianne quickly answered. "And I heard you had your say over at Hickman's."

"That rascal! I listen, so I know what's goin' on around here. That Hickman fellow is a rotten one. Now's not the time, but later, you and I can talk, and I'll fill you in on that Michael character, too, if you don't mind. You still sweet on him?"

"John, I would be grateful if you helped me with my car," Dianne responded, avoiding the subject of Michael as she reached over to her bookshelf and pulled her car keys from a bowl. "And no, I'm not sweet on Michael. Not at all!"

"Good to hear. You always put your keys there?"

"Occasionally, I forget. It's a habit my mother tried to teach me."

"Humph, Momma's smart, and daughter's smart enough to listen. You didn't waste money on that college education, ma'am. You care I bring the car back tomorrow, perhaps late?"

Dianne could only nod.

"It'll take a minute to get it together. Bobby's waiting in my truck to drive it back. You sure you're OK with us takin it?"

"Yes," Dianne responded with a weak voice.

"Well, OK. Bye for now!"

Dianne walked with John to the door. "I'm glad you want to fix it, John. Thank you again, and I'll see you tomorrow. Do you mind if I call you 'Texaco John'? It just seems to fit."

John paused and smiled. "Oh, sure. A fair amount of folks call me that." Before closing the door, Dianne watched John walk to the car. She knew she was witnessing a saint on earth doing what saints do: being extra kind and doing what they can do.

"Hey Dianne, there's a bed in here! It was covered up with boxes!" Cindy shouted like she had discovered gold, which shocked Dianne back from her gaze as she gave John a last wave.

"Let me see. Would you look at that! It's my bed from when I lived at home. I thought Mom gave that away! Is there a mattress on it? Is it any good?" Dianne said entering the room.

"The mattress is in a plastic bag!" Mel proclaimed as she peered over a few boxes.

"Oh good! No cot for me tonight!" Cindy exclaimed. She and Mel set to work restacking boxes and unearthing the bed.

"Are you two OK with continuing the treasure search without me?" Dianne asked. "I want to go in and spend some time with Mom. Anything that's in your way, put it in my room. There should be at least a little space in there."

"Go right ahead," Mel and Cindy spoke in near unison.

"We'll dust a few things and rearrange," Cindy added. "You OK with that?"

Dianne nodded and disappeared into Katrina's room. "Hi Mom. Are you awake?" Katrina didn't move. She just breathed a slow, raspy breath. Dianne believed her own words. It was only a matter of time. An hour or two passed, but Dianne didn't feel it. She was numb. She couldn't cry or keep a line of thought.

Ken appeared in the doorway, whispering, "Dianne, I'm going to run Mel back home. Cindy will be here. They got her room set up."

"Thank you, Ken," Dianne whispered back. "I'll be here with Momma. You coming back?"

"Yes. I'm going home to shower, but I'll be back."

"Thank you, Ken."

Before daybreak, Cindy also took an opportunity to freshen up at her home and pack a change of clothes before returning to the England home.

Soon after Cindy left, Ken returned. Stepping into the house felt different. It was silent and lonely. The increasing fog seemed to be thickening inside as well as outside.

Katrina's voice broke the silence, yanking Ken into her room. "Oh my God! Someone help me. Someone help me!" the dying woman repeated, seemingly trying to hold on to her last minute of life. Dianne knew she could only hold her mother's hand on this journey as Ken took her other hand.

Soon, Katrina was silent, yet she breathed—slow, strained, mucus-laden, gurgling breaths. But every shallow inhale brought her closer to peace.

Before an hour passed, Katrina slipped into her final slumber with the two lives she loved most holding her hands. Her stiff face now relaxed. Her body loosened. She was at peace.

No more labored breathing. No more guiding Dianne into adulthood. No more teasing with Dianne or Ken, or anyone—only stillness and peacefulness.

Ken placed his hand on Dianne's shoulder.

"I'm sad too," he said. "Very, very sad." The two cried together.

When Dianne was able to speak, she turned to Ken. "I loved her so much. I couldn't have asked for a better mom."

"Yes, and the world couldn't have asked for a better daughter," Ken responded. "Dianne, if you will allow me to help, tell me where's the folder that your mother left for you."

"Sure, Ken. It's in my room on the nightstand near the door."

"I'll get it. We can make these calls together if you like. OK, Dianne?"

"Yes, yes, that's OK," Dianne uttered.

With Ken designated to help, Dianne let her tears flow.

Cindy stepped in the front door just as Ken opened the folder. When she saw the folder, Cindy knew she didn't have to ask about Katrina.

"Oh, Ken, I'm so sorry," Cindy said quietly.

"Dianne is saying goodbye," he replied.

"I can make those calls. You spend time with your Trina, OK?"

"Thank you, Cindy."

Dianne and Ken held Katrina's hands watching night continue breaking into day. Before long, funeral home attendants took Katrina away into the lingering fog.

With the home in uncomfortable silence, Pastor Dawn arrived to see Dianne in the big chair, hugging covers still bearing her mother's and father's essence. She could not speak, only cry. Sometimes, an uncontrollable, wailing cry. Dawn gave her time by only holding the grieving daughter's hand. Ken remained in Katrina's room to grieve alone.

"You're going to be OK, Dianne," Dawn finally spoke gently. "You will always miss your mother, but you'll be OK. Cry if you need to. Shout. Or run 50 miles! Whatever it takes to release your emotion. Remember, you will be fine. You have friends in this town who thought the world of your mother and think well of you. It will all be fine."

Dianne looked up, paused, and took a deep breath.

"Thank you." She paused again. "Pastor Dawn, do you want some Girl Scout cookies?"

Dianne attempted to break her grief with humor, and despite her grief, she regained her sense of hunger. Her offering was as close as she could get to responding, to say she would be okay.

Pastor Dawn smiled. "I anticipated you might need some," she said. "I brought a couple of boxes with me, however, no peanut butter."

"And Ken, how are you doing?" Dawn looked up to see him entering the living room with red eyes. "You and Dianne can be a great support to one another."

"Yes, we will be," Ken said softly.

"I know neither of you asked for my opinion," continued Pastor Dawn, "but Cindy is a great person and a great luxury to have around." The pastor looked over at Cindy to catch her in a slight blush. "If Cindy can stay here a few days to help with guests and all the other goings-on, it may help."

Dianne turned to ask, "Cindy, can you do that? I could sure use your help."

"I will be happy to," Cindy responded without hesitation.

Dianne looked at Ken. "I know you have your own place and all, but can you stay for at least a few hours?"

"Sure, Dianne," he said. "I'll leave when you're ready for me to do so."

"I suggest we all have a few cookies with milk and get a couple hours sleep," Cindy said. "I mean, really, we went through all that trouble for my bed. I want to use it." She smiled and headed to the kitchen to grab glasses and milk.

"Yep. And this couch looks comfortable to me," said Ken. "We'll catch up with business later today. For now, cookies and sleep."

Pastor Dawn seemed satisfied. "Well then, I'll leave you all. Dianne, do you have a piece of paper? I will leave a sign on the door, so people won't bother you."

Dianne gave Dawn a piece of construction paper and crayons with an apology for the rudimentary tools. Pastor Dawn wrote:

Do not knock or disturb. It has been a rough night. Death in the family. Contact Methodist Church for details.

CHAPTER 15

Discovery – The Box

Dianne sipped coffee at the kitchen table, where a week before, a mix of new friends and a few strangers rotated through her small home. In her gaze, she saw signs of spring through the big picture window, which usually cheered her. Today, she didn't know how she felt. Ken moved back to his house less than a day after Katrina's death and then seemed to disappear.

After "his Trina's" funeral, he told JR he had a medical appointment at the VA Hospital in St. Louis, so he wouldn't see the gang for a few days. He eventually called Dianne during her school hours and left a message to say he was staying in Saint Louis for follow-up medical work.

When he returned to Marshfield, he called Dianne again during school hours but didn't visit. She missed him being around and wondered if he didn't visit because her mother was no longer around.

Although still depressed from losing her mother and often wondering about Ken, Dianne felt gratitude. She felt gratitude for everyone who helped her over the last month, especially Pastor Dawn, Cindy, Mel, and Ken.

They helped direct and introduce miscellaneous people from the church and mingled with people who came from the school. They directed the throng of people and supervised them doing great and small things. Pam visited with ice cream and root beer the day after Katrina's funeral. Somehow, she knew it would lighten Dianne's despair. Dawn and Mel served it up like ice cream shop pros, while Cindy kept everything on an even keel and cleaned up.

Dianne was grateful for her supervisor's generosity and greatly appreciated Texaco John's work on her car. Only Mel knew Dianne had snuck out of her house to bring John a root beer float, which he welcomed with an uncharacteristic smile.

Dianne didn't eat much of her float, or much of anything during the funeral week or the days since. However, she cherished the company and hearing how things were going with the children she was getting to know in her classroom.

One of her toughest times was after the root beer float party when Cindy announced she was returning to her house. After cleaning the last ice cream splatter, she gave Dianne the news.

"Dianne, my job here is done. I may accept a new client in a week or so. I need to return home and rest. These things take a toll on me. Alone, I can mourn like I couldn't while being your support. After resting, I will be able to energize when I meet new people to care for those who are losing their loved ones. You and Ken were wonderful to work with. May I now call you friends rather than clients?"

"I would be hurt if you didn't," Dianne said.

"That's another thing I must do: figure all this out and send you an invoice. It's tough when I like the people."

"I can imagine. Mom left me in good shape, so I'm ready to pay," Dianne replied.

It was a week before Dianne saw Cindy's bill. It arrived stealthily on the front porch, stuck to a box of Girl Scout Cookies.

What's with Marshfield and Girl Scout Cookies? Dianne thought as she opened the envelope and smiled. She responded promptly with Cindy's check and a lengthy, heartfelt letter of gratitude. Another habit that Katrina had taught Dianne was to always respond quickly to bills sent by individuals. Their work is their contribution to the community, which is more than making a living and more than making a profit. Writing the thank-you letter was therapy for Dianne. She expressed gratitude as her mother taught her and felt she could handle a new life as an adult.

From the moment Katrina died, Dianne was numb, barely able to do simple household chores and continue her teaching. However, on this day, as she tucked the letter and Cindy's check into an envelope, she decided to move on. She started by tending to her mother's room. She didn't know how to navigate life without her mother, but she knew from somewhere deep inside herself that she was now an adult and could move on.

Although hesitant at first, she opened the door to her mother's room. She knew she had to take the first step. She began by wiping every inch of the room with fragrant furniture polish, burning incense, spraying, cleaning, and vacuuming. Still, when finished, she smelled the odor of death and sickness.

The awful smell needed to go along with the reminder of her mother's last days. Although she hadn't heard from him in a while, she knew she needed Ken's help, much like a daughter would need a father.

"Hi Ken, this is Dianne and I'm glad you're home. I hate to bother you by calling so late in the day, but I need your help."

"Of course, Dianne! I always said you could call me when you need me."

"I tried to clean my mother's room today. It still smells. I believe it's the mattress and pillows. Should I put it by the curb? If so, can you help me get it out?"

"Oh no! Webster County has a special place for things like that. Let me see if I can round up someone with a truck. We'll pick up whatever you want to throw away and see it gets to where it needs to be. You can go with me to see the place next time. Not pretty, but necessary. I'll let you know in a few minutes."

It wasn't long before Ken knocked on the door with Texaco John alongside him.

"Hello ma'am. You doing OK?" John asked.

"Yes, I'm doing OK. Trying to get better than OK. Thank you very much for asking."

The men worked quickly. The bed frame, end tables, and dresser were all that remained. Even the rug was taken. "OK, the room should smell better," Ken soon told Dianne.

"John and I will wash up and head out. Pastor Dawn said she might visit to ensure you're OK. It's been too long since visiting, you know. She said to tell you she won't eat any Girl Scout cookies. You know what that's about?"

"Yes, I do. It's funny. I'll tell you about it sometime. There's something about Girl Scout cookies around here. When Cindy dropped by her invoice, it was taped to a box of those evil things."

"I look forward to hearing about the saga of cookies in Marshfield," Ken laughed. "Hugs later. I don't smell very good!" Ken pulled his shirt away from his body to air it out.

"Oh yes, hugs later. I'm not sure if I smell very good, either. I think I'll shower before Dawn comes." Although still sweaty, Dianne was breathing easier with the mattress gone.

"Thank you very much, both of you. You two are kind souls. Ken, thank you for introducing me to a fine man like Texaco John." Dianne leaned on the door frame and smiled as the men drove away. She thought, *Those two will be my lifelong friends.*

Dianne showered and put on clean clothes after the men left. As she waited for Dawn, she looked through her mother's top drawer filled with mementos, old medicine bottles, scarves, a few socks, and, to Dianne's surprise, a diary. She had no idea her mother had kept a diary. The last entry was short:

> *I guess this was my last Christmas. I know I will not see Dianne graduate, but I know she will. She wants it. She will do it.*

Yes, Mom, I will do it, Dianne answered, at first to herself. Then she repeated her commitment several times loudly as if proclaiming, "The Eagle has landed!"

A sealed letter addressed to Dianne in shaky writing fell from the back pages of the diary. With a foreboding feeling about this letter, she thought she'd better sit down in the living room where the air was fresher. She carefully opened one end of the envelope by slicing a thin sliver of the envelope's small edge. The letter slipped out easily. The shaky writing continued:

> *Dianne–my dearest daughter,*
>
> *I'm so proud of you, the beautiful person you have become and the care you are giving me. Although I've tried my best to raise you to be a beautiful person, I'm not sure if I deserve such a great person to have been born from my womb. Before it's too late, I must tell you about the box you dug up for me. I am sorry that I didn't have the guts to tell you about it when you first dug it up. Now I will.*
>
> *Momma always told me not to play near the street, and I had no idea why.*
>
> *One afternoon in the Summer, I decided to sit under the oak tree near the street and color. A man came by in a big car. He asked me if I knew the way to Marshfield. I*

pointed to town. The man kept acting like he couldn't hear me. He got out of his car and leaned over, cupping his ear. I walked closer so he could hear me. Before I could say anything, he grabbed me, put his hand over my mouth, and shoved me in the back of his car. I couldn't scream or think about what was happening. After I caught my breath, I cried and screamed. He shoved a doll at me and told me to be quiet, or he would drown me in the creek. He kept yelling at me. I was so scared. I couldn't think, but I opened the car door and rolled out onto the road and into tall grass alongside the road. I saw the man's car stop and then drive on. At about the same time, another car was coming toward me. I didn't want anyone in that car to see me and tell my mother, so I stayed hiding in the grass.

Somehow, I knew my way back home. I think I went through another farm, but I can't remember how I got back. I still had the doll in my arms and knew I couldn't explain it to my mother. It didn't matter about the torn clothes or scrapes and cuts on my legs and arms. I was always getting into something around the farm. I stole (actually stole!) a toolbox from my father. I put the doll in a couple of bread wrappers and put her in the box. At that time, I hid the box, and it stayed in a shed for many years. Even when I got older, I couldn't tell my mother, so I buried the box after putting the doll in more bread wrappers. The shame weighed me down. I don't know what to say about keeping the doll, or what to do with it. I'm tired and I had to share.

The letter ended abruptly, without a signature. It looked like it had not been written in one sitting, with some writing shakier and the spacing varied. Dianne wanted to comfort her mother and ask questions about that time in her life, but now it was too late.

Dawn's knock at the door startled Dianne in mid-thought. She went to the door and opened it to see the Pastor.

"So good to see you," Dianne managed to blurt out. "I'm feeling drained. I found Mom's diary, and it's a shock."

"I think anyone who has ever read a parent's diary is at least surprised, if not shocked. I was afraid you might be suffering from what I call 'the lulls,' so I stopped over. It looks like you're suffering a bit more than the lulls."

"Yes. What are the lulls?" Dianne asked, walking to the kitchen. "Do you want something to drink? Coke? Water? Tea?"

"Thank you. I would love some water. It seems spring has broken through and is borderline hot."

"I hadn't noticed the weather. I've just started cleaning and going through Mom's stuff. Did Ken tell you he and John moved out Mom's mattress and bedside chair?"

"No, I guess he didn't have a chance yet. Mind if I open some windows?"

Dawn didn't wait for an answer to open the windows in Katrina's former room.

"Let me tell you about the lulls," Pastor Dawn continued as she accepted water from Dianne. "It happens nearly always when someone dies. There's all the action in the last weeks of a person's life, there's the death, there's the funeral with all the guests and condolences, then there are the lulls. People have stopped coming. Cards are very few in the mail. Everyone is back to their routine. That is, except the ones closest to the deceased. They must start new routines. You are in the lulls. My guess is you have school to keep yourself busy. But you must still take care of your mom's things...and you're doing this yourself. This can bring on the lulls. I see you got a start. Do I have this right?"

"Yes. But there's this." Dianne handed the letter to Dawn. "I don't know what to think."

"Wow!" Pastor Dawn exclaimed after reading Katrina's missive. "That must have been difficult to live with all those years. Your mom never told you anything about this box or doll?"

"The first I knew about the box was the day I dug it up from her property! Remember when we had all that snow in January? I dug through a little snow and some mud. I don't even know how old Mom was when this happened. I'm guessing she may have been eight or nine at the most."

"This...this is rough, certainly adds to the lulls," said Pastor Dawn. "I don't know what to say about it, but please, Dianne, take special care of yourself, mentally and physically. As always, feel free to reach out if you need me. And don't be surprised if you find other things about your mom, dad, or family members. I support you with whatever you decide about the doll."

Dianne's voice wavered, her eyes welling up. "I don't know if I can read more."

"Certainly, it's your decision," Dawn said, placing a sympathetic hand on Dianne's shoulder. "You may want to take everything in small chunks of time. It's not necessary to do everything immediately." After the women opened more windows and chatted in the living room for a while, Dawn broke away to get to her "pastor's work" as she called it.

"I do consider you a friend, Dawn," Dianne acknowledged as the pastor exited.

"I'll see you Sunday. I'll sit at the back, so you may not see me."

Dawn, slightly surprised, stopped her exit and smiled back at Dianne before walking to the car. She lightly tapped her horn as she waved and drove away.

Dianne waved back and stepped back into an empty house. There was more than just bare furniture. There were no visitors, no loving mother, and no Springtime warmth.

Dianne wandered into the kitchen, sifting through the fridge for something edible. Amidst the spoiled food, she picked out some barely passable leftovers. Tomorrow, she promised herself, she would clean the refrigerator. After tiring herself from the unappealing culinary dish, uneaten morsels decorated a plate Dianne had used throughout her childhood as her mood descended with the sun.

Chin resting on her palm, she stared at the blue scene across her plate: two people in a boat and a man fishing on a bridge. Her mother repeatedly told her the story, but she could never remember.

She reminisced about good times at this table from childhood onward while the pain of her mother's life intertwined with her thoughts. Only a small table lamp emitted defused light from the table alongside the big recliner. Katrina's painful secret and the pain of her early marriage were now Dianne's to hold.

Tired from the day's activity and roller-coaster emotions, Dianne could only make her way to her room. She was surprised at how chaotic it was, as she hadn't seen it in such a manner since she was a teenager. Only capable of basic straightening, Dianne flopped on her bed and fell into a deep and restful sleep without her usual nightly routine or changing clothes.

"What on earth!" A loud banging on the front door startled Dianne awake. "Who would bang on the door this early?" Opening the door, Dianne squinted against the bright sunlight. "Mel? What are you doing here so early?"

"Early? It's nearly noon! They had me busy at the shop all week. I did some painting. JR seems to be an expert at everything. He showed me about prep work," Mel explained.

Despite Dianne being barely awake and not understanding much of what she said, Mel kept chattering. "Well, he became an expert after Betty showed him how it was supposed to be done." Mel laughed at her own joke.

Dianne could only nod with her eyes half open and could not comprehend Mel's words.

"Shit! You sleep in your clothes?" Mel's sudden observance forced her to take a break.

"Noon? Wow! I slept! Come in. I'll be right back." Mel made herself at home, walking around the house.

"Sorry, nature called! And I had to run a toothbrush through my mouth," Dianne explained, brushing her hair. "I'm a mess! I can't believe I slept this long. I'm tired."

"You've been through a lot lately. Kick back and breathe," Mel advised.

"I brought fresh sandwiches from the shop," Mel said, returning to a tangent while placing food items on the counter. "Then we can go over to the animal park. I'll introduce you to the folks. You might want to take your class there sometime." Mel opened the refrigerator and looked for something to drink with the sandwiches. "And when we come back, I'll help you clean your refrigerator. It looks like you have more leftovers than you could ever handle!" she observed. "Don't even think about freezing them. I know food. Some of it is near funk." Mel made a gagging motion as she quickly closed the refrigerator."

"I was supposed to go to church this morning!" Dianne exclaimed. I slept through it! I hope Dawn's not mad at me. Thanks for the sandwiches. I ate some leftovers in the fridge last night and they were far from fresh."

"Really? Dawn mad at you? Come on, girl! I don't think Dawn will mind. You want me to write a permission slip for you? They still do that in school?"

"I see you found the sweet tea in the fridge. That's not funky— not like your comment anyway." Dianne smiled, finally awakening.

After eating, Mel gave Dianne a break in her chatter so she could change clothes. Before she returned to jabbering, she thumbed through mail piled into an unruly heap and noticed an unpaid electric bill. She had to think of a way to tell Dianne about it, without knowing she had snooped in the mail.

"Come on, girl," Mel said, grabbing Dianne by her hand, barely letting her finish tying her hair back.

"We'll go in by the employee entrance," Mel said, turning the van into the park's back entrance. You can see some of the animals, and I'll take you around to meet a few of the humans."

"Wow! I had no idea so much went on behind the scenes here," Dianne said with awe as she sat erect in her seat, finally fully awake. "I'm afraid I smell like the animals. I didn't even take a shower this morning. I'm not sure anyone would want to meet me like this."

"Don't worry. No one will notice. I needed to stop in here because I have a cooler full of food scraps to take to the kitchen. I make this run about every other day. Now you know why I drive the company van, and I drive it often."

"I'm certainly not passing judgment. I don't know if you know this, but I rode in Michael's old car."

"He told me you did. He thought his car didn't ride so badly because a pretty college girl rode in it."

"It was a charity ride, I assure you. He seemed so sincere about making up for disturbing my mother. I can't say Mom discouraged it, but she seemed to think maybe, for one time, I should let the guy buy me dinner. However, when I saw him more than once, I think she started to worry. Afterward, I couldn't believe I was in such a thing. He has a souped-up truck now, so I guess he's happy. He doesn't have me in it, that's all I care about!"

"None of us think Michael is a bad guy, but we all keep him at arm's length," said Mel. It's almost like someday his brain will pop off, and he will do something stupid to get into trouble he can't escape."

"How does he run a store?"

"I know, it's weird. He's quite good at it. The store looks good, folks like going there, and sales steadily improve. I keep an eye on business stuff. Sometimes though, I wonder how much Ms. Kelly, the head cashier, really runs stuff and Michael steals her ideas and goes along with what she does."

"Then I'm impressed he doesn't get in her way, or in his own way, for that matter," Dianne agreed as they exited the van.

"What ya bring our animal children today?" a voice rang out as a big wooden gate opened.

"Oh, hey Jill! I brought the usual stuff, mostly greens. JR's supplier knows he brings stuff over here, so we have some frozen bones of who-knows-what."

Jill grinned. "We'll bring it into the kitchen and label it meat with the date. Our dietitian will use it somehow. Barb knows how to prepare the right things for the right kind of beast around here."

"Dianne, this is Jill Miller."

"It's a pleasure to meet you," Jill said. "Excuse my dirty hand. It pretty much stays that way with my job around here."

Jill's handshake was firm, not surprisingly for a woman handling big animals. Her resonant voice matched her professional confidence as a zookeeper.

"Dianne, Jill is the park's large animal environmental manager."

"Yeah, Dianne, I scoop a lot of poop," Jill interjected.

"Surely that's not all you do," Dianne suggested.

"No, I often ride to the hilly area to make sure things are good out there. I wrangle the animals for medical exams, design, build, and upkeep pens, all kinds of fun stuff. Yeah, girl! I can swing poop and a hammer." Jill smiled at her attempt at humor.

"Wow! It sounds like an overwhelming job." Dianne said, wide-eyed and with a slightly dropped jaw.

"Yes, it can be if our big animals start tearing things up. Now let's get this food inside and I'll take you two around." Jill said excitedly.

Dianne was excited at this unique opportunity. She was already thinking about her students and how they might enjoy seeing the park.

"Jill, do you have a place where kids can learn about the animals?"

Mel interjected, "Jill, Dianne just moved to Marshfield. She's interning at the elementary school. Before long she'll have diploma in hand."

"Great!" Jill said, smiling. "We have a petting zoo over by the gift shop and what we call a learning circle. We bring the tamed animals over to let the children see them up close. Not all animals can be petted." Jill smiled and gave Dianne a wink.

"I'm guessing where you live, the kids probably have animals in their backyards," Jill continued.

"Not quite, but some do live on farms." Dianne answered Jill's near-rhetorical question with a longer-than-needed answer. "According to my supervising teacher, sometimes children are late because something happened at the farm where they live. She told me the farm kids are always the most well behaved."

Dianne ended her monologue, realizing she had gone on too long. As they walked along Jill pointed to the small, paved road winding through the park. In her talk, she shared a few facts and experiences she'd had in the five years she had worked at the park.

"Oh! There's Sue Gorrell. She's our accountant and fundraiser. It seems everyone has a dual position here. Sue, this is Dianne England."

Sue's slim appearance and strong handshake seemed antithetical to a person with a desk job.

"It's a pleasure to meet you, Dianne. Sorry, I can't chat long. I just discovered one of our donations was put on hold, and I'm unsure how long it will last. I hope one of the employees didn't do something upsetting or something happened that management knows nothing about. He was contributing $2000 each month. It's small compared to our overall budget but quite helpful."

Mel jumped in. "Wait, that wasn't Michael D. Glossen—the person who cut off funds? He loves this park, and I know he lives close by."

"It's unethical to say who our contributors are, so I can't confirm or deny," Sue said.

"Well, if it was, tell him since he's backed out, another

benefactor will be jumping in and building a closed fence around the park," Mel proclaimed. "Michael is a quirky one. He likes taking pictures of the animals humping one another."

Sue's eyes widened. "Like I said, I can't confirm or deny. However, that's good information. I'm heading back to the office. See you later, ladies."

After a short silence, Jill jumped in. "I bet it was Michael. Sue wouldn't be here on a Sunday if she wasn't worried. She's so dedicated. She's even held off cashing her paychecks to make ends meet with this park. You know him, Mel. Was it him?"

"Now things make sense," Mel said, planting hands on hips, shaking, and pointing her finger in the air. Michael got that truck from Hickman. He told me he saved for it. Suddenly, he buys it and shorts his donation. His daddy isn't going to be happy. Daddy Glossen loves this park more than anything in this area. He would be sad to hear about this."

"You have his number? You can call him?" Dianne asked.

"No! I've got an easier solution I'm thinking about," Mel thumped the side of her head with her forefinger. I'm thinking about trying something a little gentler. I hate to interrupt the tour, Dianne, but I must drive you back home and head to the shop to help JR and Betty set up for the week."

Mel smiled at Jill, who seemed to know Mel's tenacity.

"Oh hell! If Mel's on the fix, it will be fixed!" Jill said with a slight laugh. "I wish you people were open Sunday afternoon. You have some great food, and folks are easily drawn into whatever talk is going on. If I even visit for a quick pop on ice, I'm there for an hour," Jill lamented.

Jill's assessment made it evident to Dianne that Jill wasn't raised in the area, so she had to ask.

"Minnesota," Jill responded. "I'll tell you about it next time we meet. And I know you want to know if we have volunteers here, and yes, that's a hint. I would love to see your name on the volunteer list!"

"Goodbye, Jill. There will be no recruiting talks this time," Mel insisted. "Dianne and I are heading out."

"See you later, friends!" Jill smiled as she shooed the women back to Mel's van.

"OK, lady, what are you going to do? Dianne queried on the

way home. "Although I hesitate to ask."

"I'm not going to say a word about any donation," Mel said. "I'm going to tell him it's buffalo mating season. Surely, he wouldn't want to miss that."

"If I were you, I'd look that up first. He may get upset if he learns you steered him wrong and gave him a bunch of bull."

Dianne laughed hard at her joke, which started Mel laughing.

"Now girl! I'm trying to drive." They agreed time together was too short before they arrived at Dianne's home. Mel began to ask Dianne about the electric bill she discovered, but still could not bring herself to say something.

"It's still kind of early. I'm going to clean up and go to the library in Springfield to see if I can find some information about buffalo," Dianne said, excited to be part of the plot while forgetting her refrigerator needed a serious cleaning.

"Oh, no problem! When I get a few minutes, I'll call Jill. She'll know when buffalo bulls fuck." Mel couldn't help but start laughing again over her crudity.

"Keep me posted on this plot," Dianne laughed. "I want to see how this turns out. And I think I'll take Jill up on her offer and volunteer. It will help keep me out of trouble. Or I can make different trouble." Dianne patted Mel's leg as she laughed before exiting the van and waving goodbye to Mel.

Mel smiled slightly and drove off, ready to complete her usual Sunday afternoon chores at the truck stop, still perplexed about whether she should talk to Dianne about her mail.

After Mel and Dianne left, Jill visited Sue in her office.

"You can't say for sure, but I believe it was Michael. Sue, I know things about Michael. I often roam this property and have taken him on tours." Jill leaned on the office door jamb as she tried to choose her words carefully.

"I know things about Michael, and it may be the ticket to reclaiming his donation. Perhaps I might get a few dollars added to it," she said with a slight grin, awaiting Sue's response.

"Jill, I appreciate what you are doing and your dedication to the animals and this park." Sue hesitated while looking directly at Jill. Not able to find suitable words, she chose to ignore Jill's offer of help.

"Jill, I think we need to apply for some grants. I know what needs to be done, but I don't have time. Could you convince the schoolteacher to volunteer for the park and write some grants? Basically, it's a matter of acting like a reporter and getting all the facts about what we do here. I can take her findings and put them into grant speak."

"Oh, you mean Dianne, the lady you met with Mel?"

Sue affirmatively nodded.

"On all fronts, I'll give it a try. We'll see what magic happens,"

"Watch yourself. Stay safe." are the only words Sue could find in her whirlwind of thoughts.

CHAPTER 16

Moving Forward

When Dianne returned home after her library visit, she curled into her usual spot on the sofa. She cozied up to one side, covering herself with a light blanket. Her glazed eyes overlooked schoolwork strewn across the coffee table and remaining sofa space. Before long, she felt unsettled and could not concentrate on preparing for class.

The beloved leather recliner lured her into its oversized leather arms, bearing her mother and father's essence and sweet fragrance. She was ready to feel comfortable for the first time after her mother's passing.

Nestling in the chair, she felt comfortable and warm with her mother's worn quilt on her lap to block a slight evening breeze. The well-built chair had comforted the England family for many years, as it now comforted her. Adjusting to a perfect position, her thoughts were interrupted by the answering machine light blinking *2*.

"Hello, Dianne?" The voice sounded like Pastor Dawn. "Of course, I always want to check how you're doing, but I'd love to visit if you have time this afternoon. I knocked earlier when I came by and saw your car, but there wasn't an answer. Anyway, I want to talk to you as a friend; I have news to share. Oh, you may have guessed, this is Dawn. Bye! Hope to see you soon."

Dianne patiently waited for the next message: "Hi Dianne, this is Ken. Can I stop by? Give me a call!"

It was great hearing from Dawn and Ken. It had been a while since they'd visited without doing something to help her somehow. Dianne couldn't remember exactly the last time she saw Dawn, sometime after her mother passed. She quickly reviewed her notes to determine if she would have time for two friends that afternoon.

"Oh no! It's been almost an hour since they called!" she said aloud, again making it evident how empty the house had become.

"Dawn? This is Dianne. Sorry, it took me so long to return your call."

"Don't worry about it. You got me now. It's your turn to play counselor. I've got a few things I want to share." Dawn sounded less upbeat and professional than she had before. She sounded like a friend who needed a friend.

"Oh wow! This sounds serious! Ken called earlier, too. He wants to stop by. Give me a minute to talk to him and come over. Please don't bring Girl Scout cookies. I still have several boxes in the freezer. Those things are dangerous!"

Dawn laughed with apparent nervousness and said she didn't mind if Ken was also there. She could use his input, too. Dianne was just as happy to speak with Ken when she returned his call. Both friends would arrive at Dianne's place soon, with Ken stopping for snacks and beer.

"I can't believe how nice the weather is! I hope we have shaken off winter!" Dawn exclaimed as she entered Dianne's house while wiping her feet on the welcome mat.

"Ken here yet?"

"Not yet. He stopped off to get some goodies. I promised I would drink a beer if he picked up something light."

"Come on in!" Dianne said with more energy than she'd had in months. "I'm so happy to see you!" Dianne hugged her friend with an extra-long, welcoming hug.

"Later, I'll have to tell you about what a great day I had," Dianne told Dawn excitedly. "Um, sorry I didn't make it over to the church. I woke up when Mel pounded on my door with lunch in her hand. Then she took me to the animal park, where I met a couple of zookeepers. I'm thinking about volunteering there! First on Saturdays, but in the summer, I might go over during the week."

Dawn could tell how excited Dianne was about making plans at the park. "I bet you'll enjoy that! I'm glad you told me now rather than later," Dawn said with a smile, appreciating Dianne's happiness.

"Will you work with the children's petting zoo?"

"Probably," Dianne said, noticing a change in Dawn.

"It will be good for you. I mean, you'll be great with children."

Hearing Dawn's lukewarm response, Dianne tilted her head, knowing something was seriously bothering her new friend. Not knowing what to say, the conversation suddenly broke off.

"Oh! I see Ken just drove up," Dawn said, breaking the silence. "Good, he has beer," she added, barely taking a breath between sentences. "I think I'll have a beer as well."

"Come on in, Ken! Dawn is here. I have glasses in the freezer."

"I usually drink straight from the bottle," Ken explained while making a drinking hand gesture.

"It's so good to see you ladies. I've missed you! I've been in St. Louis a lot. I'll have to tell you about it."

"Oh no, Dianne, don't pour it like that," Dawn instructed, interrupting anything Ken may have said. She lunged to grab Dianne's glass and beer bottle.

"Too much foam will make the beer run over. You're a wine drinker, aren't you?" she teased, taking over opening and pouring the beer as though she was a seasoned bartender.

Dianne spoke up. "Pastor Dawn, you suddenly seem different. A few weeks ago, you were so measured, even speaking, quite dignified, and ultra professional, unless it was about Girl Scout cookies." Dianne smiled, trying to lighten the group's mood.

"Seriously. You seem so nervous, perhaps upset. What's going on?" Dianne queried as she gently touched Dawn's shoulder.

As Dawn poured the beer down the sides of the two remaining chilled glasses, she explained why she had called and needed to talk with friends.

"I guess, essentially, I'm fired," she blurted out. "Pastor Greene called me aside after today's last morning service."

Dianne and Ken's eyes widened. Clearly, they were surprised.

"He didn't call me into his office," Dawn continued. "We sat on one of the benches in the hallway. It seems some individuals considered pillars of the church, talked with Pastor Greene several times. They think I'm not a fit for this congregation. They think I would be better suited in St. Louis or some other big city."

"Oh, how hurtful!" Dianne couldn't hold back her assessment and began to talk about how wonderful and valued Dawn had been to her during the journey of her mother's death.

"They don't know what a great person you are," she said. Ken jumped into the accolades and then started to ask questions.

"Did they say anything specific about something you did or didn't do? And let me poke the elephant in the room. Do they have a problem with a female preacher?" he asked.

"Possibly they do," mused Dawn. "However, it's not all bad. I was frank with Pastor Greene about my spiritual journey. I told him I was unsure if I was cut out for ministry in an organized church. I fully, honestly, and wholeheartedly believe there's so much that differs from Methodist teachings. However, in my mind, I don't believe anything that goes against the bible."

Dawn wanted to say more but paused for sips of beer as Ken and Dianne waited anxiously.

"Are you staying in town?" Dianne asked, carefully lowering her half empty beer glass to a coaster on a side table.

"Probably not. I'm unsure if there's a job I'd feel comfortable doing here, especially considering my recent position in the church. I'm thinking of heading north, perhaps to New York. I don't want to return to my family in Virginia until I get everything sorted out."

"What's the timeline for you?" Ken seemed highly concerned as he popped open another beer, raising it to his lips without the formality of a glass.

"I'll announce my departure next week possibly. I plan to be completely honest about leaving, but not about my beliefs. I'm asking you both not to discuss this with anyone. Pastor Greene will notify the board in a few days. He said I needed to give the church planning committee enough time to plan a going-away party." Dawn smiled and added, "I need to give them time for a going-away party...and they are pushing me out! Ridiculous! Perhaps it's a blessing in disguise."

"Toast to Dawn's new life!" Ken raised his half-finished bottle, and the ladies followed.

"I have finished my master's in divinity degree," Dawn continued. "Everything's done except receiving the paper. However, I'm considering working somewhere outside my career with limited responsibilities. I've got to clear my mind. And Dianne, I must confess, I am still mourning the loss of your mother. I only knew her briefly, but her spirit was strong, and I greatly miss her."

"OK, my turn." Dianne raised her glass. "A toast to one beautiful human being, Katrina England."

"Hear, hear! To my Trina!" Ken added, as glasses and bottle clinked again.

"Now that I've dropped this bomb on you two, I'm going to be rude and head home. Thank you both for listening to my confusing babble. And Ken, not bad beer! Sorry, I'm not able to finish a full glass. Too bad they don't make pretzel Girl Scout cookies. They would go well with beer. I hear chocolate mint cookies are good after smoking a little pot. Only heard. Don't know for sure."

With her eyebrows slightly raised, Dianne smiled at Dawn's statement.

Ken added, "I don't know what pairs with what cookies either. I'll report back to you both if I ever find out."

Ken and Dawn laughed, almost like they shared an inside joke that passed over Dianne's head. Soon, the trio exchanged hugs, and Ken walked Dawn to her car, laughing and chatting.

When he returned to the house, he apologized to Dianne for making his postscript longer than the letter.

"I've heard folks use that saying before. Does it mean you apologize for taking so long to say goodbye?" Dianne quizzed Ken.

"Exactly! Dianne, if you don't mind, we can talk more another day," Ken said. "For now, we can finish these beers while you give me a quick update on your life, and then I'll head out."

"I don't know where to begin, Ken." Dianne said as she sat, motioning for Ken to sit next to her on the sofa.

"Did my mother ever tell you about the box we dug up at her childhood farm and the story behind it?" She began.

"We talked a little about the box, but not much was explained. Do you know more?" Ken asked.

Dianne shared about finding her mother's diary with the letter and her feelings about the pain she must have experienced all those years.

"Here," she said, lifting the letter from the coffee table. "Please read it and tell me what you think."

The room melted into eerie quiet. The white sounds of appliances and the hum of far-off traffic made the silence more deafening. Ken's occasional sip of beer became loud. When Dianne looked at him, he appeared to be holding back tears.

"This means a longer conversation than time allows tonight, Dianne. Would you mind if I took the rest of my beer home?" Ken asked, looking distressed. He could only shake his head in disbelief.

"Oh, please, take the beer. I'll get it from the refrigerator. We can talk about the letter next time we meet." Dianne agreed.

"It's OK, I got it." Ken scurried to retrieve the beer from the refrigerator, and a puff of cold, rancid air attacked him.

"Oh, Dianne. I'm coming over tomorrow to help you with this stinky fridge! We need to dump everything."

"Yeah, I was supposed to do that today with Mel, but she had to run, and I had errands. But thank you, Ken. I can't refuse," Dianne replied, nearly mocking Ken's offer.

"Sorry! I didn't mean to be bossy. Would you like me to help you with the refrigerator?"

"Sure, Ken. I kindly accept your help," Dianne replied, emphasizing "kindly" and adding a smile and a hug.

"Good night, dear friend." She walked Ken to the door and watched him descend to the walkway. He turned back to ask, "Does Dawn know about the letter?" Dianne nodded affirmatively, then added her postscript for the evening.

"Ken, I'm not making assumptions, but if you do happen to have some pot around the house, you might want to share it with Dawn. But I'm keeping your snacks because I'm not eating anything from that fridge." Dianne rushed to her freezer and pulled a box of Thin Mints for Ken to take.

"Let me know how it pairs. Hope it didn't pick up any fridge stink."

"Dianne, you are so much savvier than you let on. Good night. Now get some rest." Ken smiled and headed to his car.

"Ken, it's bad. I mean, really bad...oh, sorry, good morning! I'm just so stressed right now." Dianne's wavering voice tumbled out words in a rushed staccato. "Thank you for offering to help throw out the nasty food in the fridge, but it looks like my refrigerator stopped working last night. It will be horrible by the time I get home. I think you should let me work on it. I don't want to put you through that mess. You have already done so much."

"OK, if that's what you want, I'll oblige," Ken lied, hoping to spare Dianne the mess. But as he hung up, he couldn't shake the feeling she'd wanted him to come anyway. After all, why else would she call him first thing in the morning?

"Thank you. Goodbye!" she said, leaving Ken to stare at the disconnected phone.

Several minutes after Dianne's call, Ken found himself at her doorstep, the house key cold in his hand. Upon entering, he hesitated for a moment, the silence of the empty house pressed against him before stepping inside.

He was determined to clear out the spoiled food and check the refrigerator while Dianne was teaching. He hoped the fridge problem was only a matter of the plug wiggling loose or a circuit breaker tripping. He'd have to show Dianne how those things worked. Unfortunately, he determined the fridge had died.

Before deciding on his next step, he needed sustenance.

"You're here a little early today, Ken. What's up?" JR greeted Ken as he collected plates for Mel and Betty to load into the dishwasher.

"Your usual breakfast will be out shortly."

"You know me, I'm always up to something. I guess I'm not behaving myself at all." Ken lowered the bread into the toaster before JR could reach it. I'm hungry today and the coffee smells extra good! Glad it's a good day out. I'm helping Dianne, but she doesn't know it."

Ken relayed the broken refrigerator story to JR loudly enough so Betty and Mel could hear and get a few laughs. It seemed JR had the solution in the time it took him to finish Ken's breakfast.

"I've got a backup refrigerator in my garage with barely anything in it," he said. "I bet we can clear the nasty thing quickly and get this replacement plugged in long before Dianne gets home. You think John can loan us a truck?"

After Ken finished scanning a crumpled newspaper another customer had left behind, he crunched his last piece of bacon and helped himself to the restaurant phone.

"It's a deal! John will meet us here at one to load up the fridge," Ken announced to JR as he hung up. "Meanwhile, I'm heading to the England house to remove the nasty food. I'll call if it turns out to be something I missed."

"Got ya!" JR shouted as Ken exited.

"Y'all care if I help Ken?" Mel pleaded to JR and Betty. "I promised Dianne I'd help yesterday, but I got short on time."

"Sure, go ahead. I'll try to stop him!" JR scrambled to the parking lot and yelled, "Hold up, Ken! Mel wants to help. She'll be right out."

"Great! Tell her to come on!" Ken yelled back.

Ken and Mel determined the refrigerator could not be revived, so he and Texaco John placed JR's refrigerator in its place. Opening the freezer, Ken placed fresh Girl Scout cookies in it. He knew the cookies needed to be replaced, but he didn't explain how or why he knew. He also knew Thin Mints pair well with quality pot, which he and Dawn discovered the night before.

"Good Move, Ken!" Mel said, not knowing Ken's recent culinary discovery.

Arriving home, Dianne opened the door and knew immediately something was different. This morning she smelled rotten food, but now she only smelled household cleaner.

"Ken! What did he do?" she said aloud. "Like, I wouldn't notice this refrigerator has a freezer on the top, and mine had one on the bottom?"

"Ken!" Dianne shouted over the phone. "I know it was you!" All Dianne could hear through the phone receiver was a man with a robust laugh. "Oh, never mind! Thank you, Ken. It was very kind of you and pretty darn sneaky! I appreciate you so much! And I must say I love you. Have a great evening."

Not long after her one-way conversation with Ken, the phone rang again.

"Hey Dianne! I have great news!"

"What? Not even a 'hello'? That's how the phone usually works, Mel."

"I've waited all day to tell you! Bison breeding season starts in June!"

"What? Did you tell Jill about your plan?"

"Yes, I did! She swore me to secrecy, though. I don't think

Sue, would be comfortable with this. She's in upper management and must watch her steps. You remember meeting her?"

"Yes. She was worried about a shortage of funds and wouldn't say it was Michael who was pulling back."

"Yep, that's her. Well, Dianne, I want to pump this up a bit! Let's raise funds for a special observation deck to see the wildlife."

"We?"

"I would love for you to help, but I know you still have your mom's affairs to tend to."

"Yes, and don't forget I'm trying to get through my internship. Let's put that observation deck dream on hold. Next week, I'm meeting with the principal for my mid-term review."

"Tell me that takes on a totally different meaning for you than it did for me a few years back."

"Oh yes, at this time in the semester, he gives me a job review, reports it back to the college, and they assign a rating. Everyone gets A's if they show up and do a halfway decent job. My only concern is that I had to take so much time off with my mother's illness."

"I hope he's good to you. I mean, you couldn't help it. Oh, I have a confession to make."

"Yes?"

"I spent a few hours with Ken today."

"You mean you were part of the sneaky fridge exchange? Where did he get it? I need to pay him for it."

"Don't worry about it. It's a loaner from JR until you can get a new one."

"I see," Dianne said. "Like usual, a gang of folks are in on this. I guess you all used Texaco John's truck?"

"You got it! But I have something more serious I must talk to you about. Before you do anything for your class tomorrow, look through your mail. It looks like you haven't touched it in weeks. Throw away the advertisements. You don't need anything they're selling. You can tell which type of mail is a card or a friendly letter. Set it aside. The things you need to open right away are the letters with windows in the envelopes. Those will be your bills. Always open the bills right away and get them paid. I'm sorry to be so bossy, but I don't want to see you get into problems down the road. You're on your own with this. I can't help. Ken can't help. This is what we do at the shop. Betty and JR said it works for them, too."

"Yes, I've procrastinated with the mail. I've got voice mails on the machine, too."

"OK, Dianne. I'm letting you go so you can work on the mail. Oh, I slipped dinner in the refrigerator for you."

"Mel, I'm blessed to tears."

"Goodbye, Dianne. Get to work!"

"Goodbye, Mel. I look forward to hearing more about the bison mating at the park."

Both women laughed as they hung up the phone.

I'm in shock! What do I do? It's Monday! Thursday, they're shutting off my electricity! Oh no! It's...It's in Mom's name! Shit! What am I going to do? Oh oh oh! I only have until Thursday!

Dianne was in a panic and couldn't think straight. Then she remembered what Dawn told her a few weeks ago when she was losing her mother. Dawn said, "Start simple. Breathe deep breaths and let the air out slowly. After inhaling and exhaling a few times, smile and tell yourself you can handle this."

Breathe.

Exhale.

Breathe.

It took only minutes before Dianne was able to make a plan.

"I know. I'll ask Pam if I can take an hour off today to pay the electric bill and get the billing under my name. OK, I need the death certificate, probably her license, and probably my license," she said as if talking to another person.

Dianne recovered from her fear and was satisfied with her plan, which helped her become less nervous and frantic about her predicament.

"And look at these cards!" After resisting opening a few and being distracted by colorful ads, Dianne found two billing notices received from the electric company before the shut-off letter.

"Hmmm. Mel said all the bills came in window envelopes. I'll look for those first." Dianne opened other bills and immediately wrote checks for each.

As Mel suggested, she placed all advertisements into the trash without looking at them. As she had hoped, the next day, Dianne received permission to leave school early so she could pay the electric bill. She was immediately ready to go after the children left for the day. Pam stopped her. "Do you mind some friendly advice?"

"Um, no," Dianne said, turning back to see her supervisor with arms folded against her chest.

"As you said Mel told you, open the bills right away and schedule them to be paid," she paused then added, "Make it a firm schedule. Say, every Thursday evening, look at your bills." It was obvious Dianne was a daydreamer and recently losing her mother, Pam suspected procrastination might happen, so she'd advised a weekly plan. Dianne confessed she does procrastinate and hesitantly asked a few questions.

"Do you look at your bills every Thursday?"

"Admittedly, I don't. However, I've been paying bills for a long time. After opening them, I ensure they're correct and schedule them to be paid. I can easily spot when something may be off by this time in my life. I advise making it a habit to look at each bill before letting it go this long," Pam said, giving Dianne the same look she gave the students when she meant business in the classroom.

"I need to practice that look you're giving me!" Dianne said with a smile.

"What?"

"When you talked about my bills, you had a stern look. It's the same look you give the class when you expect immediate action."

"Nice try," Pam said as she straightened the classroom. "I know you're only trying to make light out of a serious situation. Still, I think you understand that I care. Go get that bill paid and go home."

"I agree. I do need to get home. I've got to pay this bill, and then I've got bills to mail! Remind me to tell you about the magic refrigerator fairy who visited my home."

Pam shook her head smiling while thinking Dianne must have an imaginative children's story. The young protégé dashed out the classroom door before she could ask.

With the electric bill paid, Dianne grabbed soup and a sandwich from the convenience store before heading home. Real food shopping will wait until Saturday. At home, she organized her bills, made lists of things she needed to do, and generally organized herself. She was deep in thought when the phone rang, startling her.

"Hey! Guess what I did tonight!"

"Mel, do you ever say hello or introduce yourself on the phone?"

"Not for friends who know my voice by now."

"OK. I give up. I won't try to change you, but I will guess what you did. You took your first-ever tap-dancing lesson."

"Oh, be serious! It's even better than tap dancing lessons! I signed up for a computer course that starts this summer. Have you ever worked on a computer?"

"Yes, a little while in college. I wrote some of my papers on a computer."

"Great! You can take this course with me! It's a program that helps with bookkeeping. Betty is taking it, too!"

"That might be good to help me organize my bills," Dianne said, trying to be as excited as Mel seemed. While Mel thrived on numbers and how they worked, Dianne enjoyed written words and all the magic she felt words could conjure and hold. Mel gave Dianne the details and asked her how her meeting with the school principal went.

"It's next week. They only had time to finalize the dismissal program. As a result, things became a bit frazzled. There's a good chance our group of students may not understand what's happening, and the noise and all the moving around might confuse some of the children."

"How do they get to the bus?"

"We walk them to the bus about 15 minutes before general dismissal. And in the morning, our students arrive 15 minutes early."

"That's sweet." Mel didn't know what else to say.

"Um, hey! Do you want to go to the animal park again this weekend? Jill will set you up with a volunteer schedule, and you can stay longer."

"Yes! Let me know what time I need to be there. I need to go grocery shopping afterward." Dianne's voice beamed with excitement.

"You bet I will tell Jill and everyone! The schoolteacher will be one of us!"

CHAPTER 17

Adjustments

As directed, Michael stayed completely out of Dianne's life, not a call for condolences, a card, or a mention to anyone at the truck stop about Dianne losing her mother. Yet, perhaps to their chagrin or macabre entertainment, Michael remained a regular customer at the truck stop.

"Hey Ms. Betty...JR! I think I'll sit down for some eggs today. You got some crispy bacon to go with it?"

"Hey, Michael! How's the truck working for you?" JR yelled over his shoulder while he washed his hands to cook Michael's breakfast.

"It's smooth like a baby's butt. Pity John said he couldn't work on it. Said I'd need to take it to Springfield to the dealer. They have all the fancy machines to hook up to it. He also said the truck needs fancy tires. I got the feeling he didn't want to work on it. Maybe he's afraid to mess it up."

JR knew the truth but didn't let on. John wanted nothing to do with the truck and told JR as much when he learned Michael bought it.

"Michael, I have to ask." Betty came from the dish area to stand before Michael so she could talk without broadcasting her question to other customers. "What happened to the young lady who was Hickman's office manager? Is it true he fired her because of that truck?"

"Oh no, Ms. Betty! Scotty wouldn't do that. He fired her 'cause she was no good. She always put her nose in his business and worked on her schoolbooks during his time. She wanted to be something in a lawyer's office more than helping Scotty." Michael continued with his usual tangents, talking about his new truck. He only paused to gobble eggs and crunch bacon.

"Ms. Betty, please, may I have some orange juice?"

"You sure may!" Betty said. "And I noticed lately how polite you have become. Thank you. It makes talking to you a lot more enjoyable. And you're eating bacon. I don't remember you ever doing that." Michael could only smile at Betty as he finished his breakfast and sipped the orange juice she had placed in front of him.

"Ma'am, I appreciate you." Michael gave his movie star smile. "Is Mel around? I want to see if she wants to go to drag races tonight. The first 30 people in line get a ball cap. I could use one."

"That store of yours don't got ball caps?" JR couldn't help but jump into the conversation.

"JR," Michael started his sentence and sipped orange juice before continuing. "Winning the prize is a big deal. And it's a nice-looking cap."

"I'll tell Mel you asked about going," Betty chirped. "She's at the animal park bringing them some food scraps."

"Great! I'll stop over there and ask her." JR and Betty couldn't believe what they heard. They both knew Mel was at the park with Dianne. It wouldn't be pretty if Michael surprised them.

Thinking quickly, Betty blurted out, "Oh, that reminds me, I have to talk to Barb in the park's kitchen." JR caught on to Betty's plan without a word. Michael finished eating, paid his bill with a more generous tip than usual, and then started to leave. Betty had to slow him down.

"JR, pour Michael another glass of orange juice and have him sit for a bit. He deserves it. He's been so kind lately. He's got to wash down that bacon." Betty patted JR on his arm before going to their living quarters behind the shop. JR instinctively knew how to slow the boy down so she could warn the folks at the animal park. Betty reached Barb immediately, who understood what she needed to do. Michael was coming, and something had to be done to avoid problems if he saw Dianne at the park.

"Hi Jill!" Barb greeted her coworker as she straightened herself from leaning over a prep table sorting out restaurant scraps for the park's large animal population. "Jill, I got a call from Betty at JR's. Michael is on his way over, and Dianne's still completing her volunteer application. It may not be pretty if the two run into one another."

"No problem, Barb. I'll take the young man out to view the bison. I need to talk to him anyway," Jill said with a gleam as she pulled the jeep keys off a wall hook between the park's kitchen and the administrative office. A voice rang out from the admin office adjacent to the kitchen.

"I heard that, Jill! And don't go traveling off in a jeep. Sue stepped from behind her desk to peer out of her office and glare at Jill. Take the truck. Geez! No wonder our health insurance is so high!"

"You spoke like a true accountant, Sue. What are you doing here on a Saturday anyway?" Sue looked at Jill sternly.

"I'm reading over grant applications I got in the mail yesterday. What are you up to?"

"Don't worry, I'll be gentle...and take the truck."

Sue shook her head and then retreated to her desk. Jill bent to see if Sue was firmly out of earshot, then addressed Barb in a low voice.

"Barb, tap the loudspeaker button when a big red truck pulls in. You mind?"

"I'm packing up some goodies for the bison," Barb told Jill softly to prevent Sue from hearing.

"I'll call you to come get it when you're ready to head out. I assume you'll grab the goodies and take Michael for a chat after he arrives?"

Jill gave Barb a thumbs up, then stopped suddenly.

"Where are Mel and Dianne?" Jill's voice returned to normal volume.

"They're filling in volunteer information. One of the lead volunteers will talk to Dianne at length and then bring Dianne in to speak with Sue," Barb said with a smile.

Returning to a whisper, Barb told Jill, "All the volunteers know what's happening. They'll delay Dianne so she doesn't run into Michael." Barb returned to tearing lettuce and sprinkled the pile with vitamin nuggets for the bison.

"Jill, I don't want to, and I don't want the park to be part of whatever you're doing!" Sue called out, not knowing what the two women were up to, but heard the murmuring and suspected mischief.

"Well-oiled machine. I like that!" Jill whispered to Barb,

shrugging her shoulders. She proceeded to trade Jeep keys for truck keys and smiled at Sue with a quick peek into her office.

Sue could only respond by peering over her glasses and wagging her finger at Jill. Although Jill did not have a supervisory title at the park, her demeanor quickly brought everyone on board. Barb, in this instance and most park actions, used her command of the kitchen and her alliance with Jill to make the park run smoothly because of the staff's unspoken deference to the duo.

As always, Jill checked the truck's fuel and tires and listened to the motor before going to the "Back Lands," as park staff called it. The expansive area was far from the entrance, administrative offices, and small animal care area. The Back Lands served as a large animal habitat, with only a one-way gravel road winding through it for visitors to use when viewing the larger animals.

Two old school buses were also available to tour the park. Many visitors preferred the bus for fear of damage to their personal vehicles. Some of the Back Land's border was near the Glossen property. Sometimes, the staff could see Michael run or stroll along the fence, alone or with others.

"Jill, your package is ready for pickup." Barb's voice blared over the loudspeaker. Hearing that, Jill knew Michael had entered the park through the employee entrance. She closed the truck hood, ensuring it was latched, and walked briskly over to the area where she could pick up a package of treats for the large animals and "accidentally" talk to Michael.

"Hi, Michael! What a good surprise! You know, the bison are starting to mingle! There might be some action in the Back Lands—in more ways than one." Jill winked at Michael, and they both smiled at Jill's pun.

Without taking a breath, Jill extended an invitation. "You want to ride with me? I'm getting ready to take treats to those big boys and girls."

"I came here hoping to find Mel," Michael said as he removed his keys and locked his truck. "I want to ask her to go to the drag races tonight. She likes 'em as much as I do."

"She's in talking to Sue. She'll be a while. I'll tell Barb, and she'll let Mel know. Are you ready to ride? Get in! I'll be back with a cooler full of treats."

"I'm there!" Michael said with excitement. He wanted to see

the bison but did not want to see Sue, who knew he had not sent a check this month.

"You seem more excited than usual to see the bison. Is it because they're about to start looking for mates?" Jill already knew the answer to her question regarding the bison.

"Yeah!" Michael said with enthusiasm.

"Look, friend, I know your kink. I've seen you along the fence staring at every living thing we got here when they procreate," Jill said a short time into their ride. "You might just say you like to see them fuck."

"Yeah, I love it when they fuck."

"Oh, I can tell we're going to be friends. I don't care when they fuck; I only want to make sure they have the food they need to produce healthy offspring. I don't watch them like you do. Oh, and did you recently stop giving the park a monthly donation?" Jill jumped directly into her intended conversation.

"Yeah, I gotta start that back. I had to pay for a truck."

Jill purposely veered into a few well-known bumps in the field. Michael grabbed the truck's handle over the door.

"You're roughing me up, lady. Take it easy!"

"This ain't nothin' Mr. Glossen! When we get back, you need to write Ms. Gorrell a check. Write her a check!" she said with evident anger. "I don't care if you post-date it. Just make sure the check can be cashed! I'm serious!" Jill said in a firm voice. "You hear me?"

"Well, I got paid this week, but it's all going to stuff I need," Michael said matter-of-factly, as though Jill would believe him and empathize. Jill braked firmly with the truck angling slightly down a hill, causing her and Michael to pitch forward with the sudden stop.

"You don't want to ignore me or my request," she said, staring at Michael. "The way I look at it, you need to continue supporting your animals and your kink. I know you don't want information about your habits to get back to your store or your Daddy. Or do you?" Jill illustrated her seriousness by extending a full-hand point ending inches from the now-alarmed man's face.

"You are blackmailing me, woman!"

"Yep, and I got pictures of you. A couple of the park guys saw you jerking off at the fence. Dude! This is not normal. You need to get some help. Meanwhile, the park needs YOUR help. You see, we're a team. Want a beer? I've got some in the cooler. It'll help you relax. As teammates, I'll ensure you get more rides to the Back Lands. Wouldn't you like that? Let me get your beer."

Jill pushed a pedal on the floorboard to set the truck's brakes before sliding out of the cab and stepping to the truck bed to retrieve a beer packed among the animal feed. "Here's your beer," she said, extending her arm through the open window and tossing it to him across the seat.

"You're a rotten woman Jill!"

"No, you might say I'm quite accommodating. Look, I gave you a beer. I'd drink with you, like friends, like friends and teammates. But I'm working. You see, I'm accommodating to the park and you. Oh, another thing... the girls and I need a place to hang out on a Saturday night. I hear your place is available. You like going to drag races, and you work on some Saturday nights, right? I think between 6:00 pm and midnight, your place needs to be available and clean. We'll leave you some beer in the fridge."

"You throw me out of my house? And my dog, what about my dog?" Michael didn't think about the beer being shaken. As he opened the bottle, it began to fizz. All he could do to stop it was to place his mouth over the top of the bottle neck. Still, some leaked on his clothes.

"What about your dog? Do you care about your dog? You almost stole Brandy from the guys up at the trout farm. You thought she was full-bred, and you could make some money off her. You found out she's "just a dog" as you put it. You know, you should get her a fence and not keep her tied up constantly."

"You are throwing that into our a-comm-a-dating teammate friendship, too?" Michael seemed to be boiling with anger as he swigged his remaining beer.

"No. I'll hold off on the fence. But if you don't treat the dog right, then folks might start knowing about the real you. You understand me?"

"You give me all this bullshit. Now, where's the bison? You ain't a teammate, Ms. Jill," Michael said, trying to reclaim some ego.

"Aren't you getting feisty suddenly... and impatient! In a

minute, I'll start spreading some nice hay and leafy treats along the top of that hill." Jill said, pointing to an area in front of the truck. "You'll see them soon enough. I got a boom box in the back. They're curious. They'll come running. Usually, we play some lively jazz, and they come to find us." Jill smiled at Michael as she exited the truck, giving him a second smile through the window.

After scattering leafy treats with gloved hands across the hill, she returned to the truck, stowed equipment, and turned up the music.

"Listen! Did you hear it?" Jill asked Michael as she returned to the driver's seat. "They're thundering up the hill. I can't believe they heard the music from that far away. Or maybe they smell this truck and know good things come from it."

"Yeah! I hear 'em!" Michael said, finally mustering excitement.

"There they are! Look at those beautiful beards. They're beginning to look like Don Juan!"

"Who's that? He Mexican?"

Jill chuckled. "Oh, never mind. He's a guy in a famous book I read long ago. You think you could feed them, Michael?"

"Is this your deal too?" Michael said with a bit of trepidation. "I only watch. I don't want to get in the middle of those big boys."

"Yep! About 2,000 pounds of bull! Even more bull than you got, friend! It's not part of the deal, I wondered if you could do it. So, you won't be applying for a job here anytime soon?"

"Nope, I like my store," Michael answered quickly.

"I hear Ms. Kelly does a lot of good work over there, pretty much runs things."

"You saying something there?" Michael looked directly at Jill as more bison roamed up the hill.

"Oh, they love their treats!" Jill quickly responded, ignoring Michael's question. "I know these guys would never make it in the wild for this reason! And some of them were very young when they came here. Many came injured and were not able to make it on their own. We help them, let them breed, and sometimes send offspring on to other parks. We think some of the ladies might need some help getting pregnant."

"What are you saying? I told you I won't get near any of those guys!"

Jill laughed so hard she couldn't speak.

"OK, this conversation is over. Aren't you happy, Michael? Don't worry, I wasn't going to ask you to inseminate the ladies." Jill started the truck with her special touch, getting the clutch and gas to give it the power to start.

"You handle the truck like a man!"

"Is that supposed to be a compliment, Michael?"

Michael didn't answer.

"Truck One to base. Truck One to base. The bison look good, really good. I'm coming back." Jill radioed as Michael glowered in silence.

"Come back to momma! All is good here, too!" Jill guessed Mel and Dianne had left the park. Barb could tell everything went well for Jill, too.

Without purposely hitting every hole in the field, returning to the kitchen area near Michael's truck was faster, yet for Michael, not fast enough. With silence between them, his mind raced with thoughts on how to handle his sudden money shortage.

"I think you can find your way around here, Michael. I need to wash the cooler and truck and then update some logs. Those bison bulls looked excellent and ready to make some babies. What ya think?" Without a word and with determination, Michael headed toward his truck.

"I know you're not heading out of here in that truck, Mr. Glossen! Are you? Is your checkbook in there?"

"Um yes, right here under the seat. I gotta get it and see Ms. Gorrell," Michael answered quickly. In fact, he did plan to head out and thought Jill would let him slide.

Michael pushed aside his trusty Glock from under the seat and felt around for his checkbook. He waved a check to show Jill he was heading to the accounting office. Jill finished cleaning the ice chest and remained outside, making motions like she was cleaning the truck. She wanted to make sure Michael didn't double back.

"Hey Jill! Come in here," Barb yelled. Jill entered the kitchen, toting the newly cleaned ice chest.

"Listen!" Barb whispered while holding a finger to her lips. The women heard Michael apologize, and Sue graciously accepted a check. Eyes wide, all Jill could do was mouth,

"WOW!"

"What did you say to him?" Barb whispered.

"Tell you later," Jill whispered back, then headed stealthily back to her truck-cleaning chore.

"Hey Michael!" Jill yelled, waving a cleaning rag as she saw Michael exiting the building. "Thank you! The animals and staff appreciate you."

"No problem!" Michael responded, but he knew there was a problem. He might have to call his father to ask for money to cover the check he wrote or even eat his peculiar diet. For a minute, he thought about "borrowing" money from the store. However, he knew Ms. Kelly's efficiency at counting and accounting for every penny. He didn't want everyone in Marshfield to know his "habit." He sure as hell didn't want his father to know about it. On the way over to JR's, Michael continued to think of ways to solve his problem and save his reputation. As he parked at the truck stop, Michael mentally soothed himself, *At least I don't drink a bunch like Daddy.*

"Michael! It's kind of late to see you here, and twice in one day! What have you been up to?" JR greeted him as he exited one of the restaurant booths he had finished cleaning.

"JR, I need a big burger and some fries. Oh, and pie. I feel like having pie."

"You're a bit off your diet today, kind sir. You didn't have enough this morning, or bacon's troubling you? What's going on? You want three or four burgers? Or do you think you might want some roast beef?"

"Just one burger. I just spoke with Jill at the animal park." Mel heard the conversation but stayed hidden in the back so she could hear what Michael had to say without him knowing she had listened.

"I have one about ready that I prepared for myself. I'll fix it for you," JR said, lining up fries on a plate.

"I swear to you, JR, that woman is a witch, and I don't mean the "b" word! She starts telling me this and that, and damn! Some of it is close enough to be true! I swear she's a witch. Ain't those the women who can see into your soul?"

"I don't know. I've never met one I know of," JR said as he finished preparing Michael's food. Is there anything else I can get you? Maybe a preacher should take care of the witch? Was she mean to you for some reason?"

"Naw, she was nice, but she knew stuff!" Michael took a few deep breaths before digging into his plate of forbidden food.

"Hi, Michael! I thought I heard you come in. I had to grab the house phone, and then nature called." Mel lied on both accounts.

"You want to go to the drag races tonight? I heard you wanted to go. I'm buying! I might spring for a beer on the way home, too." This offer was too good for Michael to pass up.

"Yep, I need some loud noise and beer to cheer me up," Michael responded, then took the last bite of his burger. After a few seconds of silent chewing, Michael suddenly said he had scheduling issues he had to fix and would see Mel later.

"I got to learn how you make food so good, JR," he added as he left more than enough cash on the counter and most of his fries before dashing out.

"See you later!" Mel yelled knowing he didn't hear her. "Dad, I didn't even tell him what time! I'm driving tonight, mind if I take the van? He's crazy today. Well, crazier than usual," Mel said, shaking her head. "I'm calling Jill to find out what went on. And yes, I heard every word. I was hiding in the back."

"Kinda figured. We owe him pie. Didn't get a chance to cut him a piece." JR shrugged his shoulders and finished his cleaning routine.

"Jill, this is Mel. What happened over there this morning?"

"Oh, you wouldn't believe it!" Jill shared the entire story with Mel, who could not stop laughing.

"So, he agreed to all this and to continue his donation?" she asked. Well, soon we'll have a good time at our new club every Saturday night!" Mel still couldn't believe her ears.

"I'm not kidding, Mel! I hope the others around here are up for it. Oh, and get this," Jill continued, "I talked to the guys who drive the bus and other staff. It appears wacko Michael also takes pictures of the animals procreating! Oh, and the guys take pictures of Michael taking pictures and doing his thing by the fence."

"Poor boy, he needs help." Mel had sincere sympathy for her buddy.

"Yeah, I told him that. Oh, and another thing!" Jill's demeanor shifted into her more professional mode. "Thank you very much for introducing us to Dianne. It appears she and Sue might work on writing grants. And Dianne will learn enough to help us teach the children about the animals."

"That's wonderful!" Mel was excited for both of her friends but couldn't stay serious for long.

"I know someone who has pictures of the animals if you need them."

"Get real, Mel! Ha! Enough of you today! Talk to you later, bye."

"Bye."

After leaving the animal park earlier, Dianne traveled directly to one of Springfield's large bookstores in anticipation of volunteering at the park. She purchased several books on wild animals and one on grant writing. She looked forward to working at the park, wanted to be prepared, and was eager to take notes from her reading.

She finished her Springfield trip with a visit to the grocery store, trying to follow a meticulous list she'd devised. At home, she organized and stowed away dry goods, refrigerated items, and household items with precision. Exhausted, she melted into the recliner.

"What on earth?" knocking at the door startled Dianne. The knock did not sound like Ken, who always knocked with a certain rhythm. Dawn's knocks came in groups of three. This knock seemed continuous, giving Dianne an ominous feeling.

"Who is it?" she asked loudly.

"I need to talk to you about your mother's life insurance," a muffled voice yelled.

Dianne paused.

Opening the door didn't seem like the right thing to do.

"I need to talk to you about your mother's life insurance," the muffled voice repeated louder, with what seemed to be impatience. Dianne's better sense took over.

"I don't take guests this late. And it's the weekend!" she shouted.

"Call on Monday, and we'll meet at the bank," she said as loudly as possible.

"I need your signature now!" the voice shouted.

"Call the bank!" Dianne shouted louder.

"Now go away before I call the police!" Dianne rushed over to her phone.

Never mind, I'm calling them anyway, she thought.

Dianne was through talking to the voice, which continued to yell. The knocking continued as Dianne dialed 911 and spoke to the dispatcher as calmly as she could be under her duress.

"Ma'am, stay on the phone with me. Help is on the way," the dispatcher said.

As flashing lights lit up her living room, Dianne heard a car drive off.

"Talk to me, ma'am. Is everything OK?"

"Yes, a police car passed my house. He's chasing the car that drove off.

"Do you have any idea who it was?"

"No!" Dianne yelled nervously. A man's voice kept saying he wanted to talk to me about my mother's life insurance."

"It's alright, Hon. You did the right thing, not opening the door, not even a crack. He could have forced his way in," the professional operator said and continued her care.

"Is there a police car pulling up?"

"Yes."

"It's OK to open the door. The officer will take a statement, and the other car will continue the chase."

"Thank you. I'll talk to him," Dianne said, finally able to breathe freely. Dianne filed a report giving the officer as many details as she could. The officer promised to spend the remaining part of his shift outside her house or driving the streets in her neighborhood. He said he would pass on information to the officer replacing him when he changed shifts.

CHAPTER 18

Life Shift

Usual weekday chatter was waning as JR and Betty labored to clean dishes, sanitize tables, sweep, and perform a dozen other chores before they closed. JR was always open to good banter or conversation with the last customers of the day.

"You're Fred McCall, aren't you?" JR directed his question to a lone gentleman sitting in the farthest booth.

"Yes I am." McCall said with a smile. "And you might be able to assist me with something, JR."

"Sure, what can I help with?" JR thought he wanted food for carryout. However, the lawyer needed information, not food. McCall explained he heard a man at the counter earlier speak unflatteringly about a woman he was about to interview for an office manager's position. He was pretty sure it was the same woman.

"Do you know who the man was? The young man sat at the end of the counter and spoke while chewing. I figure he's a regular," McCall explained.

"Oh yes, that's Michael Glossen. He's a manager at MegaMart. I guarantee that's who was talking. I tell ya, I don't want to even look at the guy when he's eating. I don't want to know what he's done stuck in that ever-jabbering pie hole of his."

Both men laughed at JR's description.

"JR, I'll take it from here. Go count the register," Betty interrupted. Fred quietly sipped his coffee, taking mental notes. Now, he was listening to Betty's version of events leading to Hickman firing Mrs. Roberts.

"There is something more to the story Hickman told Michael," Betty continued as she wiped tables.

"It's too coincidental that she lost her job after helping the guys retrieve Dianne England's contract. Remember that day you were here, and we first met? That's the same crooked car dealer!"

Turning back to her husband, who had finished his register count, Betty asked JR, "Hon, since you're finished counting, can you take a minute and tell Mr. McCall what happened that day when you and the gang headed over to Hickman's? His office received a letter and resume from the lady who worked with Hickman. On paper, she seems impressive."

"Gracious woman! First, you send me away, then you pull me back." JR winked at McCall.

"Thank you, Ms. Betty, and please, call me Fred." JR barely let Fred finish when he couldn't keep himself from his dramatic reenactment of the day. He relayed his version of the story and laughed during his complete rendition about retrieving Dianne's contract. As with the other times he told the story, he emphasized certain parts to heighten his own entertainment.

McCall, lured into JR's story and laughter, cackled with him.

"That's pretty much it." Betty told Fred, then scolded JR. "The way you exaggerate things—that's going to get you in trouble one of these days! Betty gave JR a playful smack on his bottom and continued to talk to the lawyer.

"Mr. McCall, I mean Fred, Mrs. Roberts was fired because of her strong organizational skills and professionalism. There's not a thing wrong with her work," Betty explained.

"I'll never understand men. You laugh over the silliest things. I've got to get back to work."

"I see the situation," Fred responded. I'll call her for an interview. She seems like a lady of principle. I think she will be great in our new office. Oh, heavens! You're closed, and I haven't paid my bill!"

"Here's your ticket," JR said, "Pay it next time you're in here. Do your lawyer stuff. I'll stay here and see what the boss wants me to do next."

Betty wagged her finger at JR and proceeded back to work with Mel.

"Mom, I'm so glad you talked to Mr. McCall about Mrs. Roberts," Mel said as she took dishes from Betty.

"It seems like she's a great person, but her boss was not a good businessman."

"Unfortunately, that happens a lot in this world. I hope Mel, if someday you run into a creep like Hickman, you will back away quickly and have nothing to do with him."

Mel and Betty cleaned as dishes rattled, covering an uncomfortable volume of urgent-sounding advertising blaring from a radio in the kitchen. After turning the radio volume to a low murmur, the women let the sun's warm glow soften their moods as they discussed Mel's future.

"Mel, you are about to turn 19."

"Yep, I know. It's a little scary. I like working here, but like Mrs. Roberts, I need to move on. I'm not sure what I want to do or can do."

"What do you like to do, here or elsewhere?"

"Well, Mom, I think I will like the computer. That's why I twisted your arm so we could take that class together. I like playing the guitar, but I don't think anyone will pay me to do it."

"You seem quite good at the guitar, whether you play songs you wrote or ones you hear on tape or CD. But yes, a musician's life is hard and unpredictable. You'd probably have to go to college to get a good start and make connections. Taking on private students might give you a little bit of money but not enough to live on."

"Yes, I might do alright in college, but I know it's expensive, and you and JR have done so much for me. I'm not even going to ask for your help."

"We can help a little. We want to help a lot. See how you like that computer class. It's not a college course, but you can understand what you'll be up against by taking it. Oh, and there's something I want to tell you about that. I don't want to take that course. If you don't mind, you can take the course and set up this place on a computer. Maybe you could even create a little store. Whatever you want to do, tell JR and me how we can help make things run smoothly. Are you OK with that? You'll be the boss then. The big lady in charge!"

"Mom, I'm unsure if I want to do this all my life. You and JR work hard here. I don't mean to sound ungrateful, but I don't want to do this all my life. I feel there's a better life for me outside of Marshfield."

"We'd work much harder if it weren't for you helping us since day one. We have had employees in and out of here through the years. They were fine but moved on. You were the best! Now you want to do other things. That's fine. You need to decide what it is you want."

"Yeah. I'm thinking about asking Dianne if she wants a housemate. You know, a stranger came to her door the other night, wanting to get in. It might be safer if I were there."

"JR told me about that. He heard it from Ken. Go ahead and talk to Dianne about moving in. You can still work here and be almost a boss. We'll pay you fairly. Are you good with that?"

"I'm sorry. I'm starting to cry." Mel wiped tears on her sleeve. As mothers and daughters do in such moments, the two hugged. Betty pulled a fresh dish towel off the stack and wiped her tears and Mel's.

"Looks like we're finished here except for a few stray dishes. Are you calling or going to Dianne's to ask about accepting a housemate? I know you've been thinking about this or wouldn't have mentioned it." Betty smiled at her daughter as she stacked the last plate.

"You're right. I have been thinking about it. I'll call first. She likes it when I call. She always gets on to me for not identifying myself."

"Hi Dianne. How was things down at the school? You home?"
Dianne picked up the phone when she heard Mel's voice on the answering machine.

"That's "were". How "were" things at the school?"

"Whoa! She's definitely a schoolteacher!"

"Are you still not identifying yourself, Mel? Yes, I'm home. You think I'm talking to you on a car phone?"

Mel laughed, then launched a fun rant. "Hey, Batwoman! Are you on the Bat-car phone?"

"Oh, stop, woman! You know that reality isn't far off! I read a technology article about phones, and it said that by the turn of the century, the average American would have a phone in their car or anywhere they want to take a phone," Dianne responded.

Mel thought phones in cars were a far-fetched idea, so she didn't comment. "Mind if I come over? I've got things on my mind and want to run by you."

"OK, sure, come on over. I'm pretty much set for school

tomorrow. Bring the information about the computer class too."

"Sure! See ya!"

"Hey Dianne! It's me! What are you doing locking your door?" Mel said while clicking her keys on the door's peephole. "No one does that around here!"

"Well, I do," Dianne replied as she opened the door. I've been extra careful since that man, whoever he was, tried to get me to open my door the other night. I'm glad Mom installed a deadbolt." Dianne opened the door fully and motioned Mel to step inside.

"Yeah, that's a good idea, what she did. That man is partly why I wanted to visit tonight. I got something to ask ya."

"Do you think you know who it is? Tell Deputy Johnson!"

"No, slow down, my friend! Sorry to say, I have no idea. I guess you haven't thought of this, but what do you think about letting me rent one of your rooms? Hear me," Mel said, lifting her hand before Dianne as if to block her words. "It's not only the guy who showed up at your door but me. I'm ready to move from home. Betty said I could still work there, and she would pay me more so I could rent a room from you and pay for other stuff like utilities. I know this is a surprise, but what do you think?"

"Mel, I would love the company!" Dianne said impulsively, but almost immediately remembered some girls in her dorm who had left home for the first time. Have you ever lived away from JR and Betty? Have you ever gone to camp?" Dianne asked anxiously.

"Nope, never wanted to. I thought the other kids would make fun of me."

"And I thought I was the innocent, inexperienced one here! How'd you know about paying the bills?"

"I think I told you. We do this at the truck stop. It seems like I've always did that. And money stuff fascinates me."

"Whoa! Good for you!" Dianne's eyes widened as though she couldn't believe someone was fascinated with financial things. Mel smiled and tried to put her prospective "roomie" at ease.

"I can see it will be different coming into a new space every night and not having Betty to talk to. But I'd like to try if you're game."

"Sometimes I'll need some quiet time," Dianne warned. "I

need to prepare for school. And, well, at night, I sometimes wake up and call out to Mom and cry a lot. I miss her so much. And I like to write. I might need some quiet then, too."

"If I were in your place and lost Betty, I'd probably cry too. But honestly, I'm not sure how I would feel if the woman who birthed me died. Maybe I will know at some point. Shit, she hasn't even tried to contact me in the last seven years or so. Weird, I don't think bad about her, I don't think about her. Am I supposed to?"

"I don't know. We can't control our feelings, and I don't think anyone can tell us what or how to feel."

"Did you learn that in college?"

"I might have. We did have to take some psychology classes. When you move in, we can talk more about college, all kinds of mothers, fathers, whatever. Now tell me about the computer class!"

"Wow! What? What? When I move in? You mean you think I should live here!"

"Yes. I will appreciate the company. The rent will be low. Can you split electricity, phone, and all that?"

"Oh yes! Will you let me know what you pay for the utilities?"

"I'll let you know as soon as I can."

"I'll figure it out with Mom to see what they will pay me. Yes, Betty is my mother." Mel seemed to think deeply about Betty, the beautiful woman who adopted her ten years ago.

"OK, Ms. Math Lady. Figure it out." Dianne smiled as she thumped her forefinger to her temple. "Also, figure out what else you will need to buy. I'm thinking about shampoo, clothes, and drag racing money." Dianne knew Mel liked to go to the drag races. Both women continued chatting in a flurry of words and ideas, anticipating living together.

"I'm trying to think of things I experienced at the dorm," Dianne said. "But back then, I didn't have to think about electricity and trash. This home ownership thing is perplexing."

"Yeah, that's a lot to think about. Oh, and did I tell you that I play guitar too? It's not an electric one." Mel jumped in to clarify so Dianne wouldn't suddenly be afraid to move forward with their pending ideas.

"That sounds fine. At least you won't be rocking out past

midnight." Dianne laughed.

"Well, I don't know, I can get pretty wild with my folk music," Mel shot back.

"I look forward to hearing how one does that with folk music," Dianne chuckled. "We'll talk more and work out details such as rocking out and whatever. Did you bring information about the computer class over? And have you ever worked with a computer keyboard?"

"Umm, yes, I mean no, I haven't ever worked on a computer."

"Do you know how to use a typewriter?"

"Yes, but I'm not good at it."

"Look, it's fairly new, but there's something similar called a PC. That's short for a personal computer. I'm thinking about buying one. Talk to Betty and decide what you can pay. I'll get you started on whatever kind of computer is out there, and you can practice using the keyboard, which is like a typewriter. It will go smoother if you can get the hang of it before the computer class in a few months. That will also help you decide whether to go to college."

"OK. And you might want to learn more about guitar playing," Mel retorted.

"Yes, I'd like that, but I'm unsure if I could sing and strum together! It takes coordination," Dianne said, reaching for the computer class information.

"Oh yes, well, here." Mel handed Dianne a paper that described the class.

"Amy, the library lady, came by the shop and wanted us to put these by the register so folks can see what they're doing at the library. JR agreed to give them a permanent spot for library news as soon as he could clear out a space."

"The library lady? Could she be the librarian, perhaps?"

"Yes, I was being funny with ya," Mel said, smiling as she lightly play-punched Dianne in the arm. The two women talked about the possibilities the class could present for each other, then sidetracked into a friendly conversation that had nothing to do with the class, yet a lot to do with the two of them possibly becoming "roomies," as they began to call themselves.

"I'll call you tomorrow to update you on what I can pay. That OK?"

"Yes, that's fine. But before you go, Mel, why do you sometimes call Betty and JR "Mom" and "Dad" yet other times by their names?

"Honestly, it's what comes out. They said they don't mind as long as I keep loving them as much as they love me. Pretty neat, huh?"

Because life became busy for both women, a few days passed before Mel and Dianne met again; Dianne busy with school and research, Mel helping her parents with daily traffic at the truck stop.

Dianne registered for the computer class and reviewed books she'd purchased on grant writing and zoo keeping. During the review, she wrote copious notes in a notebook and on sticky papers that decorated the pages like her college textbooks. Note-taking while reading helped her keep focus, as she did in faculty meetings.

The ringing phone startled Dianne out of deep concentration.

"Hi, Dianne. This is Ken."

"Ken, hello! It's great to hear from you! What have you been up to?"

"My usual stuff. I decided to spend more time in St. Louis these past few days. I'm still sorting through things in my mind."

"Are you back in Marshfield or St. Louis? I didn't see the caller ID."

"I'm in Marshfield—it's my new home. I'm not waffling like I was. This is my family home now. You want to chit-chat this weekend some?"

"I'm happy to. Believe it or not, Mel might move in this weekend. You know her, she has to see if the money works. I hope she decides to go for it. It would be great to have the company."

"Hmmm," Ken thought for a minute. "I don't think she wants to take advantage of her parents. I think it will work out fine. If everything is a go, do you think she will need any help?"

"Yes, I think we could use your huge muscles for the move," Dianne said teasingly. "You're kind of like my dad now, you know."

"I'm feeling it, Dianne. Let me know when and where. I'll be there, me and my huge muscles." Ken laughed.

"I will, and we can set aside time to chat," Dianne said excitedly.

"I look forward to it all! Bye."

"Bye."

Dianne barely replaced the phone receiver when the phone rang again.

"Hi, sorry I haven't gotten back to you."

"Yes, Mel."

"Will you accept $75 a week and split utilities? I know it's not much."

"I'll be happy to accept! Are you thinking of moving this weekend? We'll have to shuffle things around first. I still may have to pack away a few of my mother's things to get them out of your way. I've been hesitating to do that."

"Is it something you need to do yourself, or do you want help?"

"I'm not sure. Either way, it's going to be hard. Ken called and said he would help as well."

"Let me know. I must help JR and Betty...no, never mind...I will call them Mom and Dad. They are my parents! I will help my parents with the breakfast and lunch crowd, then be over afterward. OK?"

"Great! I'm also planning to go to the park this weekend to talk to Ms. Gorrell about my research."

"She's rarely there on weekends. Can you see her during the week?"

"Oh yes. Spring break is coming up. I can do that. I'll call her tomorrow to make an appointment. I'm looking forward to you becoming my roommate and having some company. Tomorrow is finally my big day for the review from Mr. Richards. I don't know how many times he's postponed it. Can you handle it if things go south, and I rant and rave a bit?"

"I know it will be good! You are top dog in that school, my friend!"

"I'm nervous. I'm still thinking about when I had to take off."

"Good or not, call me, OK? Don't forget to identify yourself, or I'll not know who you are."

"Funny, Mel. Good night."

"Good night, dear friend."

CHAPTER 19

Disappointment

The day and hour finally came for Dianne to meet Mr. Richards for her mid-term assessment. Her trembling fingers barely held her pen and notebook. Trying to mitigate her typical earliness, her wobbly legs took measured steps. Mentally rehearsing her greeting to the principal made her nearly miss the office.

"Mr. Richards? I'm a few minutes early, is that OK?

"Oh yes, fine! I'm thinking about making better signs for the bus lanes. It seems kids are confused about where to line up, and then there's the usual tomfoolery in line. I'm trying to make the signs cute but easy to read. Hopefully, they'll positively influence behavior and get the youngsters on the correct line. Have any ideas?"

Dianne responded with a slight voice vibrato. "A sign contest for each grade? That was not my idea, but somewhere during college, I heard it was best to let the students get involved in such things. I won't feel bad if you don't want to do that. And I don't want to tell you what to do or anything,"

"Ms. England, you sound nervous. Our chat is nothing to worry about. You have a great idea. I might use it." Mr. Richards smiled and then jumped into the purpose of the meeting. "So, to help you relax, I'll get right into it. You're doing a great job and are passionate about this work. Pam Millbrook and the other teachers you work with cannot say enough nice things about you. The students love you! I could not have asked for a better intern. Oh, sorry. I should have begun by asking about how you're doing with the loss of your mother. I heard she was a great person, and it was very tough for you to say goodbye. I guess that goes for most of us when we lose a parent. Are you OK?"

"Yes. Working with the children has helped a lot. I've been very busy with them and preparing for the class. It helps."

Dianne started to relax as she talked about the children in her class.

"Keeping busy usually does. But have you had time to mourn? Do you have close friends or relatives who can help you in this process?"

"Definitely. My mother had a special friend, Ken. He's become sort of a father to me. We talk a lot. A month or so ago I met a friend, Mel. We're starting to become close. She may move in with me. It will be good to have company."

"I'm quite relieved to hear you have support. I confess, it's not only a general concern I have for you, as I do all the teachers and staff here, but I've got something to share that may be tough."

"Yes?" After feeling more relaxed, Dianne began shifting in her seat. She rotated her thumbs around one another, trying to contain her anticipation. Worse, Mr. Richards seemed to stare through her, perhaps trying as well to contain his nerves. Meanwhile, the last departing children's voices echoed in the halls, adding tension. The hall would soon become quiet, with only the rustling of teachers' papers and the realigning of desks.

"Ms. England," Mr. Richards began, "The internship program agreed to between the Webster County Schools and the University of Southwest Missouri states that interns need 90 hours of teaching time supervised by a certified county teacher and at least 20 hours of mentoring and planning time. You have put in almost 60 hours of classroom time and have far exceeded the mentoring and planning time. However, by the end of the year, I'm afraid you will fall short of the 90 hours of classroom time. There are not enough hours left in our school year.

Given your special circumstances, Mrs. Millbrook and I have talked to university administrators to let you slide with the requirements. They will not relent. You cannot graduate this semester if you don't have 90 hours.

However, Dr. Lamberth from the education department said that because of your circumstances, she can arrange for you to walk the stage at the end of the semester with your peers, but your diploma will be blank. After completing your 90 hours, whether during a summer school program or next fall, your diploma will be mailed to you. She locked herself into the requirement when, last year, an intern was short five hours. They made a similar deal with her. I'm so very sorry. I know this seems harsh, but you have done splendidly."

After Mr. Richards spoke, only the white noise of office machines could be heard. Dianne sat quietly, finally feeling the stiffness of her wooden chair.

"I, I, yes, I'm in a bit of a shock," Dianne stuttered. "I guess I should have expected some kind of problem, given how much I took off."

"I realize it's tough, but I have an offer for you. School here ends May 15th. Summer School begins the next week, so it can be finished by July 4th. Until you finish your internship hours, you won't be on the clock, but after that time, we can pay you. Some teachers who signed up to teach can take vacations while you fill in."

"My own classroom?"

"Pretty much. Understand, though, that you'll take different grades. I can guarantee that most will not be from your learning disability class. Most, if not all, students in your current class will go to special camps. After your internship, when you are in a paid position, your hours will depend on who is out. Unfortunately, we will not need you for days when no one is out. At least, when you are an intern, every day will count toward your hours."

"Thank you, Mr. Richards. I'll prepare for that."

Although trying to sound upbeat in front of Mr. Richards, Dianne was devastated. She wasn't sure she understood anything clearly, but she promised her mother that she would get her degree, and following Mr. Richards' guidance seemed to be the way to do that. After her conversation, she didn't remember driving home, pouring a glass of wine, or grabbing the potato chips Ken left behind. She only heard chips crunching between her teeth and the occasional glass clink on the side table. Her mind still raced.

A knock at the door startled her. "Dianne? Are you OK? It's Pam Millbrook."

What? What's she doing here? Dianne thought as she opened the door to see her supervising teacher. "I brought you a little plant, hoping you will watch it grow and bloom like you're doing."

"Thank you," Dianne said softly motioning Pam to come in.

"I'm so sorry. We really tried to help."

"I know you did," Dianne whispered solemnly. Dianne finally looked up and couldn't help herself. She cried almost as intensely as when her mother died.

"Yes, it's an awful disappointment. When you're ready, talk to me. Or, if you prefer that I leave, I can do that too."

"I don't know what to think," Dianne cried. Another knock at the door startled both women.

"Oh, that's Mel," Dianne said between sobs. She always taps on the peephole."

"Let her in?" Pam asked.

"Yes, she's a great person."

"Hey, girl! Look what I brought! Oh, oh, oh, what happened? Why are you crying, Dianne?"

"You tell her," Dianne said, motioning toward Pam, who then shared an overview with Mel. She didn't think going into too much detail would be right.

"Ms. England, you're a fine teacher and will only improve as time passes. I'll leave the details for you to share with Mel, unless you need me to stay.

"I brought dinner," Mel said, still searching for appropriate words.

"And some cake!" she continued. "Do you want to take a piece with you, Ma'am?"

"Thank you, but I already have too many sweets at home. However, I do appreciate your generosity. Let me say goodbye to you both. I've got a hungry husband to feed and send back on the road to protect the fine citizens of Marshfield and beyond. It looks like you're in good hands here. Ms. England, please call if you need me, OK?"

"OK. Thank you again." After a quick hug Dianne walked Pam to the door. She didn't close her front door until she saw her drive away.

"She's your boss teacher lady?" Mel asked.

"No, she's an angel. That's what she is."

Mel knew what Dianne meant.

"Do you want to hold off talking about the great move-in until tomorrow, Dianne?"

"No. It's OK. When you're finished at the diner tomorrow,

come on over," Dianne said with a forced smile. "Ken and I will start preparing the room for you in the morning. There are too many boxes in there now. And you will need some window curtains. Do you want to use my childhood bed?"

"Sure! Thanks to Cindy, it's unearthed. Can you go through the boxes before I come tomorrow?"

"Um maybe?" Dianne hesitated to commit.

"I guess there's no time like the present." Mel plopped a box in Dianne's hands before she could protest.

"Don't worry, only go through this one. It will get you primed for tomorrow's task and take your mind off your, I guess I'll call it...situation."

After looking through five stacked boxes, the women looked around at the mess they made. Paper, souvenirs, and unidentified items were strewn across the floor and into the hall.

"I think they recycle here. Mel, will you help me flatten the newspaper and boxes? We'll put the newspaper in this box." Dianne placed the box immediately outside the room's door and looked around at all her treasures, some of which she remembered from childhood.

"Mel, I like these things, but I don't think I need them. I may regret this, but I'm giving everything to charity. Let's carefully place them in a box, and I'll put it in the living room."

"Oh no! Are you sure?" Mel was incredulous. "Dianne, I have very little from childhood; sometimes, I wish I did. At some point, you might like something as well. Here, you like books. Keep these three books," Mel said, holding them in front of Dianne. "Do you remember reading them?"

"OK," Dianne said softly and fell silent, taking the books into her arms.

"Yes. I'll keep these books. I don't know if my grandparents or a babysitter read them to me, but I had a warm memory as I held them. Thank you, Mel. These will stay with me. After we clean up this mess, I'm ready to turn in for the night. What about you?"

"Oh yes. By now, I'm usually strumming on my guitar, trying to keep my eyes open."

"OK. We'll get everything we can done in 10 minutes, then leave the rest for tomorrow. Ready—Set—Go!" Mel shouted.

"Mel! I wasn't ready," Dianne shouted as she tried to keep up with Mel. The cleanup and chatter made the time pass quickly. As promised, Mel exited in about 10 minutes, leaving Dianne with empty boxes and thoughts about changes happening in her life.

Looking around at the disarray, she was tempted to continue working on the boxes. She had the energy, the curiosity, and the need not to overthink what happened at school. As she sorted, she caught a glimpse of herself in her mother's dresser mirror. Staring and contemplating the changes swirling around her as she stroked her lengthy hair, she thought about when one of the children became obsessed with her hair and constantly pulled at it. Another time, her hair became stuck in a backpack zipper. Tying it back was only a temporary solution, with her ties consistently slipping out. For the first time in many years, she thought about cutting it.

Returning to exploring boxes, she fantasized about various short hairstyles. Without thinking much further, she soon fell asleep on her childhood bed among papers and a few mementos.

Stressful dreams pierced Dianne's uneasy sleep. In her dream, she was bald, and college classmates were shooting her with strange water guns as she walked the stage to receive her diploma.

"Dianne! Dianne! It's Ken! Are you OK?" Ken's muffled voice awakened Dianne.

Pushing herself upright, she staggered to the front door. Using the door frame for support, she paused for a breath to awaken herself. She opened the front door. Squinting, she recognized Ken.

"I've been knocking for a while. Were you up late?"

"Um, maybe," she answered, fighting off a yawn.

"You still have your work clothes on. You sleep in those?"

Ken was worried. Even during her mother's demise and death, he did not see Dianne in such disarray.

"What's going on? Oh, what is all this? Did you stay up all night working on the room for Mel? No wonder you didn't give me the third degree before opening the door."

Ken placed his hands on Dianne's arms as though to steady her.

"Yes. I stayed up very late. I almost finished. I had weird dreams."

"Dianne! This isn't like you!"

"I know." Dianne instantly started crying, as she had the day before. She told Ken what had happened as soon as she could compose herself.

"Oh I'm so sorry." Ken hugged Dianne in a fatherly way, which made her feel safe.

"It's going to be OK, dear one. You have a new family to support you. We seem like friends now, but I promised your mother I would do what I could for you and protect you."

"Thank you so much, Ken. I should go in and wash."

"That's a Good idea. I'll be the gracious host this morning. I hope you have coffee because I have donuts. Oh shit, I left them on the porch!"

Ken rushed to the front porch to retrieve the treats. "They're fine, so no healthy oatmeal today—just donuts!"

Dianne finished showering and dressing in fresh clothes, the coffee was made, and Ken was in the middle of his first donut.

"Sorry, I couldn't wait for you. Pour yourself some coffee and tell me what's on your mind."

"I don't know what else to do. I'm going to get my diploma. I will finish what is required of me. End of problem." Despite her proclamation, Dianne remained bothered by what had happened and was now worried by the possibility of cutting her prized hair.

Putting worry aside, Dianne succumbed to a Boston Cream donut, the perfect complement to Ken's strong coffee and an elixir to her worries.

"Let me guess," she said, staring at Ken with a comical, wide-eyed look. "This is Army coffee?"

"Yes, I know you like it. It wakes you up good." Ken smiled. "Let's continue with the room."

Dianne updated Ken on Mel's visit the night before as they continued sorting through the boxes and miscellaneous items left in.

"Everything is finished except for some dusting and floor polishing. You might ask Betty if they have a dresser and some drapes," Ken observed. I have an idea. You finish here, and I'll meet you at the truck stop for lunch. You can ask them if they have extra furniture, curtains, or whatever you need. I must run errands on my way there. I'm still a softie, so it will be my treat."

"Thank you, Ken. OK. I'll see you after their lunch crowd. Ya think 1:00 is good?"

"Yes. See you then."

"Ken! It's about time you got here!" Dianne called from the diner's far booth. "I asked earlier about furniture. Mel is taking the dresser from her room, and Betty gave us a set of curtains."

"Well, Ms. Fast Lady, it's good to see you have recovered. Have you ordered lunch?"

"Only a salad. I think I've had enough sweets to last a while." Dianne smiled at Mel sitting across from her.

"Mel, are you riding with Dianne and me or driving yourself?"

"Ken, we can't fit much into either of your cars. Mom and Dad are letting me use the van," Mel replied, craning her neck toward Ken.

"Oh, right. Let me finish a burger, and I'll get to work helping you and Dianne."

"Well, I've never done restaurant work, but I'm certainly not going to be the only one sitting around. I'll help clean up. Mel, show me what to do," Dianne said as the two stood, leaving the booth to Ken.

"I'll put you to work stacking dishes and putting them away. Hard work is good therapy for any sadness," Mel ordered with a smile.

The others cleaned the diner as Ken surrendered his plate and munched on his burger over waxed paper. With the diner perfectly clean, the group loaded the diner's business van, along with Dianne's and Ken's cars.

"Ok, You three go over and have some fun unloading. Betty and I will stay here and mind the shop. We'll be here when you decide most of this stuff won't fit," JR instructed with a chuckle as the last item found its place in the diner's van.

After arriving at Dianne's home, unloading went easy for the trio. Betty's curtains fit the window perfectly. Mel hung a few items on her room walls, and just a few boxes couldn't be accommodated in Mel's new abode. Dianne invited Mel to place them in her mother's former bedroom until they figured something else out.

Weeks passed, and everything went smoothly for the women

and their new lives. Dianne purchased a computer and gave Mel a few introductory lessons. Mel loved working with the computer and seemed to learn more every hour. Dianne learned the guitar a bit slower, but she was getting the hang of it, thanks to Mel playing along.

"Oh my god! What did you do? Your hair! It's gone! No one will recognize you!" Mel couldn't believe what she saw when Dianne entered the house after visiting her hairdresser.

"I figured that working with the children and possibly animals, long hair would start to be a problem, so I cut it. Do you like the style? It's just a simple bob.

Mel liked it but admitted to Dianne that she looked very different. Her reception by fellow teachers was similar. One of her students cried about it yet couldn't stop touching it. Pam assured Dianne that after becoming used to her new look, the student would be less likely to touch her hair.

As the school year finished, students became more excited about attending their summer camps than Dianne's hair or any remaining lessons. Fellow classroom teachers, thankful to have a separate set of hands to help calm students, praised Dianne for her work. In contrast, the classroom energy helped to calm Dianne's anxiety about her upcoming graduation.

Dianne tried her best to prepare for graduation day. Her cap, gown, dress, and shoes were in perfect shape, ready days ahead. However, she could not prepare for a flood of emotion as she buffed her shoes one more time. She sat motionless on the floor alongside her bed. Her idle thoughts yanked her back to when she sat on the floor against her mother's bed days before she died. Possibly a plastic bag with socks sliding off the bed triggered her memories. At first, she cried lightly, then fully as though her mother had just passed.

"Oh my god! Did you fall? Mel said as she rushed into Dianne's room. "What's wrong? What can I do? Are you hurt?" Mel could not understand the emotion she was witnessing.

Dianne patted the floor next to her, motioning for Mel to sit beside her.

"What's wrong?" Mel pleaded.

"I'm just sad. I got to thinking about mom. I know she wanted me to graduate. But I want her to be here," Dianne said between sobs.

"I can understand that feeling a little. I wish my mother could have seen me graduate from high school. I'm lucky that Betty and JR were there. We don't know. Perhaps our mothers are still with us."

"True Mel. We can only hope."

Without her parents present, Dianne settled for wearing a necklace her mother cherished. As she pulled the gold chain with a star pendant set with a small diamond from her mother's jewelry box, she saw her father's watch nestled into the bottom along with a few bracelets. Oddly, the watch was set at the time her graduation ceremony would begin. *I guess Dad wants to come too,* she thought, slipping his watch onto her wrist.

"Mom and Dad just drove up with Ken! Are you ready?" Mel called out, hoping Dianne wasn't busy putting every hair in place and perfecting makeup.

"Ready!" Dianne called out, entering the living room and startling Mel.

"Ready on time! I'm impressed!" Mel exclaimed as she stepped toward the door and motioned for Dianne to exit the home. "Madam graduate, after you!"

JR took Dianne's pristine robe and hung it securely on the car's garment hook. "Sorry you ladies have to cozy up with Ken on the second row," he apologized.

"I'll be the monkey in the middle," Mel volunteered.

The trip to Springfield was quick with excited chatter among the passengers. Each congratulated Dianne and all talked about what the future might hold for her, and one another.

"Here, I'll leave you off and park the car. Listen for us screaming in the audience," JR said with a smile pulling into an area where robed young people had gathered.

"Yes, this is good. Thank you everyone. I'll see you after the ceremony." Dianne said, exiting the car and waving to friends from her class.

The speeches and ceremony seemed long at times, but when it was over and time to present diplomas, Dianne wanted the moment to last. As she left the stage, she knew she would trade in her mock diploma for a piece of blank paper and return to the reality of the work left to complete.

After Dianne's fake diploma was replaced, she stared at the blank paper in her envelope. She explained it to a classmate she hadn't met but was clearly staring at the paper.

"OK, everyone! We have a paper here with nothing on it," the woman yelled over the crowd. With barely a breath between sentences, the bold woman explained why the paper was blank to the hushed mass of happy graduates.

"I think we all need to sign it and cheer her on to finish her internship so she can have a class of her own!"

Before Dianne could object, pens were out, and the paper was passed around.

Dianne approached the instigator. "This is very nice of you. I was feeling bad about not having the real thing. I'm sorry I don't know your name."

"Not important," she snapped and smiled.

"Buy why?" Dianne asked.

"Ya see, I am, or rather was... a bit of a partier. Dr. Lamberth and I had a conversation one day. She called it an informal conversation so I wouldn't get it on my record. She said if I don't have credits by the end of my 5th year, they will give me a blank diploma, and I will get the real thing when I take and pass all my courses. I was scheduled to be at least close enough. At the same time, my parents told me there are no more funds as of June this year. I shifted into gear and dropped party time altogether. When I saw your blank paper, I felt like crap. My contact information is on the paper. Reach out and let me know how you're doing, OK?"

"Thank you, mystery woman. I will. All the best to you."

The women sealed the promise with a hug and a hearty "Good luck!" exchanged between them.

"By the way, I'm working for a year, and then I plan to go on for my master's degree that I will pay for, not my parents," the mystery woman proclaimed before disappearing into the crowd.

CHAPTER 20

Life Goes On

Life with Mel and Dianne was going smoothly for the "roomies." Chores were shared amicably, and there was a healthy exchange of give-and-take. They had similar views on cleanliness, and although a challenge, they shared the one bathroom well. The women became closer as days passed.

Mel brought a steady supply of good food into the home, enough for Dianne to "brown bag" into school. They rarely shopped for groceries, which helped save time and money.

Dianne's internship, employment, and volunteering at the animal park went well, too. Although an adjustment, she gained a special dividend of education about being an employee: paying personal taxes, having household expenses, and generally, all the adult things she had only previously glimpsed.

"Mel, life's kind of weird," Dianne remarked, emptying a spoonful of sugar into her coffee cup and watching it swirl with her spoon. "So many people hold secrets, not necessarily bad ones, just stuff unknown to most folks. You know what I mean?"

"Yes, life is weird with secrets," Mel responded, looking contemplative, trying to figure out what Dianne was talking about. The women continued chatting about secrets while sipping their coffee, enjoying one of the few mornings they had time to linger, contemplate, and rest.

The two let the conversation wane before Dianne refilled her cup. "Care for a warm-up?" She asked Mel.

"Please."

"I wonder how Pastor Dawn is doing this beautiful Sunday in upstate New York," Dianne said as she placed the now empty coffee carafe on the kitchen counter. "Surely, she must miss it around here," Dianne sighed. "It's been a couple of months since she left. No one's heard a word from her. And Cindy is getting ready to leave. Did you hear she's returning to the University of Alabama to finish her degree in social work?"

Mel thought for a moment. "Yes, I did hear that. You may have told me. I think she'll do well. Humph, a couple of months ago I might have said that she'll do good. You're a bad influence on me, Dianne."

"No, girlfriend, I'm a good influence on you. Ms. Mel you're a talented musician and computer genius. I've been reading some of your stuff on the computer. You are starting to write with skill. Are you feeling more comfortable with the keyboard?" Dianne stopped for a sip of coffee. "And grammar?" she added. "Do you feel ready for the computer class?"

"Yeah, I feel ready," Mel said, swirling her coffee. "Oh, speaking of secrets, I had an interesting conversation with Mom after I moved in here." Mel started to share with Dianne before now, but the words hadn't formed.

Mel sighed and took a deep breath.

"Mom told me more about my birth mother and how I came to be adopted," Mel said, laying her spoon on a napkin and then flipping it over several times. She decided to continue, albeit haltingly.

"I remember hanging around the diner a lot before any adoption talk. As I think you know, my father died. I don't remember how. For that matter, I don't remember him much at all. I was eight or nine. I forget. I think I told you about my mother becoming distant after his death. She arranged with Betty and JR that I stay with them while she went to St. Louis to get her life together. It turns out she was an in-patient at a hospital for a week. Mom, Betty, that is, said my birth mother tried hard to get herself right. That's when she visited me occasionally. During one of those visits, she signed over my permanent custody. She also sold her property to JR and Betty. Betty said that with only $10,000, she started a new life, rented an apartment, got a job, and was doing well. However, not too long after that, she killed herself with pills! I don't understand, especially when things were going well for her. I don't know why I'm not able to cry about it. I do know that I thank the universe daily for JR and Betty."

"And here I am, crying about the loss of my mother constantly. I'm so sorry!" Dianne reached for Mel's hand. "Mel, if you ever feel the need, please cry in this house anytime you feel like it. It's your home, too, and it's OK! A life was lost. She loved you enough to be sure you were cared for and protected you from her pain." Dianne looked directly at Mel.

"I have pictures from my early childhood," Mel continued, with a far-off gaze that discouraged direct conversation about her birth mother. "They're somewhere in the boxes stored in the other room. When it's time, will you look at them with me?"

"Of course I will," Dianne said, fighting back tears. Suddenly, she jumped to her feet. "I have Girl Scout cookies! They're good for breakfast and for chatting!"

Both women laughed, then dug into a frozen box of Do-Si-Dos. The challenging chewing brought them to laughter, just as it did with Dianne and Dawn several months ago.

"Dianne, I love you. Thank you so much."

"Likewise, Mel, likewise. Do you want to rustle around in one of your boxes?"

"Thanks, but I can't yet. Those boxes have been closed for years. I want to keep it that way." Mel popped another cookie into her mouth. The women stared at one another, transfixed, while each tried to clear the last remnants of their treats. Both sipped final drops of coffee without breaking their mutual gaze.

Dianne gently stroked Mel's face. "I'm sorry your childhood experience was so...so...heck, I don't know what," she whispered.

"No need to say anything," Mel said while transfixed on Dianne and still processing her last cookie.

Mel continued. "I was loved. That's what's important. And I feel love now. I love you, but I'm unsure what that means between us. I feel heat, but I...I don't want to make this moment something it isn't."

"OK then. Just shut up," Dianne said with authority. She stood, taking Mel's hand to encourage her to stand. Without breaking her gaze, she gently moved closer to place her hands alongside Mel's face. Slowly and with delicate passion, Dianne's lips gently met Mel's. Both were suspended in time as the world melted away. Without a word, Dianne gave Mel a heightened expression of their friendship.

Dianne's breath upon her cheeks stoked a fire within Mel. She couldn't explain herself and didn't attempt to do so. She didn't label it, she just wanted more of it.

"I hope you don't mind," Dianne whispered. "I had to let myself go. And you, Mel, so tough, yet so innocent. I want to be closer. Please tell me I didn't overstep."

"I love peanut butter cookies," Mel whispered, kissing Dianne's lips, cheeks, and neck.

"This...this is so unexpected. I feel I should have more control," Dianne apologized.

"Yeah, me too," Mel responded in a voice slightly above a whisper. Mel's smile showed she couldn't care less about self-control.

"I should have a better sense of romance," Mel confessed in a whisper as she breathed hot on the caved area where Dianne's neck and shoulder met. I don't know what I'm doing, roomie. Mel could only breathe and admire every curve she viewed up close, so personal, beautiful, and soft.

"Oh hell, girl!" Mel expressed in her normal voice. "I can't help myself. You want to get naked and feel each other up?"

"Roomie, you need to polish that a bit," Dianne said with a slight chuckle, slightly above a whisper.

"Follow me," Dianne said, gently leading Mel.

"You're such a beautiful woman. May I touch your curves?" Dianne said, stepping back from Mel.

"Please!" Mel whispered, lowering her hands to Dianne's hips. "Should I stop?"

"Please don't. It's time for both of us to get naked and feel each other up, as you call it." Dianne said, smiling.

After each satisfied their impulses and desires, they fell asleep in each other's arms. Their bodies glistened, and the room was filled with the lingering scent of their shared passion.

"Mel, it's getting close to noon. Don't you have to take food to the animals?"

"Oh, heck, yeah. I'll tell Dad I lost track of time, and I'm on my way."

Dianne chuckled. "Girl...you had better take a good shower first and wash your hair too."

Mel looked back at Dianne. "Yes. I guess I had better."

Mel darted to the bathroom, her mind racing. She couldn't

believe the time. As the warm water cascaded over her, she mentally rehearsed her excuse.

"I'd go with you, but then you would be later than you already are. And I'm sure they'll know what delayed you." Dianne shouted.

Mel moved with lightning speed to dress and head out.

"At least you're only about 20 minutes late," Dianne shouted as Mel exited.

"Well, hey Mel! Traffic bad on your way in? Those church people can cause quite a traffic jam on a Sunday morning. Employees nowadays! No respect for time." JR shook his head smiling and hugged Mel.

As JR teased her, Mel felt a pang of guilt mixed with the warmth of his embrace. She wasn't just late; she was torn between the life she was building and the one she'd left behind.

"So how are things going over in town?" JR said as he continued inventory of restaurant spices.

Flustered, Mel struggled to respond. "Umm, fine, Dad. Sorry, I ran late. You know, I miss it here, but I'm OK with living on my own...somewhat, anyway," Mel said while pulling old stock from the restaurant refrigerator.

"You and Dianne OK? No fights about the bathroom or anything? I see your hair is still wet," JR said starting to post the upcoming week's specials.

"No, no fights. No problems. But having more than one bath in that house would be nice. Dianne had to get into the bathroom, and I didn't have time to dry my hair."

"Well, that's how they built them back then," JR said without further commenting on Mel's hair.

"You going back, um, home...to your new home right away after the animal park? You want to stay for a few minutes to catch up with each other? Mom made some delicious apple cobbler."

"Dad, are you missing me?"

"I miss you too," Betty said, setting a cobbler-filled pan on the counter.

"Oh, so that's what I smell! I could jump into that right now!"

"Don't worry, dear; I made a small pan for you to share with Dianne." Betty smiled while covering the piping hot pan of sweetness.

"I can't wait until fall when we'll have fresh apples to make cobbler. Duane will bring us a bunch of apples when he makes a run from Pennsylvania. I hope he's able to do that. Those long-haul fellows can never predict their routes, it seems."

Mel recognized her parents' chatter as small talk and sensed they wanted her to return after delivering to the animal park.

"Mom, Dad? I think I'll stop by after feeding the animals if you don't mind. I'll have a sandwich then and take the cobbler with me."

"Wonderful! We'll look forward to seeing you in about an hour!" JR seemed giddy when he heard Mel would be returning.

Mel left to make the delivery before returning to the diner in almost record time.

"I wondered if you were going to make an excuse and head on to your new home," JR said, welcoming Mel back. "I thought we might sit out on the patio, but it looks like we might get rain."

The kitchen felt cozy and warm, the smell of apple cobbler still lingering in the air as JR guided Mel to her old spot at the table. Outside, the sky had darkened, hinting at the rain that might soon patter against the windows.

"Your Mom packed up goodies you can take to your new home." JR motioned toward an almost overflowing bag of groceries beside the promised cobbler.

"Hon, I think your dad is stumbling around. I've got something to show you," Betty said, seeming nervous. Betty placed three brochures in front of Mel.

"We thought about doing this in a couple of years, but things are changing around here, and we may do it sooner than planned."

"What? What is this?" Mel couldn't believe what she saw laid out on the table.

Mel stared at the brochures, her mind spinning. She'd always assumed the truck stop would be a constant, a place she could return to whenever needed. The thought of it changing hands, of her parents living on the road, left her feeling unmoored as if the ground beneath her feet was shifting.

"We're thinking about getting this 32-foot Airstream. Gotta get a good truck first," JR said, pointing to a deluxe travel trailer.

"You see, I've promised your mother for years that we would travel and finally see the country. We might even see the Florida Gulf Coast that Dianne talks about."

"Well, I'm in shock! But I'm happy for you both. I know you've worked so hard here. Is that why you were dreaming about me taking over this place, Mom?"

"Yes, but I didn't want to force it on you." Betty looked down, not knowing what to say next.

As Betty talked about selling the property, Mel noticed the slight tremor in her mother's voice. This wasn't just an adventure for them, it was a leap into the unknown of a totally different life.

"And let me stress this is totally between us. As of last evening, things started to change. We were offered an excellent price for this property. Before releasing the property, we'll have time to plan, pack up, sell furniture, or do whatever we want. The buyer— a corporation—will disburse cash in chunks until we sign everything over. That smart Fred McCall and some of his partners are reviewing everything to see if it will benefit us. Meanwhile, I'll do all the finances and planning, and JR will continue to serve customers. You do understand the importance of keeping this to yourself, right?"

"Oh, yes, Mom. So many things can change in an instant. Is it OK if I tell Dianne? I totally trust her."

"Yes. Make sure she doesn't utter a word. That could ruin a lot. At this point, Ken knows, and John knows."

"Texaco John?"

"That's the one!" Betty said, raising her eyebrows in a way that told Mel, *What other John do we know?*

Mel turned her excitement toward her plate. "Wow! I'm almost choking on my sandwich here. I didn't realize how hungry I was!"

"As we go on, we'll talk more about your plans, college, a job, whatever. We won't abandon you, OK?"

"I didn't even think that," Mel said after gulping nearly a full glass of water.

The remaining part of the family visit was spent discussing travel plans, the new trailer and truck, and the changes to the diner and Marshfield as a whole. Whatever daylight could be seen through the parting clouds started to fade as the trio said goodbye.

Mel barely remembered her drive home, with all that was

swimming in her mind, the fantastic morning she'd had with Dianne and now, a new life facing her.

"Oh, goodness! What do you have there?" As she approached the front steps, Dianne lifted the bag and the cobbler pan from Mel's hands.

"I kept watching for you all afternoon. You were gone a long time. I assumed you were with your parents and I see you indeed were. That cobbler smells great! Baked this morning?"

"Yes, you should have smelled it coming out of the oven! Mind if I give you another kiss, Dianne? I promise it won't take as long as this morning. I've got so much to tell you," Mel said as she placed the cobbler on the stove top, then gave her roomie a kiss.

"So, what's up, Mel? I figured you'd be ready for some dinner, so I made a quiche. It's my first ever! I hope it came out OK." Mel glanced up and down at Dianne's ruffled apron and smiled.

"You look great!" she said, almost letting herself get distracted. "Betty packed some melon slices and other food. Oh! Have I got news!" Mel immediately jumped into her thoughts.

"OK, spill it, girl!" Dianne looked directly at Mel, interrupting their dinner preparation.

"I can only have a small piece. I overate at Mom and Dad's."

While barely nibbling at her dinner, Mel relayed the entire story to Dianne, who didn't know what to think or say about the news.

"Umm, have you ever thought that whenever there's an important conversation, people eat something?" Dianne said, avoiding an actual comment.

"Yeah, I guess that's right. I can understand that, with Mom and Dad running the diner, but we have also done that. We need to change our ways a bit before we get fat."

Mel couldn't say much more. She was still shocked, and Dianne had yet to process the news.

"We can't do too much about your parents' plans." Dianne opened the conversation. "When do you think they'll shut things down?"

"Possibly next spring, less than a year, at any rate."

"Where will you work then?"

"There's bound to be someone who needs a bookkeeper who

can fix some mean grub. Perhaps I'll be in school by then. I need to make up my mind."

"I hope you're still living here, and we can repeat this morning occasionally." Dianne interrupted Mel's thoughts with her wish.

"Oh yes, that would be nice!" Mel showed her excitement with an impromptu dance step that resembled a band drum major on too much caffeine.

"Heck! I hope I'm still living here too! I don't know what will happen if I don't have a job."

"Mel, would you say we're friends for life and lovers for as long as it's good for us?"

"Yes, I like that."

"As near as I can tell, unless you make other plans, you have a place here. At some point, though, we may have to build another bathroom somehow," Dianne said, taking Mel's hand in hers. "Oh, and if you're later than expected, please call. I was a bit concerned."

"OK," Mel replied sweetly, blowing Dianne a kiss.

Dianne responded by gently kissing Mel on the forehead. "I look forward to what comes next," she half whispered.

"Oh! I can't wait to finish this conversation," Mel said.

CHAPTER 21

Marvels

Ms. Kelly waited for this day at MegaMart when Wendy would no longer be her employee. There would no longer be strife between department managers. There would no longer be arguments to settle. If it were up to her, Ms. Kelly would have walked her out months ago when it was evident that Wendy was the problem behind many employee-to-employee issues. Being in retail for most of her life, Ms. Kelly knew there would always be a "Wendy," but she was tired of this Wendy. Wendy had excelled in being a problem employee. General Manager Michael D. Glossen did not want to fire her for unknown reasons. Hopefully, today he will follow through.

"Wendy, to the front, please. Wendy to the front for a pickup," Ms. Kelly blared her request over the store's speaker. After waiting a few minutes, she repeated her request: "Wendy, to the front, please. Meet Mr. Glossen at the front."

"Oh hey, Ms. Kelly. I was setting up a new display. You said Mr. Glossen needed me?" Wendy was a little out of breath.

"Yes, he's on his way in. Clean and tidy what you have back there, and be up here at 6:00, about ten minutes from now."

Ms. Kelly suspected Michael D. Glossen would wear his General Manager hat and walk Wendy out. She did not want her to leave a mess for others in the store to clean up, least of all herself.

General Manager Glossen and problem worker Wendy were punctual.

"Hello Wendy, you doing a good job back there?" Michael smiled at the young clerk. "Yes, sir, I am." Wendy ranted about her display capabilities and how much she loved the store.

During Wendy's tainted dissertation, Ms. Kelly couldn't stand hearing the falsehoods, so she stepped over to one of the registers clearly out of earshot and started helping the other cashiers process customers through the line. She was afraid that, again, Mr. Glossen would not fire Wendy.

"Well, Ms. Wendy, do you like organizing things, talking to customers, and kinda taking charge of things?"

"Yes, sir, you know I do!" Wendy responded energetically.

"Well, a good friend of mine lost his office manager recently, and I think you might like that kind of thing. You get to sit down, answer phones, greet people, and be in charge. The pay would be about twenty cents more an hour than you're paid here. You think you'd like that job?"

"Yes, it sounds great! How do I interview? Wouldn't you miss me here?"

"Things would be a lot different here without you, but Ms. Kelly can handle it. Do you know the Scott Hickman car dealership on the way to Springfield? He needs someone right away. He's willing to hire you just on my recommendation. I don't do this for everyone, you know."

"But don't I need to give two weeks' notice here?"

"You're a special case. I'd let you go right now if you want to quit."

Wendy thought for a moment. *Well, that car place is a little closer to my home. I could see myself working there.*

Glossen pushed. "So, knowing about this good job...are you quitting? Don't worry about us now. I'm just interested in helping you and my friend Scotty. I already told him about you. Go on down and see him tomorrow morning at about ten, ready to work. Got that? Here's the information."

Michael handed Wendy a note with Scott Hickman's name and contact information.

"I'll stop in later this week to see how you're doing. You care if I do that?" Michael gently touched Wendy's arm.

"Yes. I'd like that. OK then. I quit!"

"This is good. I know you'll be happy. Scribble out your quitting note here at the desk, and I'll walk with you to the lockers to make sure no one gives you a hard time," Michael said. His real motivation was to see Wendy clock out and to give everyone the impression that she was fired.

"Mr. Glossen, everyone here might think you're firing me."

"Oh no! We can't think that! I'll tell everyone that you are quitting to go to another job. Does that help you any?"

"Umm, yes. You want me to clock out?"

"Yes, please. I'll pay you for the rest of your shift, but to keep things legal, you need to clock out."

"OK. Thank you so much for your help, Mr. Glossen. I'll see you down at the car lot." Michael walked Wendy from the store to her car, shook her hand, said goodbye, and watched her leave the parking lot.

"Ms. Kelly, please place this note of resignation in Wendy's folder," Michael said, handing her Wendy's note as he entered the store.

"I need to make some phone calls. Can you stay a few minutes while I finish up?"

"Yes," Ms. Kelly said agreeably. "Let me know when you're done."

"Hey Scotty! I got something good for you!" Michael said, barely letting the man say hello when he picked up the phone. "A lady here at the store just quit. She's a good lady, likes organizing things, and isn't bad looking! I think you need her to straighten up the mess Roberts left."

"Under normal circumstances, Glossen, I'd tell you to go to hell, but I probably can use her. You say she's pretty?"

"Yes, you'll like her. Her name is Wendy. She'll come see you at ten in the morning."

"Good. I look forward to it. Gotta go. Bye."

"Bye."

"OK, Ms. Kelly, you can take off," Michael called out.

Ms. Kelly walked toward Michael and whispered.

"How did you get her to quit? We might escape a hassle with unemployment insurance, you know."

"Yes, I know. Good night, Ms. Kelly," Michael said with a smile.

"Oh hey, Dianne, why don't you come with me? Friends from the animal park and I are getting together to bullshit and play music, you wouldn't believe where. Come on, you never seem to go out on Saturdays!" Mel pleaded with Dianne.

"Well, we're finished with the school year, and next week, summer school starts. And I'm working on grants for the park," Dianne responded looking up from her book.

"Look, dear friend. It's OK to go out and have fun! You're not still feeling bad about your mother's death, are you?"

"Sometimes I think about it, and I miss her so much. Pastor Dawn said I may always miss her, but the pain gets easier. Generally, I'm moving forward. So where do you have these shindigs?"

"Michael's house."

"That's a complete and hard NO! N period! O period! NO!" Dianne roared, slapping her book closed.

"Wow! I didn't know you had a voice like that. OK, you'll pass this time," Mel smiled as Dianne glared at her tease.

"How did you talk Michael into that?"

"Jill did. She told Michael he needed to work on Saturday nights or go to the drag races with me so she could use his house to party in."

"Mel, does she have something over him that he doesn't want to be broadcast? I don't picture Michael doing that from kindness," Dianne said.

"Neither do I, but I don't ask questions, and neither does anyone else. We'll probably get tired after a while, but it's our party place for now. You should hear his dog, Brandy, sing along with us. She's quite a talent!"

"I'm sure she loves the attention." Dianne stood to fold the towels she left on the sofa earlier.

Mel slipped behind her for a sneak embrace, a kiss on the cheek, and a quick caress on her breast.

"We all love attention, my very special and very dear friend," Mel whispered in Dianne's ear.

"If you're going to start something, be ready to finish it, lady," Dianne admonished folding the last towel.

"Perhaps tomorrow morning I will, little Miss Bookworm. We both need to be relaxed for the computer class next week."

"Go, Mel. Goodbye. Have fun!"

"Yep! More fun than drag races!" Mel quipped as she grabbed her guitar and took off to the van.

"Mel, how is it going...being on your own?" Betty asked as she pushed the start button on the dishwasher.

"Mom, I love living with Dianne. However, she's always studying or some smart-girl thing. I hope college isn't this intense for everyone. I'm not sure I could hack it. She wouldn't even go out with me last Saturday."

"Wait! You say that and always stick your nose into the financial scene. Talk about intense!" Betty smiled at her daughter. "I guess it's what she must do to keep her mind off losing her mother. Did you go over to Michael's?"

"Yeah, we all had a great time. I'm unsure why I do what I do with financial stuff, Mom."

"Me neither. So, you say you are still going to Michael's with a group from the park? I can't see any good coming from that."

"He's not home, you know. He decided to work on Saturday nights, and Jill asked if we could all use his place. He said yes."

"From my point of view, it doesn't feel right," Betty said, shaking her head and staring straight at Mel. Betty's brow furrowed as she wiped her hands on a dish towel. She trusted Mel, but something about this group—about the freedom they seemed to have at Michael's—unsettled her. She didn't want to come across as overbearing, but her mother's intuition was rarely wrong.

"OK, Mom, I'll keep eyes, ears, and feelings open if something goes wrong. Meanwhile, you know we started the computer class, right?"

"Yes! How's that going?"

"Thanks to my intense roomie, I can handle the keyboard. These first two weeks have been OK. I struggle a little, but mostly it's been OK. Of course, smarty-pants roomie helps me a lot." Mel smiled at her attempt at a joke.

As Mel reassured her mother, a small voice whispered in the back of her mind that maybe, just maybe, Betty was right to be concerned. But she pushed the thought aside, focusing instead on convincing Dianne to join in the fun.

"I wish she would go with me over to Michael's for our

Saturday night parties. I think she'd have fun."

"Perhaps she's not only a smarty-pants, but she's also a smarty-brain," Betty shot back.

"Don't worry, Mom. I'll get her there. I know she'll have fun."

The roomies' lives continued to go smoothly, both domestically and at work. The computer class finished with both women brandishing a certificate of completion and an entry-level certification that they thought would bolster their resumes. Dianne had come to peace with her diploma challenge.

She was sad to say goodbye to her regular class but embraced the summer school classes. Often, she taught English to an entire classroom, which she liked the most of her varied experiences.

Mr. Richards did not formally meet with Dianne when she completed her 90 hours. Instead, he brought the students and faculty cupcakes to celebrate her internship completion. She was especially moved when Pam came to the school for the celebration and presented her with an oversized card with all the students' signatures, both from her and the summer school classes. Not long after the celebration, Dianne's diploma arrived in the mail.

Betty and JR celebrated the new college graduate's degree with a dinner at their home. The entire family attended—JR, Betty, Mel, Ken, and Texaco John. They bemoaned not having Pastor Dawn or Cindy there since they'd gone off to their new lives. They saluted Katrina, Dianne's chief motivator and life mentor.

"I still think your haircut is really cute! I bet everyone at the Saturday night parties would swoon over you!" Mel couldn't help herself with continuous and aggravating invitations to Dianne, even weaving her pleas into compliments.

"Mel, you're a pain in the ass!" Dianne did not hesitate to respond to Mel when she yet again asked her to go the party at Michael's.

"The group has gotten large. There are at least 20 of us who go. Sometimes, we play music on the eight-track. Sometimes, I sing and play. We've even built a bonfire outside. Jill said Michael wasn't pleased about that. We always stocked his refrigerator, so he wasn't too mad."

"Can't you sing and play here, at this house?"

"No. Twenty people can't fit in our house. And I don't want people snooping around here."

"Actually, neither do I. Don't look at me with your sad puppy dog look!"

Mel started whining like a puppy to tease Dianne, then started to lick her arm.

"Eww, stop that! You're not a dog! I'm making a deal with you. If I go just once, do you promise never to ask me again?"

"I promise!"

"Nothing crossed? Good heavens! I'm reverting to my student's age."

"Aww, schoolteacher, you'll have so much fun! It will be a night to remember!"

"Yeah, the night I was bonkers."

"Hi, Wendy. It's good to see you," Ms. Kelly lied. "How is your new job at the car lot going?"

"Well, I'm here to talk to you about that. A few days ago, we essentially got raided, locked out, or whatever you want to call it. I never got to see Mr. Hickman's paperwork, so I never knew what he was up to. A lawman in a suit showed up and said Hickman had a couple of stolen cars and didn't pay taxes. Any chance I can work here again?"

"Let me get an application for you. Unfortunately, everything is filled, but I can keep your application on file," Ms. Kelly responded, knowing there was no way she would rehire Wendy.

"Thank you. I really appreciate it. I can't wait to get back there dressing those mannequins again."

"Don't you worry. Those mannequins aren't going anywhere," was all Ms. Kelly could say.

"Bye, Ms. Kelly! Hope to see you soon!"

Ms. Kelly only waved.

"Look! See? I told you you'd enjoy it!" Mel was delighted to finally convince Dianne to go to Michael's for a Saturday night gathering. They both enjoyed riding together to the party and, on the return trip, talked about the various people they'd met.

"Mel, that is a weird place," Dianne shared her observations.

He has no family pictures around, only pictures of animals. Even some of the artwork wasn't much, only animal paintings. The people were fun, but the place was creepy. Not everyone was from the park, right? That girl, Millie, is she a truck driver?"

"That's right. I talked to Millie a few weeks back and convinced her to come over and meet some locals. She wasn't as hard to convince as you were."

"Yeah, she can hop in her truck and move. I gotta live here."

"So, you game for next Saturday night?"

Dianne remained silent until the women were inside the home. After brewing a cup of tea, she addressed Mel.

"Look, you said that if I went with you one night, you would never ever ask me again."

"What's one little lie between best buddies and close roomies?"

"Mel, stop, OK?" Dianne had become irritated.

"OK! I don't want to make you mad. You'll throw me out on the street."

"That's right, I would," Dianne said as she smacked Mel's butt. Mel bent over and wiggled her backside toward Dianne.

"Smack me, baby, smack me!" she teased.

"Oh yes, I will!" Dianne took Mel's bait. The women's horseplay predictably turned into a night of lovemaking in Dianne's bed, still a new experience for Mel and a seldom-felt experience for Dianne.

"Who's Jennifer?" Mel asked when they both awoke.

"How do you know that name?"

"You called me Jennifer several times last night when you fell asleep."

"I'm sorry." Dianne seemed to search for the right words to explain Jennifer.

Dianne paused, her gaze drifting away from Mel as if searching the past for the right words. "She was my first real love," she began, her voice tinged with mixing fondness and pain. "I thought it was the real thing, but...I guess she didn't feel the same way. She graduated before me, and I missed her so much."

"Is she a teacher?"

"She might be. She didn't know what she wanted to do, so she majored in history. I don't know what that gets you. Last I heard, she returned to her home along the Mississippi, possibly Cape Girardeau. Our time together was short-lived, only a few months, but it was intense. I'm surprised we both passed our final exams."

"Wow! I guessed you were experienced, but now I know you are. You make love with such grace, and making love to you is beautiful."

"Thank you, Mel. I thought you had been down this road before as well. What's your experience?"

"I don't want to say who, but I was 'introduced' to this life by someone at the park. The fun part worked fine, but neither wanted a relationship."

"That's unusual. Lesbians tend to stick to one another like glue, and the rest of the world goes away," Dianne said as she left the bed.

"It's Sunday! Don't you want to hang out here a bit?" Mel pleaded, not wanting to say anything more about her earlier experience.

"Mel, you're such a romantic." Dianne backtracked and kissed Mel on the forehead.

"Hanging out here is nice, but I want to get out and do something," Dianne said with anticipation. "What do you think about going canoeing today? Can you deliver the animal feed later or earlier? Have you ever paddled a canoe?"

"Sure, let's go canoeing. I've been several times. If you don't know a rental place, I do. I'll call Mom and Dad to let them know I'll be late today. Do you think we can do all this by four or five?"

"I'd say five! Let me get a map from Mom's room, or rather, my office." Dianne hesitated for a moment, then continued to the other room.

"Found it! Dianne unfolded a Missouri rivers map on the bed to show Mel the various canoeing areas. Here's a place! Two Rivers! We can drive down there with some gear and sandwiches to see what they have. If we find a place to rent canoes, then we do it. If not, we head home."

"Sandwiches? No time!" said Mel. "We'll stop and get some fried chicken."

"OK, we'll jump into shorts, grab some beach towels and swimsuits, and head to the rivers!"

A little after six, Dianne and Mel returned to the house.

"What a day!" Dianne said. "I'm so glad JR made the animal park run for you. I'm happy we didn't rush back and had so much fun. I don't know what our muscles will feel like tomorrow."

"I could barely keep up with you! You're quite a swimmer Ms. Bookworm, girly-girl turned nature woman! And girrrrlllllll! You can J-stroke that paddle! Let's plan to do this regularly! Ya know we gotta do something more than eat and make love." Mel said as she turned to Dianne with a gentle smile.

"I accept that compliment," Dianne said with a slight curtsy. "You're not so bad yourself!...no matter what you're doing," Dianne returned a smile with soft eyes toward Mel.

"I hope to enjoy many more rivers with you, my love." Dianne couldn't help herself. She had to hug Mel and stroke her hair. "OK, I gotta control myself," Dianne said, taking a deep breath, hoping to shake her desire. "I'm gonna take a shower and watch TV."

"Mind if I join you? Oh …" Mel smiled. "I mean in front of the TV."

"Yes. I figured that's what you meant," Dianne chuckled.

Seated comfortably on the sofa, both ladies nodded off in less than an hour after their showers. Neither could remember what they had watched.

"Share my bed, roomie?" Dianne asked, poking Mel awake.

"Can't both fit in mine," Mel murmured, half asleep.

The two slept soundly until Mel's obtrusive alarm squawked.

While Dianne and Mel were canoeing, Ken rode with JR to the animal park. It was one of those times when Ken needed a confidant. They talked a little about their Army life, something they often did when no one else was around.

"I can't shake this feeling, JR," Ken said, running his hands along his thighs. "Mel and Dianne go over to Michael's place when he's not home. I sense trouble. I shared this with the shrink in St. Louis, and he agreed."

"I'd worry even more if he was home," Ken confessed. "After Dianne's last encounter with him, I don't trust that boy."

Ken further confided to JR that he stopped near Michael's house on his way back from Springfield on Saturday to stealthily observe the party.

"They didn't seem rowdy," he told JR, "… and only a little bit loud. From what I could see, Michael came in not ten minutes after the last person left. That whole arrangement is uncomfortable. I wish the girls would find something else to do on weekends."

"I agree," JR remarked. Then he fell silent as he remembered his first meeting with Michael and shared it with JR.

"When he first drove up to the truck stop, he was a sight to behold," JR shared. "At the time, I had known Michael for a few years. He had been odd since the first day he ate at our place. You know, he was driving that same car he traded in," JR smiled and gave Ken a quick side-eyed look.

"How long had he owned that car?" Ken asked as JR stopped the van in front of the side door to the truck stop. The men continued talking in the parked van.

JR looked puzzled as he gave Ken's question some thought. "About seven years since he was a senior in high school. It was in bad shape, but he kept fixing it. Each time, he was as proud as a peacock. Gotta hand it to the young man. He stuck with it. The first time he and Mel went to the races, I was as worried as any father would be. Like you, I followed them and watched from a distance. I don't think they knew they were being watched. Not long after that, I figured they were friends and would stay that way."

With a furrowed brow, JR gripped the steering wheel with both hands, his mind racing with worry about what Michael may be capable of. "Ken, I got a bad feeling," JR shared, fiddling with the keys he had pulled from the ignition. We need to convince the girls to do something else on Saturday."

"I'm with you. Let's talk more about this," Ken said lifting himself from the van. He closed the door a bit too solidly, seeming to express his anguish.

After settling into his car, Ken, as was his style, added a postscript to his conversation with JR. Parking beside him and blocking his path, he lowered his car's passenger window to call out.

"Hey buddy, you know about the gun that boy got?" Ken said to JR.

"Yep. He keeps it in the kitchen drawer next to the back door when he ain't toting it under his truck seat. That's a well-known secret, according to Mel."

Ken frowned. "I'm worried. That boy's unpredictable. He might still boil inside from Dianne giving him the boot."

"Buddy, you gotta keep up on the secrets around here. Now go home and leave worry alone," JR slapped the car door as though he had told a horse to giddy up and move out.

As JR inserted the keys into his living area door, he stopped, sighed, and thought to himself, *I hope Ken is worried needlessly.*

CHAPTER 22

Inevitable

Michael D. Glossen considered himself the store's cornerstone. He never acknowledged Ms. Kelly's value to the store's success. Although every retail worker in the store propped him up, they all knew Ms. Kelly was the true authority. Wendy instinctively knew she had to speak with Ms. Kelly, not Glossen.

"What can I help you with, Wendy?" Ms. Kelly said in a somewhat curt manner after Wendy hailed her on the way to assist a cashier. Ms. Kelly was tired after a long day dealing with the store's usual Saturday hubbub.

"Don't worry, I'm not asking for my job back. I know you won't hire me back. And I think Mr. Glossen led me wrong when I quit. After talking to my mom, after a lot of talking, she made me realize I wasn't a good worker here." Wendy looked down, seeming to have remorse. "Mom told me I always bragged about my work and complained about everyone else. She helped me realize that I'm the problem. It took some time, but I saw things more clearly—especially after I stopped drinking. I'm trying my best to hold steady in AA and stay sober. I hope to have a sponsor in the next couple of days. At this point, I needed to apologize to you and a few coworkers. I'm sorry, Ms. Kelly, for all I have put you through. Hopefully, I'll see some of the others today so I can also apologize to them too."

"So, what are you going to do?" Ms. Kelly asked without commenting on Wendy's past behavior.

"Not sure if you'll believe this, but I'm considering going to school for criminal justice. I hope I can get a grant or loan to help me."

"Wow! That's not something I expected. You want to be a cop?"

"For many years, I wanted to be a detective. I got sidetracked when I worked here. I gotta get back on it."

"Oh hey, Mr. Glossen. You're in a bit early tonight," Ms. Kelly greeted the general manager, interrupting the conversation with Wendy.

Unready to speak with him, Wendy quickly slid behind a product display.

"Why are you here, Ms. Kelly?" Michael asked, hanging his jacket in the manager's office.

"I went over last week's reports. There were some errors in them I had to correct before the district manager came down on us."

"Oh, those are the reports I did last week. I came in to do them this week before getting distracted. And I hope to leave early tonight," Michael said.

"Yes, you're looking tired. Ms. Kelly observed. "All you need to do is enter tonight's receipts, and the report is good. On Tuesday I'll show you what happened in the last report. Oh, and Wendy is here. She wants to speak with you, but not about a job." Ms. Kelly motioned with her head over to the display she knew Wendy had slipped behind.

"Oh, this can't be good," Michael mumbled, directing a louder voice toward the former clerk.

"Wendy? You want to talk to me?"

"Yes sir. I want to apologize." Wendy walked hesitantly toward Michael.

"I was a creep when I worked here," Wendy said, with a bit of a shake in her voice. She continued to talk, apologize, and share her plans. Michael listened to her, not because he cared what she had to say but he succumbed to his curiosity.

"That's very nice of you, Ms. Wendy. I suspect you'll do well in criminal justice. Didn't the office job at Hickman's work out?"

Michael knew what went down at the car lot but wanted to get Wendy's inside take on the shutdown.

"Oh, you didn't hear? His lot is shut down," Wendy replied. "Can't say much more. I don't know much more. But it's OK. I needed to say goodbye to that place anyway. Scott Hickman is a very odd man."

"Well, I wish you luck in college, Ms. Wendy. When you're in the store, give me a wave, OK?"

"I will do that. If you don't mind, I will hunt down a couple of co-workers. Thank you, Mr. Glossen, Ms. Kelly."

Wendy sought out her former co-workers, who accepted her apology with polite indifference, though she sensed their disbelief. While Marty wasn't there, the others promised to relay the message, but her words quickly became gossip, with Marty remarking, "We'll see how she is a year from now."

"Did I hear you say you were going to party with us one more time, dear, sexy roomie of mine?" Mel asked as she removed towels from the dryer.

"You're an insistent little bitch," Dianne teased, snapping Mel with a towel.

"Ouch! I'd get you back, but I want you to come with me tonight without any excuses." Mel rubbed her hip while overreacting to any pain the towel snap may have caused.

"It's pitiful that your party is the only thing in Marshfield for us. How about we drive into Springfield and go to a movie?" Dianne offered her an alternative as she began helping to fold the towels.

"OK, let's do that Sunday afternoon," Mel said, with faked enthusiasm.

"Mel, I love hearing you play and hanging out with everyone, but the place makes my skin crawl!"

"That's because you have a history with the owner...a whopping two months of dates with him. You didn't fuck him, did you?"

"Nope. The opportunity didn't present itself. Well, not really. I could have, but I needed to get back home to Mom. Anyway, the guy is too strange. It's a lot to overlook, no matter how horny a person is. Did you ever fuck him? You asked me. Now I ask you." Dianne said, turning away to stack towels in the linen closet.

"No, I didn't. We were only friends from the start. We've never kissed or hugged or any of that. The most contact was an occasional peck on the cheek or forehead. It was almost like he purposefully wanted to make people think we were dating by doing these things. We did not date in the traditional sense; we just did things together," Mel confirmed with a confident voice.

"I would have been surprised if you had. You two never

seemed like lovers to me. Have you had any female lovers?"

"Well, sort of, but not long or deep, just more like checking things out than anything else. You know Jill from the park?"

"Yes?"

"I drove the van to the park regularly after leaving high school. I'm not sure if Jill saw an opportunity for someone new or if she really liked me. She took me out to the backlands to observe the bison. About the second or third time we visited the bison, she made her move, and I let her. It was fun, sorta." Mel shrugged, then smiled. "We fooled around a few other times, but our interest fell. We didn't date or see each other sexually, other than that. It was just one of those things. I wouldn't do it again because I won't risk what we have," Mel said, momentarily serious, taking Dianne's hand.

"Would it upset you?" Mel asked.

"Not sure," Dianne said, looking down.

"So, Will you come with me tonight?"

"OK, Ms. Insistent, but we'll take my car. I don't want to see that van rocking out by the roadway without me," Dianne teased Mel.

"Warm up on your guitar or whatever you do before playing. I've got some stuff I want to do before we go to Satan's Den."

"Girl, that's a little strong."

As Mel predicted, they enjoyed the party. The crowd wasn't as large as it had been on some nights, but at any given time during the evening, about 15 people gathered around, chatting, listening to Mel play, and playing their music. Some group members surmised that the usual attendees may have been preparing for the fall semester start-up at universities outside the area.

Although Jill had little respect for Michael, she respected his place. She ensured everything was cleaned up, returned Brandy to her chain, and ensured no spills were left unattended.

"Mel, I'll be right out," Dianne announced. "I must make a quick stop in the bathroom. Do we have everything? Here, take my bag."

"OK, girlie! Hurry, it's about to rain, and Michael is about to come home."

"Remind me to spank you when we get home," Dianne said

with a smile, entering the bathroom.

"I'll see you in the car," Mel responded, nearly out the door.

"OK, see you there!" Dianne's muffled voice came from the bathroom.

Oh shit! Michael's home, Mel said to herself as she unlocked the car's door. She became increasingly worried about Dianne.

Michael didn't notice Dianne's car parked in front of his home. He was barely able to navigate his driveway, given his condition. Still, he was able to perform his usual habit of retrieving his pistol, storing it, and removing his shoes by the back door. He staggered toward his room before catching Dianne as she exited the bathroom.

"Oh, hey, babe! Are you looking for me? It's about time you came around. I knew you would." Michael slurred his words as he leaned against the hallway wall.

"No, I was just leaving." Dianne attempted to go around Michael as he encircled her with both hands anchored firmly against the wall, trapping her. His breath was putrid with beer as he pushed against her, pinning her to the wall. Dianne attempted to slip under his arms but was blocked by his knee.

"Michael, please! You don't know what you're doing. I can smell the beer on you. Let me go!"

"You here playing with Jill and the girls tonight? You are turning that way, ain't you? I see your hair cut short now. I'll give you dick. That'll change your mind," Michael said, pressing harder against her.

"Michael! I said no! Let me go!" Dianne broke loose but did not escape. Michael pushed her into the front bedroom and onto the bed.

"No, Michael! Leave me alone!"

"You said you didn't want to see me, but now you're here. You want my dick, don't you!" Michael pulled his belt from his waist and whipped the bed beside Dianne, catching part of her leg, eliciting a piercing scream from Dianne.

Standing with one knee on the bed, he yelled, "Take off your clothes! I'm going to fuck you good, you trashy bitch! That will take the queer out of you!"

"No!"

Dianne's protest barely finished. Michael reared his arm, this time with the leather part of his belt in his hand. He swung at Dianne with a force so swift she couldn't avoid contact. The buckle hit her face with a vicious sting, drawing a gush of blood. Frightened, she pulled her strength together and uprighted herself. Enduring more stinging lashes, she shoved open a window a few steps from the bed.

"Mel! Help!" She yelled in a booming, panicked voice. Whack! The buckle hit Dianne's back several times, tearing her shirt and skin.

In the shadows, she saw Mel running toward her. Not waiting for another second, Dianne pushed through the screen and rolled out the window into the bushes, falling onto the lawn and suffering additional cuts from the screen and bushes.

"Dianne! Oh my god, Dianne! What did he do to you?"

A neighbor's dim security light exposed Dianne's torn clothes and the blood streaming down her face. As Dianne tried to catch her breath, Michael continued to rant incessantly.

"I'm going to fuck you yet, schoolteacher! You think you are so smart! I'm coming out there to fuck you right there. Don't you move!" Michael yelled out the window, then turned away, seemingly heading toward the back exit of the house.

Moments later, a loud bang rang out.

"What was that? It sounded like gunfire!" Mel whispered to Dianne.

"Is he coming out here with that gun? We gotta get out of here!" The fear in Dianne's voice was obvious.

Mel held Dianne securely while placing a sleeve against her bleeding face, trying to contain her bleeding as they ran.

"Get in the car!" she ordered.

After sliding into the car's back seat after Dianne, Mel couldn't find the keys. "Shit! I must have lost them in the grass. Get down, Dianne, so he doesn't see us!"

Meanwhile, hearing gunshots, Mr. Colson grabbed a walking stick to steady his arthritic legs through tall grass to neighbor Glossen's place. He called out, with only silence answering. Barely opening the back door, he gasped at the scene of Michael lying sprawled in a lake of blood, forming a river that flowed toward the door.

"Well, he real dead," Mr. Colson muttered, staring at the

carnage as a blood-splattered Glock pistol in an open drawer caught his eye. He succumbed to his instinct to recover the weapon he long ago sold to Michael on a promise and a note.

The man got shot with his gun. No, my gun! Colson thought, remembering his neighbor never finished paying him.

"The asshole never paid me for it. I'm taking it back. It stayin' here ain't gonna save him," he mumbled to himself. "Startin' to rain. Guess I need to hurry."

Mr. Colson pulled a kerchief from his back pocket, grabbed the gun and wrapped it securely before retrieving his walking stick to slog through the tall grass back to his home. Before entering the house, he swung open a false padlocked shed door. Gently, he placed the recovered gun into a bucket and poured kerosene over it as he thought, *I'll cover it good for some cleaning*. He carefully closed the shed door and fully locked the padlock, intending not to see the pistol soon. The rain came slowly at first before dark skies opened with a vengeance just as he stepped onto his porch.

"Steve! I was scared," his wife scolded upon seeing him enter their home. "I called the police. What's going on?"

"I went up to Glossen's driveway and called and called, but no answer," Colson replied, trying to calm his wife.

"I didn't see anything off—the barking and soaked dog is all. I guess he was in the crapper. I'll ask him tomorrow. I hope he gets the dog out of the rain."

"As long as you're OK. I hate it when you talk so crudely like that," his wife frowned. "Anyway, let the police handle it. I got a terrible headache. I'm going to bed. You talk to them."

"Go on to bed, sweetheart. Looks like cops driving up. You go on and rest. I'll stay up if they come knocking at our door."

The downpour brought Dianne to reality as it pounded on the car's roof. "Mel, I'm so glad you're here!"

"Yes, I'm here."

While the two women hid and tried to understand what was happening, two police cruisers arrived with lights ablaze. Sirens from more responders could be heard in the distance. Looking huge in his safety yellow raincoat, Deputy Johnson flashed a light into the car. He tapped on the window with his oversized flashlight, bright enough to light up the inside of the car.

"Mrs. Colson called and said she thought she and her husband heard shots. Ma'am! What happened to you?" The deputy was shocked to see Dianne's bloody face.

"I'm calling an ambulance for you. You two stay right there!"

"Deputy!" Mel shouted, letting the pounding rain hit her face when she opened the car door. Michael Glossen did this! He's in the house! He always uses the back door! We heard shots fired, too. That's when we ran to the car. I can't find the keys, or we would be out of here by now."

"Deputy Johnson called to the other officers for backup as he rushed down the driveway, gun drawn, adrenaline pumping. He silenced his radio and took cover against the house before turning the corner. Several officers were behind him. Reaching the home's back corner, he swung his arm around and pointed to the other home entrance through the plastic-covered weight area. The lead officer reached to try the doorknob. The door was unlocked. The officer, with two others behind him, entered the house. Johnson listened for an intruder but only heard Brandy barking desperately while straining on her chain. Other backup officers stealthily cleared the house.

Stepping out from the wall's protection, the deputy took an aggressive defensive stance with his weapon drawn in a steady grip. With left arm extended and slightly bent knees, he pointed his bright flashlight forward. Maintaining a controlled breath, he was ready to shoot if necessary.

"All clear in here. Think he's out the window!" an officer yelled from inside the house. Finally breathing, Deputy Johnson shouted for the officer to get a statement from the ladies in the car.

"See if they saw anything!" Pushing the door open carefully, the Deputy sighed nervously. "Glossen, what the hell happened to you?" He whispered, as if Michael could answer, as he lay across the kitchen floor. An oozing river of blood found its way over the threshold, spreading along the ribs of the aluminum door plate. The body appeared stiff and lifeless.

Johnson, still with his weapon drawn, checked for a pulse and found none, confirming his observation. Trying to process the scene mentally, he slowly returned his gun to its holster.

Only rain dripping through gutters and Brandy barking broke the silence of thick, humid air.

"Don't think there's anyone around," another inspecting officer said as he entered the kitchen. "Holy shit! He's shot up good!"

"Don't step into the kitchen." Johnson cut him short. "Go out the front or the door you came in. Get a leash for the dog. Bring it over to the ladies in the car. Get everyone on comms!"

"Copy."

"Johnson to all units. Johnson to all units. We have a homicide. Get everything taped off, get a wagon from state or up the road, and we'll need pictures."

Texaco John's police radio soon blared urgent updates, making airways busier than they had been in years. He wasn't the only Marshfield resident with a police radio screaming these messages. Cars soon began a slow parade as close as they could get to the Glossen home.

"This is not a drive-in theater!" Deputy Johnson sent an angry message over the radio.

"Someone get medics over to the girls in the car! One is hurt bad!" Deputy Johnson continued control of the scene as best he could.

"Set a perimeter! I don't care where they detour. We need traffic control—vests, flashlights, roadblocks! We're not anyone's show!" Johnson commanded.

Soon after the ambulance arrived, JR, Texaco John, and Pastor Greene convened in the chaos and caught up with Ken, who was already near Dianne's car.

"Ma'am! Ma'am!" An EMT tapped on the car window. "Which one of you got hurt? Can you come with me to where I can look at you?" Dianne and Mel peeled themselves out of the car and walked silently with the EMT's over to the ambulance in the soaking rain.

"Ladies, I suggest you ride over to Springfield with us," the lead EMT said after getting both names and a basic medical history. "I believe you're both experiencing shock and Ms. England, you need those wounds looked at. Is there someone we can call for you?"

Overhearing the EMT's questions, JR and Ken answered in unison, "Here!"

"Dianne, you got a purse in the car?" Ken asked.

Dianne nodded.

Mel reached into a back pocket and pulled out her wallet with ID while still staring, trapped in a far-off gaze.

"Dad, I think I lost the keys in the lawn," she said to JR, breaking her gaze. "I can drive it home."

"We'll find them," JR answered. "Don't worry about the car. I'll see you ladies at the hospital. John's got Brandy!"

CHAPTER 23

Planning

EMTs wheeled Dianne, strapped to a gurney, into a private room in the emergency department for her wounds to be assessed. The pastel walls and antiseptic smell made the experience more nightmarish than what had already taken place. The antiseptic-filled air and fast-moving attendants added to Dianne's confusion about the night's events. She barely remembered x-rays or bandages being applied. Only Ken's arrival eased her confusion, that was, until he shared information about Michael.

After a nurse was assured Mel had not been physically injured, she escorted her to a comfortable private area known as a "Grieving Room." As Mel paced the dimly lit room, Pastor Greene entered minutes afterward.

"Melanie, perhaps you don't know who I am, but I am here to assist you...only if you want me to do so. I'm Reverend Thomas Greene, head pastor at the Marshfield Methodist Church. Soon, a police deputy will come in to ask questions about what happened tonight. Do you want a lawyer or anyone else with you? After Dianne is examined, the deputy will also speak to her."

"Lawyer? I want my dad! Or mom! What's going on?" Mel said, continuing to pace the room while not able to settle into any thoughts.

"Is your father JR from the truck stop?"

"Yes."

"He followed us here. He'll be in shortly."

"Where's Dianne? How bad is she hurt?"

The pastor talked to Mel as gently as possible, telling her it would be a few minutes before Dianne could come in. Mel couldn't listen, only worried about her friend. She stared at the nature prints hanging with precision on the wall in the softly lit room after she forced herself to stop pacing. The pictured streams, lakes, and mountains helped her detach from the evening's experience, yet she was far from calm. Mel's trance broke when the door cracked open, letting in a blinding light. She looked up at the officer and wondered aloud what she had done wrong.

"Ma'am, you have done nothing wrong," Deputy Crystal Tillman said, anticipating Mel's assumption. She readied her notepad and plucked a pen from her shirt pocket.

"I'm from the Sheriff's Department in Springfield. We have cooperating agreements with Webster County, so if you agree, may I ask you about what happened tonight? I know it's late but try to remember everything you can. Do you mind if I record what you say?"

"No, I don't mind," Mel said, still with a far-off gaze. Officer Tillman tested a hand-held recorder and then read the information from Mel's license that she had given the EMT earlier.

"Please state your given name and your nickname."

"Melanie Joy Rodriguez. My original name was Melanie Joy Brown. JR and Betty adopted me when I was ten. Everyone calls me Mel."

"Given names of your parents?"

"JR is Juan Rodriguez. He might be here soon. My mother is Betty Rodriguez. I think she might be at home."

"Thank you. Mel, Tell me what happened tonight."

"Dianne and I were at a party at Michael's house. We do that every Saturday night while Michael is working."

"Does he know?"

"Yes. It's mostly women from the animal park and a few others. I sing while some folks drink a little beer and tell each other 'BS' stories. Jill from the park arranged it with Michael so we could do this while he works on Saturday nights. Did you arrest Michael for what he did to Dianne?"

"I need Jill's full name," the officer asked without replying to Mel's question.

"Jill Miller."

As Officer Tillman continued writing, Mel recounted the time from the party's end to when they walked to the ambulance.

"Terrible night for you, Mel. Is Pastor Greene your pastor?"

"I never met him before. He followed the ambulance here."

"How much beer, drugs, or other beverages did you consume

tonight?"

"No officer, I'm a singer. I only drank water. Anything else makes my throat tighten."

The officer looked at Mel with some disbelief, thinking she was possibly covering up for underage drinking.

Pastor Greene explained how he knew of Mel and knew Dianne through her mother and Pastor Dawn. Officer Tillman nodded as she wrote copiously in her notebook.

Closing out her recording device, the officer requested the Pastor's confidentiality. "Because this is an ongoing police investigation, Pastor, I ask that you not pass on any of the information about this evening," she said.

"Certainly, Officer," Pastor Greene agreed.

As Officer Tillman started to leave the room, JR came in.

"Dad!" Mel hugged JR tightly. It appeared her shock was lifting.

"It's awful Dad, it's awful!" Mel cried.

"Oh, Sweetie. I know it's awful."

"There's more to what happened." JR, in a move unusual for him, held Mel's hand. "I'm not sure if anyone told you. Michael was shot. Someone killed him." JR tried to give the news gently.

"What? How can that be? I saw him. I heard him say nasty things to Dianne. How could someone kill him?" Mel was dumbfounded.

"Did you tell the officer this?" JR asked, "I think I did." Mel, still wide-eyed and more confused, turned toward Pastor Greene.

"Pastor?"

"Yes, you went into detail about Dianne going through the window, being injured, and about the parties."

"Yes, Mel, you told me in detail. Is there more that you remember?" Officer Tillman again pulled out a pen and notebook.

"Where's Dianne?" Mel asked anxiously.

"Oh shit! He beat her, Dad! I never thought he would do such a thing! It's my fault! She didn't want to come. It's my fault!"

JR, continuing to hold his daughter's hand, explained. "The nurse said that as soon as the officer finished speaking with Dianne, she'd bring her in. Ken is with her."

Although broken out of her trance, Mel still couldn't make sense of anything. In her mind, she repeatedly relayed every minute from the time she left Dianne. "Does Dianne know about Michael?"

"Thank you all for your time. I'll go out to speak with Dianne now," Officer Tillman said, opening the door. "Um, Who's Ken?"

JR explained Ken's close friendship and his role after Katrina's death.

"Please contact me or Deputy Johnson if you think of anything else." Officer Tillman said, exiting the room.

"Ken said he would tell Dianne about Michael. You two will need each other for a long time, perhaps years, after this tragedy," JR said.

Mel was still trying to make sense of the evening. "This is a terrible thing! I thought Michael was becoming more...well...human lately. He wasn't as crude. Then all this!"

Tears began to form in Mel's eyes. Then the door cracked open, again letting in a sting of bright light. Dianne peered in. Recognizing her silhouette, Mel gasped.

"Dianne! Are you OK? What did he do to you?" Dianne, dressed in scrubs and sporting a large white bandage on her brow, hurried to Mel and looked directly at her.

"I'm OK. The doctor said all the wounds will heal nicely but may be painful. He prescribed a couple of painkillers, and the nurses gave me these scrubs. They're keeping my clothes because of...of Michael, you know, Michael. Oh, Mel." Dianne paused, fighting back tears. "The doctor was surprised I didn't break something going out the window like that!"

"I am so sorry. I shouldn't have twisted your arm to go."

"What he did isn't your fault, Mel. It could have happened any time I was with him. When he drank, he got more stupid. And he was drunk! At least you were there to help. Did your dad tell you that Michael was killed?"

"He just told me. I don't know anyone who genuinely liked the guy, but no one I knew hated him that much. And I've known him for a long time! Did Officer Tillman ask you what happened?"

"Yeah. I think they wanted to make sure neither of us killed him," Dianne said, shaking her head in continued disbelief.

Yet again, the room's door opened. A nurse in deep blue scrubs walked in and introduced herself.

"Hello, I'm Jasmine Belk. I'm a psychiatric nurse. Dianne and

Mel, you have been through a tough event tonight. I'm not sure if you remember, Dianne, but I met you when your mother left the hospital."

"Oh yes, you helped me with Mom when we left."

"Yes, that was me," Ms. Belk smiled softly. "I'm now a psychiatric nurse practitioner. If you and Mel need to speak with someone...either together or separately...I want you to know I'm here to help without judgment or expectations. Dianne, you have been through several life-changing events this year. It's going to be tough. And, I hate to say this, Ms. Rodriguez, Officer Tillman has requested that we bag your clothes as well. Here's a set of scrubs to change into."

"Thank you," Mel said.

"And here's my card. Please call—even if it's a quick conversation to let me know you're doing OK," The nurse continued. "For tonight, anytime you feel up to it, you can leave. A discharge nurse will come in right after me to finish the paperwork. If one of you gentlemen is driving …" Nurse Belk scanned the room, looking at Pastor Greene, JR, and Ken "… by the time you get to the car and drive to the discharge circle, Mel should be changed, and we'll be there to meet you."

"Thank you, Nurse. I'm driving. I'll see everyone there," JR said without hesitation.

"And it looks like my work here is done. I'm offering a couple of good ears as well," Pastor Greene volunteered. "Dianne, I understand you were close to Pastor Dawn. She promised she would call. Have you heard from her?"

"No sir, I haven't, but if you hear from her, please ask her to call. I miss her and want to fill her in on everything."

"Will do. Gentlemen, Dianne, I mean it. Don't hesitate to reach out if you need me, any of you," Pastor Greene said.

"Thank you, Pastor." Ken and JR said, extending their hands in gratitude. Dianne nodded and breathed a soft, "Thank you."

The bewildered friends remained silent in JR's car for most of the journey home. When they reached the area near Michael's house, they saw that the road was open only in one lane, with officers letting only a few cars through at a time. Traffic had thinned. Local broadcasting stations had warned drivers to seek other routes, which helped clear the roads.

"Ken, isn't that your car over there? Want me to let you off?"

"Thanks, JR. Oh, I forgot to say, Deputy Johnson asked that we leave Dianne's car parked where it is until tomorrow."

After Ken exited to recover his own vehicle, JR drove the ladies home. The now quiet storms left an eerie air blanketing the night in an unnatural stillness.

JR knew it would be hours before he could sleep, so he drove by Ken's house to see if he had arrived and was still awake. Ken's lights remained on, indicating he was still awake and possibly up for a beer.

The two exhausted men talked through the night's events and made some parallels with their night operations experienced in the Army.

Opening his second beer with a hiss from the bottle separating from the cap, Ken shared an experience he'd had in Vietnam when a Vietnamese friend was killed. He didn't know it for days. JR listened sympathetically as he shared details about the friend and the situation.

JR and Ken's conversations often extended beyond surface chats at the truck stop and into difficult war situations. Ken needed JR's camaraderie and ear to listen. Both men had served in Vietnam on multiple occasions, making shared experiences a pillar of their friendship and, sometimes, their sanity.

Texaco John served in combat as well and needed friends. However, John held onto his feelings and experiences more tightly than the other two men. JR and Ken often worried about John because he hadn't shared much. They knew that no one left service in Vietnam without being scarred in some way. Both men also felt strongly that Dianne and Mel might be scarred by their experience and would need their empathetic ears and friendship.

Sleep eluded Dianne and Mel. "I've got to sit for a while before going to bed," Dianne said, dropping onto the sofa. "I'm still trying to make sense of what happened tonight."

Dianne's mind flickered between images—Michael's face twisted in rage, the glint of the belt buckle, the blood. It felt like trying to piece together a dream.

"I've got to get some water. Want some?" Mel said, opening

the refrigerator to pour from a chilled carafe."

"Please," Dianne responded with a blank stare.

The cool glass of water against her lips felt grounding to Dianne, but the taste was hollow, like drinking air.

"I don't know what to think or feel. I want to wake up and let this be a horrible nightmare," Mel said sipping her last swallow of water.

"Yes. Mel, would you sleep with me tonight? I don't want to sleep alone."

"Of course," Mel quickly responded and moved to hold Dianne in her arms.

The night's stillness stole time from the women as they sat in silence. At last, Dianne spoke.

"Mel, let's try to get some sleep."

Try as they could, neither slept well. Dianne awakened as the sun peaked above the horizon but returned to her restless sleep. Her body felt leaden, her muscles sore like she'd run a triathlon. When her sore muscles quieted, letting her succumb to sleep, flashes of the night jolted her awake. Mel sensed Dianne's roller-coaster sleep. Yet, it was her guilt constantly jolting her awake. The women's uneasy sleep let the morning slide away.

The following day, when he finally awoke close to noon, Ken's first concern was Brandy. During the previous night's confusion, he had hurriedly parked Brandy with Texaco John.

"Hey buddy! How's Brandy? This is Ken. I can come over to get her if she's a bother."

"Nope. I'm keeping her. She needs me," John said abruptly. "I'm taking her to the vet today. She's going to be an indoor and fenced-in dog. No more chains for her. She's such a good girl."

"Well, that seals it then. She's no longer just a dog. She's John's best friend."

"Yep. Must get back to work. The station is busy today."

"OK, talk to you later," Ken said, replacing the phone receiver and smiling like he hadn't in a long time...since dancing with his Trina at the church potluck, anyway.

Still tired, Ken slumped on the sofa with his hands behind his head, trying to make sense of what had happened since he saw Dianne and Mel park at Michael's house. Before long, he dozed off again.

After Ken's call, Texaco John returned to bathing and brushing Brandy in a sink usually used for shop cleanups. He carefully trimmed away the matted patches of Brandy's fur. Brandy shook her head, and her furry body sprayed water droplets on John and the car hoods near them. John chuckled at Brandy's new-found energy.

After thoroughly towel drying his new charge, John awarded her "people food" treats. Fixing cars would have to wait. He had to shop for dog food, bowls, a leash, chew toys, and whatever caught his eye for his new best friend.

"JR, don't worry about going over to the park. You sleep. I'm delivering the animal food," Betty said, slightly nudging JR. She wasn't sure JR heard her, so she left a note taped to the bathroom mirror.

"Hey Barb! I have a delivery!" Betty said, peering into the kitchen door. Although she had not done so in almost a year, delivering greens was welcome normalcy. Making plans for a new life in an RV was challenging enough without adding Michael's demise to the impending changes.

"I hope the traffic didn't slow you down, Ms. Betty. For a long time, they had the street down to one lane," Barb said. "What are you doing with JR's big car?"

"The road is fully open," Betty said, placing the cooler beside Barb's prep table. "Mel has the van. I guess she's slept in today," Betty replied quickly, almost snapping at Barb.

"Isn't that Michael's house with all the crime tape? What happened?"

"Well, yes." Betty hesitated, trying to gauge how much she wanted to share.

"Michael was murdered last night." Hearing the words, she was smacked with the reality of never seeing Michael again. Nearly in tears, she had to exit.

"I suspect the law will come over here and start asking questions 'cause you're the next property over."

Betty didn't want to say another word, not knowing if Barb knew about the Saturday night parties at Michael's house.

"Oh heavens!" Barb exclaimed. "I can't believe this! Are you sure?"

"Very sure." Immediately, Barb called for Jill on the radio.

Betty needed to exit and told Barb to hang on to the cooler with the greens. She didn't want to get caught up answering too many questions from Jill or be subject to more curiosity from Barb.

"JR is not feeling well. I need to get back," Betty lied and quickly left.

Attempting to wipe sleep from her eyes, Mel called her mother immediately upon waking. "I knew you'd be worried," Betty said, knowing it would be Mel on the phone. "I already brought the food over to the park. JR is still sleeping. Why don't you and Dianne come over for an early dinner? I've got some pent-up energy, and I would love to cook a family meal for you both."

"No, I'm not sleeping!" JR called out. "Tell those ladies to come on over!"

"Hi, Dad! Mom, tell him I heard him in the background! I'm pretty sure Dianne would love to come over. I'll let her know when she wakes up."

Barely getting his opinion heard, JR almost instantly fell back asleep.

"Great! I'm calling Ken and Texaco John, too. We can all enjoy a home-cooked meal." Betty's energy was evident.

Mel was energized after talking to her mother. After showering and brewing coffee, she scrubbed the kitchen, tidied the living room and dusted the furniture—tops sides and underneath. Dianne eventually awakened and scuffed into the living room as Mel wiped the last table leg.

"What are you doing? The place looks and smells great! How long have you been up?"

"Just a little while. I confess, it's a habit I picked up from Mom. We often clean when things start buzzing in our minds! I still need to vacuum."

"Nice," Dianne said, shaking her bandaged head and surveying the room. Dianne gingerly touched the bandage on her forehead as she entered the kitchen. The throbbing had dulled, but every movement was a reminder of a terrible night.

"Oh, Mel, what happened last night?" Dianne approached Mel, looked into her eyes, and placed her hands on the sides of her face.

"We'll get through this. We'll get through this." Mel repeated and wrapped her arms around Dianne, gently kissing her head.

"Oh, be careful, he got my back too. It all stings," Dianne said, wincing.

"I'm so sorry for all of this." Mel was sincerely remorseful for her involvement with the parties at Michael's. "If you're ready, I have coffee made," Mel said, guiding Dianne to the kitchen table.

"That sounds good, and I'm so hungry."

"Leftover cobbler for breakfast?" Mel asked.

"Can't think of anything better," Dianne mumbled.

"Mom invited us for dinner. She's also asking Texaco John and Ken."

Dianne blinked her eyes, still trying to awaken. "Your mother is a wonderful cook. I guess she's had some practice. I'd like that."

"Alright! Now eat and get yourself put together. Then we'll go over to Mom's to eat some more." Mel smiled.

Mel finished her cleaning and gave Dianne time to change into fresh clothes before they headed over to the truck stop.

"Brandy!" Both ladies exclaimed in unison as they arrived and jumped out. "Oh, girl! You're looking good!" Mel reached a hand toward the dog's snout so Brandy could sniff and recognize her human pal.

"Dianne, this is Brandy."

"I know. I met Brandy once a few months back."

"This girl looks so good!" Mel turned to John and JR. Did one of you do something different to her?"

"I bathed her, brushed her, and put some shine on her coat," John replied, boasting. "She wasn't in the house ten minutes and told me she wanted to be my new best friend."

"I'm glad you listened to her," JR quipped. "She certainly seems like she attached herself to you."

"It's been a long time since I had a dog. I hope she stays with me for a long time," John said, stroking her coat. "I got something to share with y'all when Ken gets here."

"He just drove up, so get your words in order," JR said with a wink.

"The pot roast is about done, and everything else is on the stove keeping warm," Betty called out from the kitchen. "We have a little time for conversation."

After Ken came in and the chatter settled down, Betty joined them and couldn't help herself. "OK, John. Spill it! What you gonna tell us?"

This kind of assertiveness wasn't typical of Betty, making the group chuckle. "All right, Ms. Betty, I won't keep you any longer." John took a deep breath. He wasn't used to talking to a group of people all at once. And what he had to say may not be well-received.

"I don't know where to start. My brother. You know he was an Army lifer, right?" Ken and JR nodded their heads.

"Lifer? He was in the Army, like 20 years?" Betty asked.

"Yes. He stayed almost 30. Anyway, he's moving to the Old Soldiers Home in Biloxi. He's waited over six months to get a spot there and is now moving. He's got a house down south there and is willing to sign it over to me, furniture and all. All I got to do is pack tools...and my buddy here. It's a small place but has a nice garage. I figure I can sell everything here and pay bills with the money and retire, but I'll still tinker with cars."

"Like...leave Marshfield?" Mel said with obvious shock.

"Yep. You see the changes here. Betty, JR, you two are leaving. You're hitting the road for adventures. Brandy and I will go south for our adventures." Brandy heard her name and jumped up to lick John's face.

"Not sure if I'll get used to that, but I know it's cause she likes me," John said with a smile while patting his new friend.

"Ken, you're not going anywhere, are you?" Dianne asked. John didn't give Ken a chance to respond.

"I guess you'll see my taillights going down the road about when JR and Betty are hitting the trail. Like their plans, I want you all to keep my plans to yourself. Oh, and you know who else is about to skedaddle?"

"John, you have the scoop on everyone in this little town," Betty said.

"Yep. Folks think cause I'm quiet, I'm not hearing what's going on, and I'm only a grease monkey, so I know nothing. I do know how to listen, and I do listen."

"OK, OK! Who's leaving?" Mel asked anxiously, unprepared to hear what John was about to say.

"You know that lady at the animal park, Jill? She got a job in Cincinnati. She'll be out of here in a few weeks."

"How do you know that? I'm kinda friends with her and she never told me," Mel said, surprised.

"A week ago, she brought her car in for an oil change. She wanted to use my phone. Didn't ask if she could call long distance, but she did. She left me a note with $20 and said she did that so that I could keep the change. She could've asked before she did it, but I guess she thought I'd say no. She didn't know I was listening to her chatter. She'll be out of here in 'bout three weeks."

"Well, John, I haven't known you for long," Dianne broke the silence after John's revelations. "But yes, I think of you as a man of few words. But gracious! Your words pack a wallop!"

"Yes, they do! Now, let's eat and keep talking about positive things in the future," Betty said, motioning the crew to the table she'd set.

"You going to let Dianne and me clean up, Mom?"

"It's my absolute pleasure! I will sit with the guys and pump John for more information!" Betty smiled and ordered the group to the table.

"Everyone sit where you want and eat everything! The girls will clean up and don't need to start putting away a bunch of leftovers!"

"Your turn, Ken. Answer my question!" Dianne said, in near panic.

"Honestly, dear friends," Ken addressed the group. "If I left, I don't know where I would go. So, you might say I'll be the one here who keeps the warm home fires burning."

The evening continued with excited chatter about new lives and adventures. As promised, Dianne and Mel cleaned the kitchen to perfection after packing dinners that were easy for Ken and John to heat. No matter how much Betty begged for the ladies to take home leftovers, Dianne and Mel resisted.

The evening ended early in hopes all would catch up on sleep.

Monday at the truck stop appeared typical but with a higher volume. With every theory and quip on Michael's murder, the conversation increased to an uncomfortable intensity. Heads shook from side to side, and amateurs conjectured reasons and suspects for Michael's murder, some voices out-shouting one another.

Before long, Ken had about all the buzz he could stand. He asked JR if he was OK.

"And are you OK?" JR asked in return. "I think I feel my blood pressure going up. I gotta leave. I'll be home if you need me. I'll go work in the yard to get some of the cobwebs out of my mind and the weeds out of the yard. The landlord thinks I'm a nice guy, keeping the fence tidy. He doesn't know it's my therapy." Ken and JR smiled at each other and said goodbye.

CHAPTER 24

Suspects

Mel and Dianne were startled when they heard a demanding series of knocks at their door. Dianne feared it might be some creep, like the one she encountered a few months ago.

"Ms. England, Ms. Rodriguez! This is Deputy Johnson. I need to ask a few questions and get some things cleared up."

"Thank God!" Dianne said with a deep exhale. She opened the door wide to let the Deputy in.

"Would you like to sit down?"

"Thank you. It'll only be a minute. It feels good to stand. I've been in the car too much. Is there anyone else in the house?"

"My housemate, Mel...Ms. Rodriguez is here. She's in her room. Do you want to speak with her as well?"

"Yes, I'll ask her some questions after I talk with you." The Deputy apologized for asking Dianne again to say what happened.

"Can you remember any other details? You said you heard the shots soon after you dove out the window. As near as you can remember, how many minutes?"

Dianne did her best to recount her experience and put an approximate number of minutes to the events, but admitted she'd been terrified at the time, so she felt her timing wasn't exact. As Dianne was ending her statement, Mel came into the living room.

She gave her recounting of events as well. "OK, ladies, I believe I've clarified some things. Now, for the important question. Do you know of anyone who has made threats against Mr. Glossen or wanted him dead? Was he in a dispute with anyone?" Dianne told the Deputy about her date with Michael and the issue at Benny's. She also shared what appeared to be a disagreement with Scott Hickman, which she witnessed on her second date.

"Oh, and wait, that one time when I was over at Michael's, I thought I saw Mitzi from Benny's pass by. Michael blew it off and said she didn't live around there, so it wasn't likely her."

"I'll note that. Server at Benny's?" he asked.

"Yes, a tall blonde with what I call 'fluffy' hair. At first, she treated me poorly, but it was fine the next time we met. Although, I think she knew Michael was about to propose to me by how she acted."

Dianne told the Deputy all the details she could remember about the night. She promised to write everything down and drop it off at his office.

"Ladies, these things are essential. I certainly appreciate your time. Lately, it seems that this area has fallen to the grim reaper. There were the murders back in 87, Glossen's murder, then just last night Mrs. Colson, the lady next door to Michael's, had a brain aneurysm and died there in the house.

Odd to say, but at least Mrs. Colson's death wasn't a murder. Unfortunately, after losing her, Mr. Colson isn't doing well mentally and is not making much sense. Perhaps he could have added some information, but not now. We're trying to locate his son, hoping he can help him make some sense."

"I am so sorry," Dianne expressed empathy for the neighbor. "I hope all the problems from the other night didn't bring it on."

"We'll never know," the Deputy replied. "You ladies doing OK? JR, Betty, and Ken helping you out?"

"In so many ways," Mel said. "They continue to be great to me and Dianne."

"Oh, I want to ask you about one thing, Ms. England. My wife told me you had a doll you dug up at the farm where your mother was raised?"

"Yes, it's the strangest thing. My mother felt bad about how she got it. She wrote a letter about it that was tucked into her diary."

"I don't mean to take up more of your time, but may I see the doll? Deputy Johnson seemed intrigued. "There is a weird cold case about a serial molester, and possibly a killer, of young girls back in the 1960s. Most cases happened closer to Saint Louis, but he could have come out this far. May I see the doll?"

"Sure! And I'll show you the note, too." Dianne brought out the old toolbox from her office along with the note her mother wrote.

"Sir, I haven't seen the doll. I only know it's in here from my mother's note.

"Oh, no! It looks like your mother narrowly escaped a horrible situation," the Deputy said after reading the note.

"May I take these items with me?"

"Sure. I would appreciate it if you could get the note back as soon as possible so I can keep it with my mementos. The doll you can keep."

"Yes, I'll make official copies of the note and return the original to you. Also, here's a receipt. In case I'm unavailable, whoever is at the desk can help. If there's nothing else you ladies want to share, I'll head out."

"Wait, Deputy!" Dianne seemed to have remembered something.

"Yes, Ms. England," The Deputy said with raised eyebrows.

"Do you know the kind of gun that shot Michael?" Dianne asked.

"Yes, I thought that information was common around here by now. It was a 9mm Glock."

"You know Michael owned one of those, right?" Dianne said. "I saw it the night we broke up. It gave me the creeps."

"Do you know who sold it to him?"

"No sir, I don't. Other than seeing it that night, I know nothing about it." Dianne responded.

"Everyone knows about that gun," Mel said, "… but no one knows about it, like where it came from or anything."

"Yes, that's what I've found so far. Of course, if you hear more or think of any other detail, no matter how small, give me a call," Deputy Johnson said as he began to exit.

"Yes, we certainly will, Deputy. Bye now," Dianne said, escorting him to the door.

Later that night, both women were propped up on soft pillows and laid comfortably wrapped around one another. Dianne stared at her friend, turned roomie, and lover. She couldn't shake the feeling that there was more behind Deputy Johnson's questions earlier. Was he here to clarify details or because they were suspects?

"My head is still spinning about all this," Mel said fiddling with a little bow on Dianne's nightgown as she rested in the crook of her arm.

"Me too, Mel. I wish I could figure out who did this thing."

"Dianne, I knew him most of my life, and there were plenty of times when I wanted to bop him, but damn! Kill him? No. Weirdly, I miss the guy. Betty and I thought he was simmering and hoped he would someday be considered close to normal."

"You and Betty are far more generous than I could have ever been." Dianne adjusted her position on the pile of pillows. After a few minutes of silence, Dianne looked over at Mel, trying to show some compassion for Mel's loss, and squeezed her with a side hug. Mel gently kissed Dianne's forehead, then her lips. The two comforted one another in their loss, each caressing the other's face and then arms.

Their reassuring comfort slowly, gently turned passionate, albeit delicately. Concerns and worries disappeared for several hours as the two, with gentle passion, vanished from their grief and worry deep into the night and each other.

"Mel, are you awake?" Dianne whispered after half awakening.

"Yes, I fell asleep, but I've been awake for a while. What time is it?"

"It's 3:30, and I'm having trouble going back to sleep," Dianne said as she righted herself and propped pillows behind her.

"I'm up with you, so tell me what's on your mind," Mel said as she returned a pile of pillows from the floor to the bed so she could lie comfortably next to Dianne.

"I think Mr. Richards should have called by now to offer me the job at the school. I may be unemployed. After four years of school, working summers, and having all my time occupied, I'm uncomfortable."

"When Dad and Mom shut down the truck stop, I'll also be among the unemployed. So, you see, I'm not far behind you."

"That's another indication you should go to college. Humph, maybe I should go back for my master's degree. Wouldn't hurt."

"No! I think you should go to the destiny place you talk about." Mel paused.

"And take me with you!" she finally added. "I need to get out of this area. I can't hang around here anymore!" Mel was excited by her thoughts about moving away from Marshfield to someplace with a beach in Florida.

"That sounds like fun. But let's not imitate Thelma and Louise. Have you seen that movie? I saw it when it first came out. It ends tragically. I don't want that to happen with us."

"I haven't seen it, but I've read about it. I hear the ending is a surprise. What happens?"

"Nope, not going to give it away. Geez! What would I do with this house and my stuff? It's not like I have a place to move to."

With the new adventure percolating in the women's minds, they could not sleep for continuing to discuss the possibilities.

"Dad gave me a few days to recoup from what I will call 'the event.' I think today I'll go back to work. I'll talk to him about leaving during a break or after the breakfast crowd. I want to leave and not say a thing, but you know how kind they are and how they would be hurt if I didn't talk to them first. It will be so hard. Just walking away from them, from everything, is exciting but terrifying."

"Yes, they will be hurt if either one of us just disappears, especially you!" Dianne playfully scolded Mel.

"And Ken will, too," Dianne added. "Hey, it's Wednesday. If you all get slammed down there, give me a call. I'm an experienced restaurant worker since I helped you the other day." Dianne smiled.

"I'll remember that, Dianne. Meanwhile, get out those brochures and start thinking about a new life with me dragging along," Mel said with a grin.

When Ken answered his phone, he didn't anticipate what he was about to hear.

"You're doing what?" Ken asked in disbelief. "When? Look, you two have been through a trauma. Moving is not the solution! I know. I can't tell you how many times I tried to run from my problems, but it catches up with you, and then everything is worse—much, much worse." Ken was shaking after Dianne told him of her and Mel's 'spur of the moment' plans.

"Wow, Ken, I didn't expect that reaction! I guess I didn't know what to expect. And to be honest, I'm starting to feel uncomfortable around here. Not because you got upset or anyone has done or said anything. I feel it in the air, staring at me." Dianne tried to explain her feelings.

"Young lady, You haven't been much of anywhere for people to stare at you, but I can guarantee that most everyone knows Michael was murdered. I can't stop the talk, and I can't stop you. But like everything else, let me know if you need my help," Ken offered as he calmed. "My unsolicited advice is not to tell anyone your plans. Just do it. That is if I can't talk you out of it," Ken said.

"When Mel comes home, we'll start figuring it out. You want to be here?"

"Hell, no. I'm going to be over at JR's house, drinking beer."

"If this move really happens, you promise to still be my friend and substitute Dad?" Dianne asked.

"Of course I do!" Ken said before saying goodbye.

"Ms. Kelly, you got a moment I can talk to you?"

"I figured you'd come around with questions, Deputy. Please come into my office. I need to finish pulling these receipts. Marty, are you comfortable pulling the receipts and entering the numbers?"

"Yes, ma'am."

"Thank you, Marty," Ms. Kelly said with a smile.

"Deputy, do you want water, or to sit down? Suddenly, taking over as general manager and pulling someone up from the floor to do my job has made things a little hectic here."

"This won't take long. I have a few questions to ask you. Do you know anyone in the store who hated, or at a minimum, disliked Mr. Michael D. Glossen?"

"A few days back, without hesitation, I would have said that one of our teammates, Wendy, who recently resigned, disliked him. He kinda led her on a wild goose chase, sending her to another job at Hickman's Auto Sales," Ms. Kelly explained as she pulled water for herself from a little refrigerator she kept in her office.

"What happened? Did she come back to the store?"

"Yes. She came back at first to ask for her job back. Then she returned to apologize for her behavior while employed. I didn't think much of it then, or really, until you asked. I'm glad she's no longer here. She said her mother made her see what a problem she was. And, she said she's now going to AA."

"I see. Do you mind if I talk to other employees while they're in the store?"

"Not at all. Let me know if you need my office."

"Thank you. One last question: Did you work the night Mr. Glossen was killed? Oh, and let me talk to Marty if you don't mind."

"No sir, I didn't work that night. Sure, I'll ask Marty to come in."

"Marty Sims to the front office. Marty, to the front office, please," Ms. Kelly announced on the store's intercom. Before Marty came in, Ms. Kelly explained how Michael had suddenly switched his schedule so he could work on Saturday nights. She didn't know why he'd done that.

"I was happy to have the time off. And, before you ask, after leaving the store and Michael earlier that evening, I went home to have dinner with my family—one of the few times I could do so since I started work here! The hours here are brutal."

"I think we both understand brutal hours, Ms. Kelly," Deputy Johnson smiled. "I thank you for your time. Please let me know if you hear anything, including what may seem like rumors. And, if any of your other employees want to talk, call me, OK?" The Deputy looked at Ms. Kelly directly and shook her hand.

"OK, Deputy. I'll ask Marty to come in...and will call if I get wind of anything."

The conversation with Marty went smoothly. Nothing she said jumped out for Deputy Johnson. However, he thought Marty was a bit too kind for having had to work with Wendy when she was a problem employee. Like Ms. Kelly, she gained a promotion after Michael's demise. He made a note to speak with Wendy and her mother.

"OK, ladies, tell me about this place you want to run off to. And don't make it sound too good or warm. Betty already has her bag packed and wants to run off with you," JR said as he scooped ice cream onto a warm apple cobbler.

"No, Betty, you stay seated. Ken and I got this," JR insisted when Betty motioned toward the kitchen.

"You baked the cobbler. Ken and I will serve it up and wash the dishes. In return, you gotta talk the ladies into staying. That is, at least until we leave for life on the road."

"Hon, they will do what they want when they want," Betty replied. "We've got no control over them."

"Mel, I'm having trouble letting go," JR admitted.

"Dad, thank you. I'm having a little trouble with that myself. But, ya know, I need to get out and see what's beyond Webster County and Springfield. Even Springfield, I haven't explored much." Mel tried hard not to sound like a 12-year-old pleading to go to the movies.

"I'll have my chance to explore the world with Dianne. She's a smart lady, and I think we can have fun enjoying warm sands and a different life."

"Let's not get carried away," Dianne chimed in. "Remember, Ken had to bail me out of buying a truck,"

You almost had to walk to the school in the snow, girl!" Ken reminded Dianne. "I hear that thing is in police impound now."

"I don't think you would have let me do that," Dianne patted Ken's arm as he set the last dish of cobbler on the table.

The friends, who were more like family, were quiet, slurping and chewing a satisfying treat. Several times, it looked as though Ken was starting to say something.

"OK, let me put this before you," he began. "The three of you arc my witnesses. I'm not trying to take advantage of Dianne or the situation here. I've lived in my little house without a lease for the last three months," Ken talked around what he wanted to say.

"Spit it out, Ken! And I don't mean the cobbler," Betty demanded, which drew a laugh from the group.

"OK, OK! Dianne, would you consider selling your house to me? If you'll sell it to me, I could make renovations, like adding a bath."

"Good lord, Ken! I proposed to JR with less fanfare," Betty said impatiently.

"What?" Mel, Ken, and Dianne said in unified amazement.

Betty smiled. "That's another story for another time. For now, let's hear what Ken has to say."

"Thank you, Betty, but I sure do want to hear about this

marriage proposal," Ken said, trying not to chuckle at Betty's revelation.

"Well, this is how I figure," Ken explained. "You can put whatever you don't take on your adventure in my Trina's room for storage. Sorry, I mean your office, Dianne. Meanwhile, I'll live in and fix up the house. If I decide to sell it, I'll give you plenty of time to move things. We'll talk about household stuff later. Ken seemed physically relieved to have spilled his idea.

"It certainly seems attractive, but I've never sold a house before," Dianne said, looking confused.

"Wow, this makes the move sound real," Dianne breathed deeply. "Before I say yes or no, let me check with Mr. Richards to confirm if I have a job. And I haven't even thought about what to do with my stuff. This must be only a dream we're having."

If Ken purchased her home, it would make the idea of leaving feel too real. She hadn't considered the logistics. Could she really sell her home? Could she actually move? What would be left for her in Marshfield if she had stayed? Was she ready for that kind of step in a sea of unknowns?

"All of us together? Same dream?" Ken said, smiling.

"Fair enough. You talk to the lawyer at the bank to see who he recommends representing you. If you decide to go through with this, Maybe Mr. McCall will help me with my end of it." Ken said.

"He's a good one, and I think he's helping Julia and her husband, Carlos, with jobs and citizenship," JR interjected.

"I'm so glad to hear that, JR. Those two deserve it so much after putting up with Michael's antics and, basically, assault over the years. Ladies, I'll tell you about that sometime." Ken didn't want to disclose what he and JR had occasionally discussed about Michael's behavior.

JR shifted in his seat, obviously uncomfortable with the whole subject of Michael.

"And, Dianne, it wouldn't hurt for you to call the folks over at Case Realty to find out what the property is worth. I might not be able to afford it." Ken smiled at Dianne.

"Things are happening fast," Dianne said.

"What? The senior Glossen tried to get into the house? He's in town?" Deputy Johnson was perplexed when one of the officers called to tell him that Michael's father was insistent about entering the house.

"I'm glad we got the perimeter fence up. Make sure we have a good local and permanent address for him," the deputy ordered. "I need to think about this situation. Just write it up. Thanks for working past your shift." Deputy Johnson said before closing out the call.

"Kinda strange. Senior Glossen landed in St. Louis the same day his son was killed. I need to draw a timeline," Deputy Johnson said to himself, scratching his head.

Johnson couldn't shake the feeling that it was too much of a coincidence. Why show up on the day of your son's murder, and why insist on getting into the house? He wasn't buying the "concerned father" routine. Something else was at play, and Johnson intended to find out what.

Days passed without progress on finding Michael's killer or figuring out why the senior Glossen wanted into the house. The elusive elder Glossen had allegedly returned to his home in the Washington, DC area after staying only a few days.

Deputy Johnson called the District's Metropolitan Police Department and the Maryland and Virginia Motor Vehicle departments for assistance with finding Glossen's address. He received no information in return. At least the departments are now aware that Glossen is wanted for questioning.

CHAPTER 25

Reluctant Goodbyes

"Are we really doing this?" Dianne asked rhetorically as she taped another box.

"I think we are. I'm so glad I unpacked all this stuff to pack it up again," Mel replied with sarcasm and a smile.

"We're kinda doing a crazy thing, taking off and not planning a hotel stay or anything. Dianne paused and belted out a few sneezes. "How can this stuff get so dusty? Well, we have some plans in place. We will wiggle our way over to Nashville, then south on 65. Let's plan to stay a night or two in or around Nashville. What ya think? We can party like college girls. For you, we'll call it a college prep adventure."

"Humph! And I thought you were a serious nerd in college. Seriously, did you party?"

"After the finals I did, somewhat. I was into political stuff and wove some party time into that." Dianne smiled, then poked Mel in the ribs a little to tickle her.

"OK, don't start anything. We need to be packing nerds right now," Mel scolded.

"Helloooooo?" A voice followed the front door clicking open. "That sounds like Mom," Mel said.

"May I come in?"

"Oh, yes, Betty, please do!" Dianne rushed to welcome her in and assist her with placing some fresh sandwiches on the table.

"I thought I'd invite myself over for lunch." Betty smiled as she unpacked goodies from the truck stop. "We had a bit of a shock this morning," she said. "We need to announce our closure sooner than we had planned."

"What? What happened?" Dianne prodded while Mel washed her hands and placed a roll of paper towels for napkins on the table.

"Fred McCall stopped by. He said the corporation buying our place had to file the offer publicly. He said that someone may get wind of it before long, and the newspapers will want to report on it. Especially with Michael tied into the story, things may get uncomfortable soon. Words leak easy around here."

"Oh, Mom!" Mel gently held her mother's shaking hand. Not knowing how to react or respond, Dianne mechanically pulled drinking glasses from the cupboard.

"We're thankful McCall said he would be our spokesperson if we wanted him to be. Oh, and you know what else that man did? His law firm hired both Julia and Carlos!"

"Wait, Mom! You're jumping stories here. OK, so you're not doing anything about reporters, Fred McCall is handling everything. Right?"

"Yes."

"Julia and Carlos...Julia is the lady who worked for Michael?" Dianne asked.

"Yes, McCall is helping them set up a cleaning company. They will be the contractors to clean and maintain their new law offices."

"Wow! They sure are in a better position away from Michael. I guess they're happy about that," Mel said.

"Yes, and McCall is helping Julia with a visa, green card, then citizenship."

"Woah! Happy ending! Julia had slipped into the country?" Mel asked. "I'm happy she can get everything straightened out. I had no idea and, quite frankly, didn't even think about that possibility."

Betty shrugged her shoulders and smiled. "They're a great couple. I wish them the best."

"So, we pretend nothing is happening with the truck stop?" Dianne asked.

"Yes. And that includes you two. Have you told anyone you're leaving?"

"No, not even when I talked to Mr. Richards about the possible job. I couldn't get a straight answer out of him, so I told him that I needed to make plans and would get my master's degree. Therefore, I will not be available to work for him," Dianne explained. "I guess I sounded a bit uppity at that point, but I no longer care."

"He's probably succumbing to the gossip and rumor mill," Betty speculated. "He didn't want friction if you taught there."

"I haven't said anything to anyone at the animal park either, Mom. Shit, I don't even want to talk to Jill. She's leaving soon anyway. That girl has become worrisome," Mel said, pondering Jill's involvement.

"Could be," she continued. "Barb said when I delivered greens the other day that Deputy Johnson has been to the park several times to speak with her and a few others."

"Mom," Mel said, taking the last sandwich from her mother's hand and placing it on the table.

"Mom....Mom."

At a loss for words, Mel hugged her mom like she'd never let go.

"Mom, you were right when you told me nothing good would come out of us being at Michael's place," Mel apologized.

"Sweet daughter, I would never throw that in your face. I was young once, too. However, when I heard what you were doing, I felt like slapping you." Betty smiled.

"Thanks, Mom," Mel said, still holding her mother.

"You gals need some help?" Betty said, releasing Mel's grip then picking up food wrappings and cleaning off the table as she fought back tears.

"Not sure if you want to help us, Mom. It's a dusty job."

"I've never moved, except from my parents' house long ago. But I've helped others pack. Yes, it's dusty. And I want to talk to you two."

"About?" Mel asked.

"I guess that you two have become closer than just friends. I see the sparkle in your eyes and how you speak to one another. I'm not making a judgment. I want to offer my support and love. If you need to speak frankly, please do. And please, don't ever purposefully hurt one another. You can never take back hurtful talk or actions."

Betty turned to face Dianne directly.

"Dianne, I think you'll always miss your mother. I certainly can't take her place, but please allow me to be that special person you can go to."

"Wow!" Dianne said, not believing what she just heard. Dianne felt her chest tighten. She hadn't realized how much she needed to hear those words until they were spoken. She feared having to navigate this new chapter without guidance or support. And now, here was Betty, offering her a guiding light.

"I second that!" Mel said. "Mom can be your mom too!"

"JR and I will miss you both. You two are incredible ladies. Whether in a committed relationship for years or going your own ways. I want to stay close, no matter where we might be on earth."

Dianne was visibly touched. She had to put down her box and tape to run to the bathroom to wash her face.

"Momma Betty, how could we ask for more?" Dianne said, returning to the living room. "You, JR, and Ken are my family now. And Mel, you're my chosen partner."

"I'm glad you're thinking like that, Dianne. I want to be with you for a very long time," Mel said, nearly bringing herself to tears, with Betty close to crying too.

"Hey, ladies! Your princes are here! Both of us, Mr. Charming and Mr. Handsome!" JR announced their arrival.

"JR don't take that too far! These three will have you tied to a utility pole and let the wild animals get you if you irritate them," Ken quickly retorted.

"Dad, we're not like that! We're nice little princesses!" Mel laughed.

"We're almost finished packing. I hope our necessities will fit in the car tomorrow," Dianne said to the two father figures turned imaginary knights.

Turning serious, Dianne changed gears and became the chief organizer.

"'Ken, I'm leaving you the dishes, linens, and Christmas stuff in the attic. I'll wash the towels and sheets before we go." Dianne's tone was matter-of-fact, but Ken could see the moment's weight in her eyes.

"Another thing, I've been thinking about Dawn. No one's heard from her. No one knows how to reach her. Ken, when you do hear from her, I want to know."

"That will be fine. All will be fine! I see you filled the office room. Everything else looks so sparse. Not to worry. I'll 'man up' the place before long," Ken assured her.

"Then you'll trash it with construction debris," JR teased.

"Yes, and proudly so. I've arranged for a shed to be delivered to hold tools starting tomorrow," Ken explained.

"You didn't take long to jump in," Dianne teased, cutting him off.

"You're right. I appreciate you making it easy for me to jump in. I hope you never think I took advantage of you." Ken looked directly at Dianne with apparent sincerity.

"I've learned a lot from you, Ken," Dianne reassured him. "Ever since I met you, I've learned a lot. You truly have been like a father to me during these tough months. Do you mind if I refer to you as 'Dad Ken' from this point?"

"Ma'am, I will be honored," Ken said with a sweet bear hug for Dianne.

"Can I be your Dad Ken, too, Mel?"

"Of course! I hereby dub you 'Dad Ken'," Mel said, as she picked up an empty wrapping paper tube and lightly knighted Ken's head and shoulders with it, making the others laugh.

"I hear a party going on," Texaco John said, bursting through the door with Brandy trailing close behind.

"John!" both girls exclaimed. "So wonderful of you to come over!" Dianne said with exuberance as both she and Mel hugged him.

"Girls! You know I ain't much for hugging! Back off before you make me cry. You ain't gonna believe who followed us over here. They'll be coming through the door any minute." John had barely finished his announcement when Benny burst through the door carrying bags of sandwiches, preserves, and various snacks.

"I'm sorry, girls," Texaco John explained. "It's one time I let my mouth run. Benny comes over with a rattle in his car. I fixed it and told him I was leaving. Then I told him you two was leaving."

"No apologies necessary, John," Dianne said with a smile and a hug for Benny.

"I figured you'd be hungry tonight and need snacks for the morning, so I ran real quick over to my shop," Benny said.

"Don't know where you'd get good stuff like we got here," Benny smirked, obviously baiting JR.

"Hey! Watch that!" JR said, smiling.

"That is so kind of you," Betty shouted over the noisy excitement. "Benny, let me put this in the kitchen. Anyone hungry?" JR and Ken barely let Betty set the bags down before they were digging through the goodies.

"Yeah, you two got to keep your school-boy figures," Benny said, wagging his finger toward the men.

"Don't forget to leave our travelers some. And Ms. Dianne, I am so sorry about what happened at our place when you came in there with Michael a while back. We should've treated you better. I saw Mitzi when I picked up the sandwiches. She sends her apologies as well. She didn't think you'd want her here." Benny said as he helped Dianne with a box.

"That whole thing with Michael was bad, Benny. I don't hold anything against you or Mitzi. Everything is good."

"Ms. Dianne, I got a confession to make," Benny said as he restacked a tilting column of boxes.

"Confession?" Dianne asked.

"Yep. You know those ribs Michael brought in? He'd been doing that for a few months before he brought you in. Well, they weren't that great. And my insurance company and good conscience wouldn't allow me to serve them up to customers. Seriously, I fixed them up and sent them over to the soup kitchen. They were good, but not like the ones I had."

All Dianne could do was laugh a full snorting, nose-running laugh. She patted Benny on the shoulder without saying a word.

"And that stuff Mitzi served you the first night. They were soup bones. I braised 'em, ready to go into a stew, not to customers to eat plain. They had already left the kitchen, so I finished cooking 'em and Mitzi brought them over to Brandy. She did that occasionally with a few pieces of meat."

The festive atmosphere quieted when Deputy Johnson drove up.

"Greetings," the Deputy began, sticking his head inside an already open door. "Dianne, I'm returning your mother's letter. You need to sign a receipt stating that I returned it to you. Also, I have some information for you. Do you want to step outside?"

"Um, OK. Can Betty and Mel listen in? They are family to me now, and it will mean a lot."

"That will be fine. I think having some ladies with you will be good," Deputy Johnson replied.

"Let's go to the front yard," Dianne said, taking charge of the conference.

"The doll in the wooden box …," Deputy Johnson began. He shared the story about where the doll had originated and how his suspicions panned out. Indeed, the doll was given to her mother by a child molester and serial killer.

"I'm sorry I can't return the doll to you. It's now considered evidence. Although the prime suspect has passed."

As Deputy Johnson spoke, Dianne's mind wandered to her mother. How close had she come to something terrible? The weight of the doll's history settled over her like a wet blanket, but she forced herself to nod.

"Oh, no problem," Dianne was quick to retort. "I don't want that doll. Send it wherever it needs to be sent. Thank you for following up on it. Oh, and I guess you wonder what's going on here."

"Yes, I am wondering," the deputy said, returning to his investigator persona.

Dianne explained that she and Mel are going on an adventure to Florida and may not return but Ken will be here and now owns the house.

"Now I'm reading you, sir. You seem concerned," Dianne said to the Deputy.

"I've got nothing holding you here," Deputy Johnson replied.

"Will you ladies keep up with Ken? I believe his last name is Simpson? Let him know your contact information and address. I may have more questions. And I think my wife will miss you, Ms. England."

"Yes, Ken's last name is Simpson. We will keep in touch. I guess Pam told you that I was attending grad school. Before that, I needed time to think everything through. Ken is our anchor here. He'll know how to reach us."

"Will he be able to get ahold of JR and Betty? I heard they may head out as well. They'll be living in an RV?" Deputy Johnson questioned, looking at Betty.

Mel and Dianne were surprised that Deputy Johnson knew about their departure. Dianne again took charge, "Betty, do you mind talking to Deputy Johnson? Mel and I need to continue packing."

"Of course!" Betty responded. "JR, come over here, please, and talk to the Deputy." Betty called out, beckoning her husband.

"Thank you for everything, Deputy Johnson. I guess this means goodbye." Dianne reached out her hand.

"Yes. But let's say farewell, and I'll see you again soon. Both of you young ladies would be great citizens for Marshfield." Deputy Johnson shook Dianne and Mel's hands and smiled in one of his rare moments.

After a short chat with Deputy Johnson, Betty and JR returned to the group to help Dianne and Mel pack.

"Would it be fitting to say the evening was more than enjoyable? It was a totally unexpectedly joyous send-off for Mel and Dianne," Betty proclaimed to the group.

"Toasts to the ladies, to one another, and Deputy Johnson in hopes he can find Michael's killer!" Betty said to close the celebration.

Deputy Johnson returned to his office, poring over his notes and giving his chat at the England home deep thought. It was congenial. Everyone appeared genuine and forthcoming, but he wasn't 100 percent comfortable about most of the group leaving for unknown destinations. *What am I missing?* he thought.

To help define what could have made him uneasy, he added more events to the timeline he had plastered across the squad room wall. He paid detailed attention to each event and statement. Nothing pointed to Michael's killer, yet he had a general uneasiness about the group at the England home. They seemed to know Michael best.

Mel had grown up around Michael, and Dianne had been involved with him for a while. Ken and JR knew him from the truck stop and the local scene. They all had ties to him—different kinds of relations. And Johnson couldn't help but wonder if one of those ties had been cut more permanently.

It didn't help that the murder weapon was yet to be found. One individual, Mr. Colson, could help but was not mentally able to do so.

Officers occasionally roamed the Glossen property in the

coming weeks, looking for clues. They searched for anything missed, perhaps footprints, dropped personal effects, and things out of place. Michael's weapon hiding place was well-known among a large group of associates, making things more perplexing, yet the gun could not be found.

Mel and Dianne were too excited during their impromptu going-away celebration the evening before, making waking up difficult.

"Oh heavens, Mel. Let's get some coffee in us," was Dianne's first greeting, perhaps prompted by the smell of coffee brewing in their kitchen.

"Good morning, ladies! I hope I didn't wake you. Coffee is about ready," Ken said, his heart pumping harder as he quickly tucked his pistol into a kitchen cabinet just in time for Mel to stagger in with eyes half closed against a bright morning sun.

"I have orange juice and was lucky to find a coffee scoop with the potholders," Ken said.

"Wondered where that was," Mel murmured. "Only coffee, please. You scared the crap out of me—I didn't know you were here."

"Almost ready," Dianne yelled from the bathroom over running water. "I'll be out in a minute!"

"I think Dianne misunderstood me," Mel responded and shared a quick laugh with Ken.

"You here to see us off?" Mel asked.

"Yes, and your parents are heading over with fresh biscuits."

"Not sure if I can handle that," Mel said. "We already have a ton of food. I'm going to start pulling sheets. Ken, you'll have many leftovers—we can't take it all with us."

"Not for long my friend. My work around here will surely work up an appetite. Oh, I think Dianne's done with the shower."

Dianne emerged, patting her hair dry. "I'm sorry. I took a quick shower. I forgot you had to get in there," Dianne said, leaving the bathroom.

"OK, girlie. Finish your hair. Our guardian angels are sending us off with a good breakfast," Mel said, still groggy, as she headed to the bedroom, coffee cup in hand.

"You'll be fine after a shower. I packed my stuff, so the room is all yours," Dianne said, gesturing to the bathroom.

"And the sheets are now in the wash," Mel proclaimed after a few minutes of tugging and stuffing in the washing machine. "I'll wait until I finish another cup of coffee and the water gets warm again."

After their routines, the women gathered their last few things, packed and repacked the car, before taking a last inventory through the car windows.

"You two have your small suitcases? Are they easy to find when you find a place tonight?" Ken asked.

"Yes, we do. Oh, Mom and Dad just pulled up!" Mel dashed over to the delivery van for her last goodbye. She embraced Betty first, then JR, barely letting them get their feet on the ground.

"Mom, am I doing the right thing?" Mel asked, tears finally flowing freely. Dianne looked at the trio, all in a bundle, while holding back her tears.

Ken placed a hand on Dianne's shoulder. "It's all OK, Dianne. I know your mother is proud. I am, too, and I know I'll miss you greatly." Ken said, giving Dianne a comforting hug.

"Goodbye, Dad Ken," Dianne said, stepping back and turning to Mel. "Mel, I think it's time."

"Oh, wait," Betty said through tears. "Take these biscuits, and here are more things you can use—a map, a TripTik, and a few brochures you might want to look at on the way. Oh, and you're now Triple A members. Here's the envelope. You can call them if you have problems on the road. And stop at welcome stations. They're full of information."

"Drive carefully," Ken said as the women settled into the car. "You two sharing the driving?"

"Yes, Dad Ken," Mel said with a wink.

"Wait! I have something for you," Ken called out, ducking back into the house. Betty took the opportunity to lean into the car window for a final kiss on Mel's cheek.

"Frozen Girl Scout cookies? Do-si-dos! Our favorites!" Dianne shouted, laughing when Ken handed her his parting gift.

"I'm keeping the Thin Mints," Ken smiled.

"Alright, let them go! I think they have enough food to last a week!" Betty said with a shaking voice bordering on tears.

"Goodbye all!" Dianne called, waving out of the car window.

"Goodbye," Mel echoed softly with a slight wave.

The long, winding road stretched ahead as they pulled away from the house. Mel glanced in the rearview mirror, watching the view of her parents shrink. For the first time, the weight of the unknown settled over her. There was no turning back. She and Mel were traveling to Destin, Florida.

Ken watched Dianne and Mel drive out of sight, knowing he would soon bid goodbye to JR and Betty when they leave Marshfield. As he climbed the steps to the house that was now his home, he paused on the last step as memories flooded through him. He reminisced about the many times he knocked on the door, the days he held Katrina's arm going up the stairs, and the final assist—the night before his Trina died. He winced when he thought of moving smelly furniture out of the home with Texaco John. He chuckled when he remembered moving a refrigerator up the stairs with John. Stepping inside, the home's silence was heavy. In hopes of relieving the heaviness of memory and farewells, he unpacked a microwave purchased explicitly for his new home, the home with so many memories.

While positioning the microwave on the counter, the giant lollipop Michael purchased on his first date with Dianne fell from a countertop canister resulting in an unexpected clatter that turned memories into irritation. He flung open the back door pitching the candy far into the backyard. Without pause, he grabbed the pistol he stowed in the cabinet earlier and shot the candy with precision, shattering it into tiny shards. The sight brought only fleeting satisfaction.

Unable to contain his growing agitation, he laid the gun on the dining table, before furiously shoving the final packing from the new oven out the backdoor. Hands shaking, he placed his coffee in the microwave, punching in too much time. As he lowered himself on to a kitchen chair, his deep breaths fogged a Blue Willow dish he used with Dianne and her mother. Unable to shake his agitation, he raised the dish over his head and was positioned ready to smash it to the floor. Trembling, he hesitated, slowly drawing it close to his chest as tears welled in his eyes. His gaze locked onto the Blue Willow plate, and haunting memories dragged him back to the night Michael died. Horrifying thoughts broke through the dam of reality and collided with the present whirring of the microwave.

The memories hit hard, pulling him back to that night—the night he watched from the trees, unseen, waiting. Stealthily that Saturday night he watched from the tree line as misty night air foretold impending horror. Standing guard in Marshfield mimicked many nights years ago in Saigon. The lunacy of party goers entering and leaving a home without the owner present heightened his senses, just as it often did outside small villages.

As the ground dampened, he watched Mel leave the house, place her guitar in the back seat, then lean against the car hood fiddling with car keys while appearing to wait for Dianne. The oddly normal night turned ominous when Michael drove into the driveway. Not long after hearing a truck door slam, Ken heard yelling. "No! Stop it! Let me go!" Pleas for help and seeing Dianne roll out of the window, ignited Ken into action. He had to protect her!

Vietnam flickered through his mind, memories playing like a broken film strip. The mission became clear—neutralize the enemy as he had many times before. War-time instincts took over. He moved along the tree line, each step solid, despite the slick undergrowth. His heartbeat quickened with each step, thumping harder with each breath, every step. He focused on the kitchen door and what might lay beyond. Flickering visions pushed him onward. He had an objective, a duty. Michael was just another enemy. Saving Dianne was the mission.

After hearing several gunshots, Ken retreated to the tree line with clenched fists holding a weapon not there. He opened his hands, cramped by stress but no weapon. Had there been a gun in his hand the night of Michael's death? His fingers clenched as if remembering the weight of one, but when he looked down, they were empty. He questioned if he had killed again or if they were just racing thoughts. If he had killed, with what? The jumbled filmstrip of past events faded as microwaved coffee boiled over unnoticed. Visions ceased when the sharp ding of the microwave returned him from hazed memories.

The acrid smell of scorched coffee permeated the kitchen air adding to Ken's trauma. He didn't want to kill again—not that night, not now. Echoes of the past barely faded, just suppressed. They rose and fell, always waiting. Trying to overcome a clouded mind, he reached for the kitchen phone. He stared at the buttons, suddenly unsure how to dial a number he had memorized for years. His gaze shifted—gun, plate, microwave, gun, buttons. He instinctively dialed.

"JR," Ken whispered, straining his shaky voice. "Come get my Colt. I need you to take it."

"Buddy, I'll be right there." JR knew he had to act fast.

In slow movements, Ken gently placed the phone receiver on the plate he had earlier embraced. Ignoring the phone's mechanical buzzing, he cradled the Colt. Rising, he stepped away from the kitchen in a gentle, no longer military stride. As he opened the front door into bright, warming sunshine he noticed the door creaking, something he meant to address a day earlier. Fixated on the door's hinge, he absentmindedly caressed the pistol's engraving, finding peace with each curve and flourish.

"Shit!" he shouted robustly throwing the weapon into the grass as he expelled his last ounce of stress. He plopped to the steps and leaned against the railing staring at the gun, still trying to settle his thoughts.

"Your brother's here, Buddy. Are you OK? The Colt is secured."

Ken didn't see JR drive up and barely saw him now as he sat silently comforting his brother in arms for many minutes. JR didn't know what to say to his dear friend, yet words fell from his heart.

"You've spent so long doing things for others, brother. Maybe it's time to do something for you, just you. Are you hearing me?" JR tried his best to be cheerful.

Ken raised his head with his face directly absorbing the sun's rays. Turning his head slowly toward his very best friend, brother, and life saver, he only muttered a promise.

"Yes, I need to do that."

With those words, each man knew this was not the day another goodbye would be said at the England house.

THE END

265

ABOUT THE AUTHOR

Throughout grammar school and college, Helen Gillespie loved developing story sketches or full stories but kept them hidden within herself. That creative spark proved valuable in unexpected places, first on assignment as a musician in the US Army, and after leaving the Army, when she earned a degree in elementary education. After reentering the Army in 1981, she put pen to paper, or rather, "fingers to an Olivetti." She officially learned the art of journalism to serve the Army, but it quickly became a personal passion. Interviewing fellow soldiers, exploring their jobs and personalities, and publishing useful information for the military community formed the basis of her skill and enjoyment. Those years of thought, training, education, and experience laid the foundation for crafting her first novel, *The Goodbyes*.

Social Media

Email: helengillespie256@yahoo.com
Facebook: Facebook.com/profile.php?id=61565442142189
LinkedIn: Linkedin.com/in/hgillespie/
Website: helengillespiewrites.com/

Personal Social Media

Facebook: Facebook.com/helen.gillespie/
Instagram: Instagram.com/hgillespie/